MOMOTA INOUE

ARTIST

I loved Pokémon as a child and would draw Pokémon manga on my notebook.

So I never imagined that I'd have the opportunity to actually draw a Pokémon manga like this after I grew up.

Born on June 19, 1985, in Saitama Prefecture, Momota Inoue received the 58th Shogakukan Rookie Comic Grand Prize for the Children's Di___ ___ 2006 for *Red Enza*.

POKÉMON—ZOROARK: MASTER OF ILLUSIONS

VIZ Kids Edition

Story and Art by **MOMOTA INOUE**

Original Japanese edition "GENEI NO HASHA ZOROARK" published by SHOGAKUKAN Inc.

Translation/Tetsuichiro Miyaki
Touch-up & Lettering/Vanessa Satone
Design/Sam Elzway
Editor/Joel Enos

Printed in the U.S.A.

Published by VIZ Media, LLC
P.O. Box 77010
San Francisco, CA 94107

10 9 8 7 6 5 4 3 2 1
First printing, September 2011

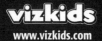

www.vizkids.com

www.viz.com

RATED A FOR ALL AGES

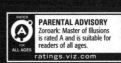

PARENTAL ADVISORY
Zoroark: Master of Illusions is rated A and is suitable for readers of all ages.

ratings.viz.com

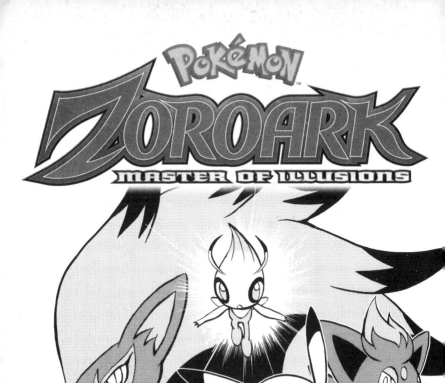

Pokémon™ Zoroark

Master of Illusions

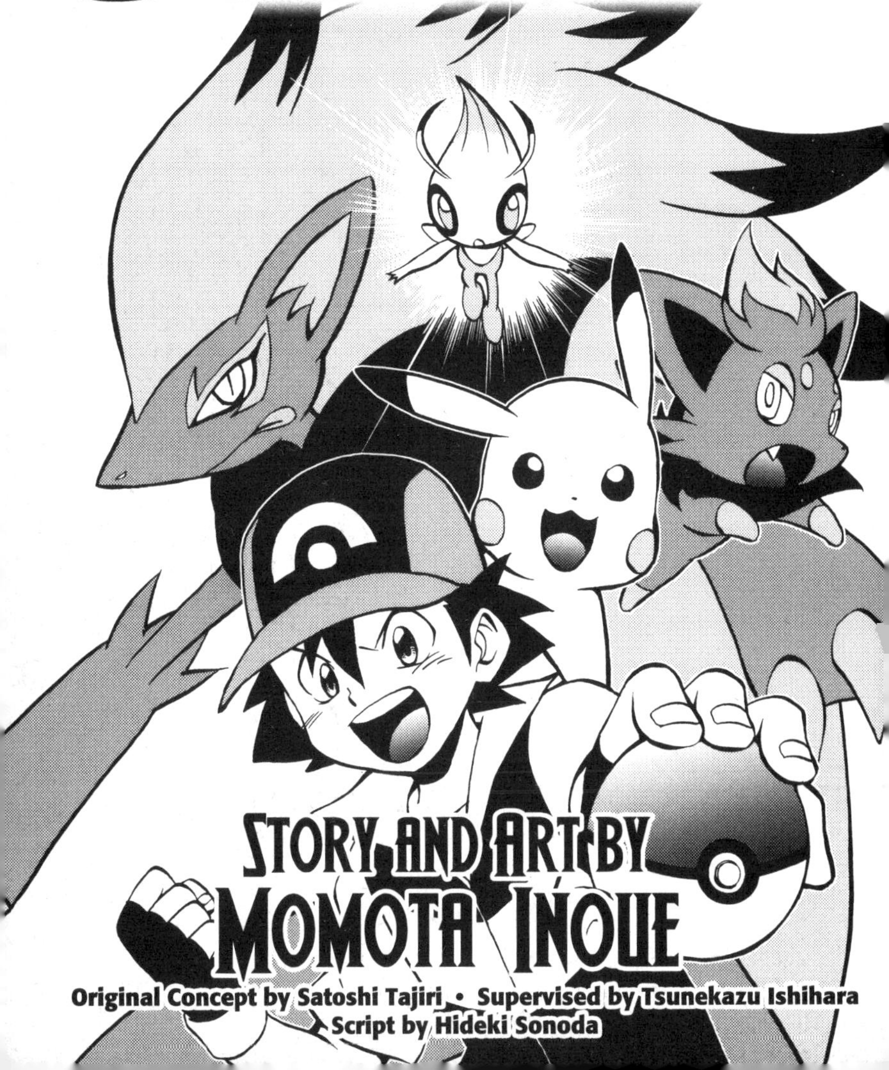

Story and Art by Momota Inoue

Original Concept by Satoshi Tajiri • Supervised by Tsunekazu Ishihara
Script by Hideki Sonoda

Characters and Pokémon

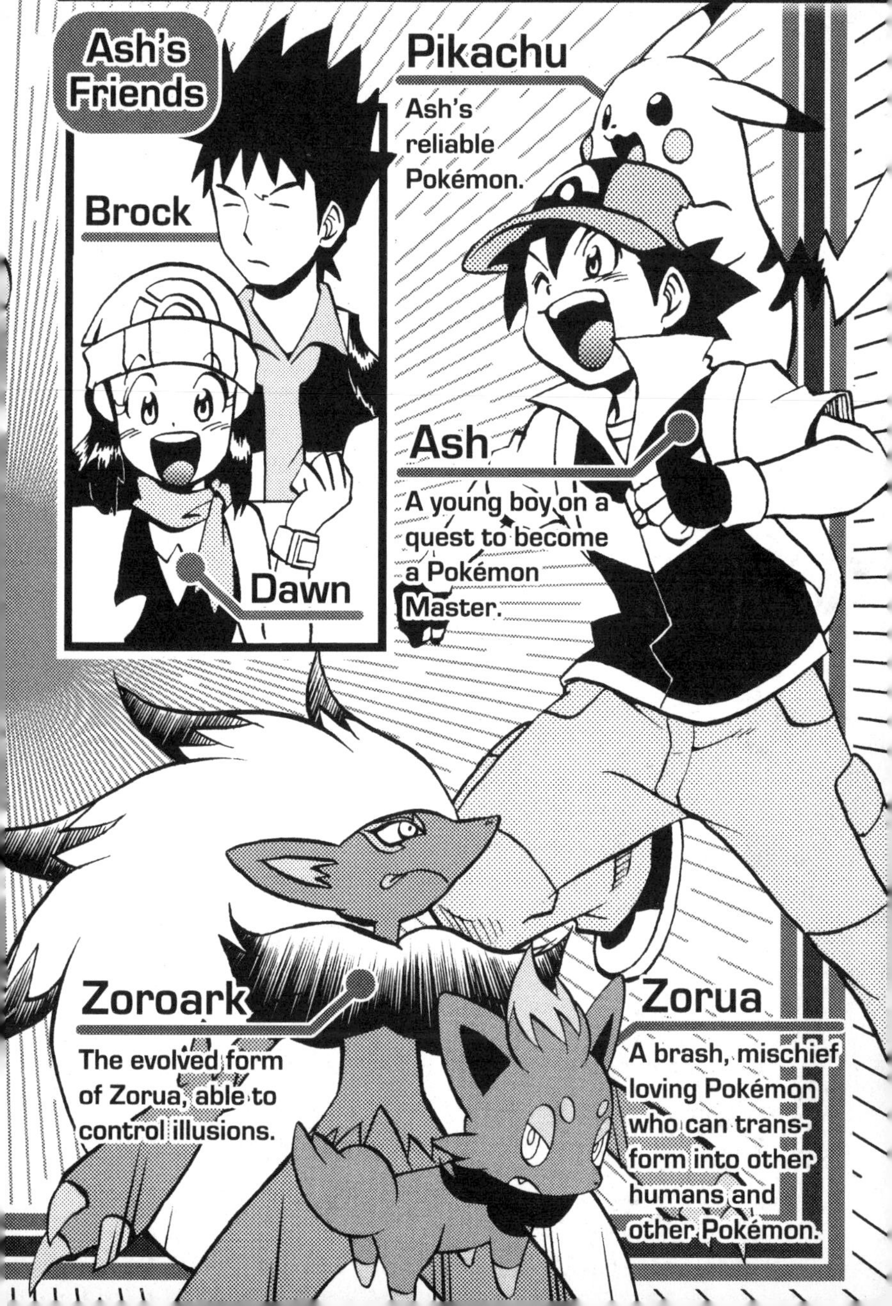
Pikachu
Ash's reliable Pokémon.
Ash
A young boy on a quest to become a Pokémon Master.
Ash's Friends
Brock
Dawn
Zorua
A brash, mischief loving Pokémon who can trans-form into other humans and other Pokémon.
Zoroark
The evolved form of Zorua, able to control illusions.

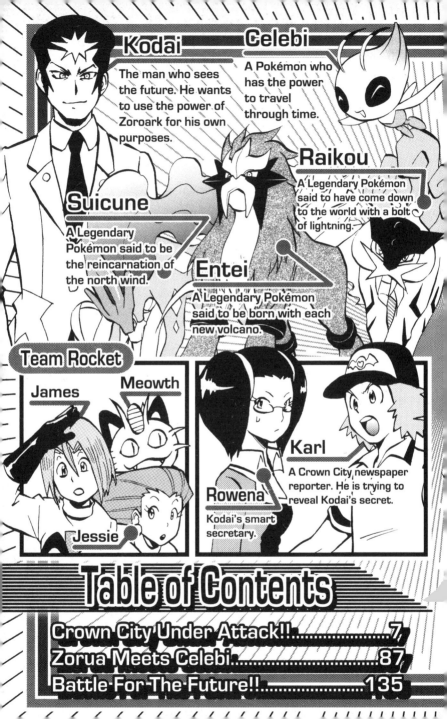

Kodai
The man who sees the future. He wants to use the power of Zoroark for his own purposes.
Celebi
A Pokémon who has the power to travel through time.
Raikou
A Legendary Pokémon said to have come down to the world with a bolt of lightning.
Suicune
A Legendary Pokémon said to be the reincarnation of the north wind.
Entei
A Legendary Pokémon said to be born with each new volcano.
Team Rocket
Meowth
James
Jessie
Karl
A Crown City newspaper reporter. He is trying to reveal Kodai's secret.
Rowena
Kodai's smart secretary.

Table of Contents

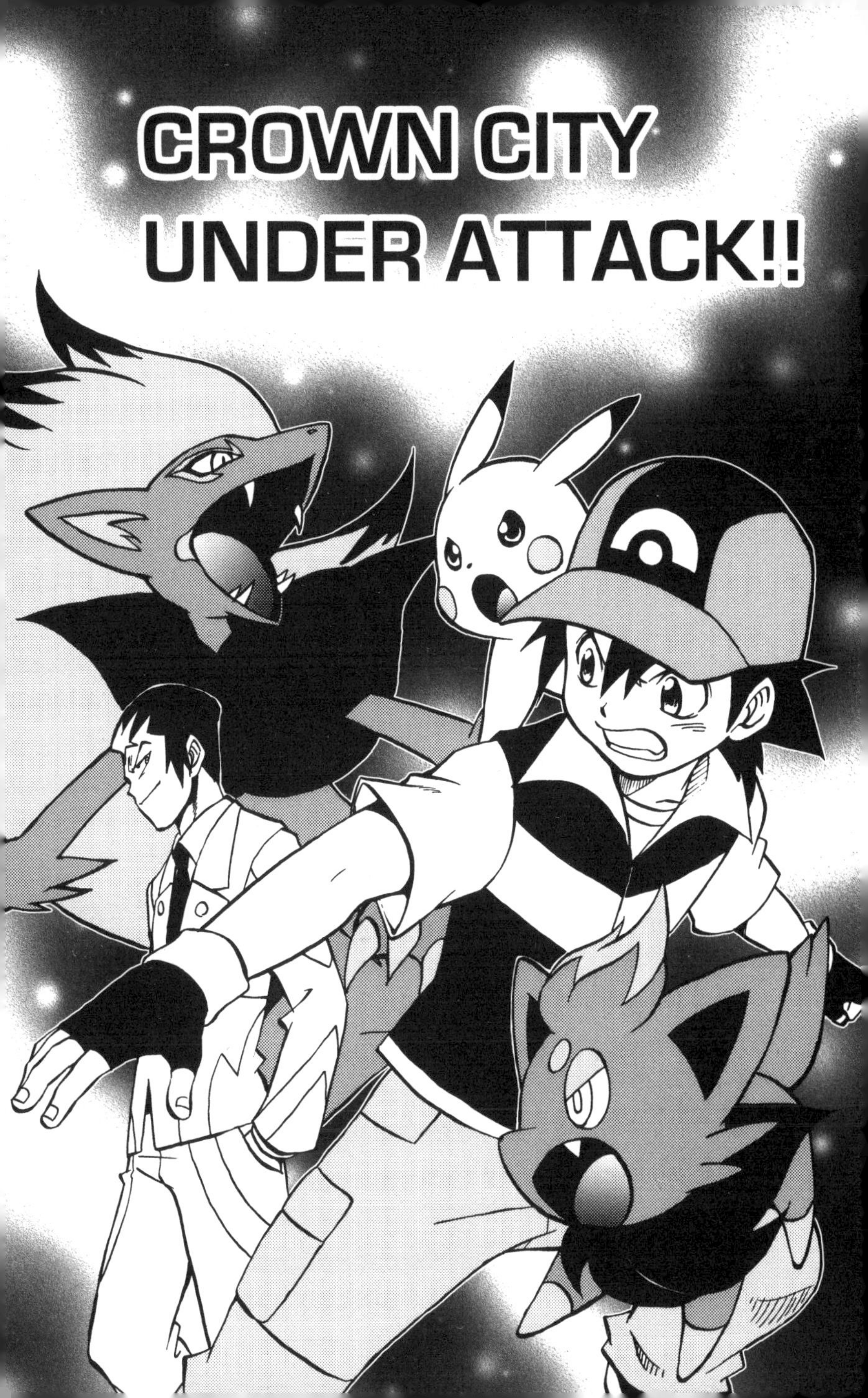
CROWN CITY
UNDER ATTACK!!

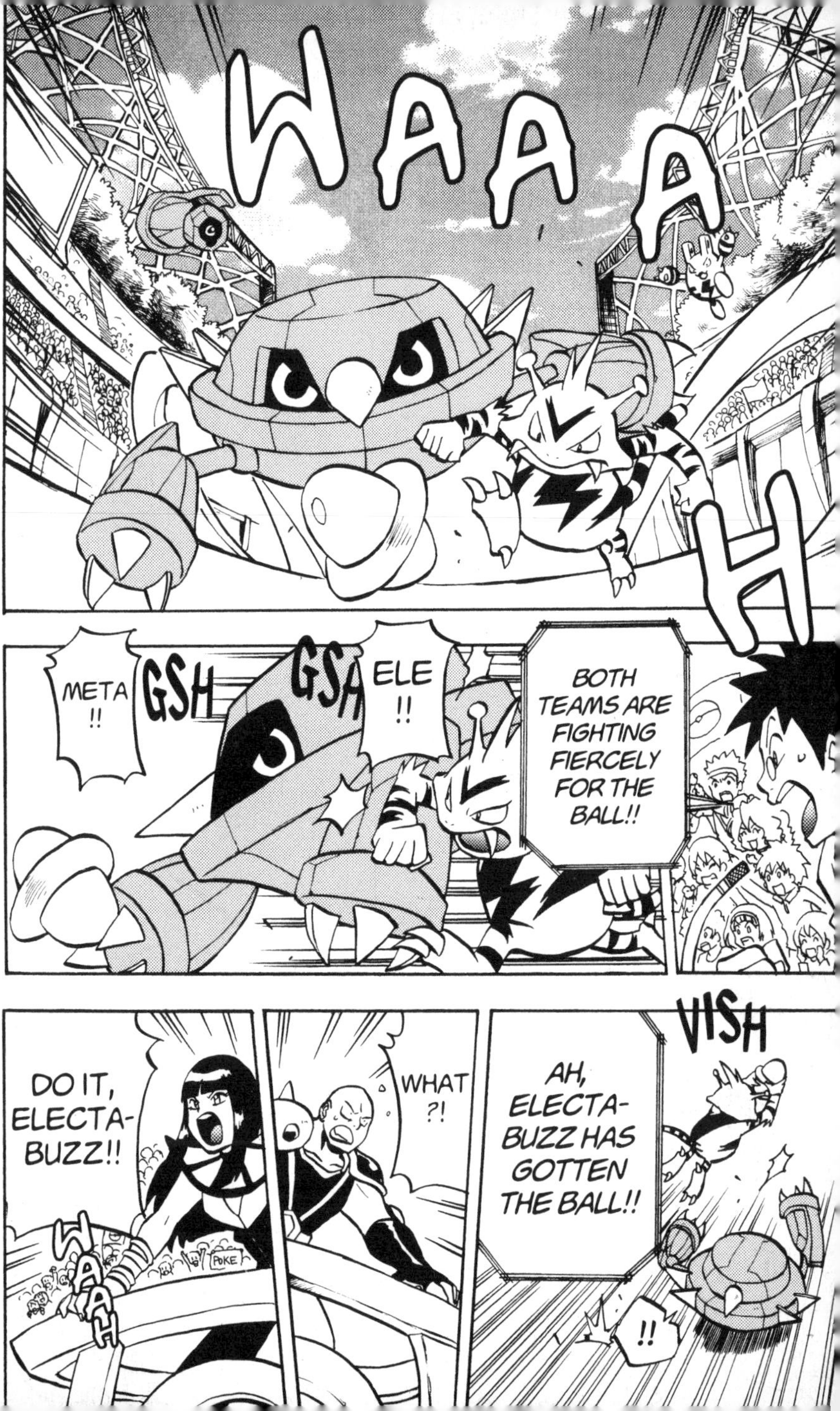
WAAAAH
BOTH TEAMS ARE FIGHTING FIERCELY FOR THE BALL!!
ELE !!
GSA
GSH
META !!
VISH
AH, ELECTA-BUZZ HAS GOTTEN THE BALL!!
!!
WHAT ?!
DO IT, ELECTA-BUZZ!!
WAAH
POKE

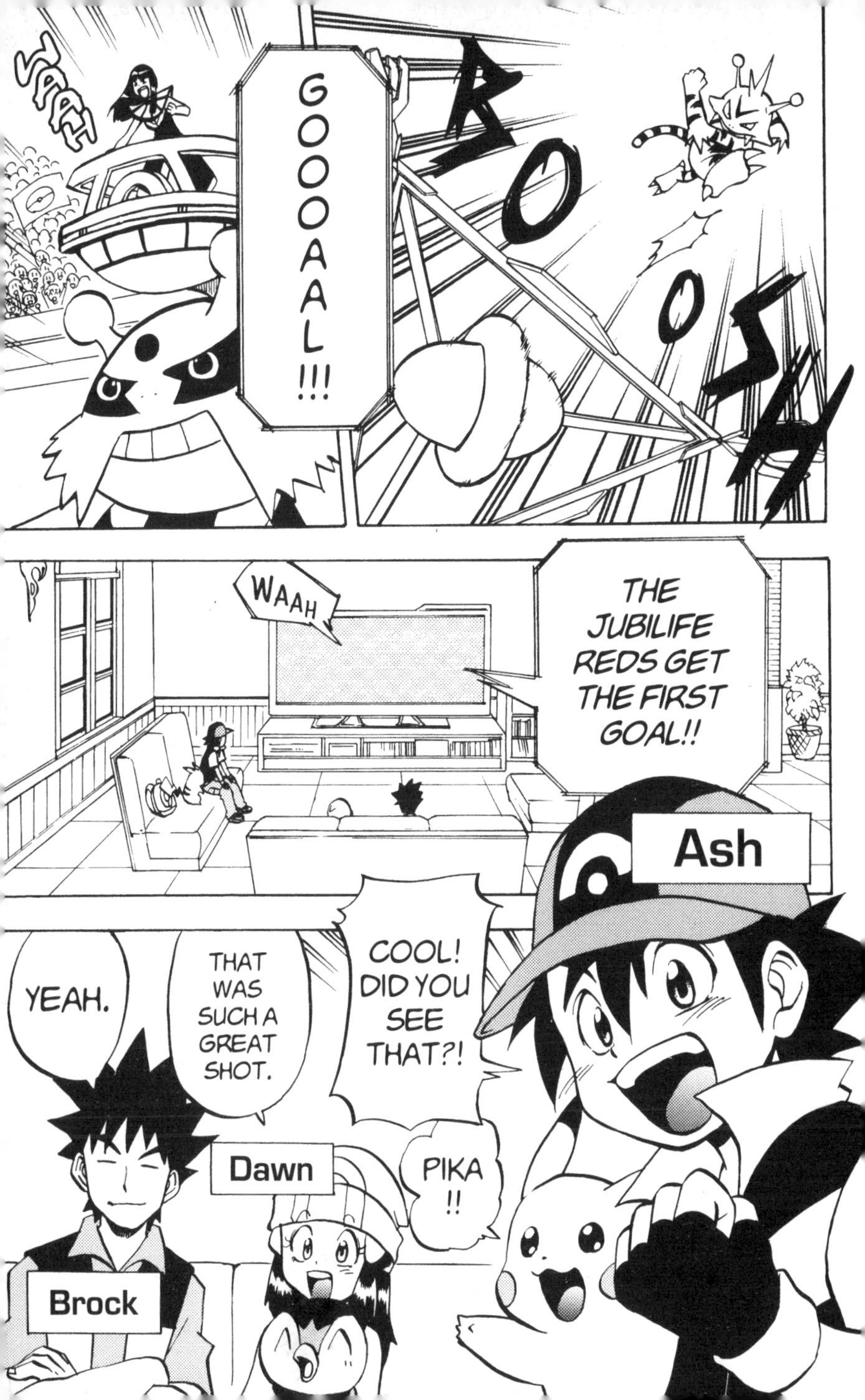
BOOSH
GOOOAAL!!!
YAAH
THE JUBILIFE REDS GET THE FIRST GOAL!!
WAAH
Ash
COOL! DID YOU SEE THAT?!
PIKA!!
THAT WAS SUCH A GREAT SHOT.
Dawn
YEAH.
Brock

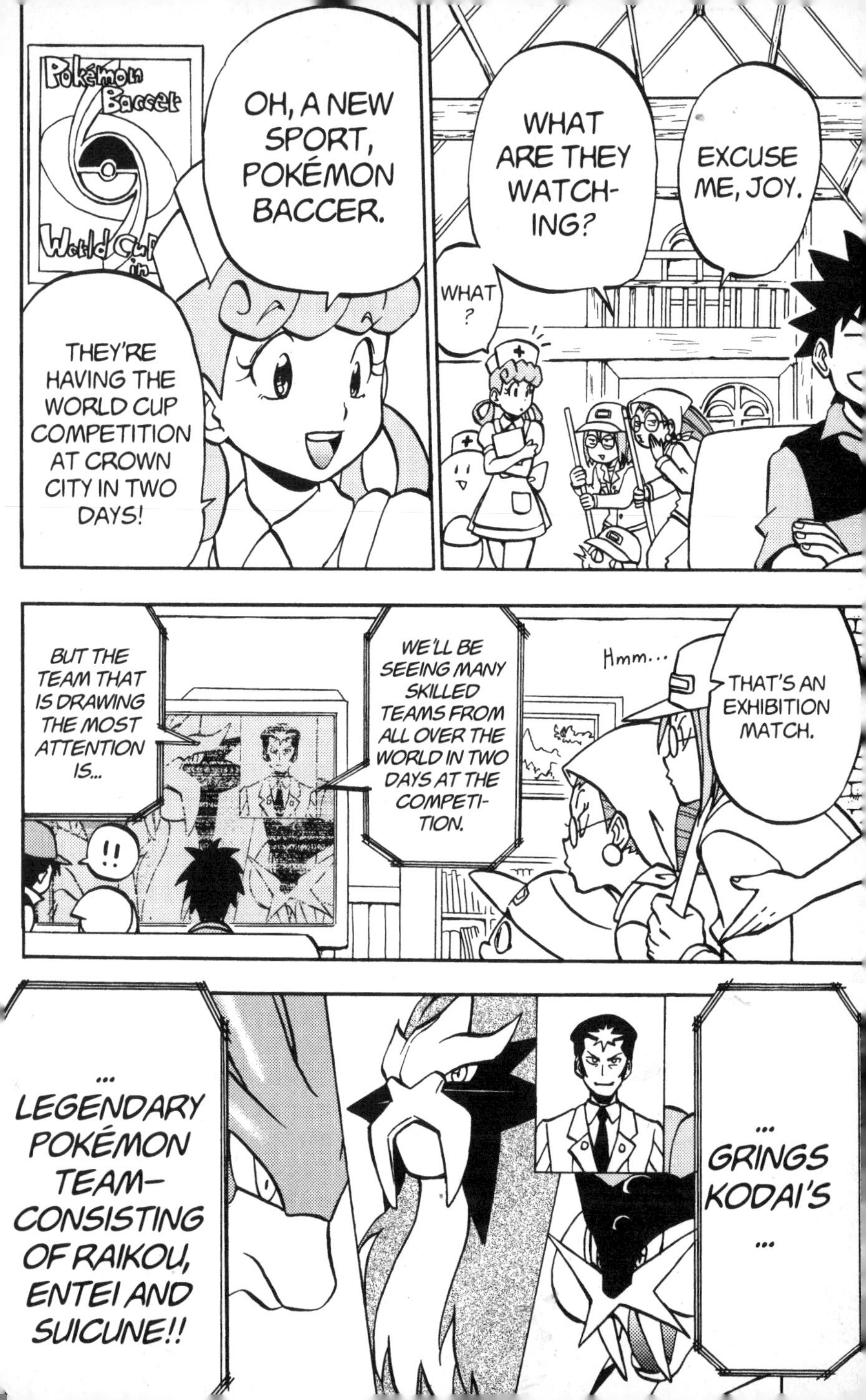
EXCUSE ME, JOY.
WHAT ARE THEY WATCHING?
WHAT ?
OH, A NEW SPORT, POKÉMON BACCER.
Pokémon Baccer
THEY'RE HAVING THE WORLD CUP COMPETITION AT CROWN CITY IN TWO DAYS!
THAT'S AN EXHIBITION MATCH.
Hmm...
WE'LL BE SEEING MANY SKILLED TEAMS FROM ALL OVER THE WORLD IN TWO DAYS AT THE COMPETITION.
BUT THE TEAM THAT IS DRAWING THE MOST ATTENTION IS...
!!
... GRINGS KODAI'S ...
... LEGENDARY POKÉMON TEAM—CONSISTING OF RAIKOU, ENTEI AND SUICUNE!!

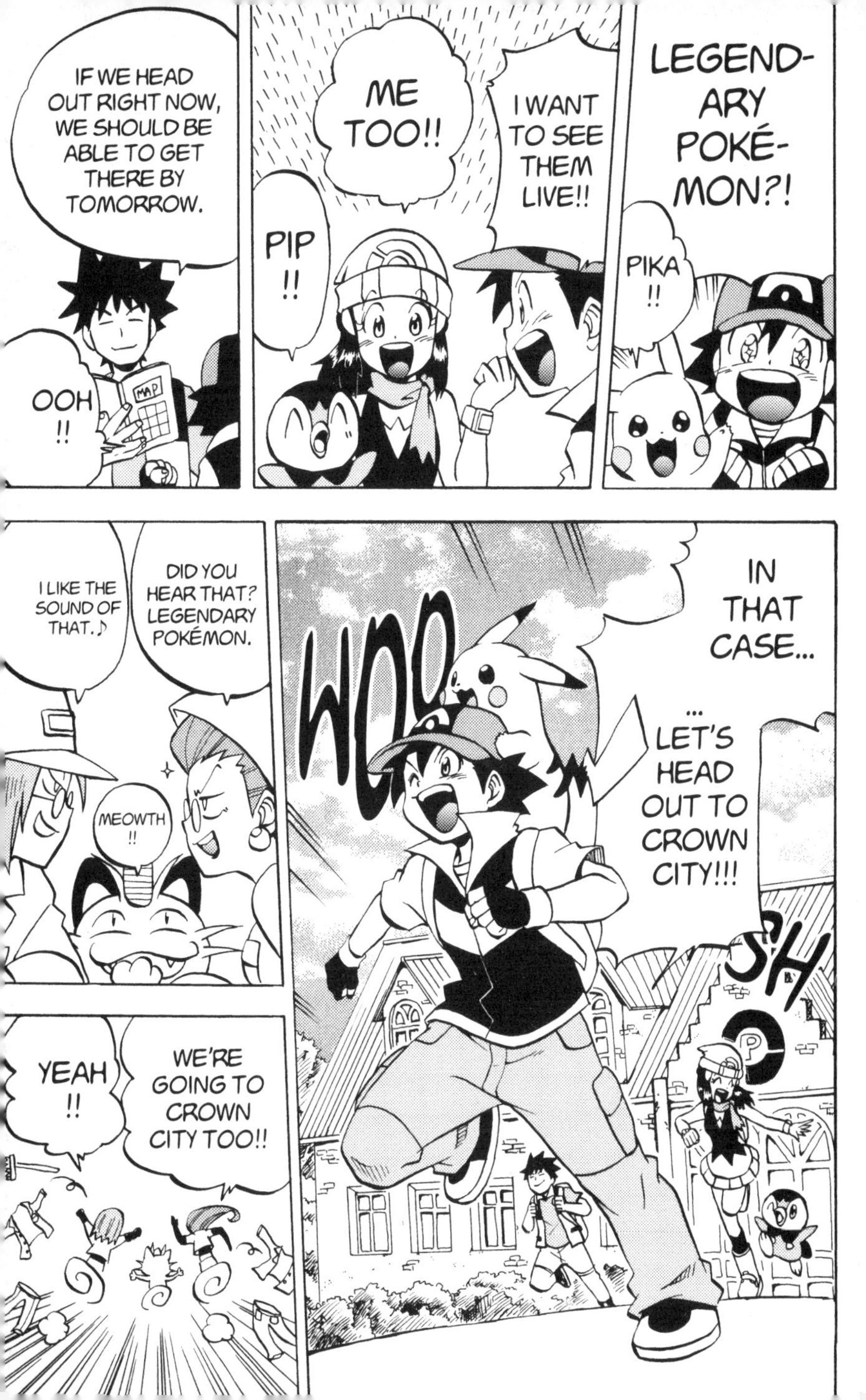
LEGENDARY POKÉMON?!
PIKA !!
I WANT TO SEE THEM LIVE!!
ME TOO!!
PIP !!
IF WE HEAD OUT RIGHT NOW, WE SHOULD BE ABLE TO GET THERE BY TOMORROW.
OOH !!
IN THAT CASE...
...LET'S HEAD OUT TO CROWN CITY!!!
WOO
SH
DID YOU HEAR THAT? LEGENDARY POKÉMON.
I LIKE THE SOUND OF THAT.♪
MEOWTH !!
WE'RE GOING TO CROWN CITY TOO!!
YEAH !!

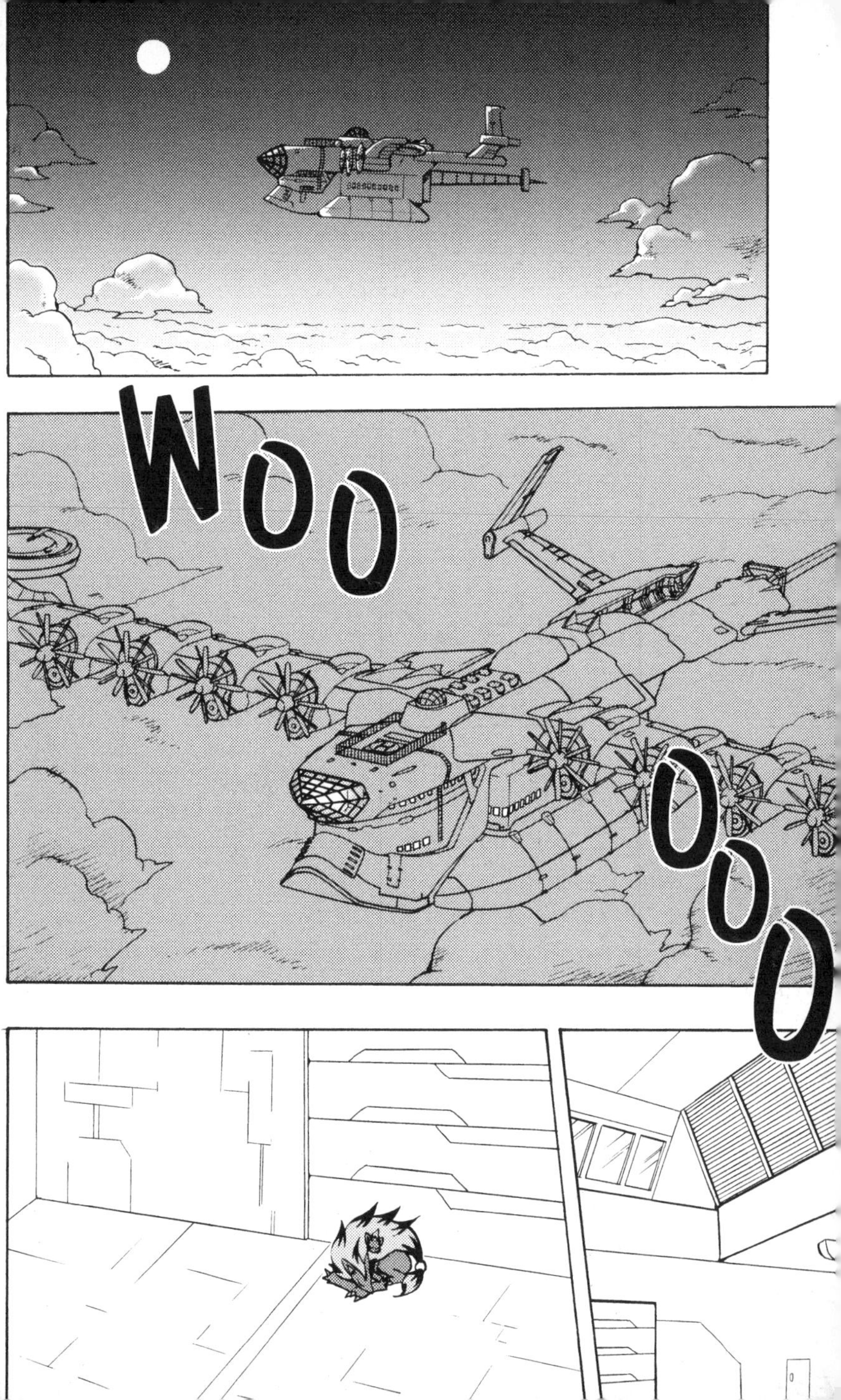
WOO
OOO

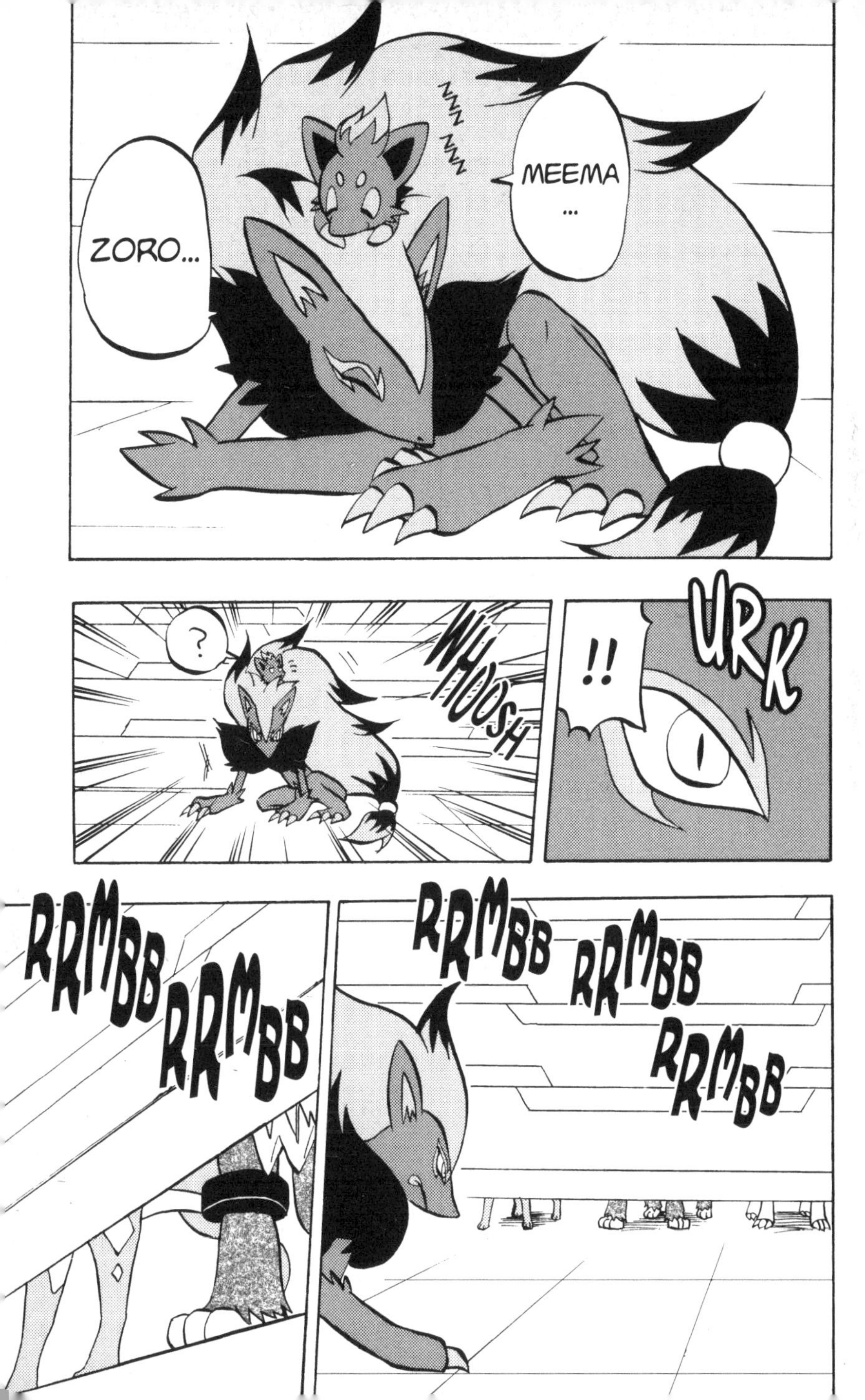
MEEMA
...
ZZZ ZZZ
ZORO...
URK
!!
WHOOSH
?
RRMBB
RRMBB
RRMBB
RRMBB
RRMBB

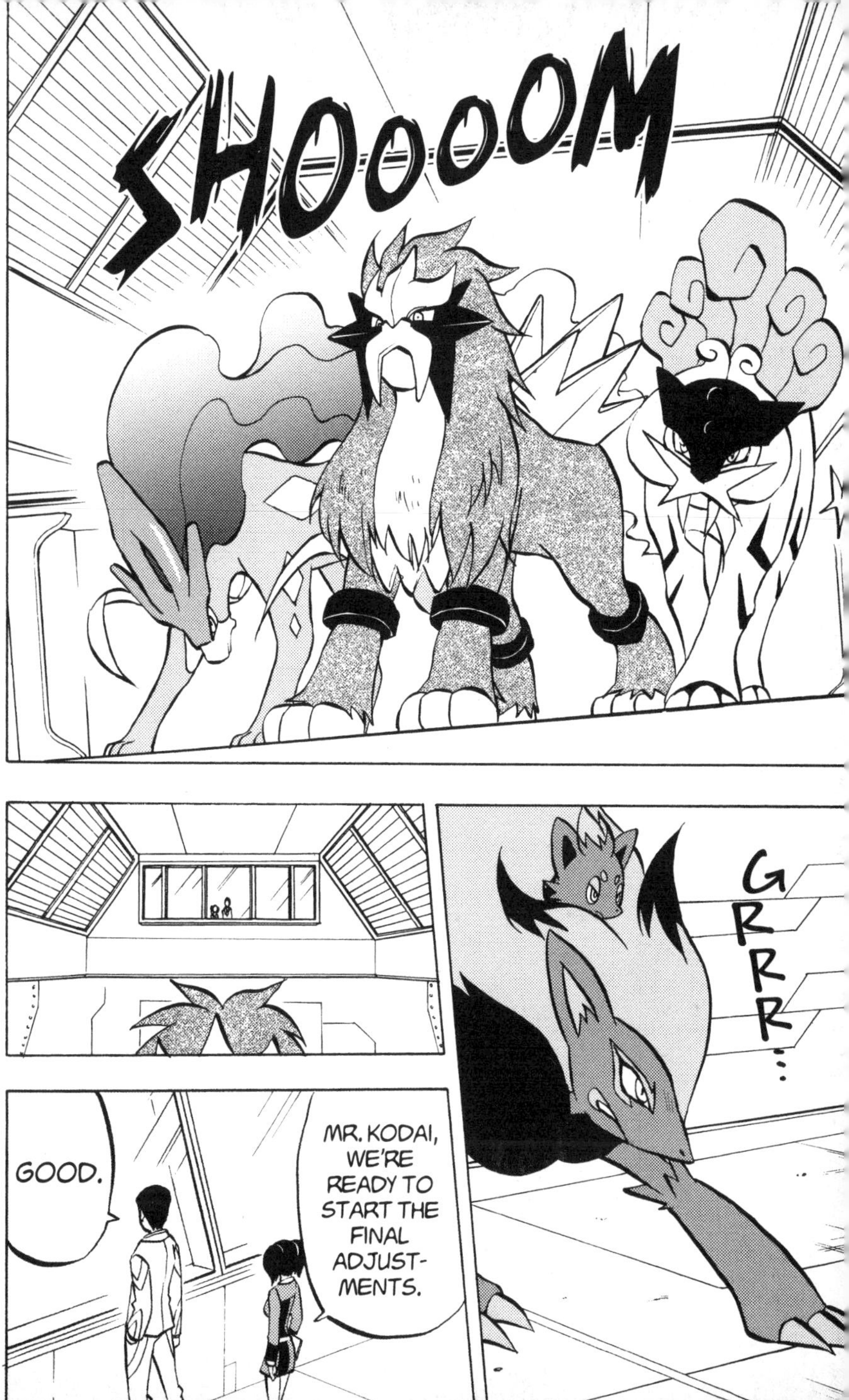
SHOOOOM
GRRR...
MR. KODAI, WE'RE READY TO START THE FINAL ADJUSTMENTS.
GOOD.

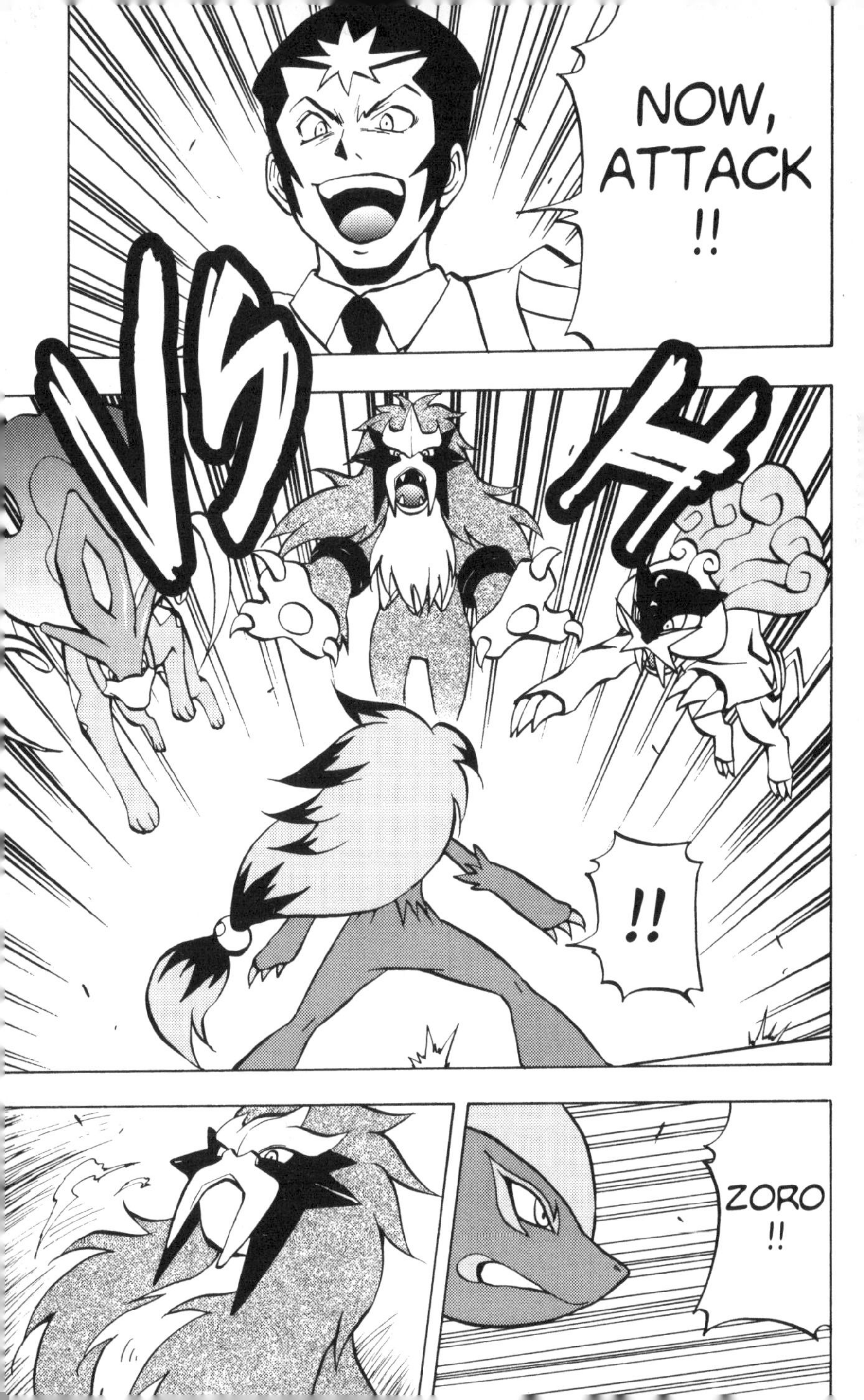
NOW, ATTACK !!
!!
ZORO !!

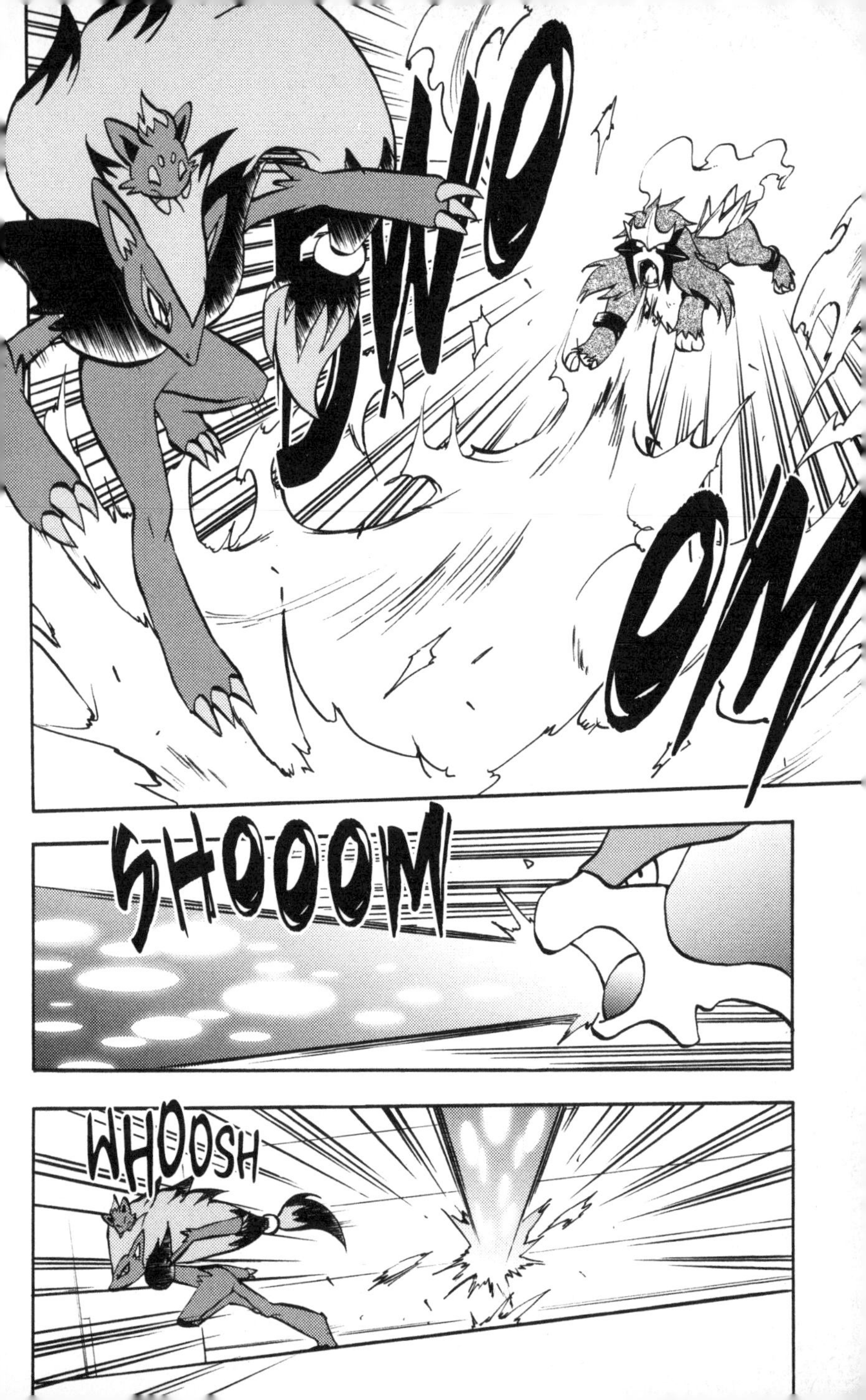
SHOOOM
WHOOSH

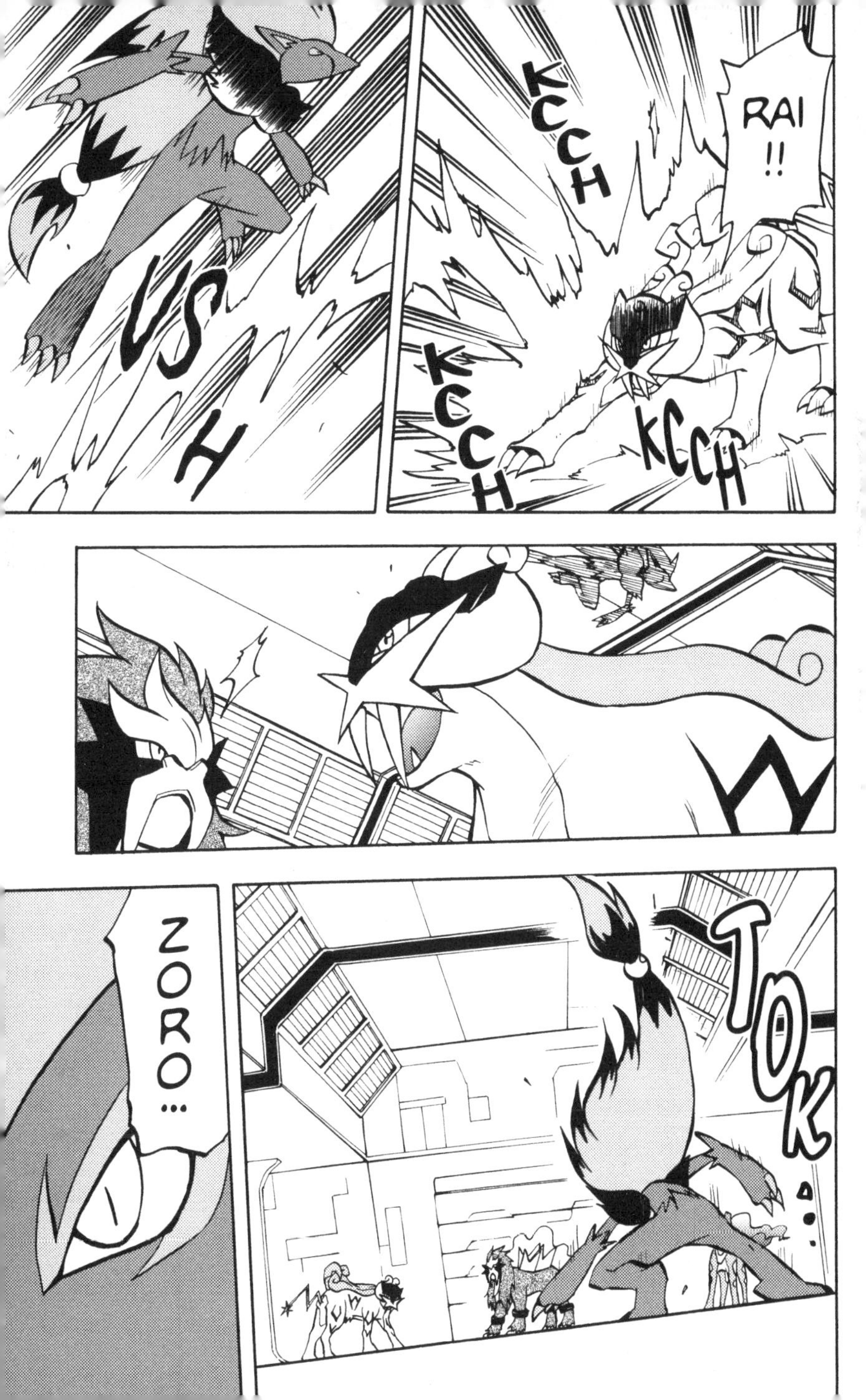

RAI !!
KCCH
KCCH
KCCH
USH
TOK
ZORO...

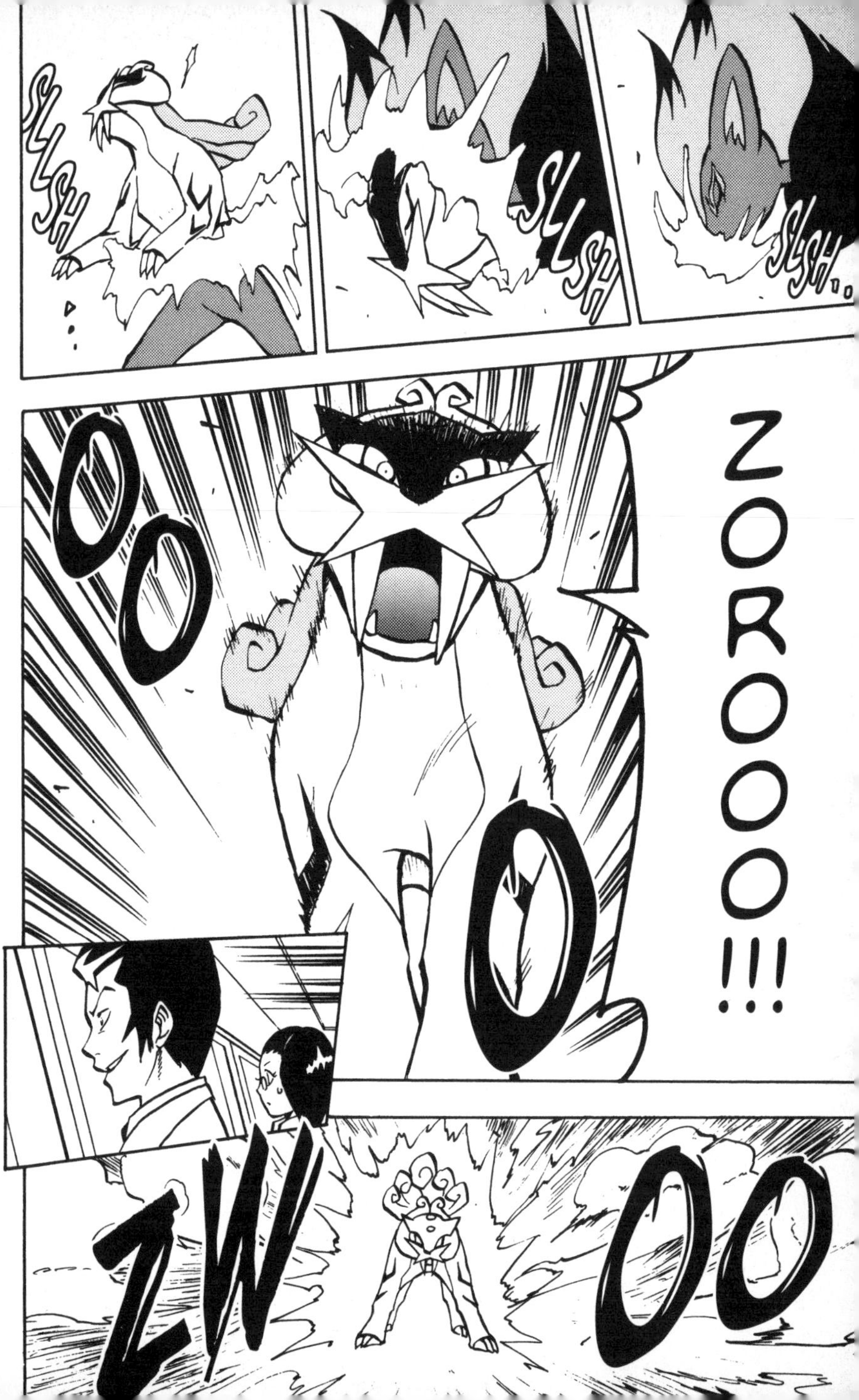
SLSH..
SLLSH
SLLSH
ZOROOOO!!!
OOO
ZW
OO

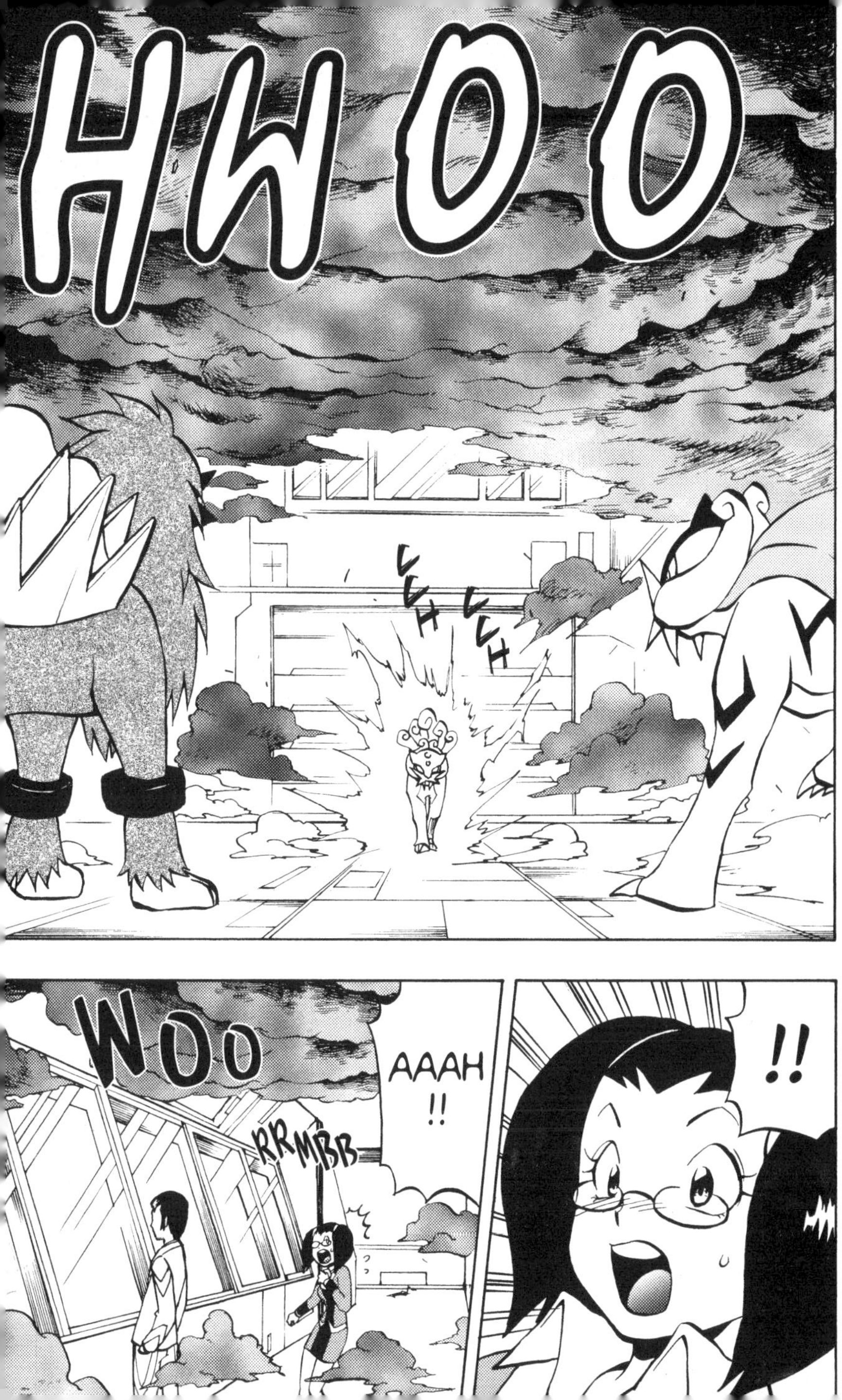
HWOO
!!
AAAH !!
WOO
RRMBB

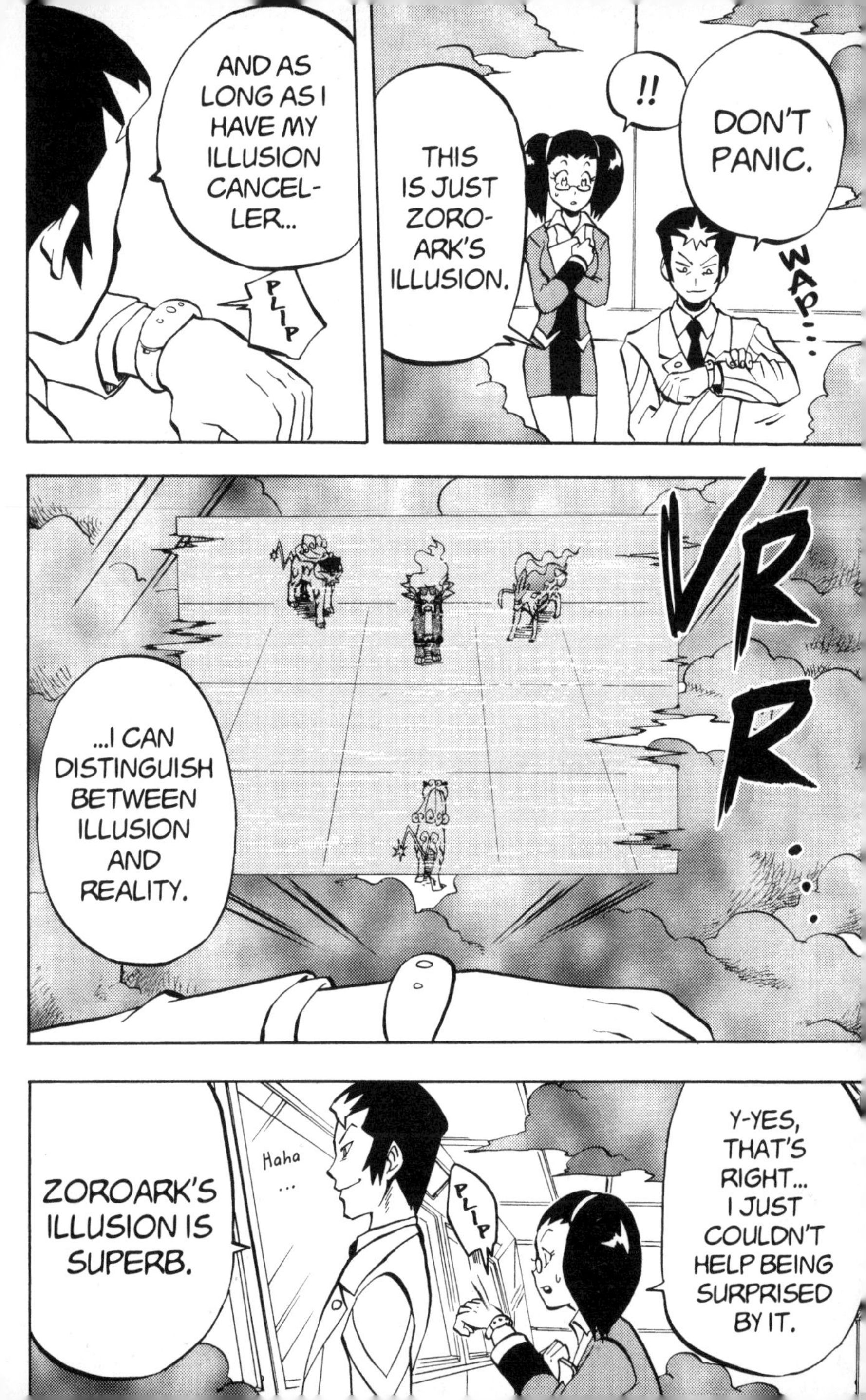
DON'T PANIC.
!!
WAP...
THIS IS JUST ZOROARK'S ILLUSION.
AND AS LONG AS I HAVE MY ILLUSION CANCELLER...
PLIP
VRRR...
...I CAN DISTINGUISH BETWEEN ILLUSION AND REALITY.
Y-YES, THAT'S RIGHT... I JUST COULDN'T HELP BEING SURPRISED BY IT.
PLIP
Haha...
ZOROARK'S ILLUSION IS SUPERB.

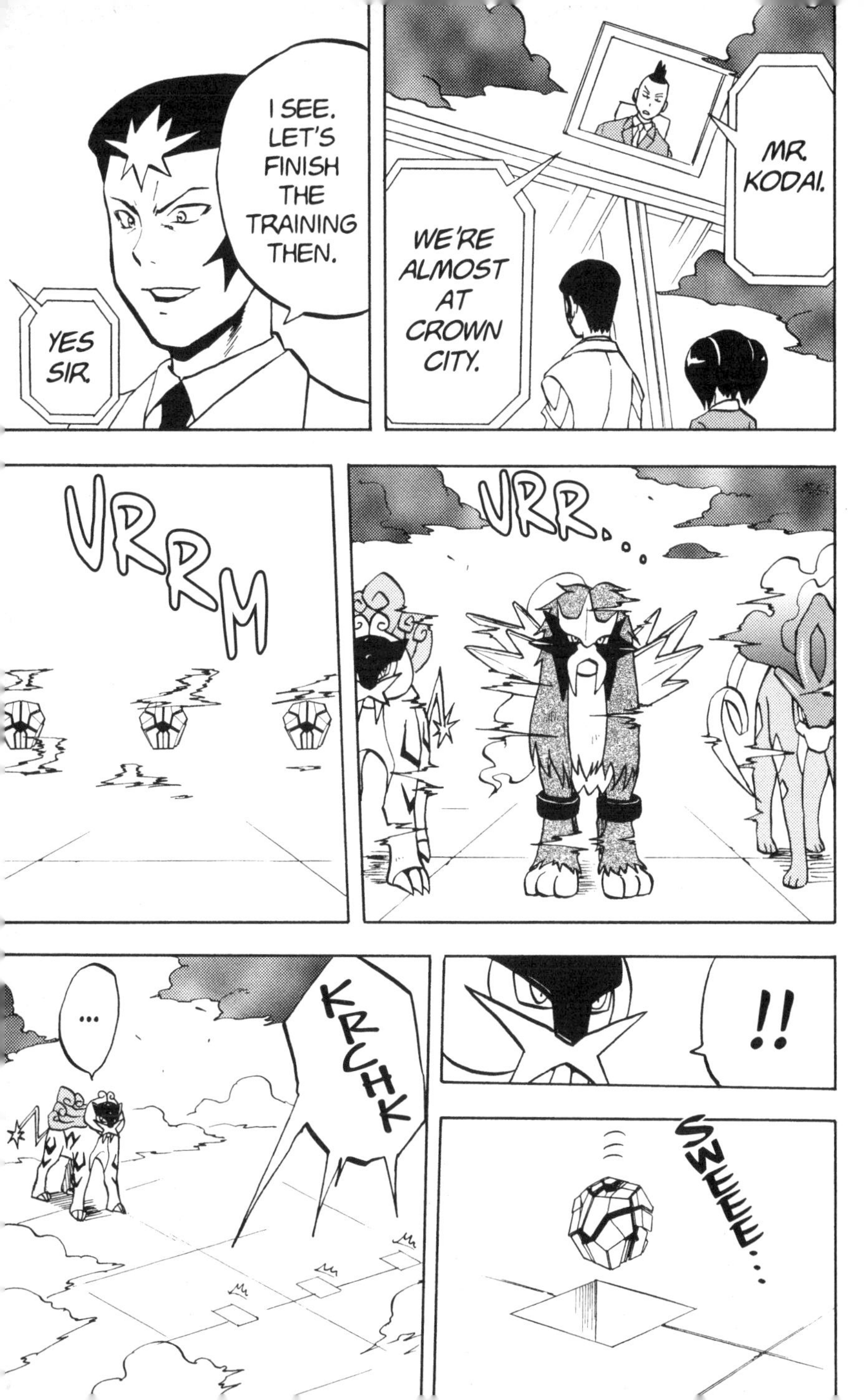
MR. KODAI.
WE'RE ALMOST AT CROWN CITY.
I SEE. LET'S FINISH THE TRAINING THEN.
YES SIR.
URR...
URRM
!!
SWEEE...
KRCHK
...

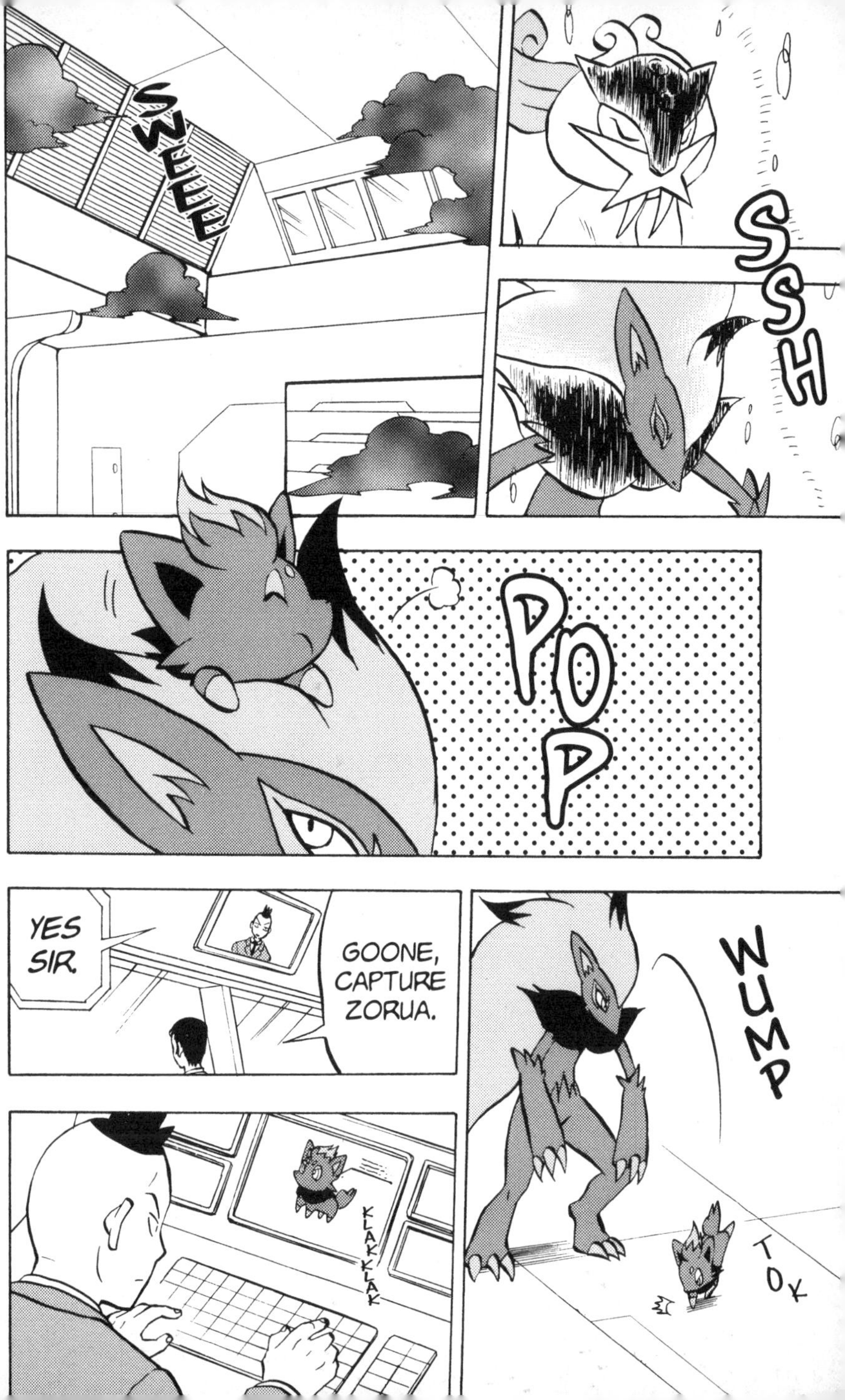
SSSH
SWEEE
POP
WUMP
TOK
GOONE, CAPTURE ZORUA.
YES SIR.
KLAK KLAK

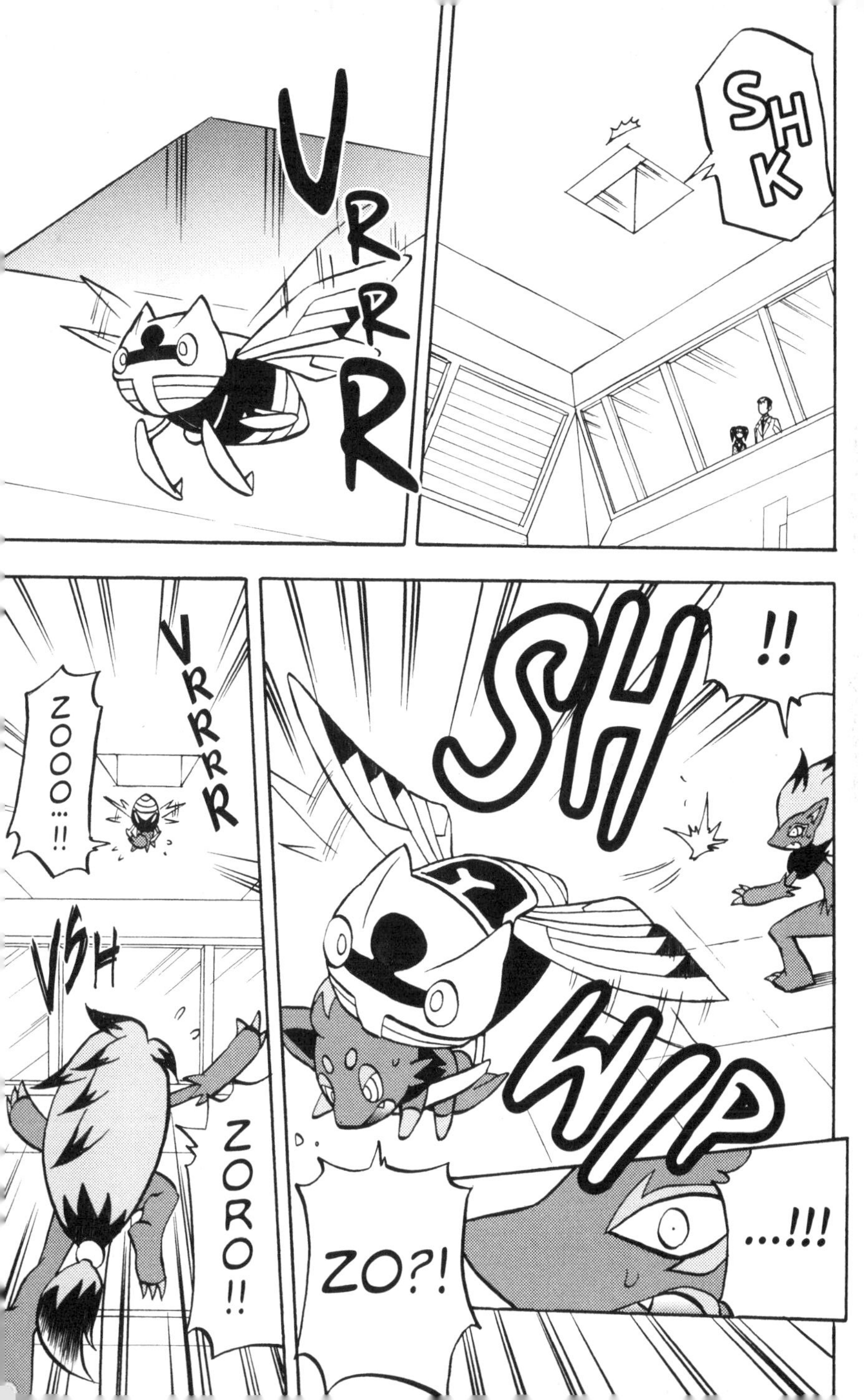
SHK
VRRRR
!!
SHWIP
...!!!
ZO?!
VRRRRR
ZOOOO...!!
VSH
ZORO!!

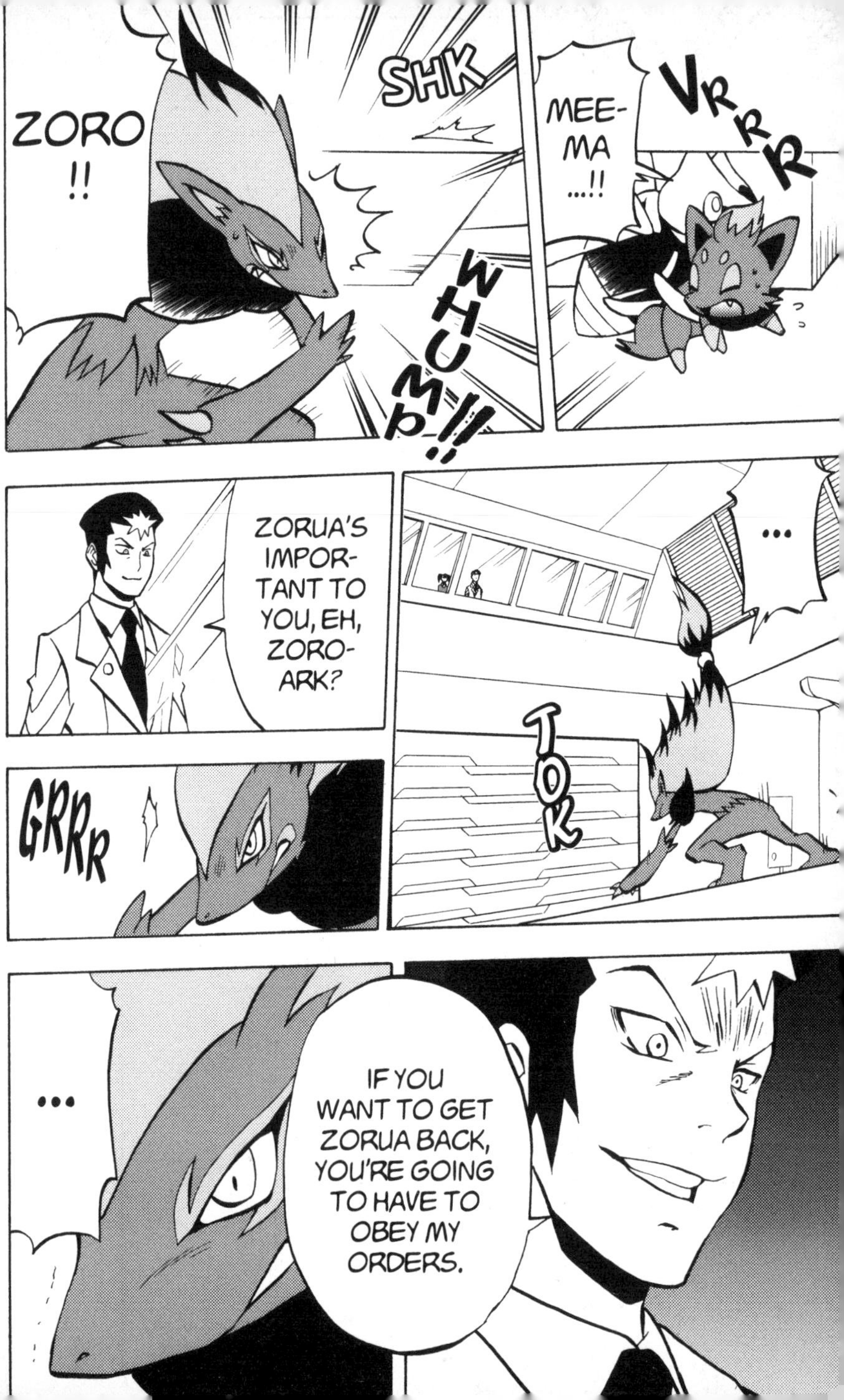
VRRRR
MEE-MA ...!!
SHK
WHUMP!!
ZORO !!
...
TOK
ZORUA'S IMPORTANT TO YOU, EH, ZOROARK?
GRRRR
IF YOU WANT TO GET ZORUA BACK, YOU'RE GOING TO HAVE TO OBEY MY ORDERS.
...

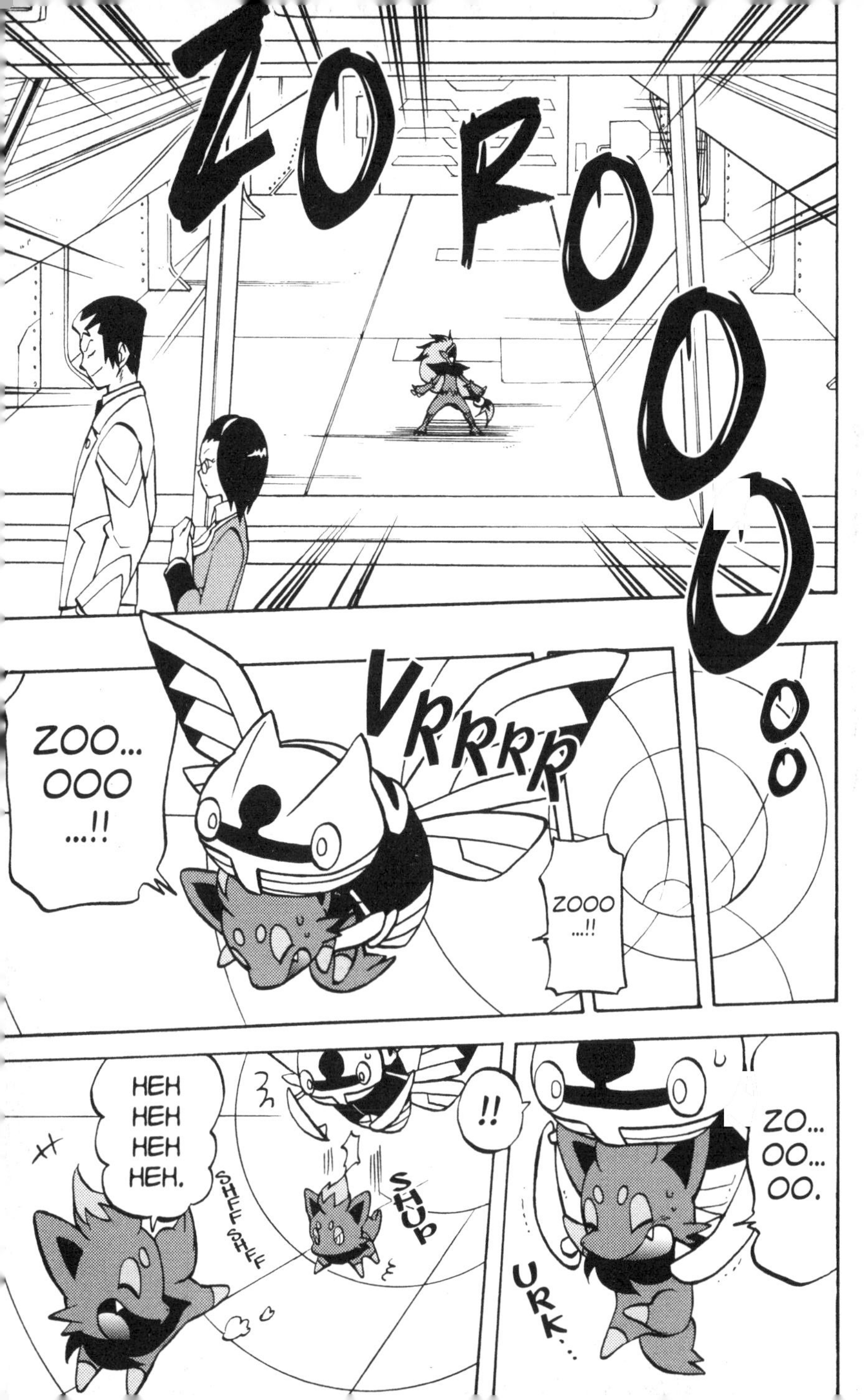
ZOROOOOOO
ZOOO ...!!
VRRRR
ZOO... OOO ...!!
ZO... OO... OO.
URK...
!!
SHUP
HEH HEH HEH HEH.
SHEF SHEF

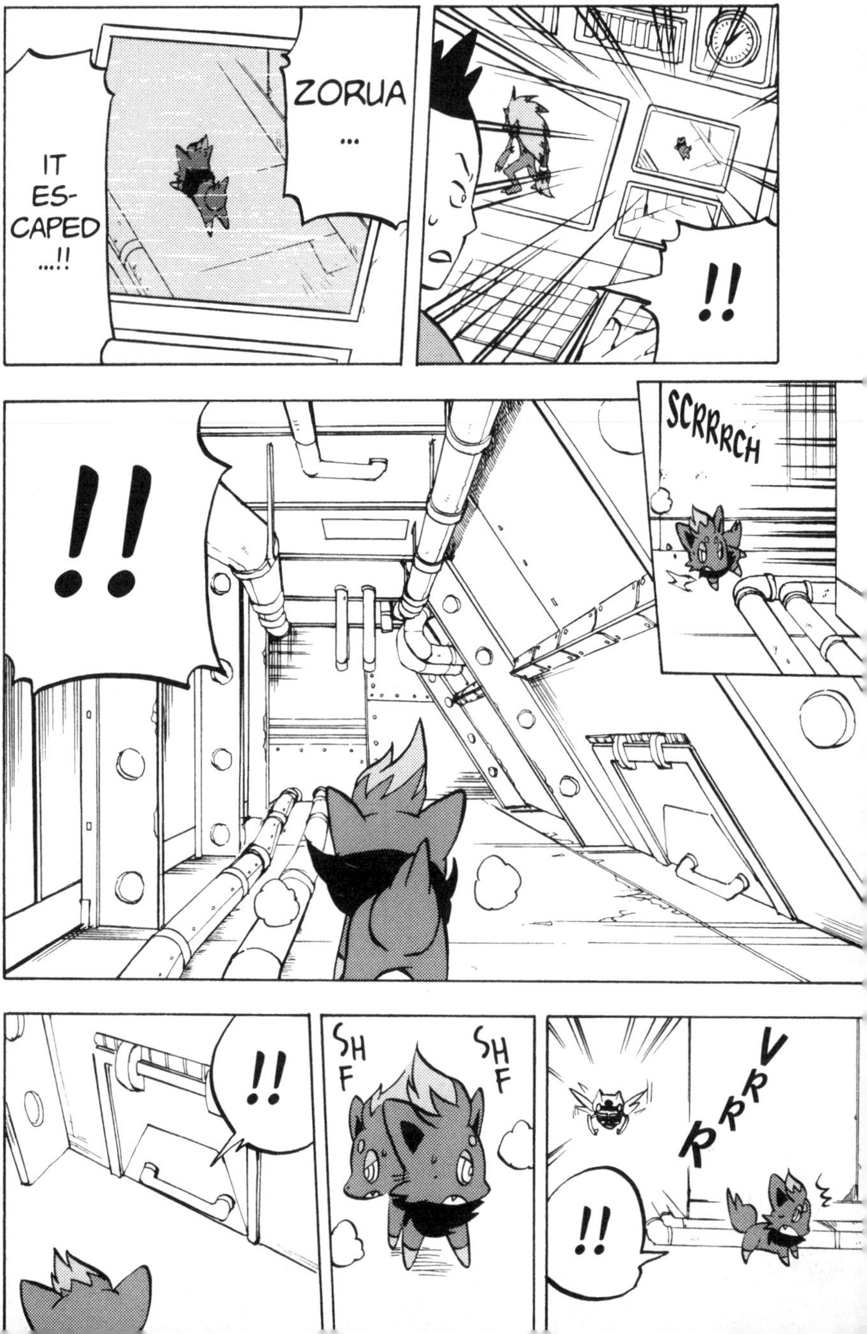
!!
ZORUA
...
IT ES-CAPED ...!!
SCRRRCH
!!
RRRRV
!!
SHF
SHF
!!

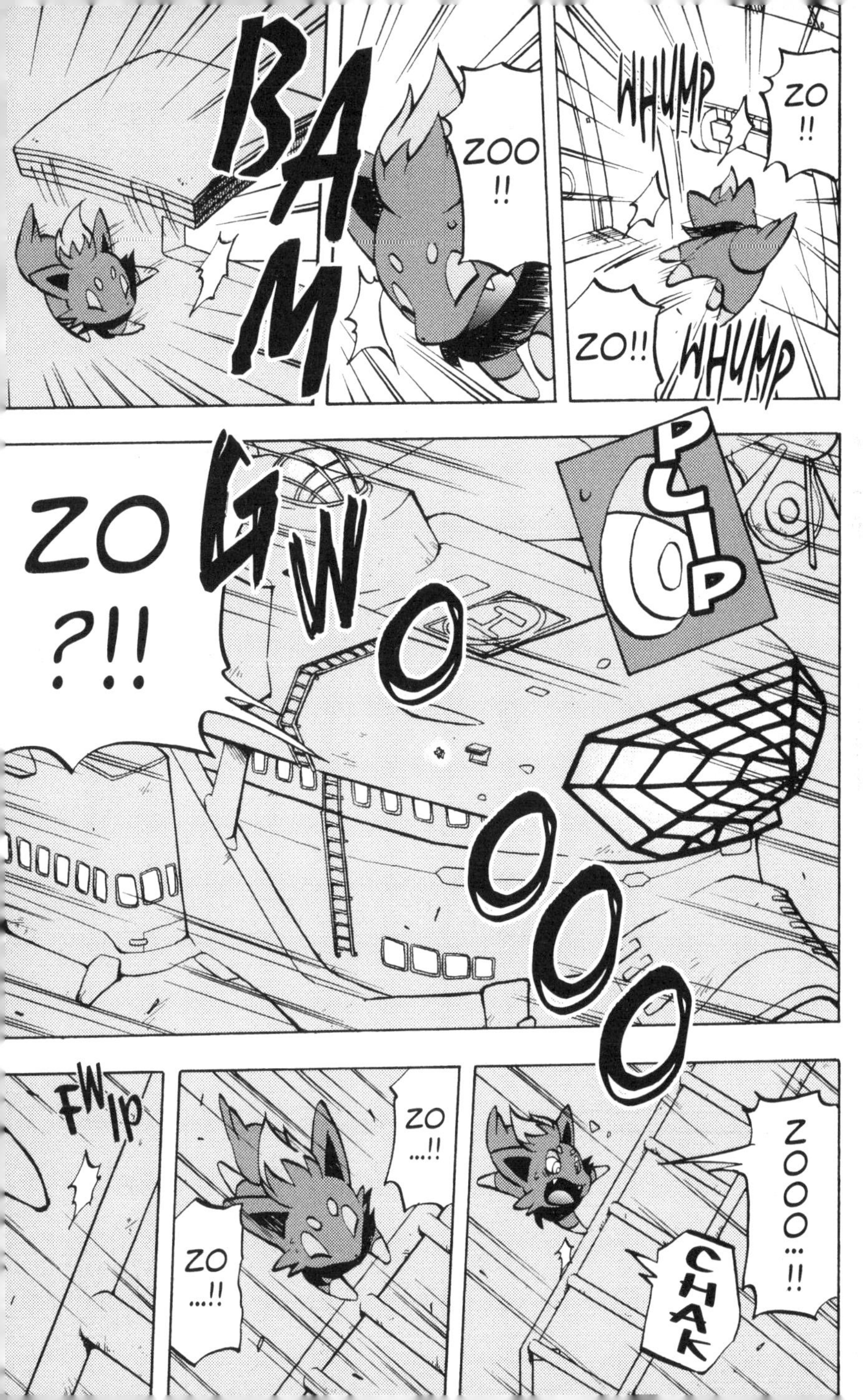
ZO!!
WHUMP
ZO!!
WHUMP
ZOO!!
BAM
PLIP
GWOOOOO
ZO?!!
ZOOOO...!!
CHAK
ZO...!!
ZO...!!
FWIP

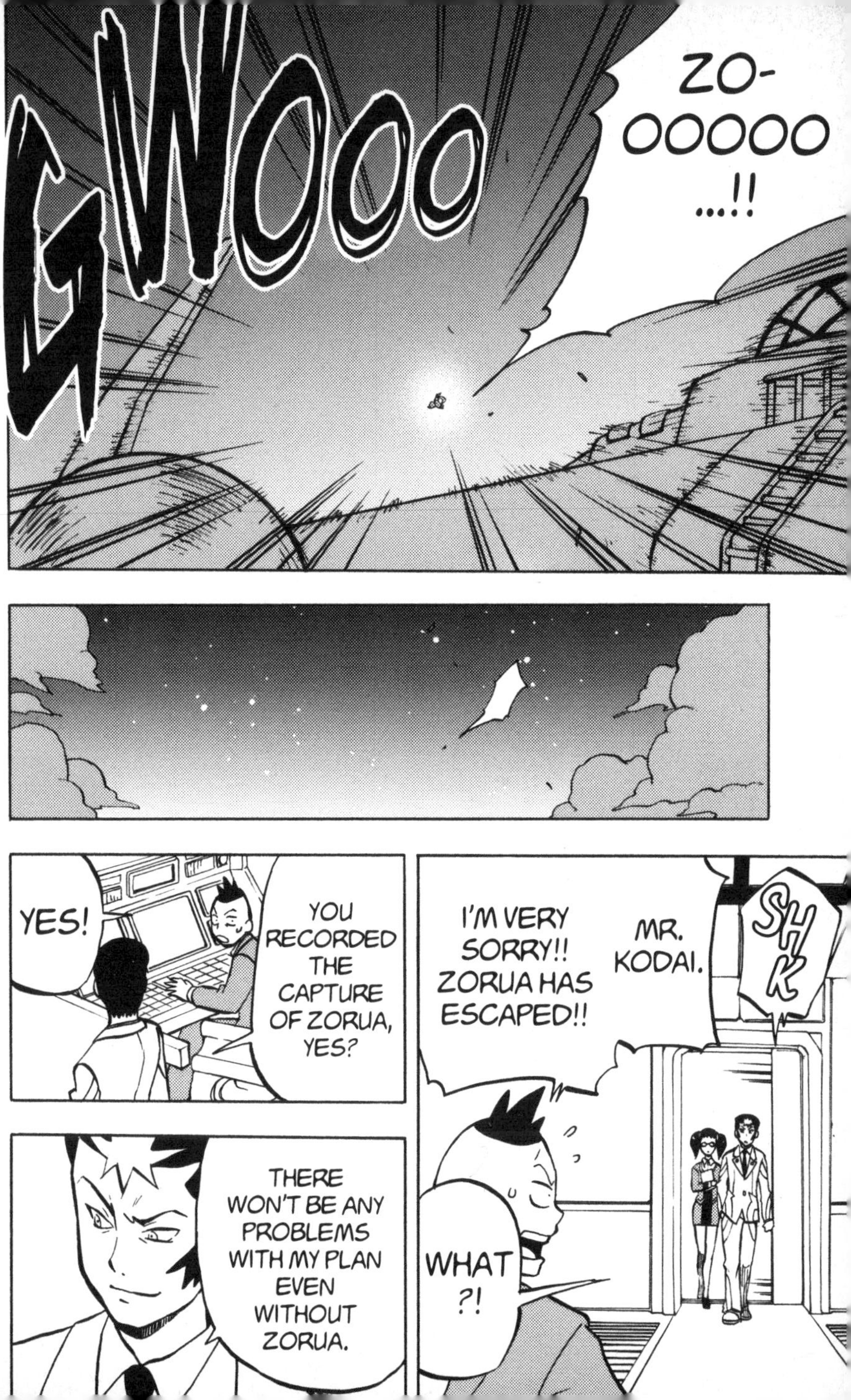
ZO-OOOOO...!!
GWOOO
SHK
MR. KODAI.
I'M VERY SORRY!! ZORUA HAS ESCAPED!!
WHAT?!
YOU RECORDED THE CAPTURE OF ZORUA, YES?
YES!
THERE WON'T BE ANY PROBLEMS WITH MY PLAN EVEN WITHOUT ZORUA.

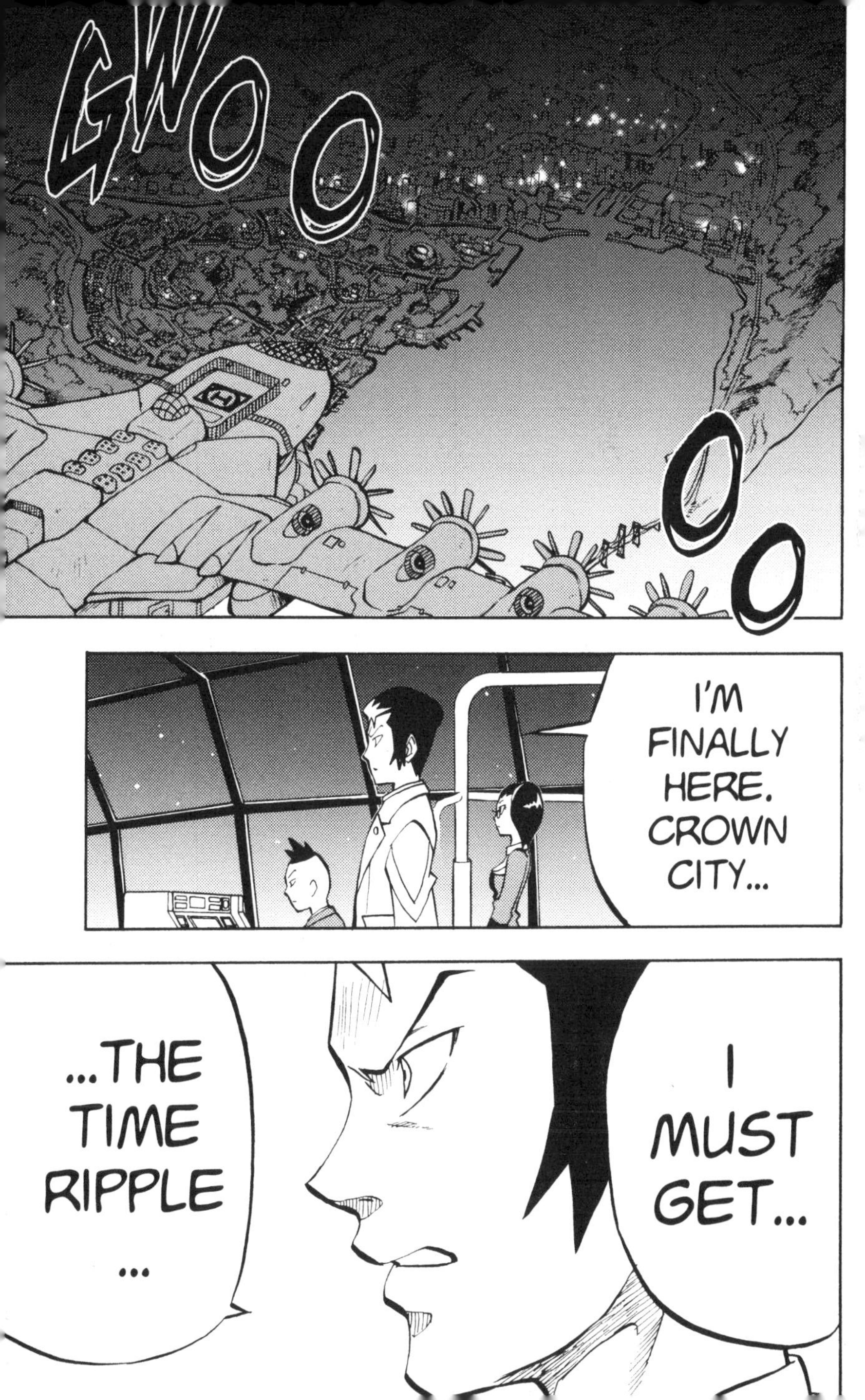
GWOOOOO
I'M FINALLY HERE. CROWN CITY...
I MUST GET...
...THE TIME RIPPLE ...

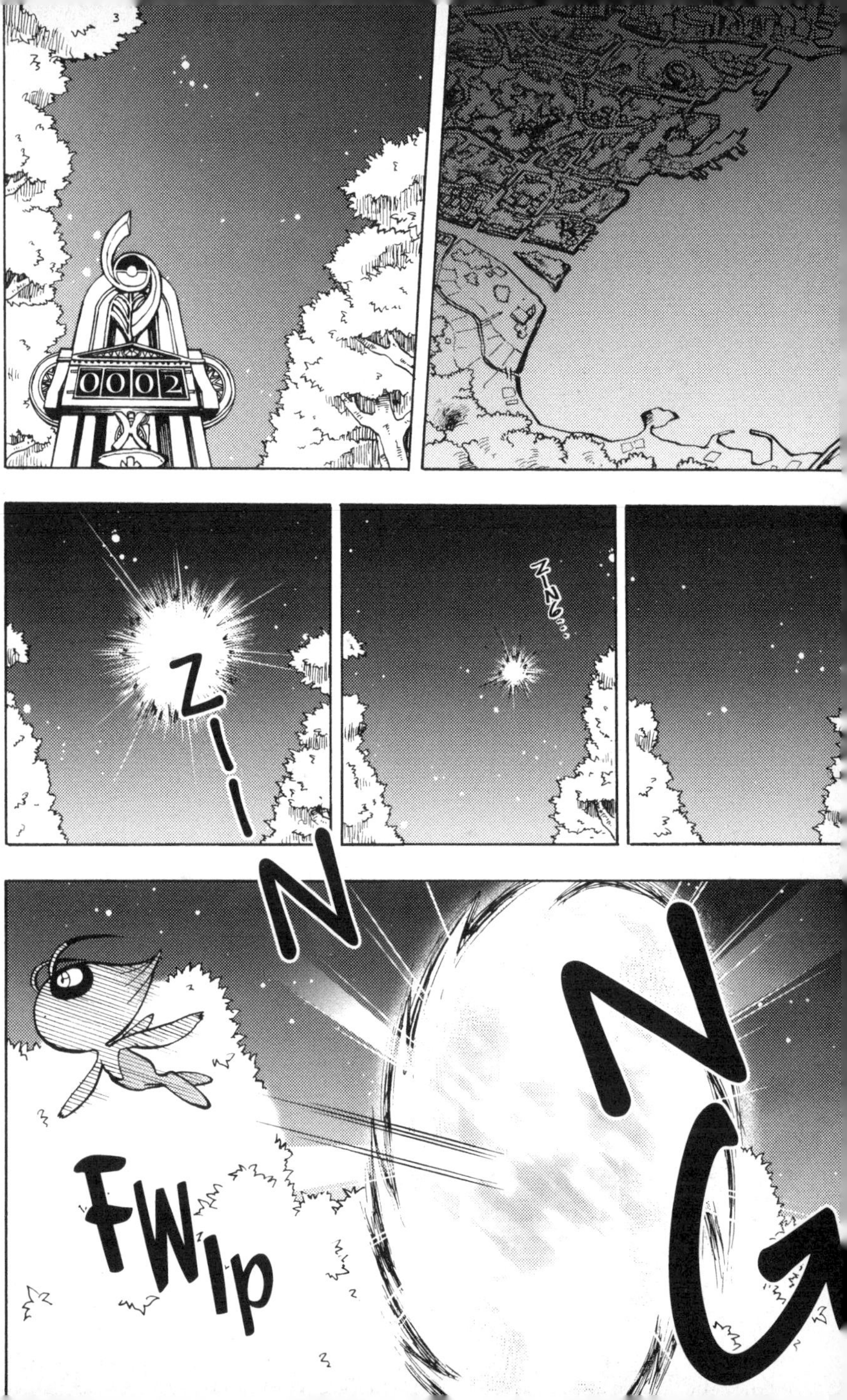
0002
ZING...
ZIINNG
FWIP

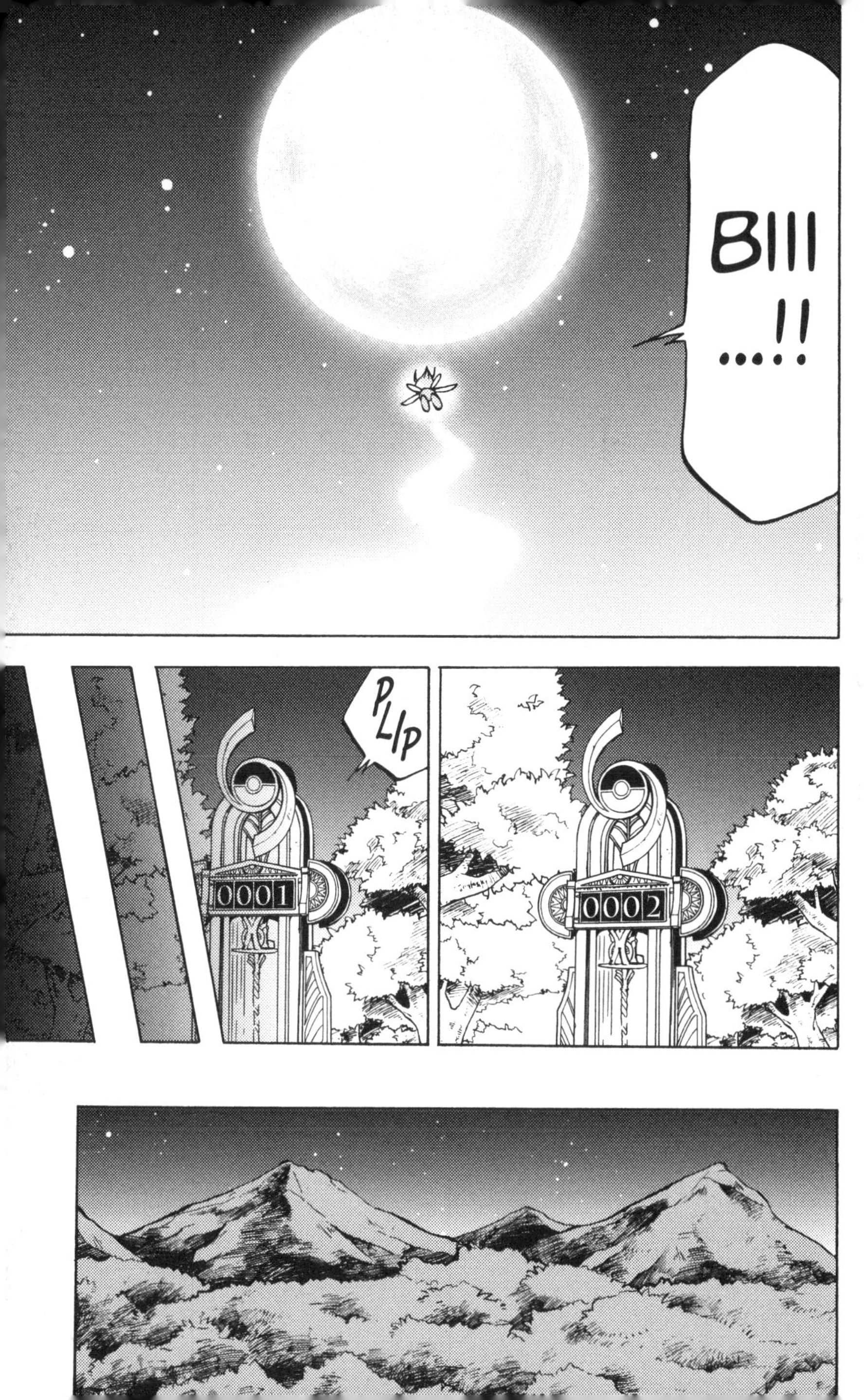
BIII ...!!
0002
PLIP
0001

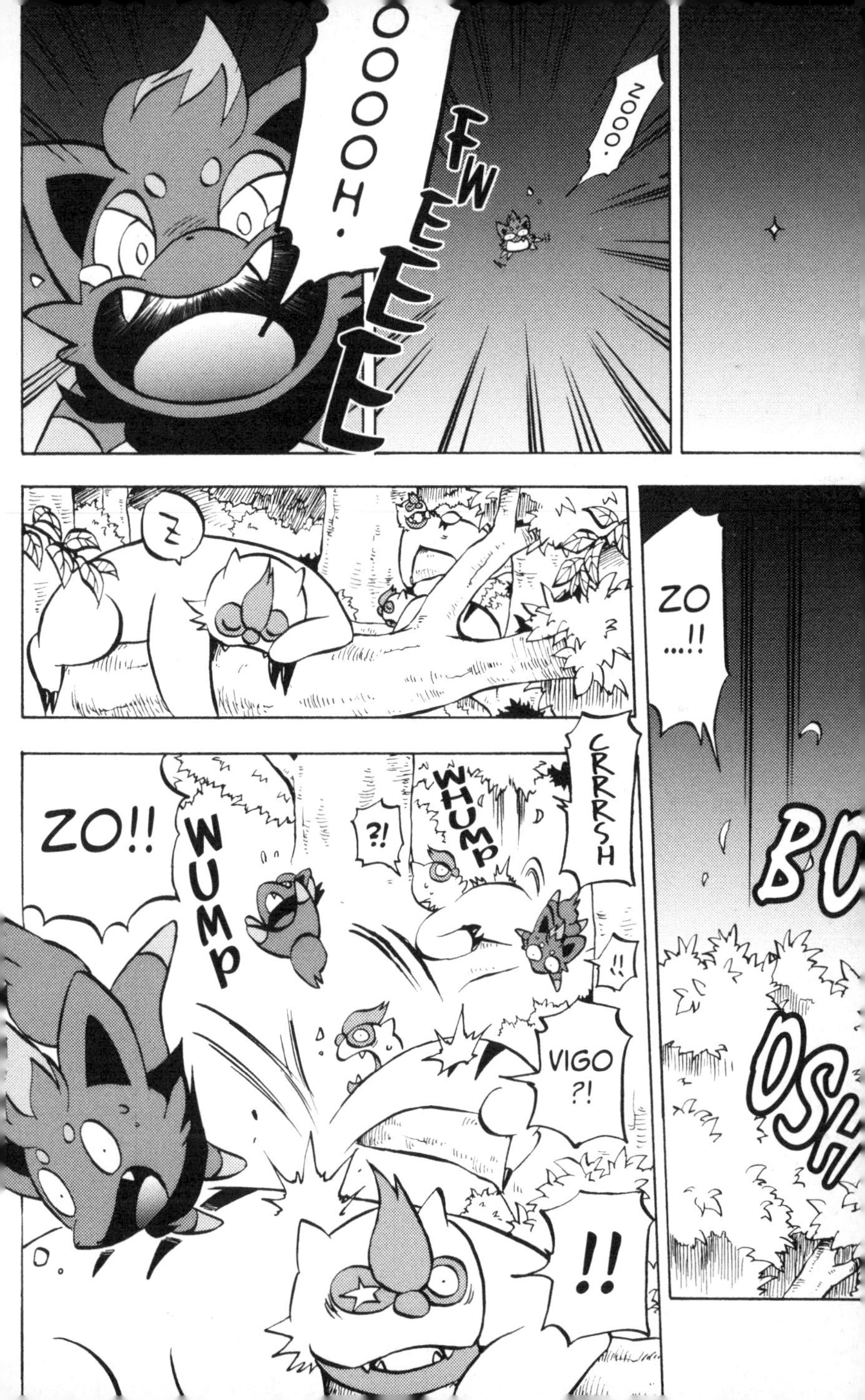
ZOOO...
OOOOOOH.
FWEEEEE
ZO ...!!
BO
OSH
Z
CRRRSH
WHUMP
?!
WUMP
ZO!!
!!
VIGO ?!
!!

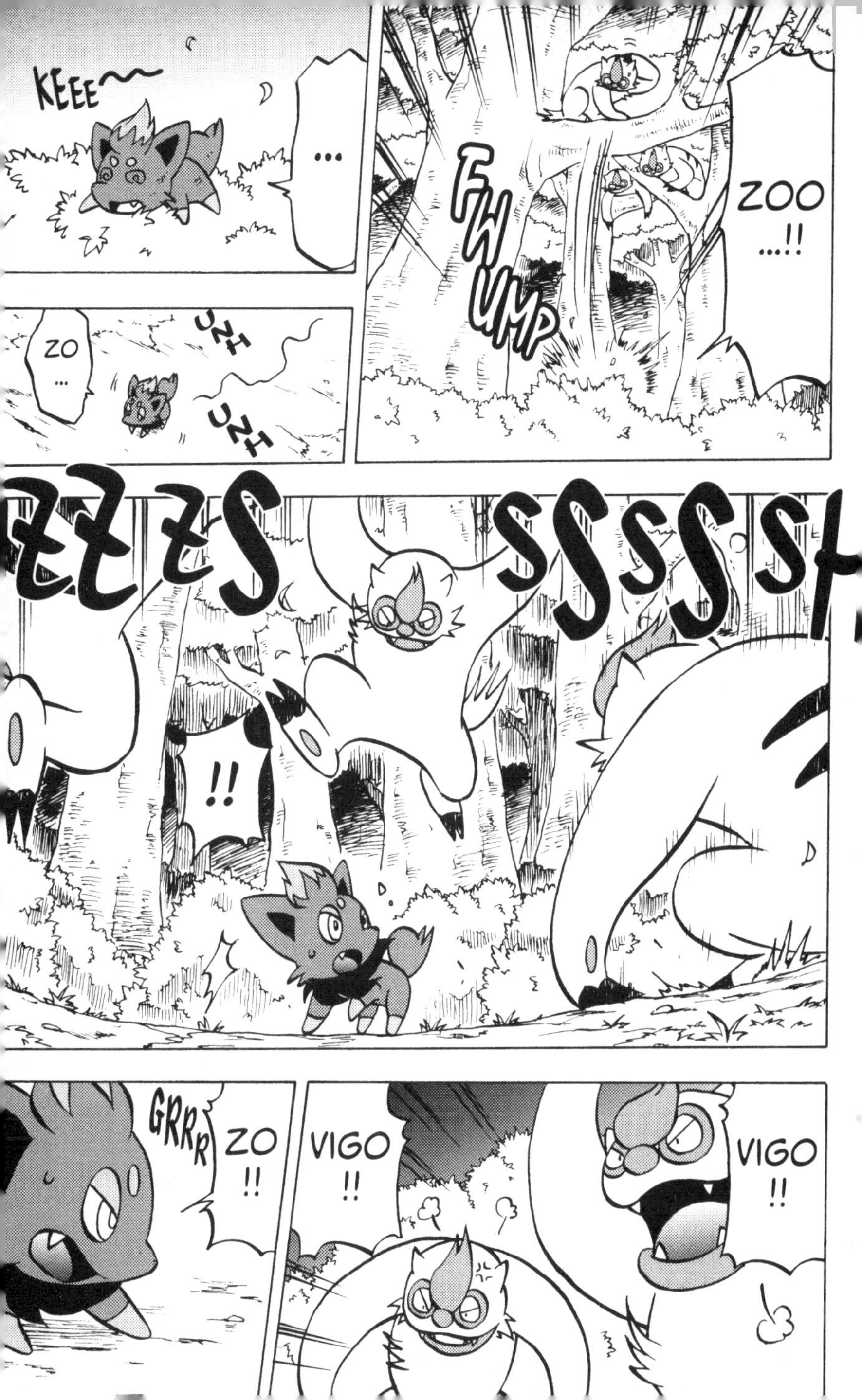

FWUMP
ZOO ...!!
KEEE~~
...
ZO ...
SSSSH
!!
VIGO !!
VIGO !!
GRRR
ZO !!

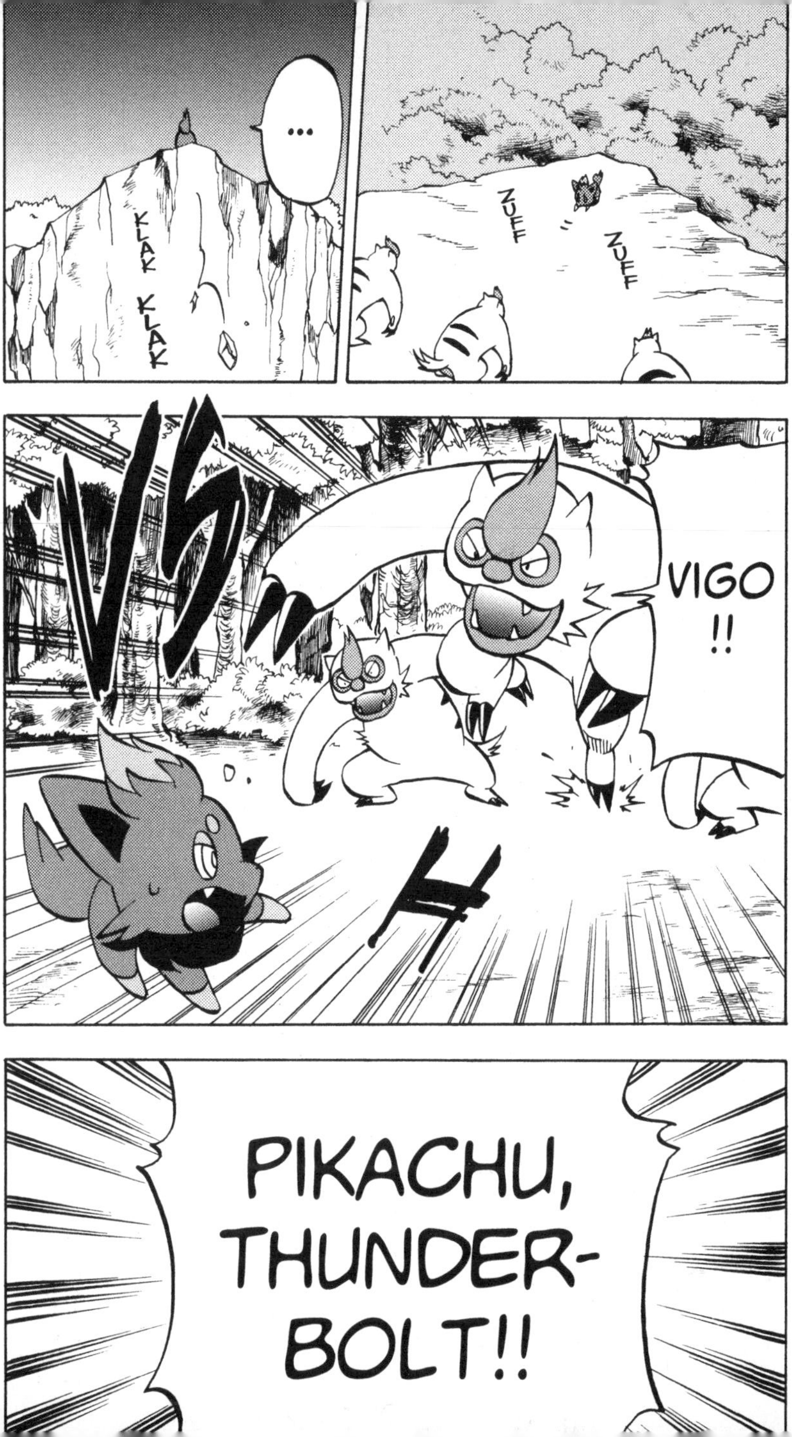
ZUFF
ZUFF
...
KLAK KLAK
VIGO !!
PIKACHU, THUNDER-BOLT!!

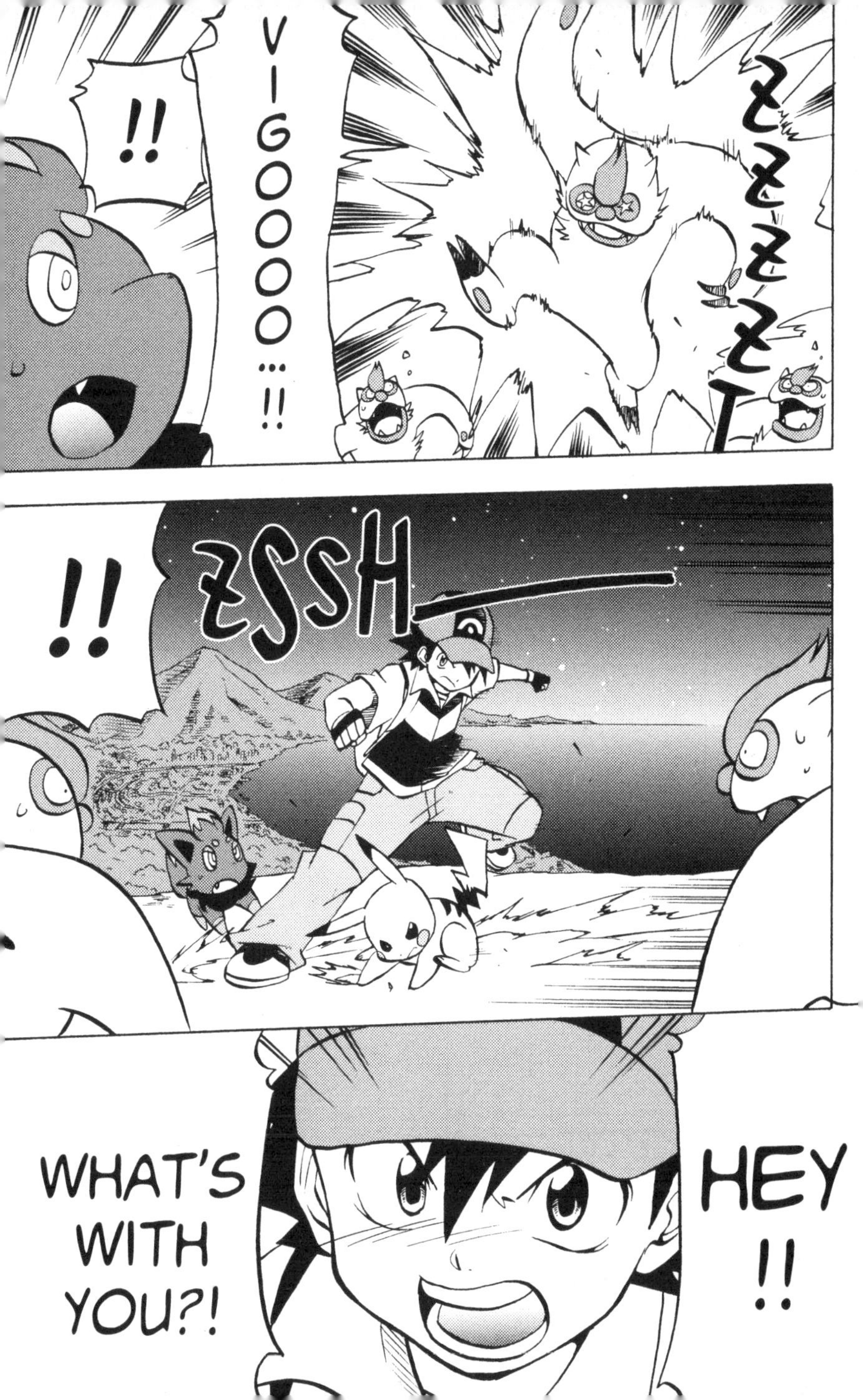
VIGOOOOO...!!
!!
ZSSH
!!
HEY !!
WHAT'S WITH YOU?!

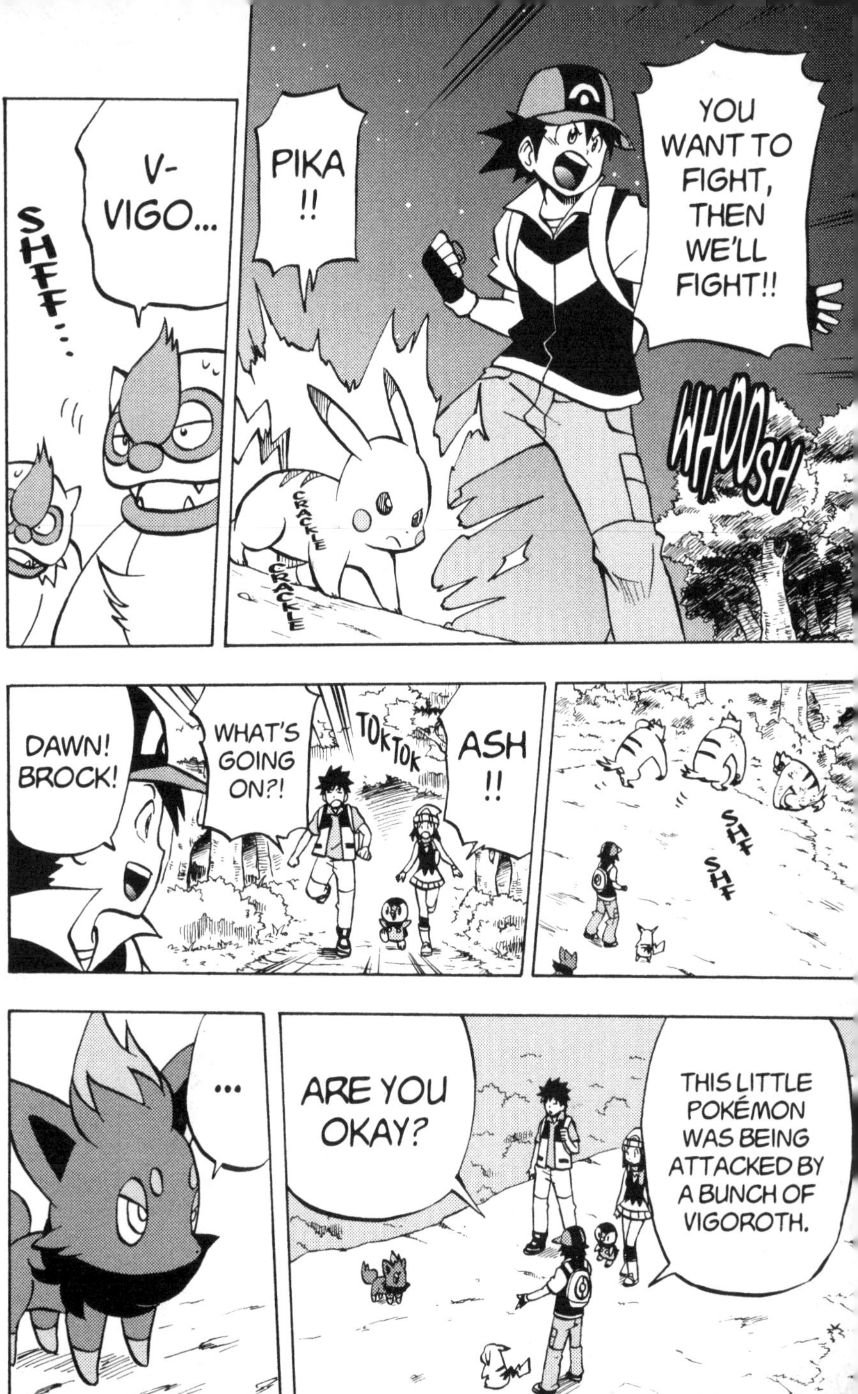
YOU WANT TO FIGHT, THEN WE'LL FIGHT!!
WHOOOSH
PIKA !!
CRACKLE
CRACKLE
V-VIGO...
SHFFF...
SHF
SHF
ASH !!
TOKTOK
WHAT'S GOING ON?!
DAWN! BROCK!
THIS LITTLE POKÉMON WAS BEING ATTACKED BY A BUNCH OF VIGOROTH.
ARE YOU OKAY?
...

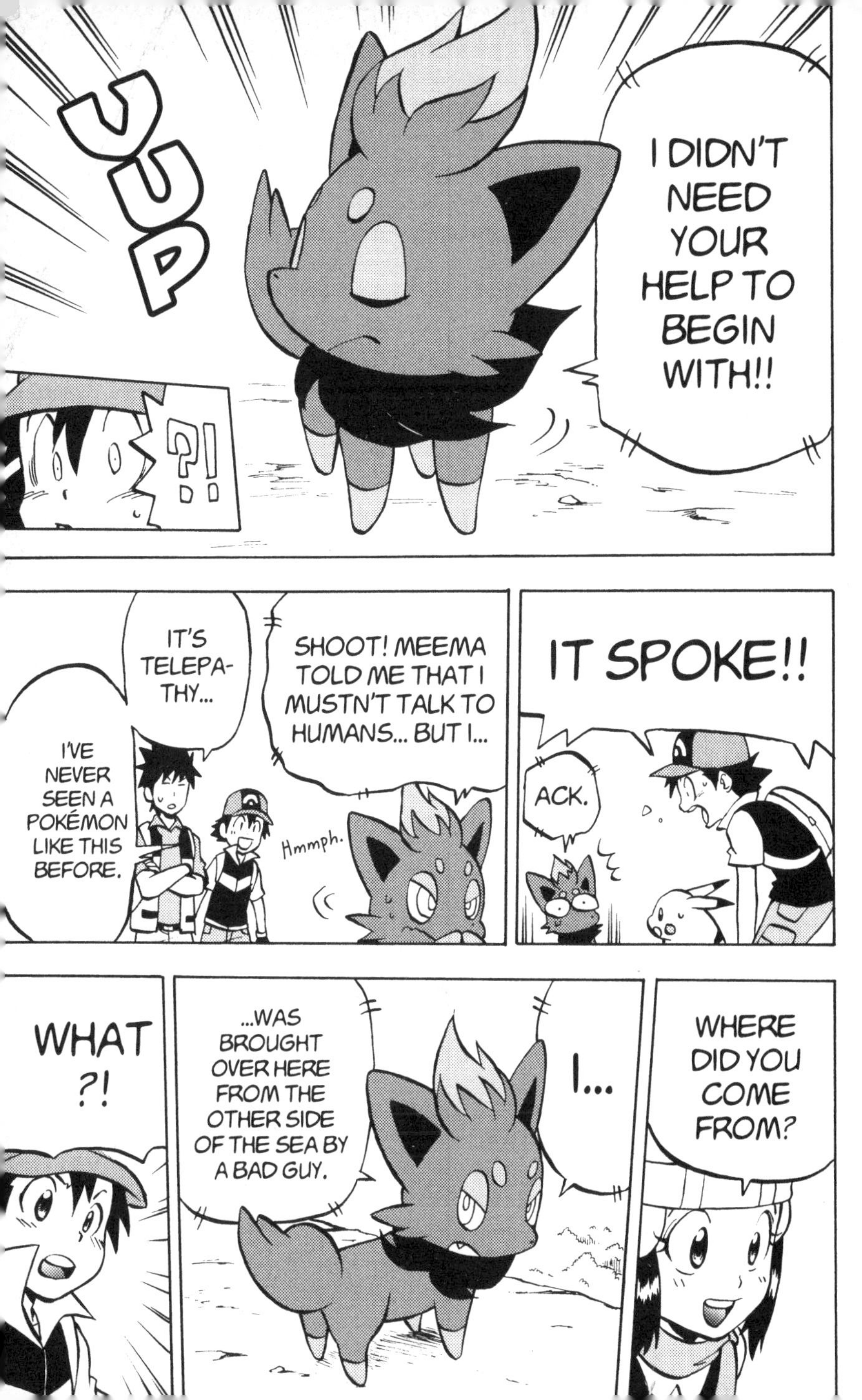
I DIDN'T NEED YOUR HELP TO BEGIN WITH!!
JUP
?!
IT SPOKE!!
ACK.
SHOOT! MEEMA TOLD ME THAT I MUSTN'T TALK TO HUMANS... BUT I...
IT'S TELEPA-THY...
I'VE NEVER SEEN A POKÉMON LIKE THIS BEFORE.
Hmmph.
WHERE DID YOU COME FROM?
I...
...WAS BROUGHT OVER HERE FROM THE OTHER SIDE OF THE SEA BY A BAD GUY.
WHAT ?!

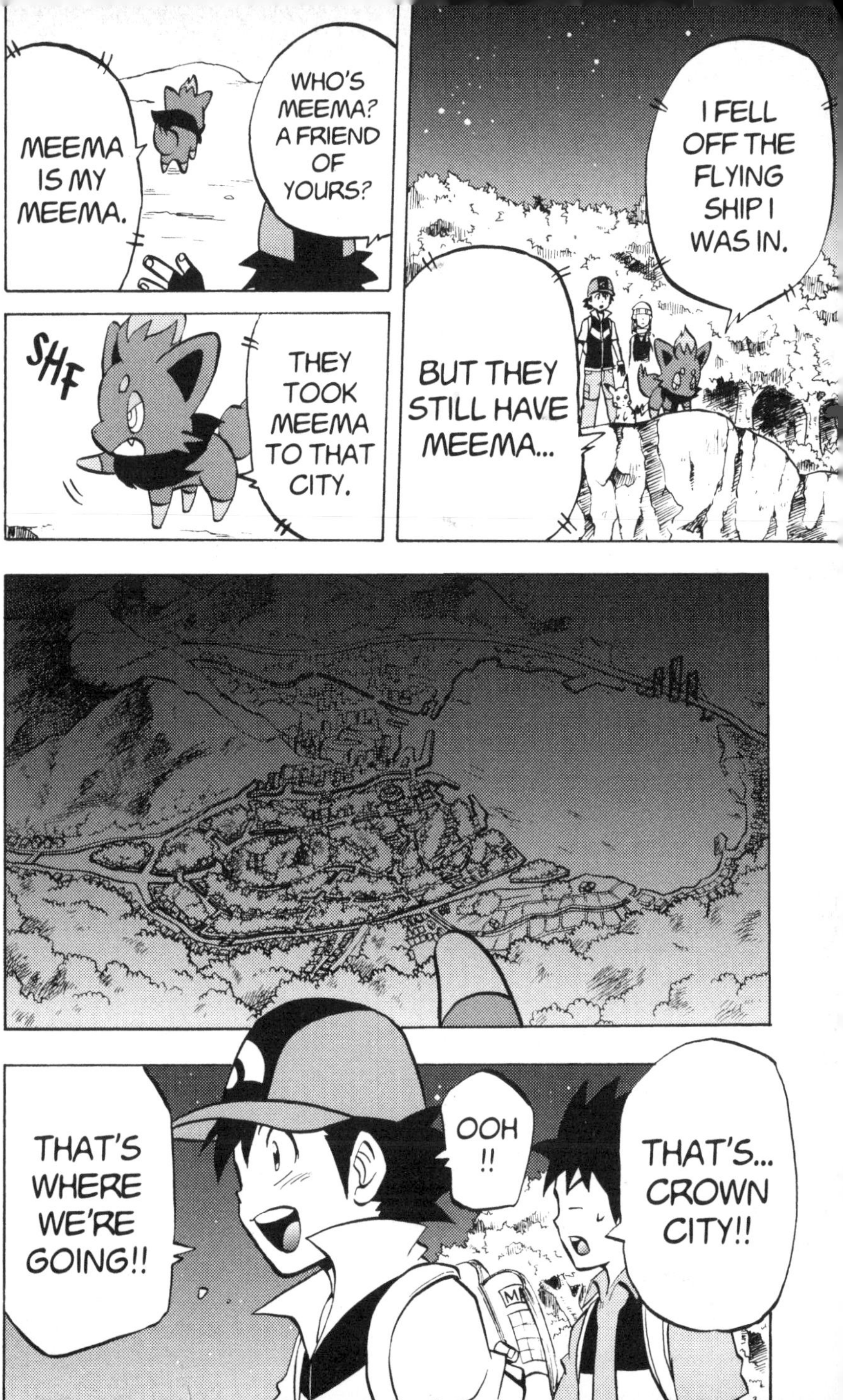
I FELL OFF THE FLYING SHIP I WAS IN.
BUT THEY STILL HAVE MEEMA...
WHO'S MEEMA? A FRIEND OF YOURS?
MEEMA IS MY MEEMA.
SHF
THEY TOOK MEEMA TO THAT CITY.
THAT'S... CROWN CITY!!
OOH !!
THAT'S WHERE WE'RE GOING!!

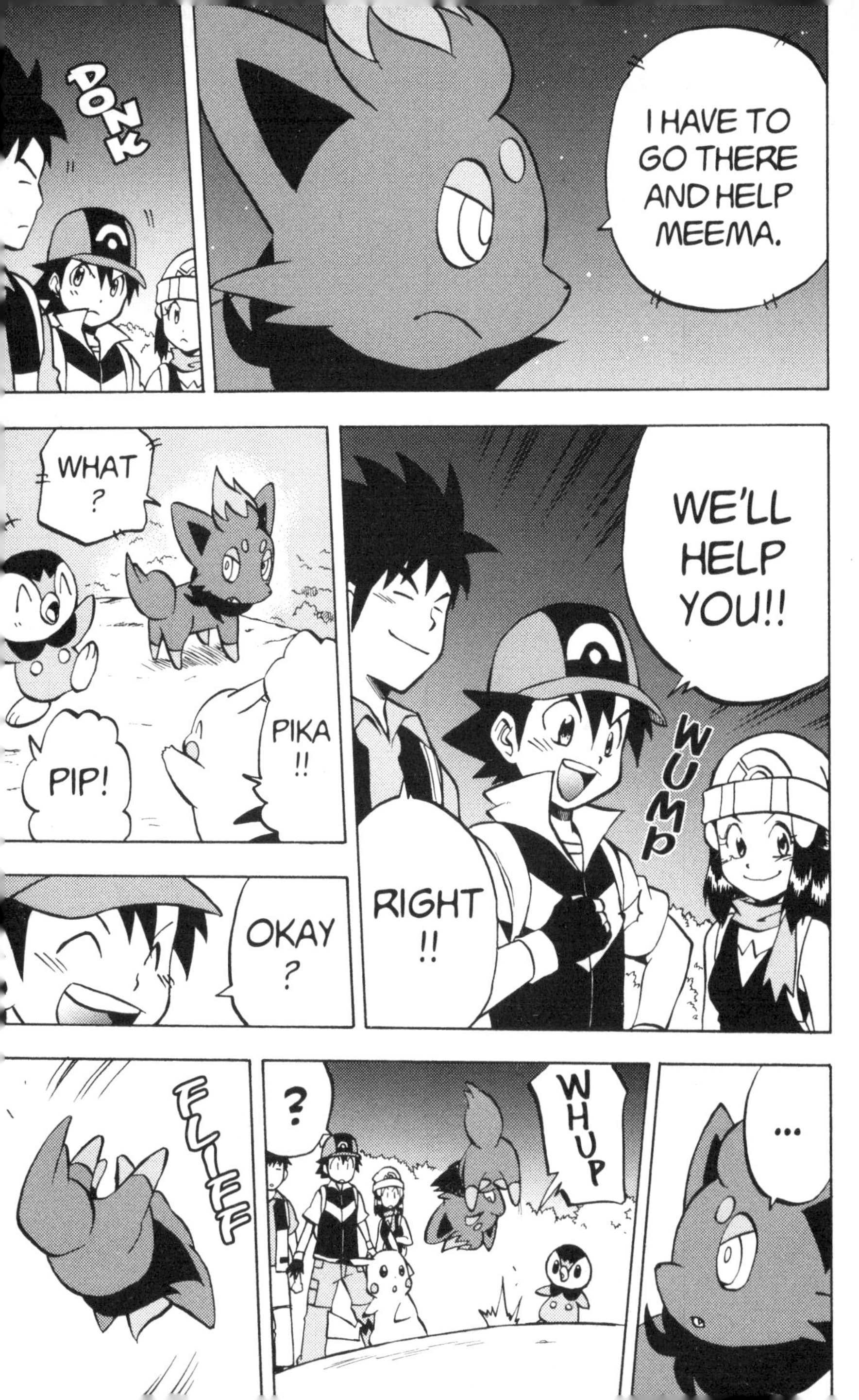

I HAVE TO GO THERE AND HELP MEEMA.
DONK
WE'LL HELP YOU!!
WUMP
RIGHT!!
WHAT?
PIKA!!
PIP!
OKAY?
...
WHUP
?
FLIFF

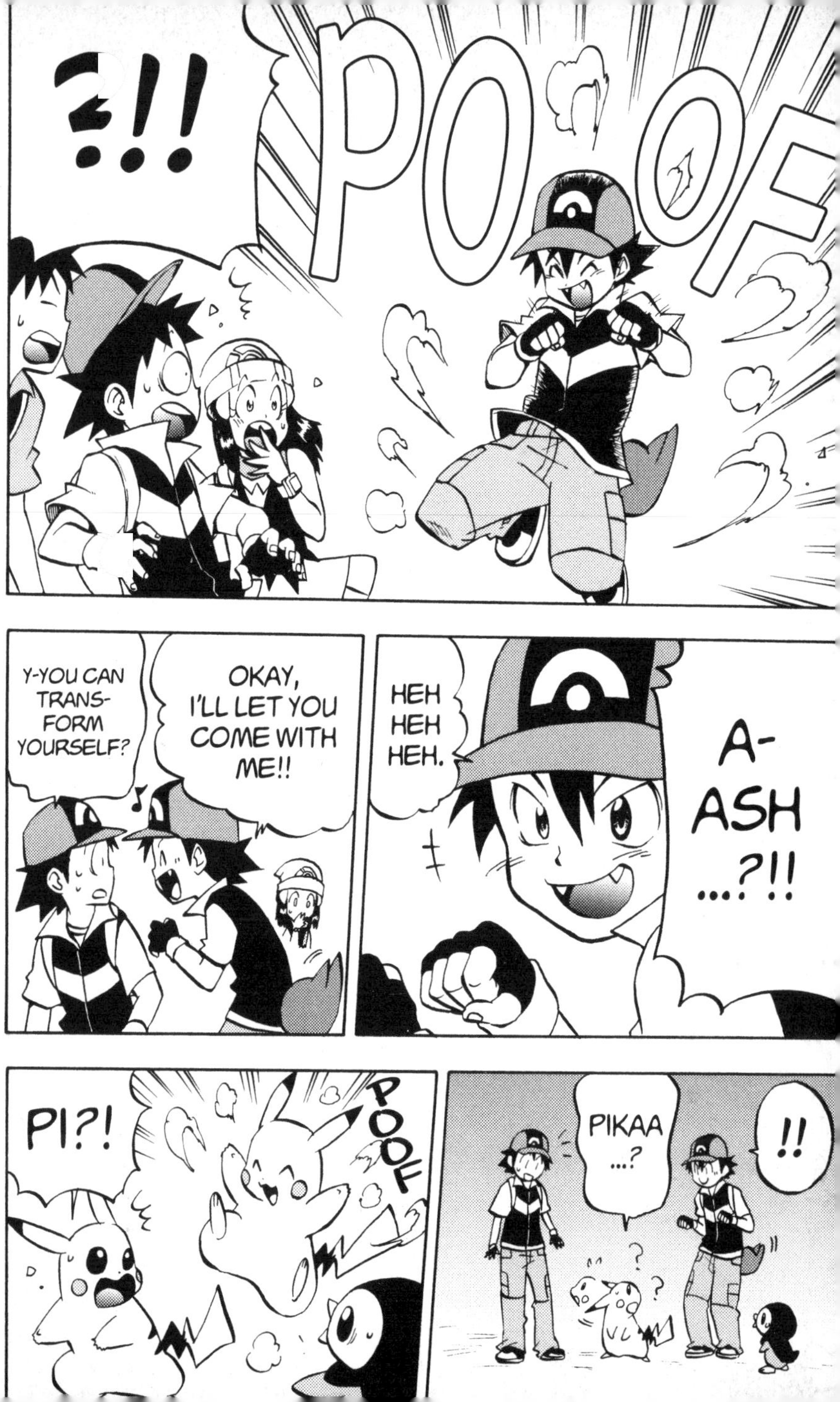
POOF
?!!
A-ASH...?!!
HEH HEH HEH.
OKAY, I'LL LET YOU COME WITH ME!!
Y-YOU CAN TRANS-FORM YOURSELF?
!!
PIKAA...?
POOF
PI?!

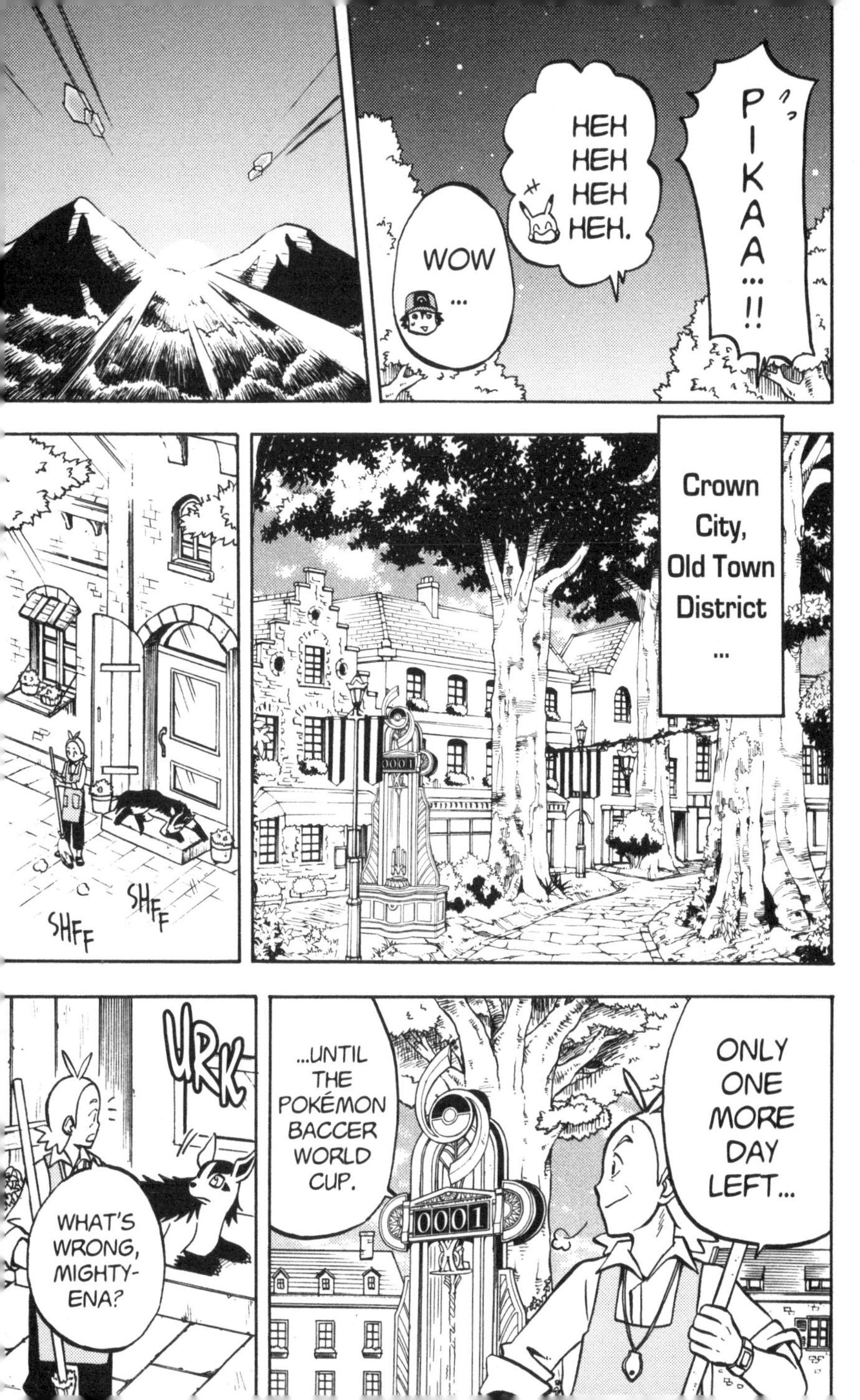
PIKAA...!!
HEH HEH HEH HEH.
WOW...
Crown City, Old Town District ...
0001
SHFF
SHFF
ONLY ONE MORE DAY LEFT...
...UNTIL THE POKÉMON BACCER WORLD CUP.
0001
URK
WHAT'S WRONG, MIGHTY-ENA?

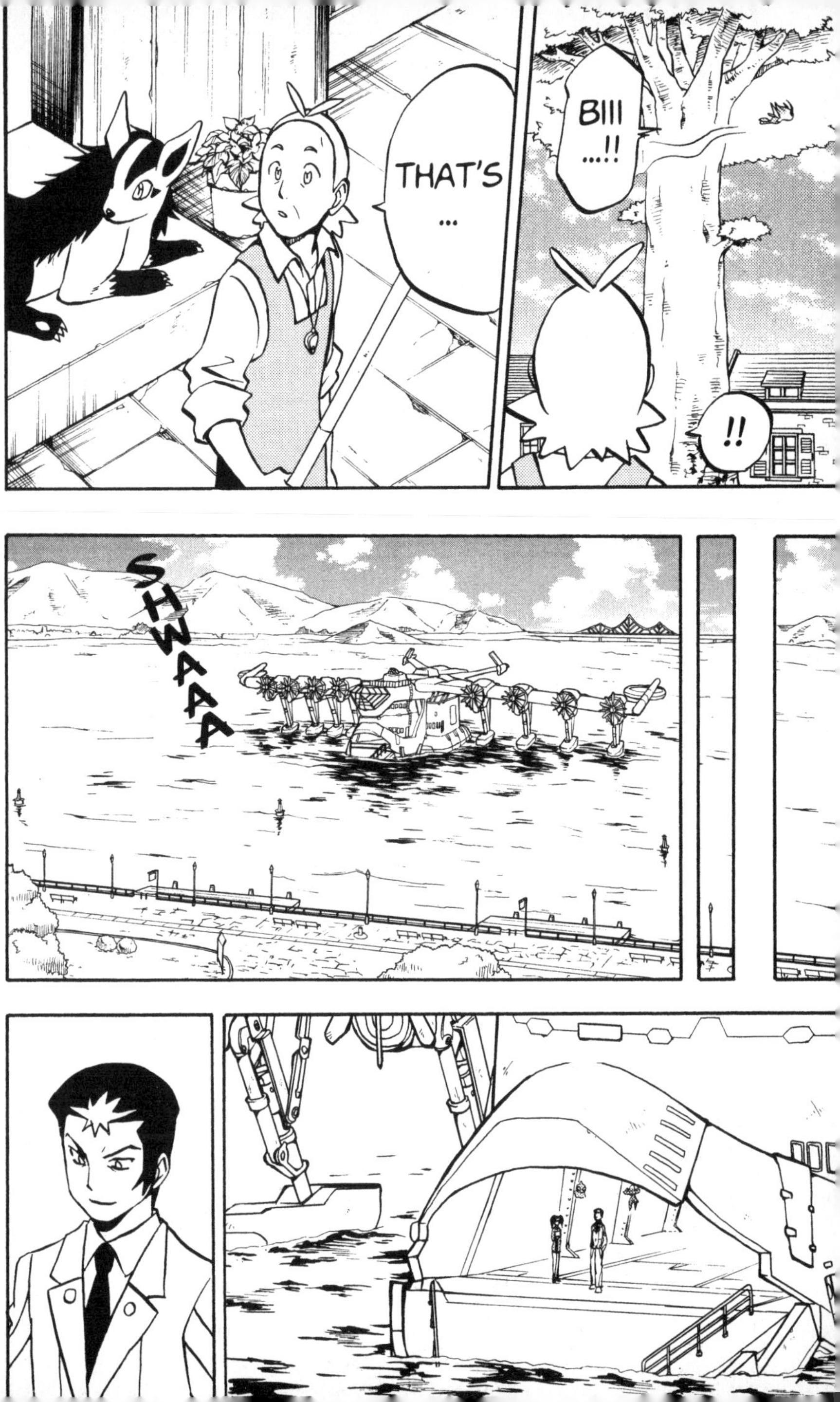
BIII ...!!
!!
THAT'S ...
SHWAAA

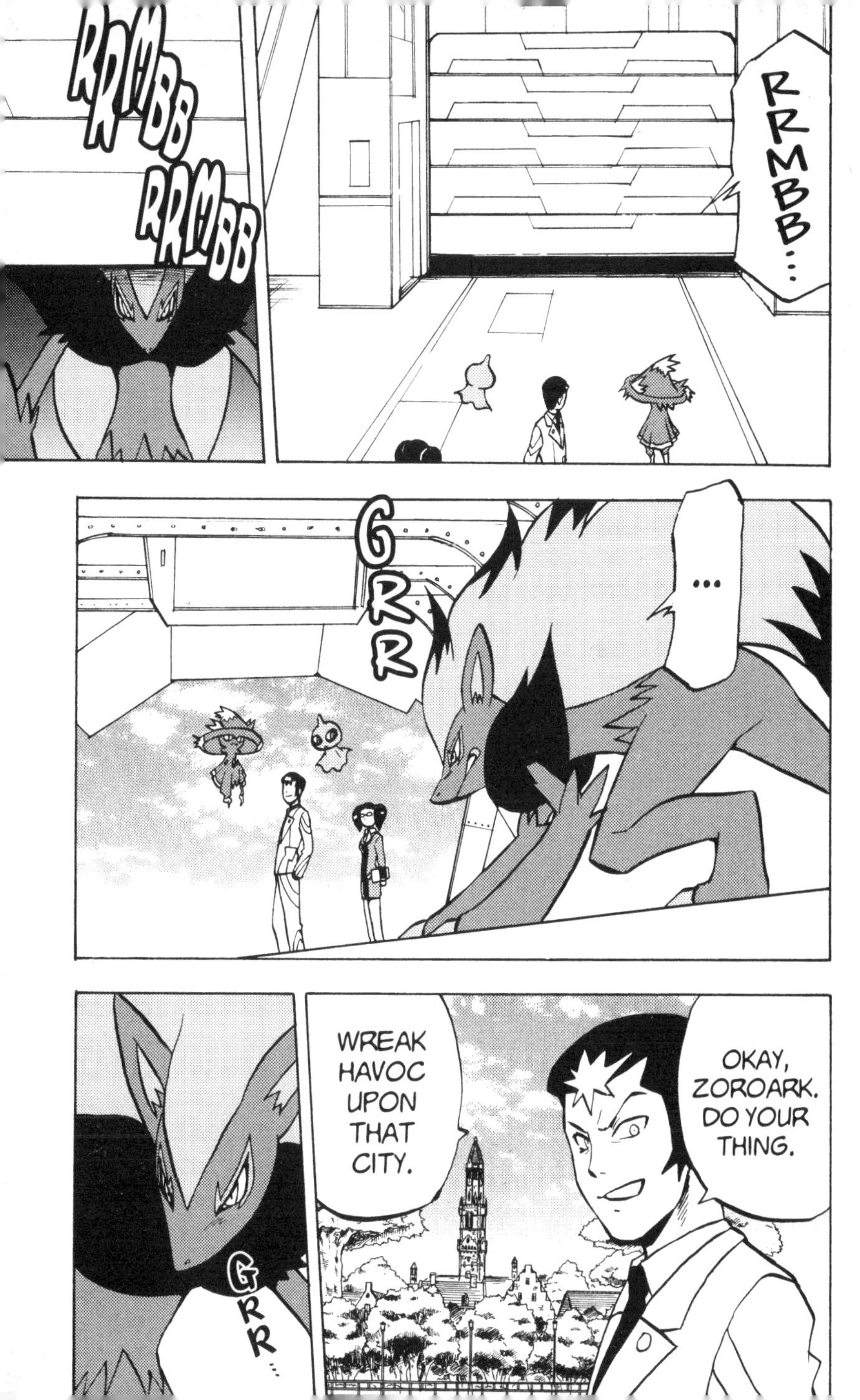
RRMBB...
RRMBB
RRMBB
...
GRR
OKAY, ZOROARK. DO YOUR THING.
WREAK HAVOC UPON THAT CITY.
GRR...

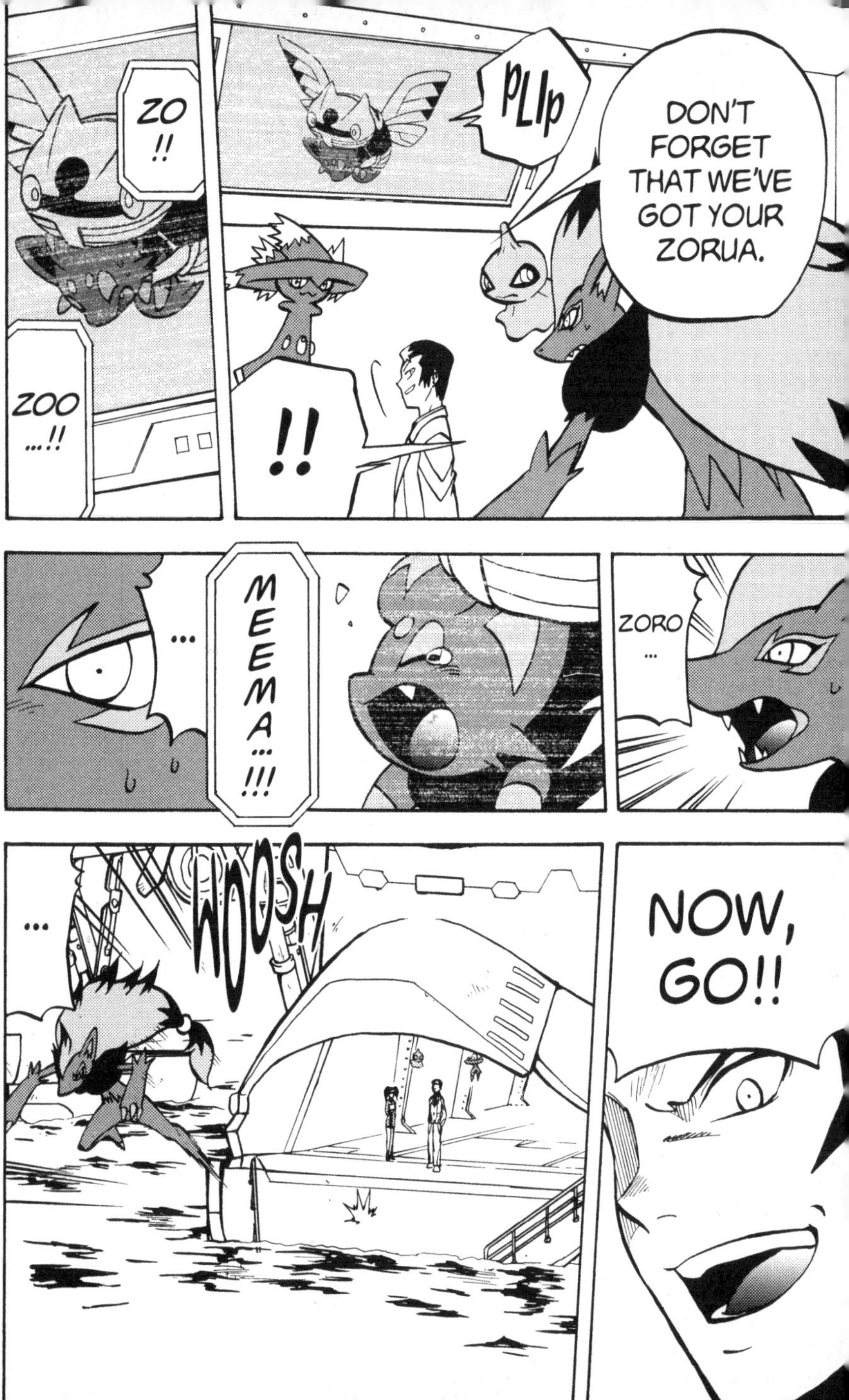

ZO !!
PLIP
DON'T FORGET THAT WE'VE GOT YOUR ZORUA.
ZOO ...!!
!!
...
MEEEMA...!!!
ZORO ...
...
WHOOSH
NOW, GO!!

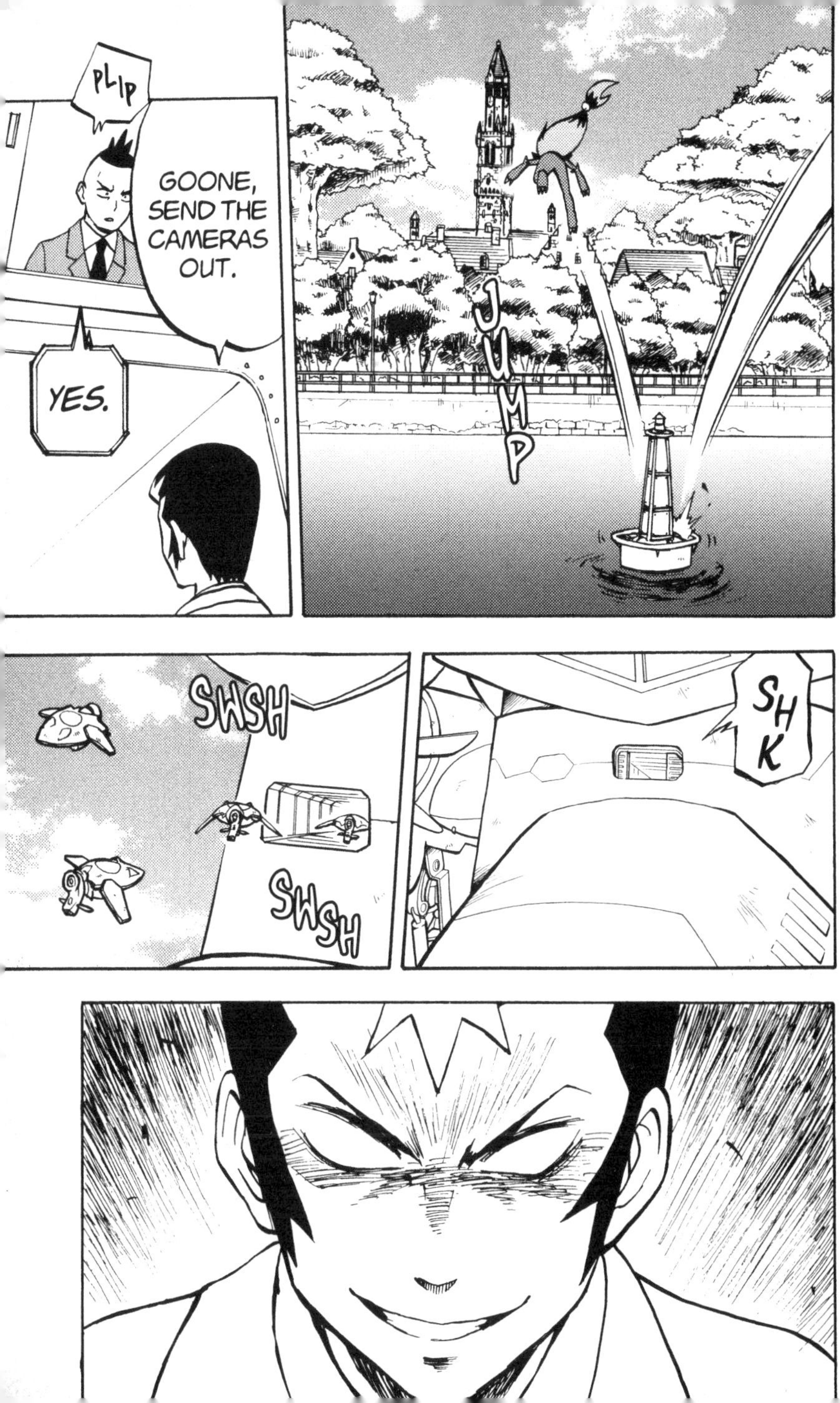
JUMP
PLIP
GOONE, SEND THE CAMERAS OUT.
YES.
SHK
SWSH
SWSH

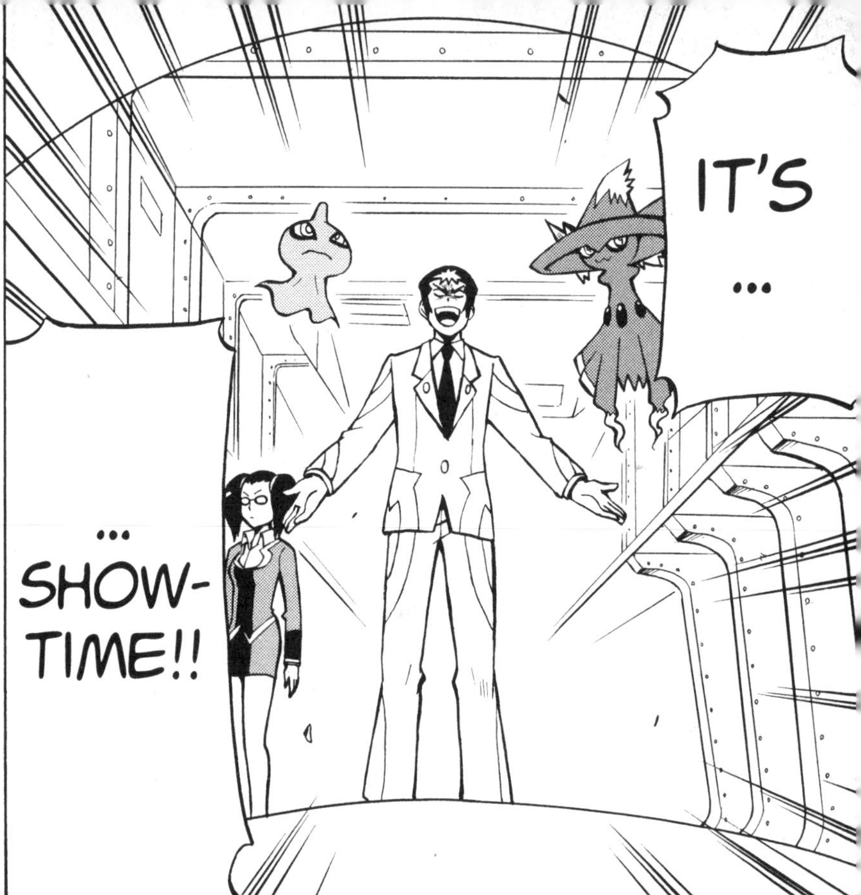
IT'S ...
... SHOW-TIME!!

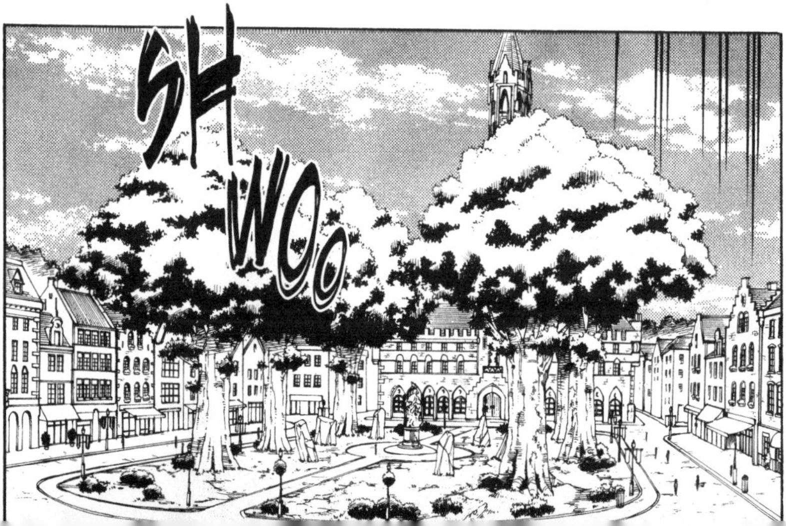
SHWOO

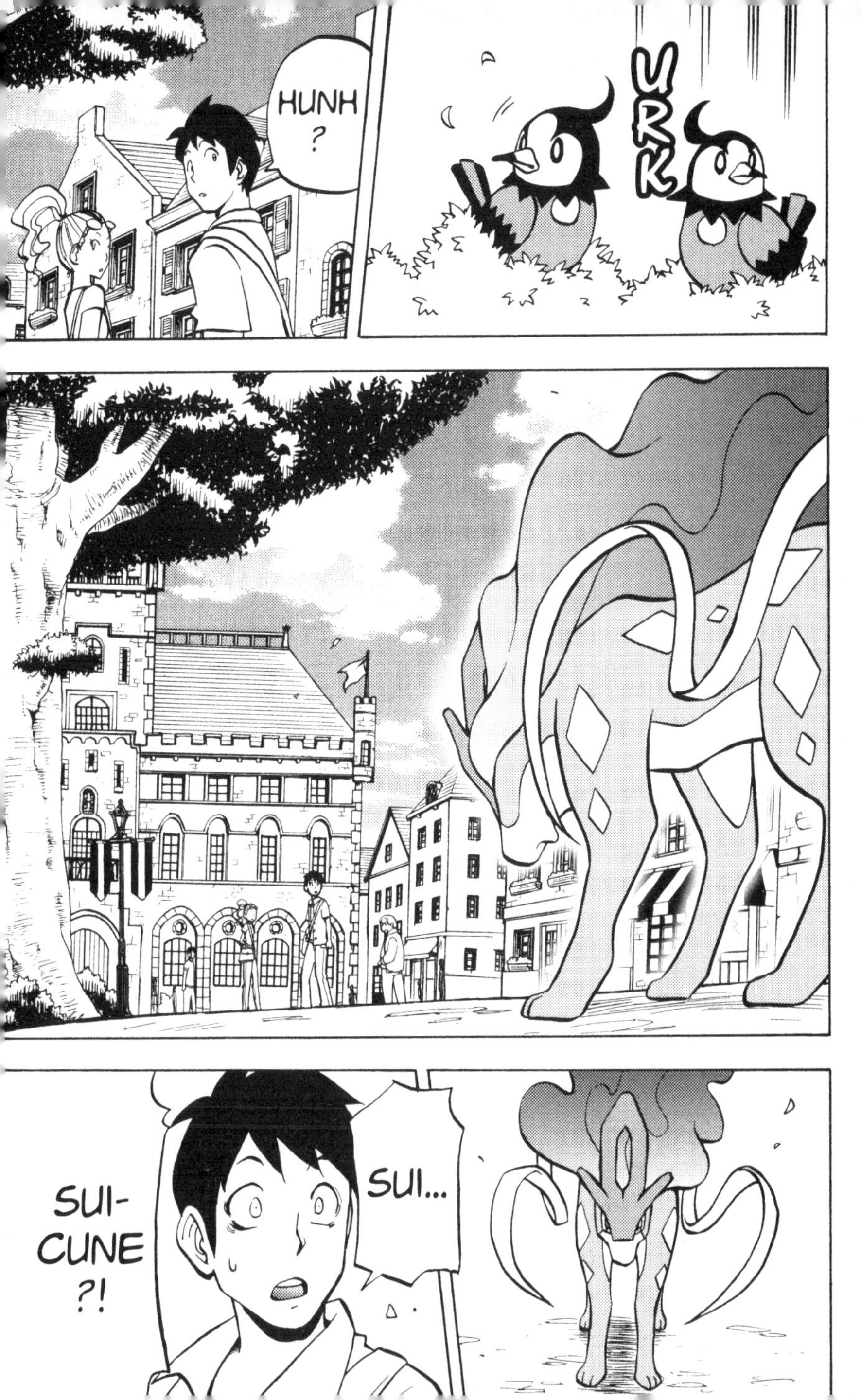
URK
HUNH ?
SUI...
SUI-CUNE ?!

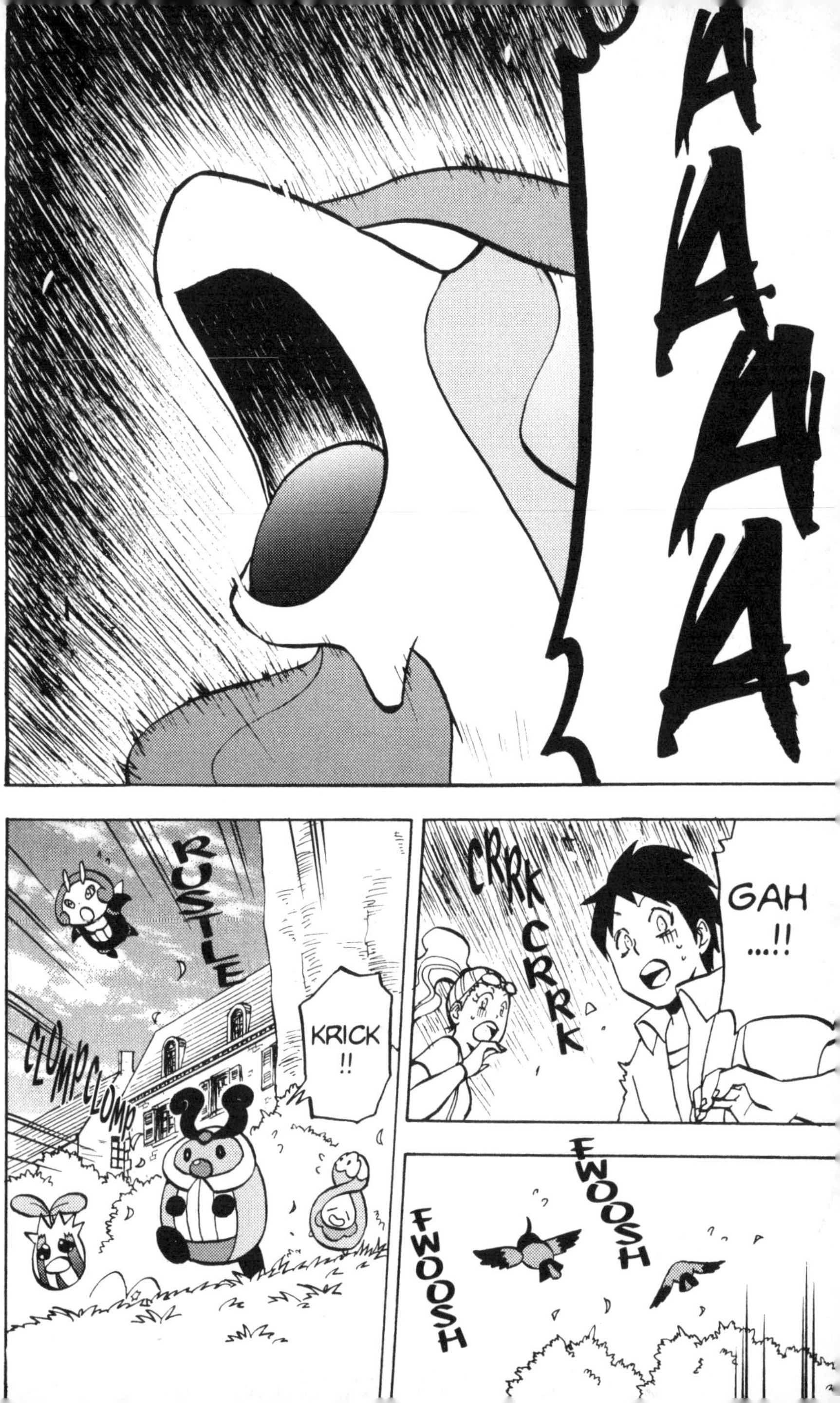
GAH ...!!
CRRK CRRK
RUSTLE
KRICK !!
CLOMPCLOMP
FWOOSH
FWOOSH

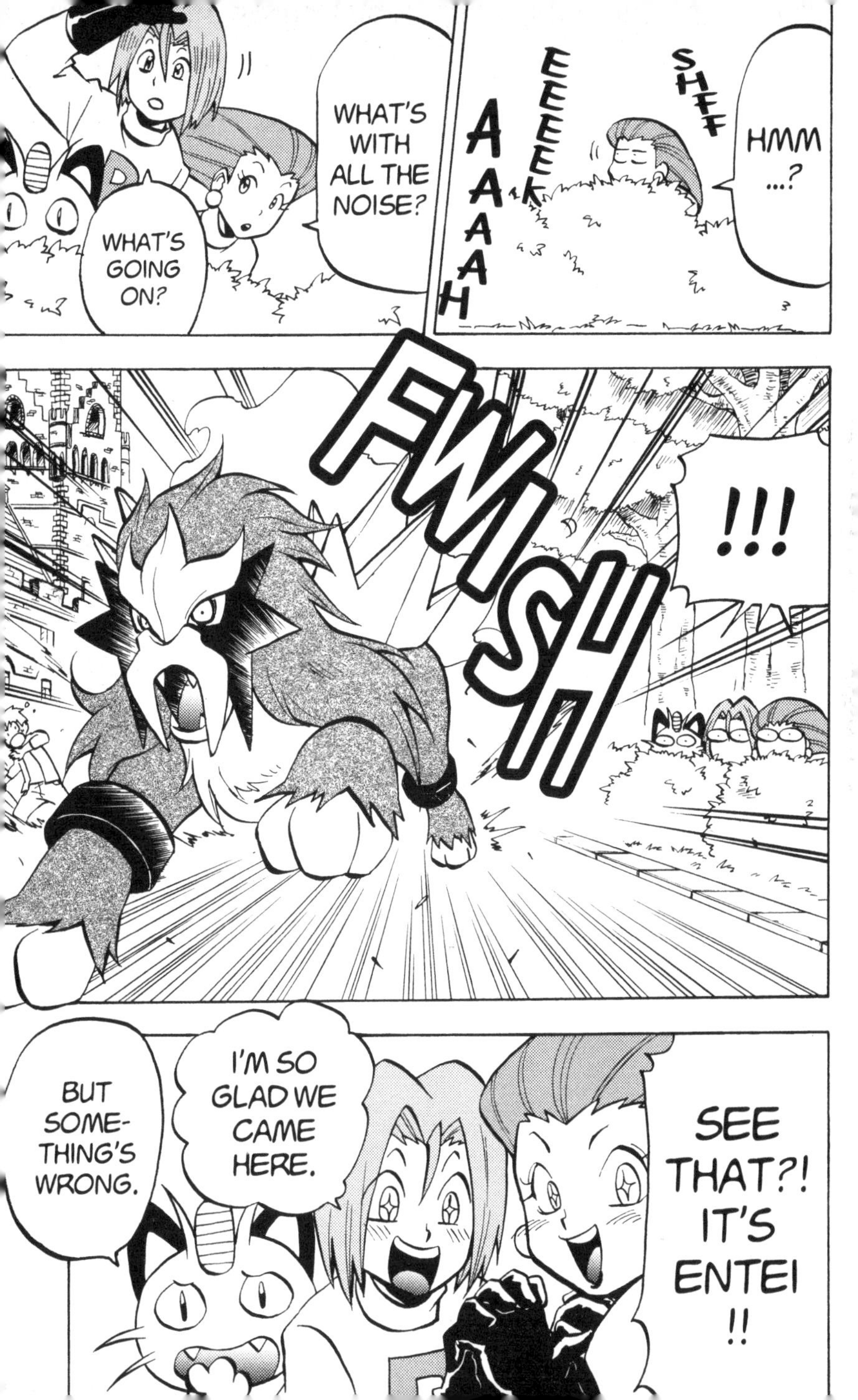
SHEFF
HMM ...?
EEEEEK
AAAAAH
WHAT'S WITH ALL THE NOISE?
WHAT'S GOING ON?
FWISH
!!!
SEE THAT?! IT'S ENTEI !!
I'M SO GLAD WE CAME HERE.
BUT SOME-THING'S WRONG.

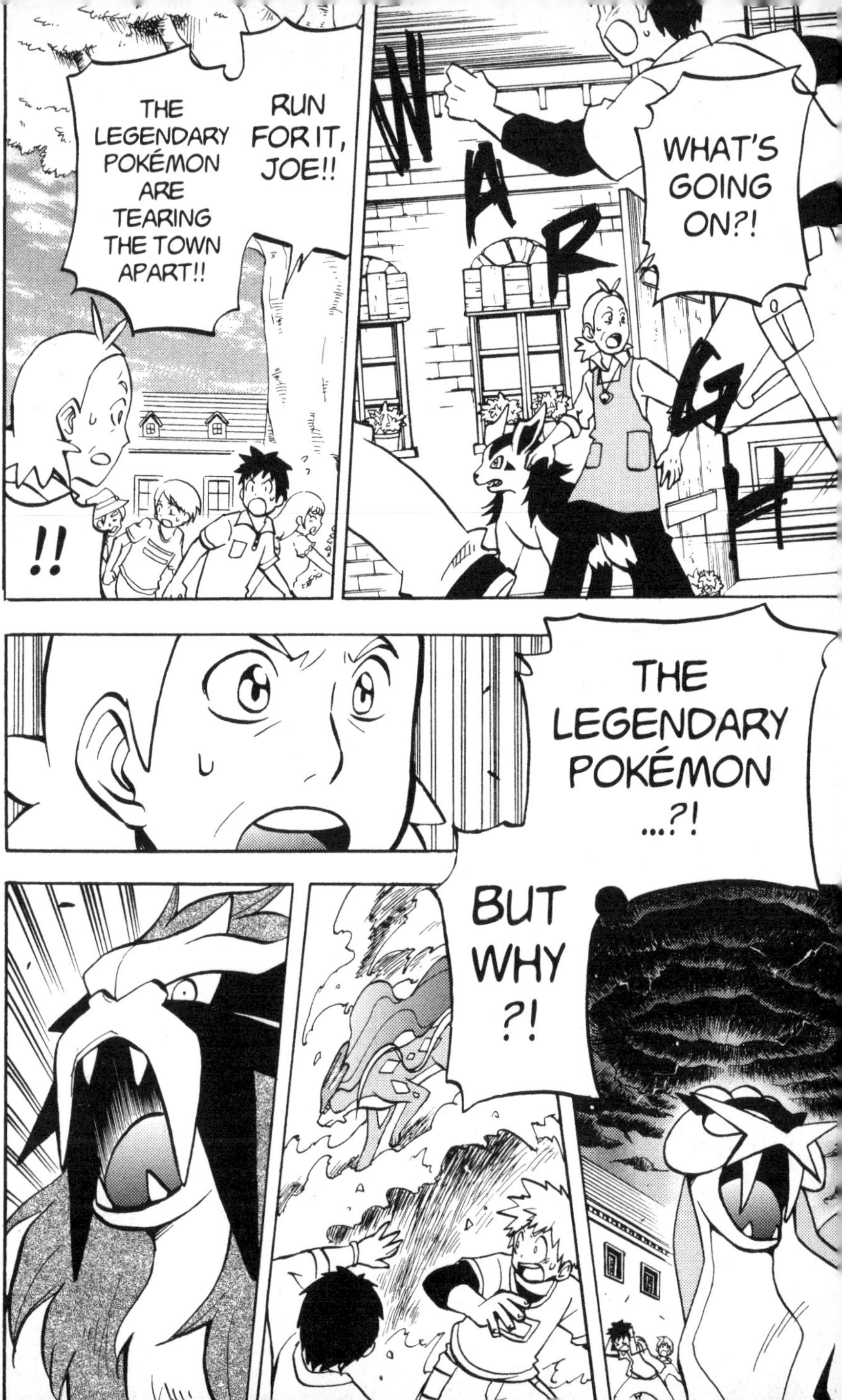
WHAT'S GOING ON?!
WARGH
RUN FOR IT, JOE!!
THE LEGENDARY POKÉMON ARE TEARING THE TOWN APART!!
!!
THE LEGENDARY POKÉMON ...?!
BUT WHY ?!

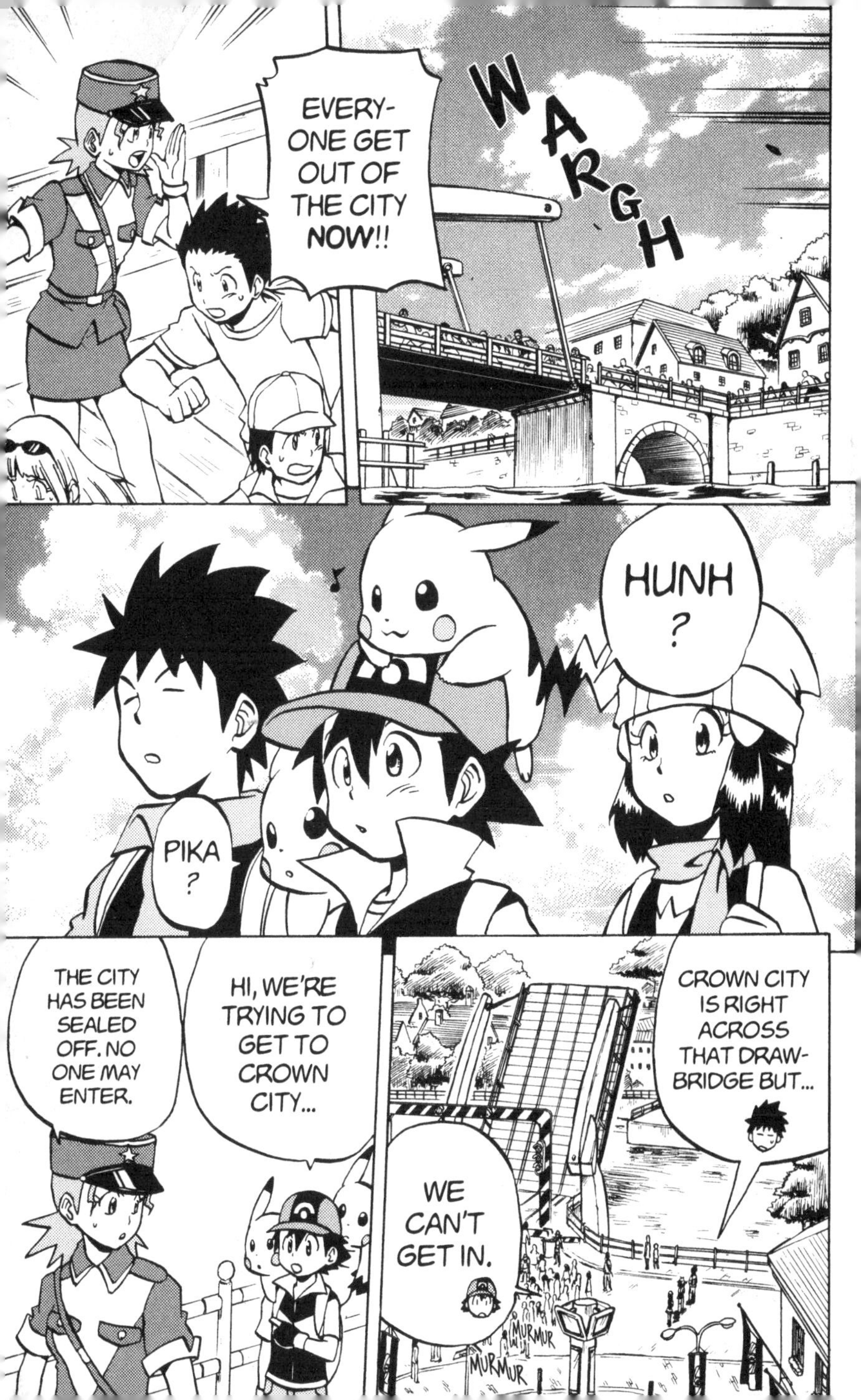
WARGH
EVERY-ONE GET OUT OF THE CITY NOW!!
HUNH ?
PIKA ?
CROWN CITY IS RIGHT ACROSS THAT DRAW-BRIDGE BUT...
WE CAN'T GET IN.
MURMUR
MURMUR
HI, WE'RE TRYING TO GET TO CROWN CITY...
THE CITY HAS BEEN SEALED OFF. NO ONE MAY ENTER.

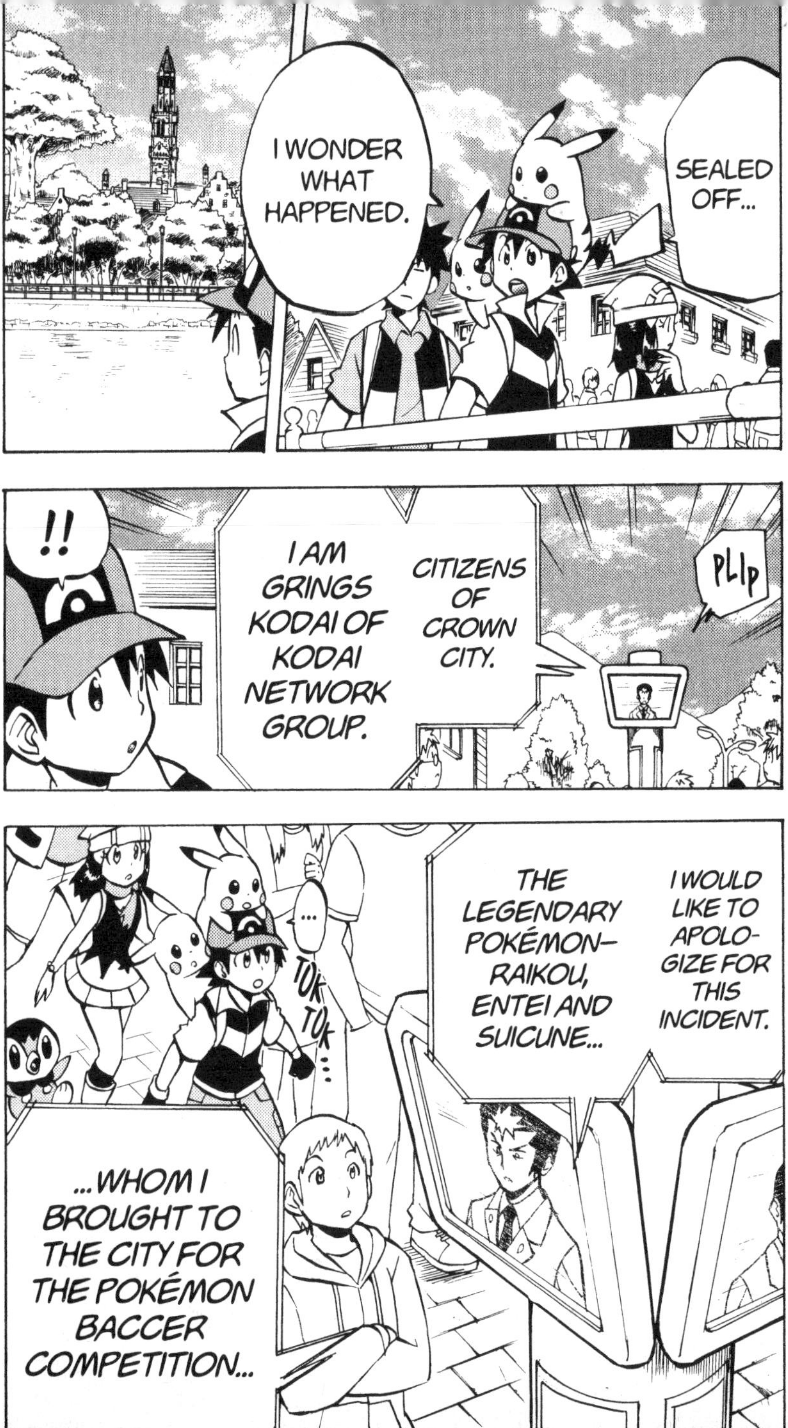
SEALED OFF...
I WONDER WHAT HAPPENED.
PLIP
CITIZENS OF CROWN CITY.
I AM GRINGS KODAI OF KODAI NETWORK GROUP.
!!
I WOULD LIKE TO APOLO-GIZE FOR THIS INCIDENT.
THE LEGENDARY POKÉMON-RAIKOU, ENTEI AND SUICUNE...
...
TOK TOK...
...WHOM I BROUGHT TO THE CITY FOR THE POKÉMON BACCER COMPETITION...

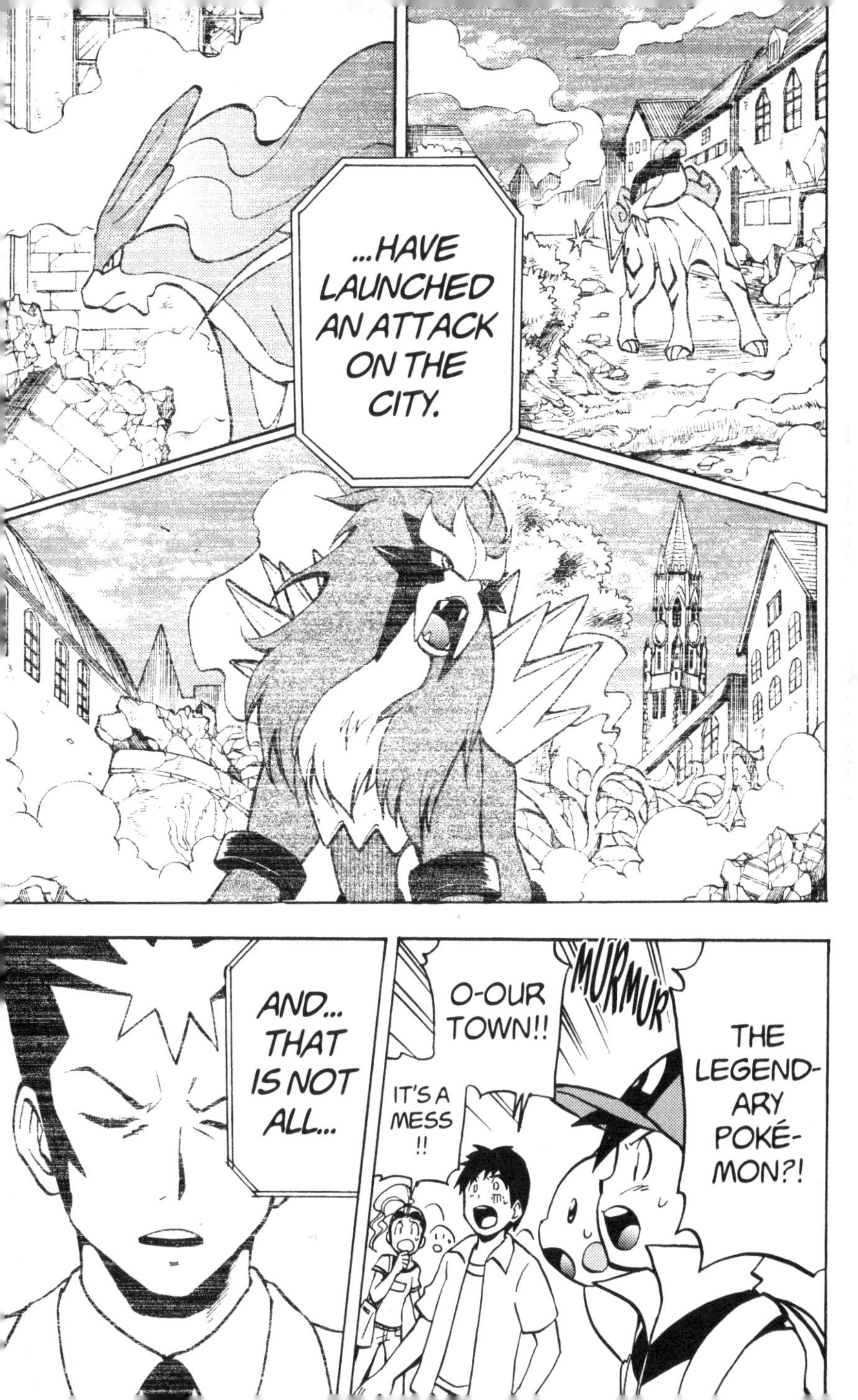
...HAVE LAUNCHED AN ATTACK ON THE CITY.
MURMUR
THE LEGEND-ARY POKÉ-MON?!
O-OUR TOWN!!
IT'S A MESS !!
AND... THAT IS NOT ALL...

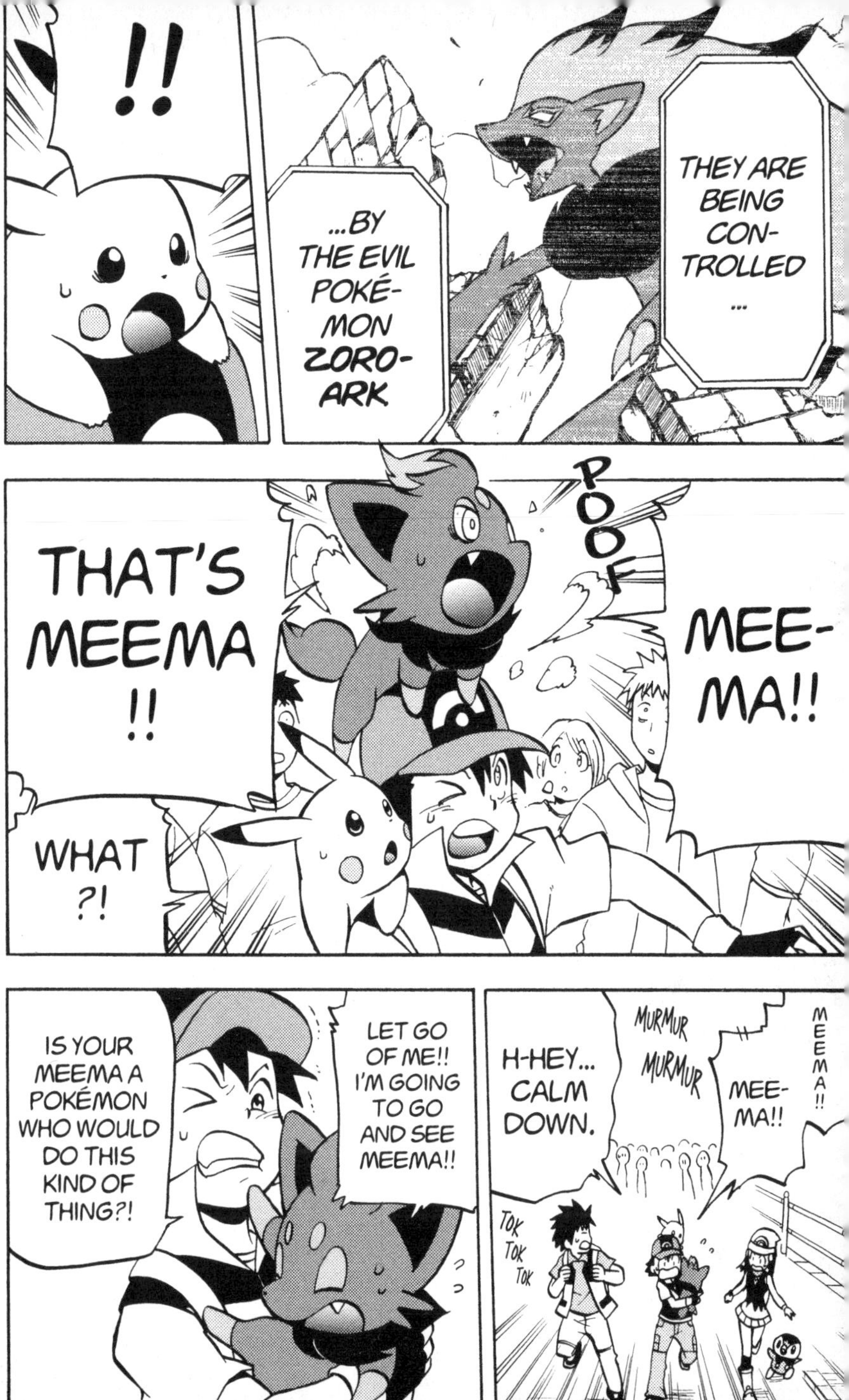
THEY ARE BEING CON-TROLLED ...
...BY THE EVIL POKÉ-MON ZORO-ARK
!!
POOF
MEE-MA!!
THAT'S MEEMA !!
WHAT ?!
MEEMA!!
MEE-MA!!
MURMUR
MURMUR
H-HEY... CALM DOWN.
TOK TOK TOK
LET GO OF ME!! I'M GOING TO GO AND SEE MEEMA!!
IS YOUR MEEMA A POKÉMON WHO WOULD DO THIS KIND OF THING?!

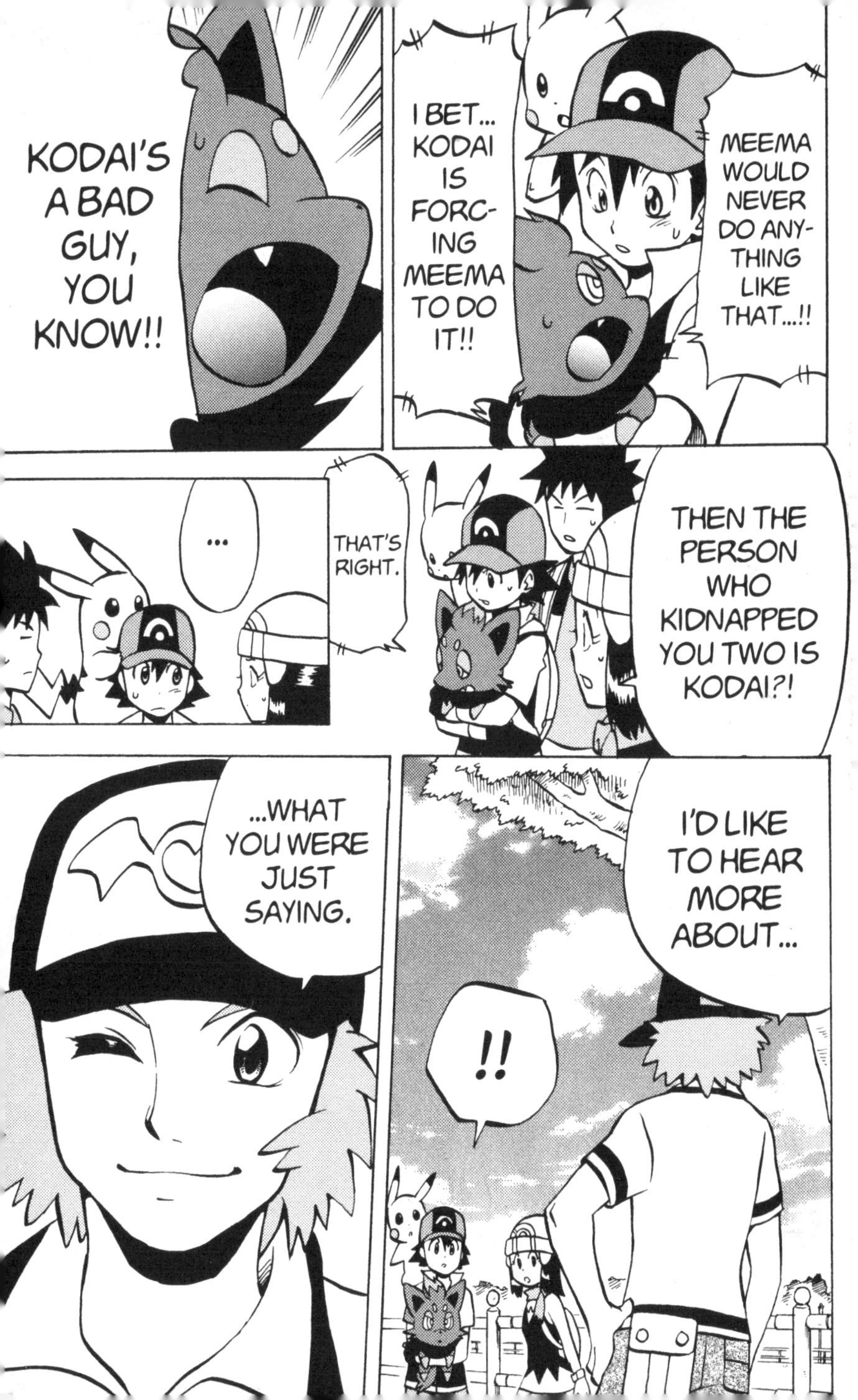
MEEMA WOULD NEVER DO ANYTHING LIKE THAT...!!
I BET... KODAI IS FORCING MEEMA TO DO IT!!
KODAI'S A BAD GUY, YOU KNOW!!
THEN THE PERSON WHO KIDNAPPED YOU TWO IS KODAI?!
THAT'S RIGHT.
...
I'D LIKE TO HEAR MORE ABOUT...
!!
...WHAT YOU WERE JUST SAYING.

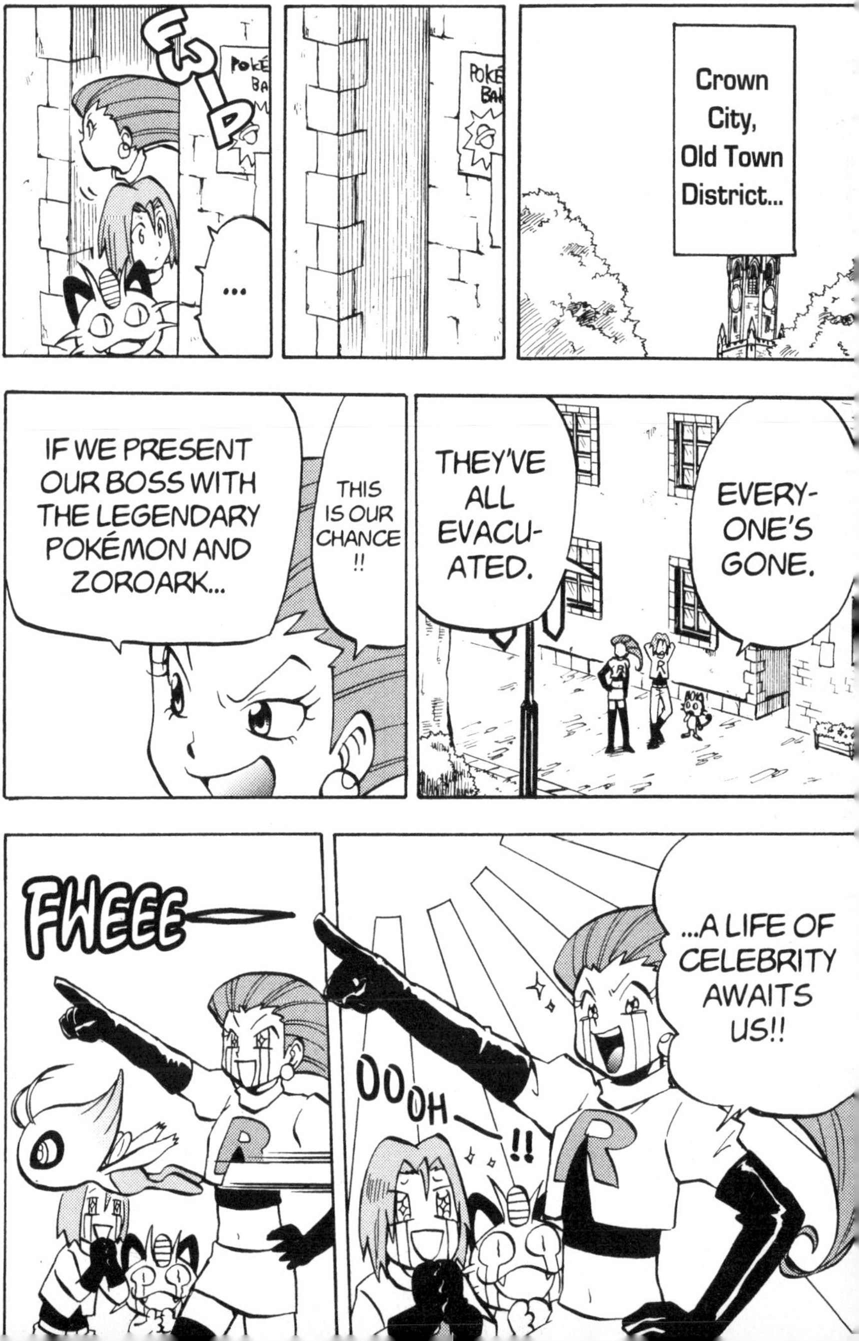
Crown City, Old Town District...
FWIP
...
EVERY-ONE'S GONE.
THEY'VE ALL EVACU-ATED.
THIS IS OUR CHANCE!!
IF WE PRESENT OUR BOSS WITH THE LEGENDARY POKÉMON AND ZOROARK...
...A LIFE OF CELEBRITY AWAITS US!!
OOOH—!!
FWEEE—

READ THIS WAY

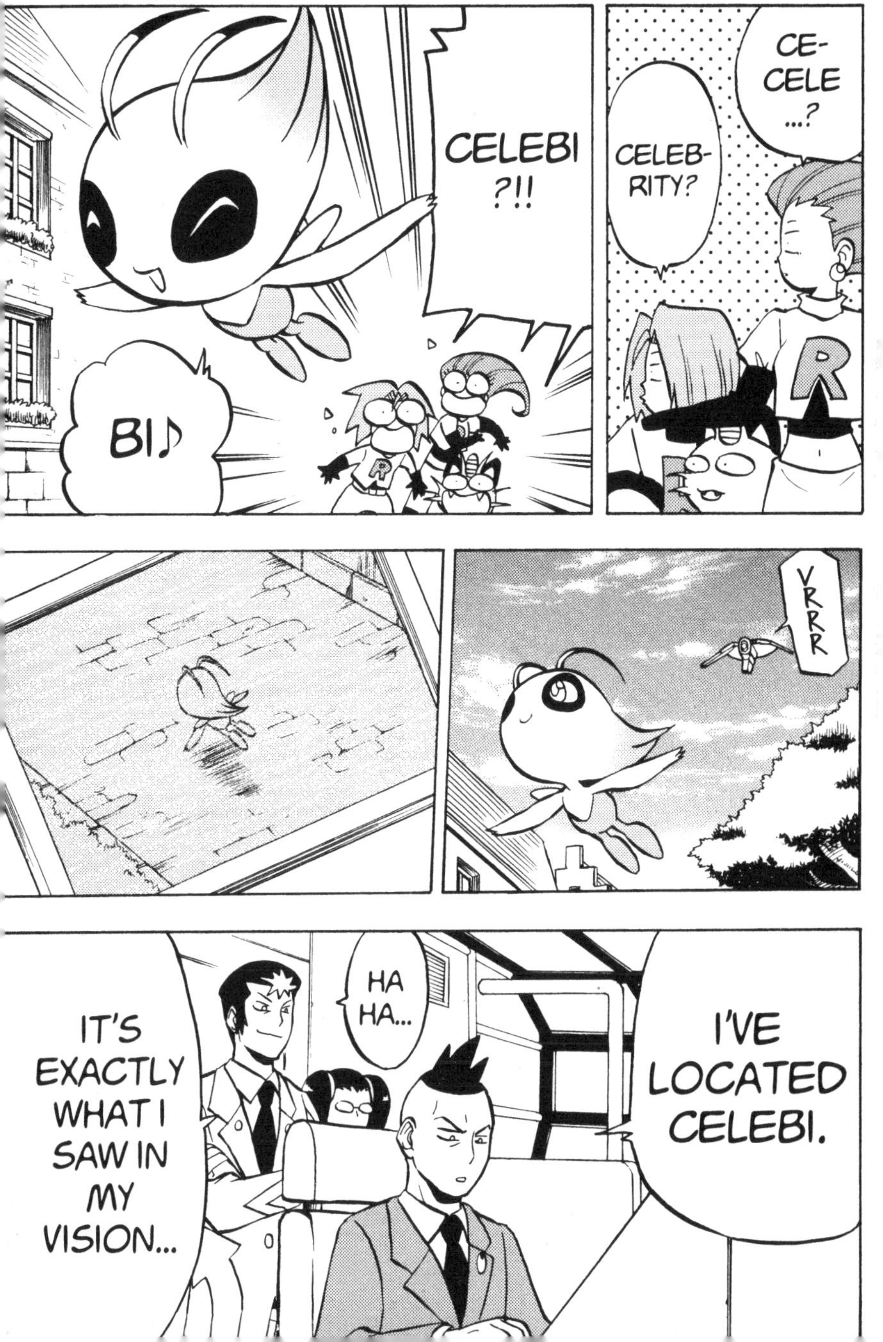
CE-CELE ...?
CELEB-RITY?
CELEBI ?!!
BI♪
VRRR
I'VE LOCATED CELEBI.
HA HA...
IT'S EXACTLY WHAT I SAW IN MY VISION...

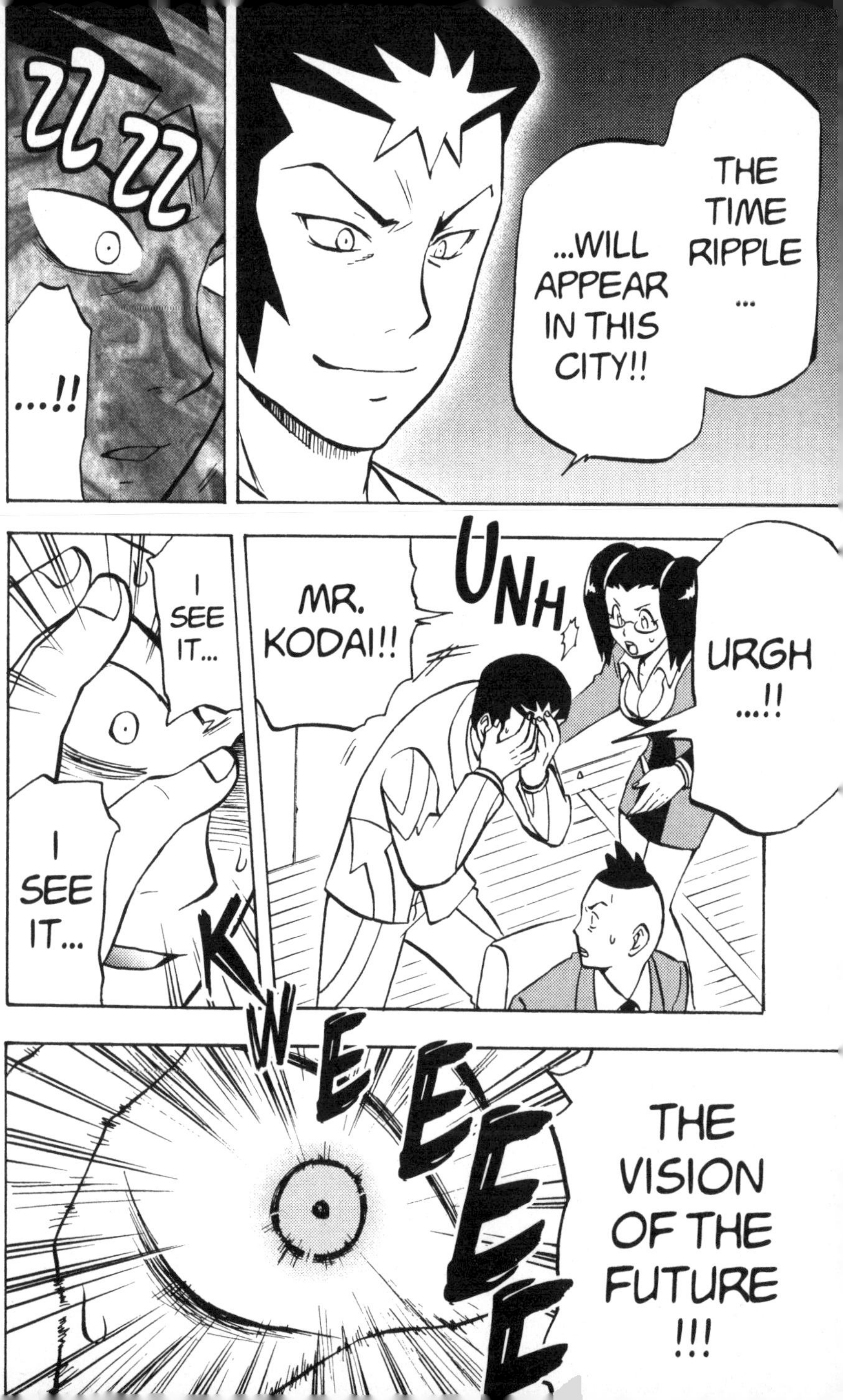
THE TIME RIPPLE ...
...WILL APPEAR IN THIS CITY!!
ZZZZ
...!!
UNH
URGH ...!!
MR. KODAI!!
I SEE IT...
I SEE IT...
KWEEEEEE
THE VISION OF THE FUTURE !!!

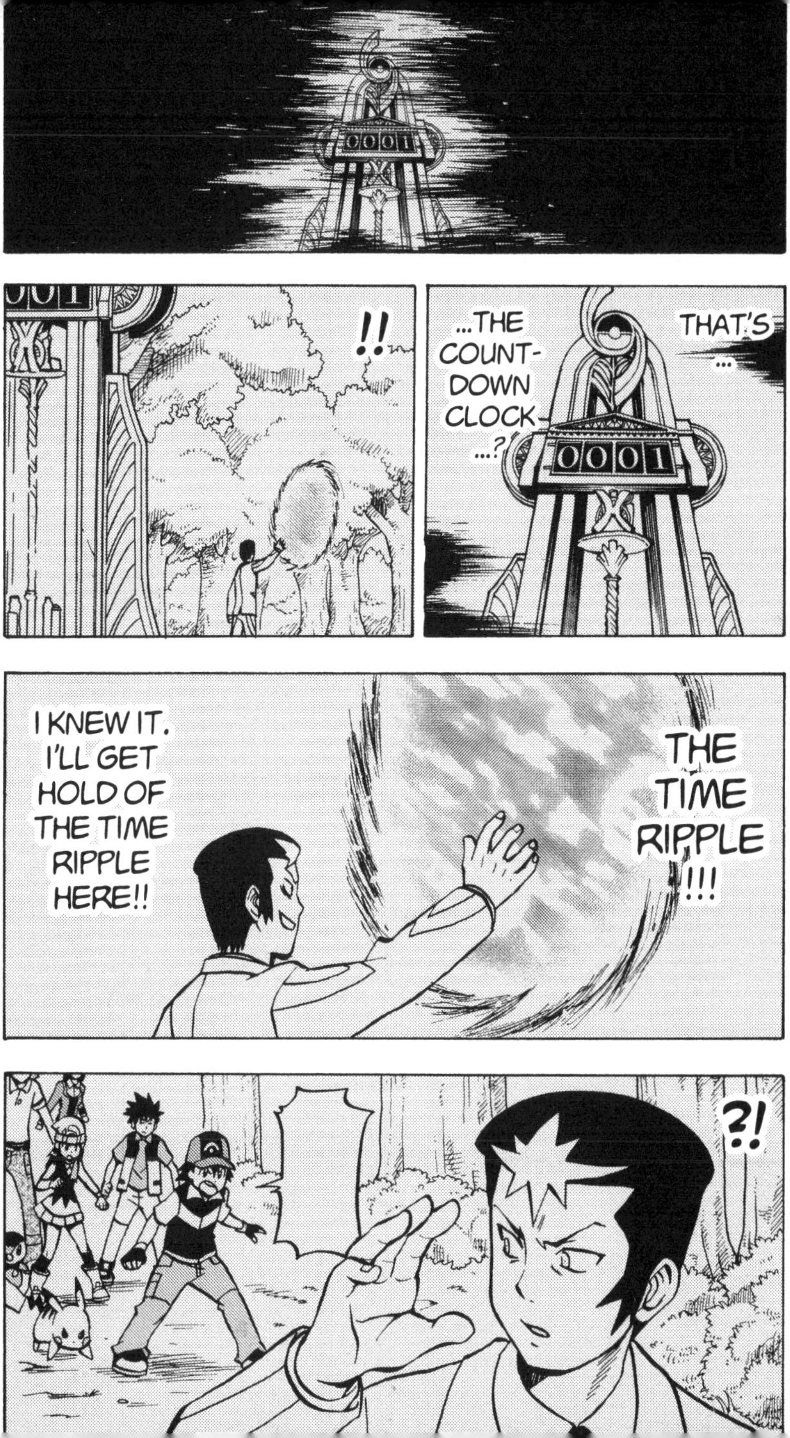
0001
THAT'S ...
...THE COUNT-DOWN CLOCK ...?
!!
THE TIME RIPPLE !!!
I KNEW IT. I'LL GET HOLD OF THE TIME RIPPLE HERE!!
?!

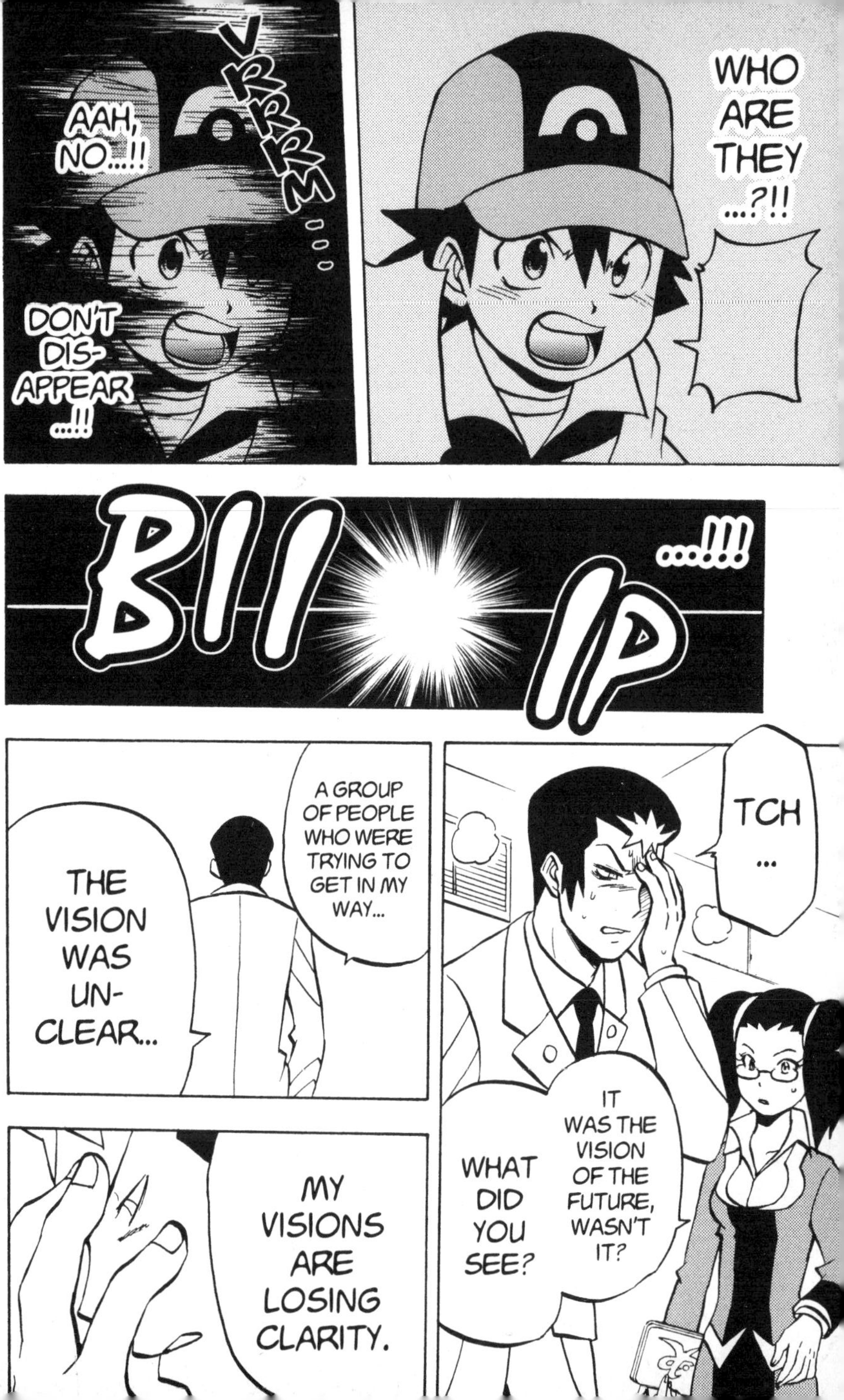
WHO ARE THEY ...?!!
VRRRRM
AAH, NO...!!
DON'T DIS-APPEAR ...!!
BII IP ...!!!
TCH ...
IT WAS THE VISION OF THE FUTURE, WASN'T IT?
WHAT DID YOU SEE?
A GROUP OF PEOPLE WHO WERE TRYING TO GET IN MY WAY...
THE VISION WAS UN-CLEAR...
MY VISIONS ARE LOSING CLARITY.

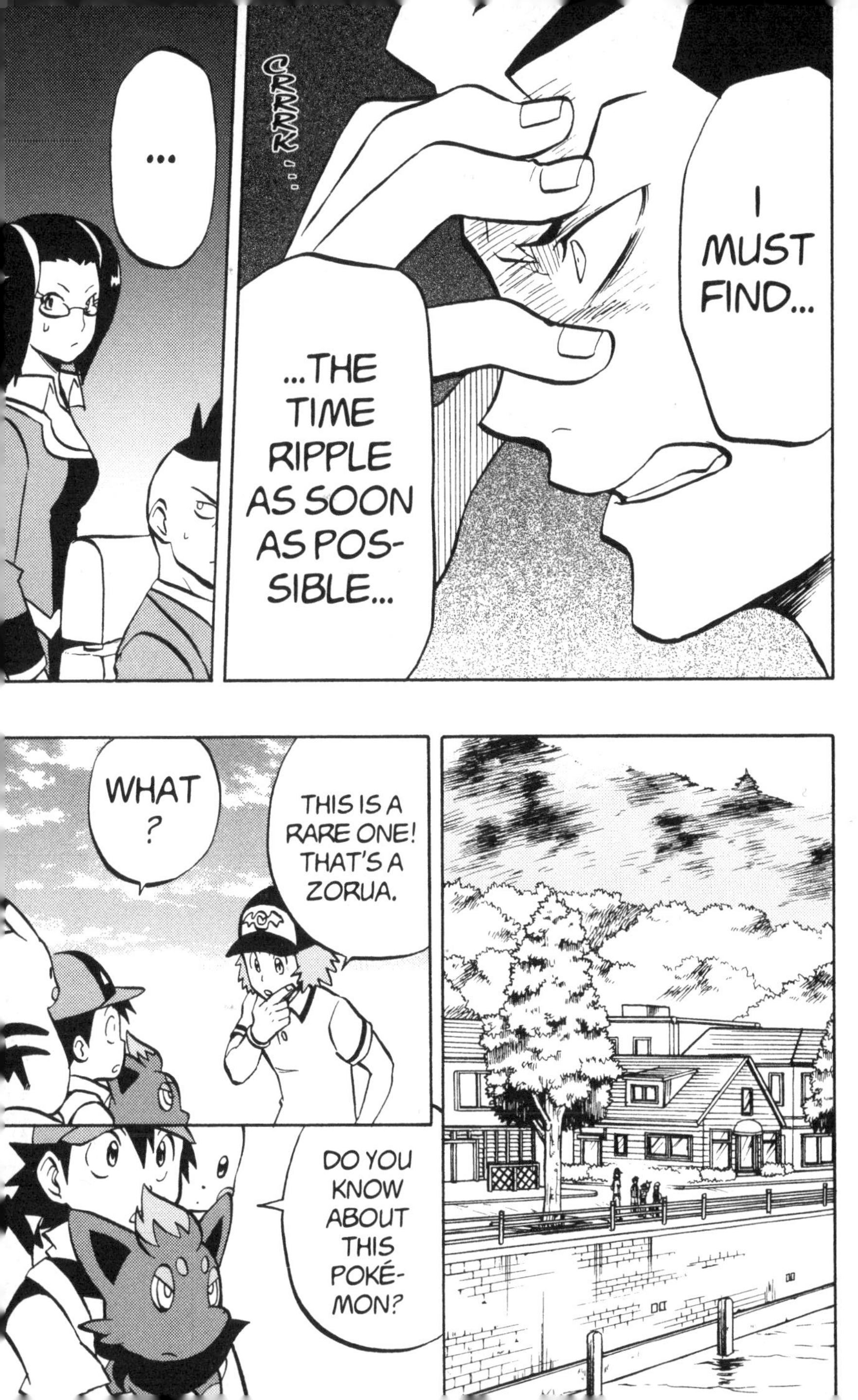
I MUST FIND...
...THE TIME RIPPLE AS SOON AS POSSIBLE...
CRRRK...
...
THIS IS A RARE ONE! THAT'S A ZORUA.
WHAT?
DO YOU KNOW ABOUT THIS POKÉMON?

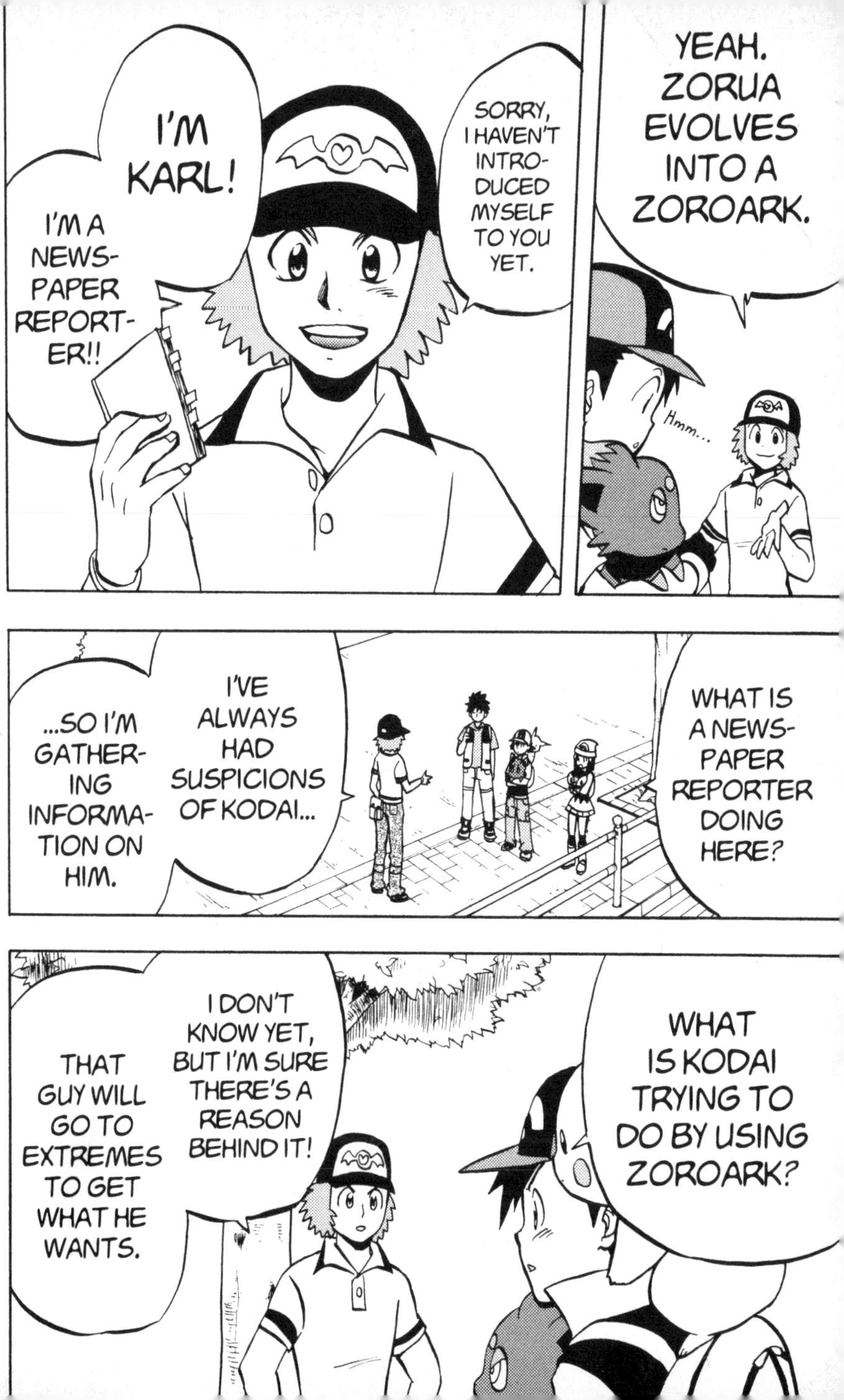
YEAH. ZORUA EVOLVES INTO A ZOROARK.
Hmm...
SORRY, I HAVEN'T INTRO-DUCED MYSELF TO YOU YET.
I'M KARL!
I'M A NEWS-PAPER REPORT-ER!!
WHAT IS A NEWS-PAPER REPORTER DOING HERE?
I'VE ALWAYS HAD SUSPICIONS OF KODAI...
...SO I'M GATHER-ING INFORMA-TION ON HIM.
WHAT IS KODAI TRYING TO DO BY USING ZOROARK?
I DON'T KNOW YET, BUT I'M SURE THERE'S A REASON BEHIND IT!
THAT GUY WILL GO TO EXTREMES TO GET WHAT HE WANTS.

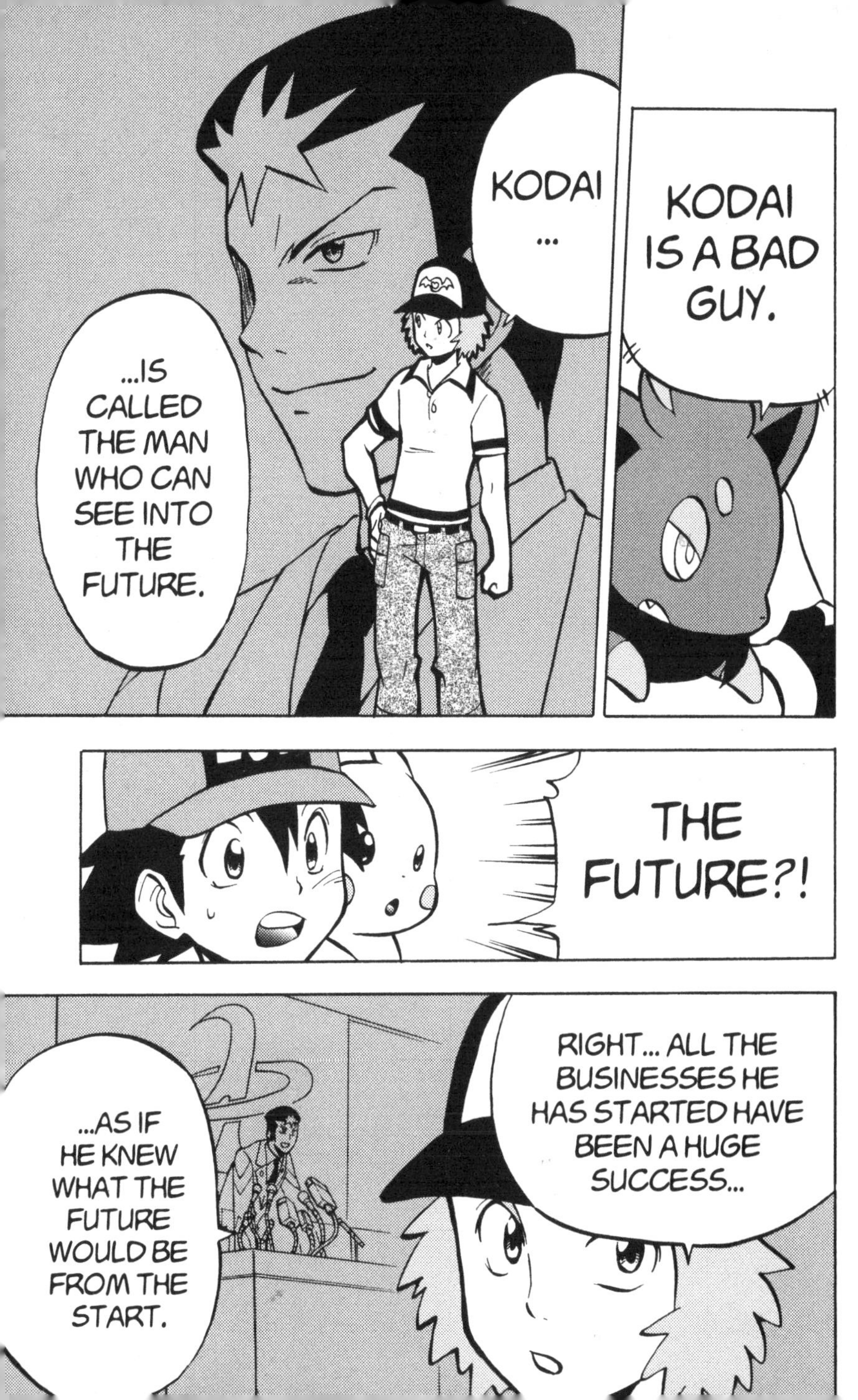
KODAI IS A BAD GUY.
KODAI ...
...IS CALLED THE MAN WHO CAN SEE INTO THE FUTURE.
THE FUTURE?!
RIGHT... ALL THE BUSINESSES HE HAS STARTED HAVE BEEN A HUGE SUCCESS...
...AS IF HE KNEW WHAT THE FUTURE WOULD BE FROM THE START.

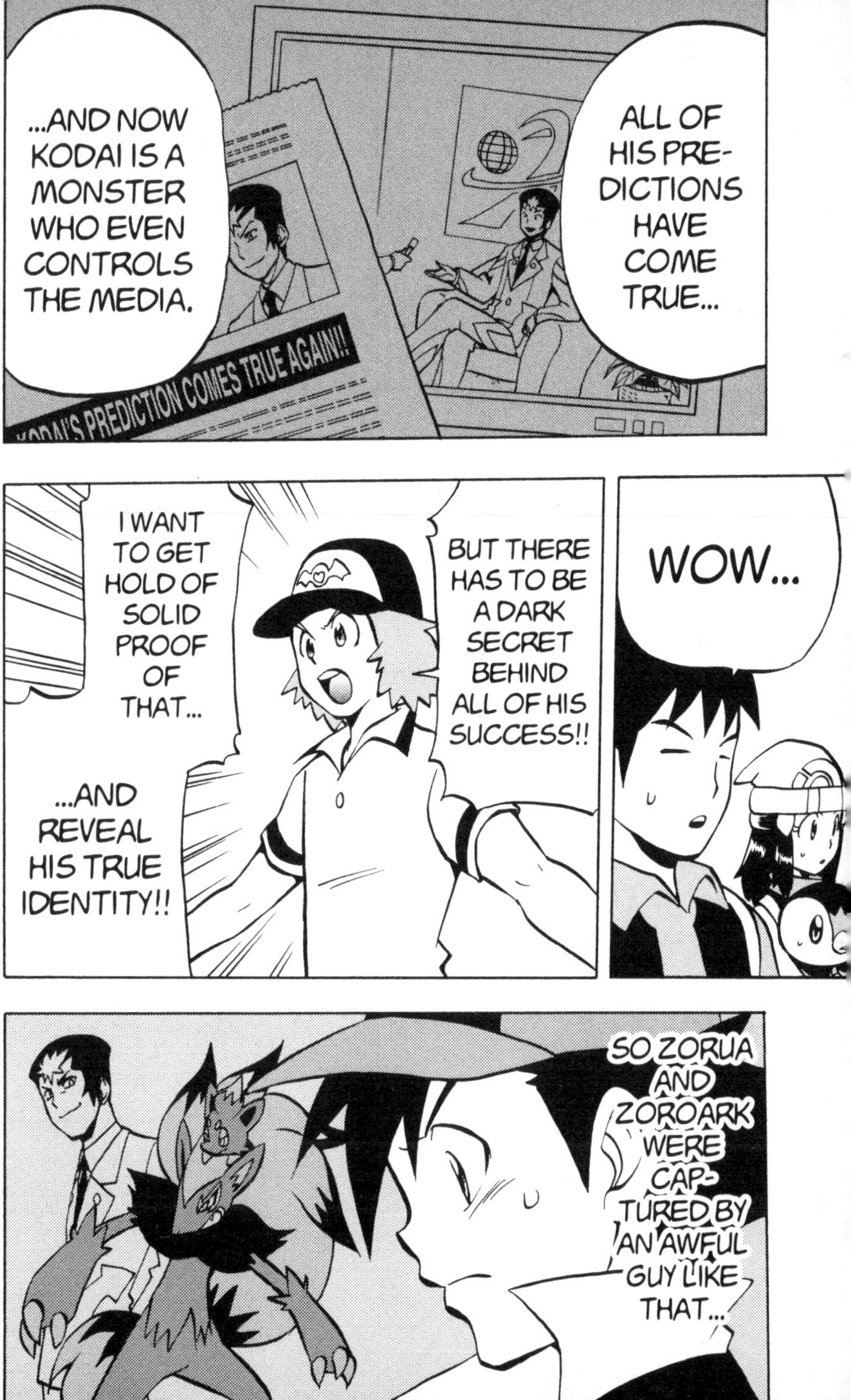
ALL OF HIS PREDICTIONS HAVE COME TRUE...
...AND NOW KODAI IS A MONSTER WHO EVEN CONTROLS THE MEDIA.
PREDICTION COMES TRUE AGAIN!!
WOW...
BUT THERE HAS TO BE A DARK SECRET BEHIND ALL OF HIS SUCCESS!!
I WANT TO GET HOLD OF SOLID PROOF OF THAT...
...AND REVEAL HIS TRUE IDENTITY!!
SO ZORUA AND ZOROARK WERE CAPTURED BY AN AWFUL GUY LIKE THAT...

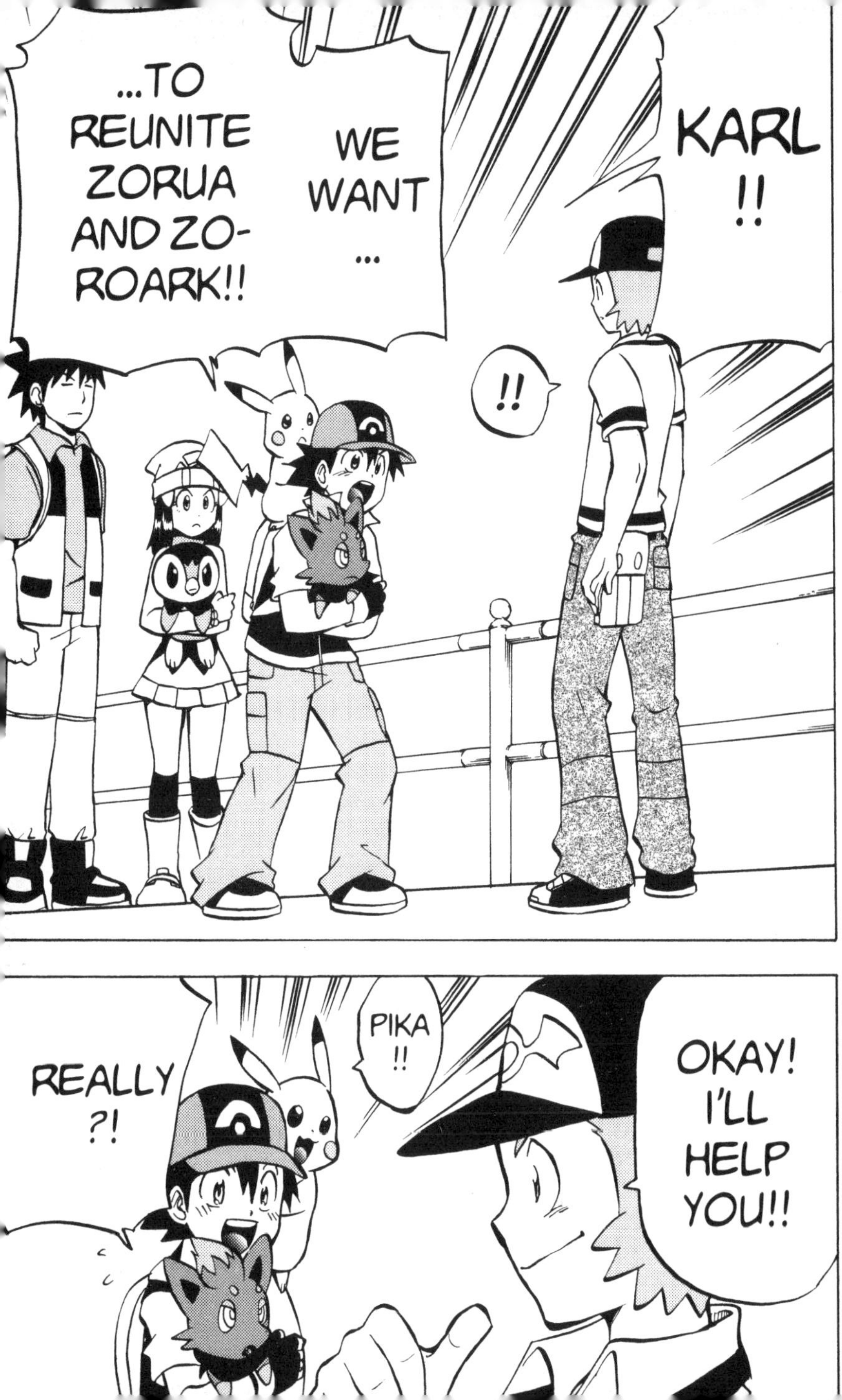
KARL!!
WE WANT...
...TO REUNITE ZORUA AND ZO-ROARK!!
!!
OKAY! I'LL HELP YOU!!
PIKA!!
REALLY?!

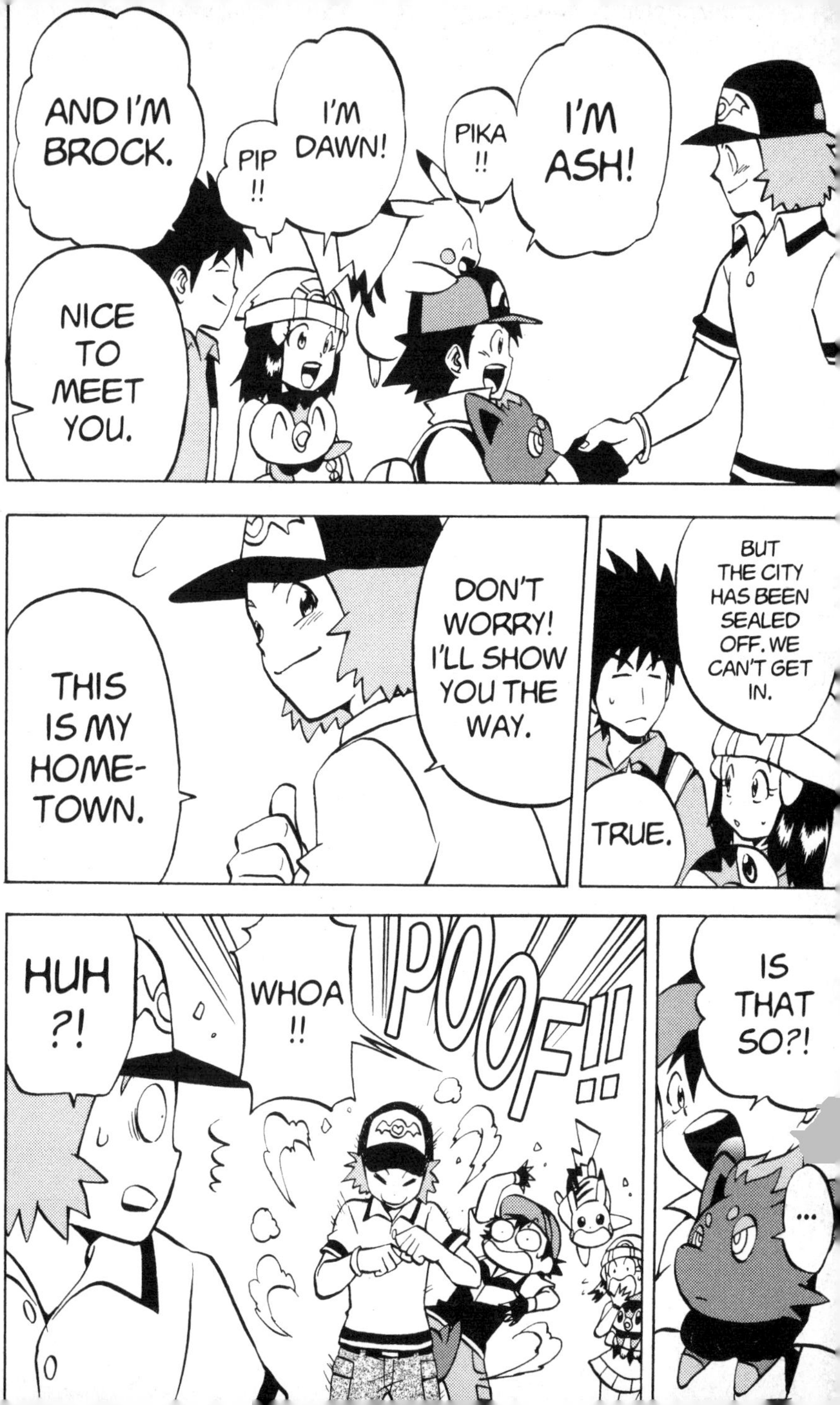
I'M ASH!
PIKA !!
I'M DAWN!
PIP !!
AND I'M BROCK.
NICE TO MEET YOU.
BUT THE CITY HAS BEEN SEALED OFF. WE CAN'T GET IN.
TRUE.
DON'T WORRY! I'LL SHOW YOU THE WAY.
THIS IS MY HOME-TOWN.
IS THAT SO?!
...
POOF!!
WHOA !!
HUH ?!

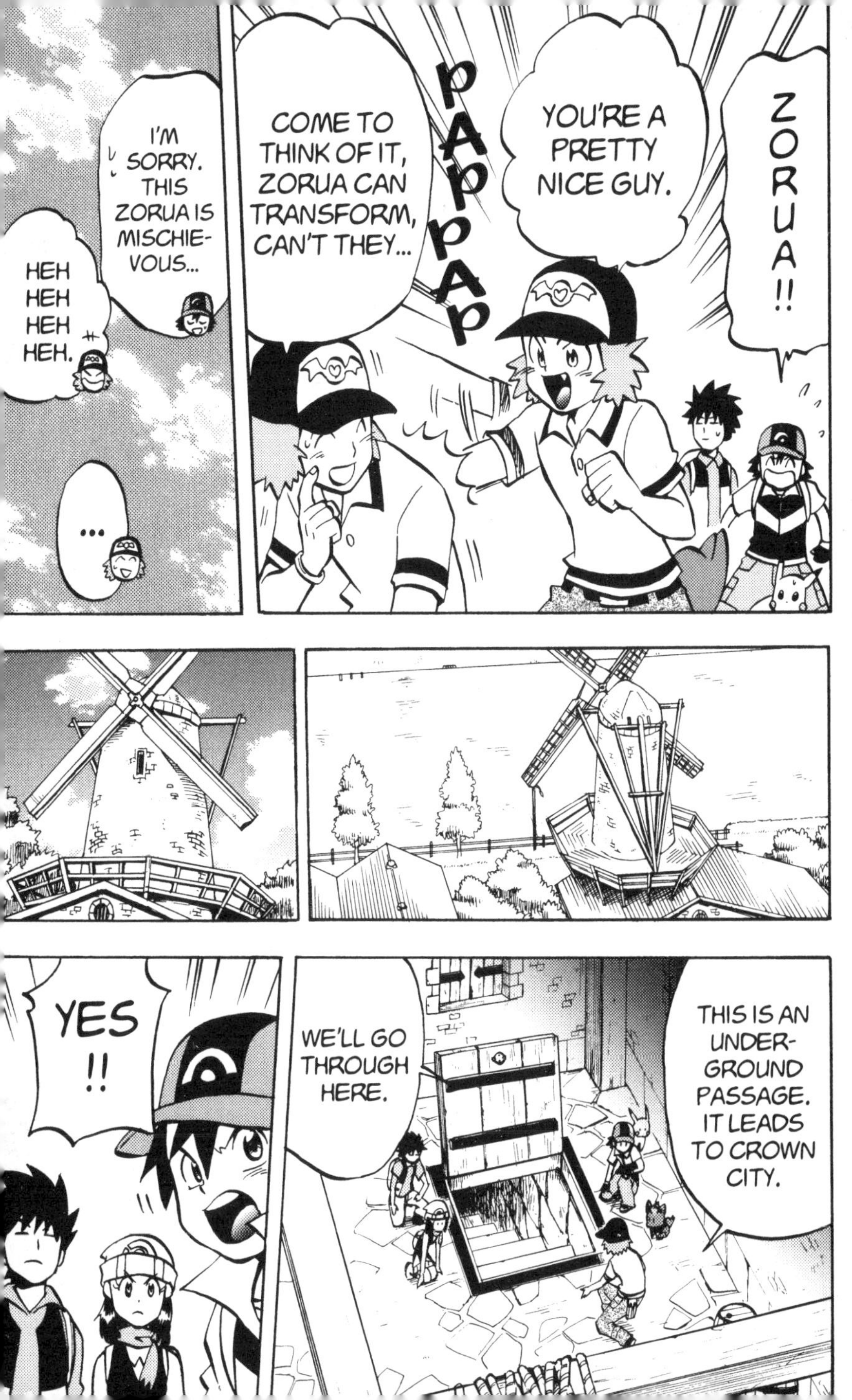
ZORUA!!
YOU'RE A PRETTY NICE GUY.
PAP PAP
COME TO THINK OF IT, ZORUA CAN TRANSFORM, CAN'T THEY...
I'M SORRY. THIS ZORUA IS MISCHIE-VOUS...
HEH HEH HEH HEH.
...
THIS IS AN UNDER-GROUND PASSAGE. IT LEADS TO CROWN CITY.
WE'LL GO THROUGH HERE.
YES!!

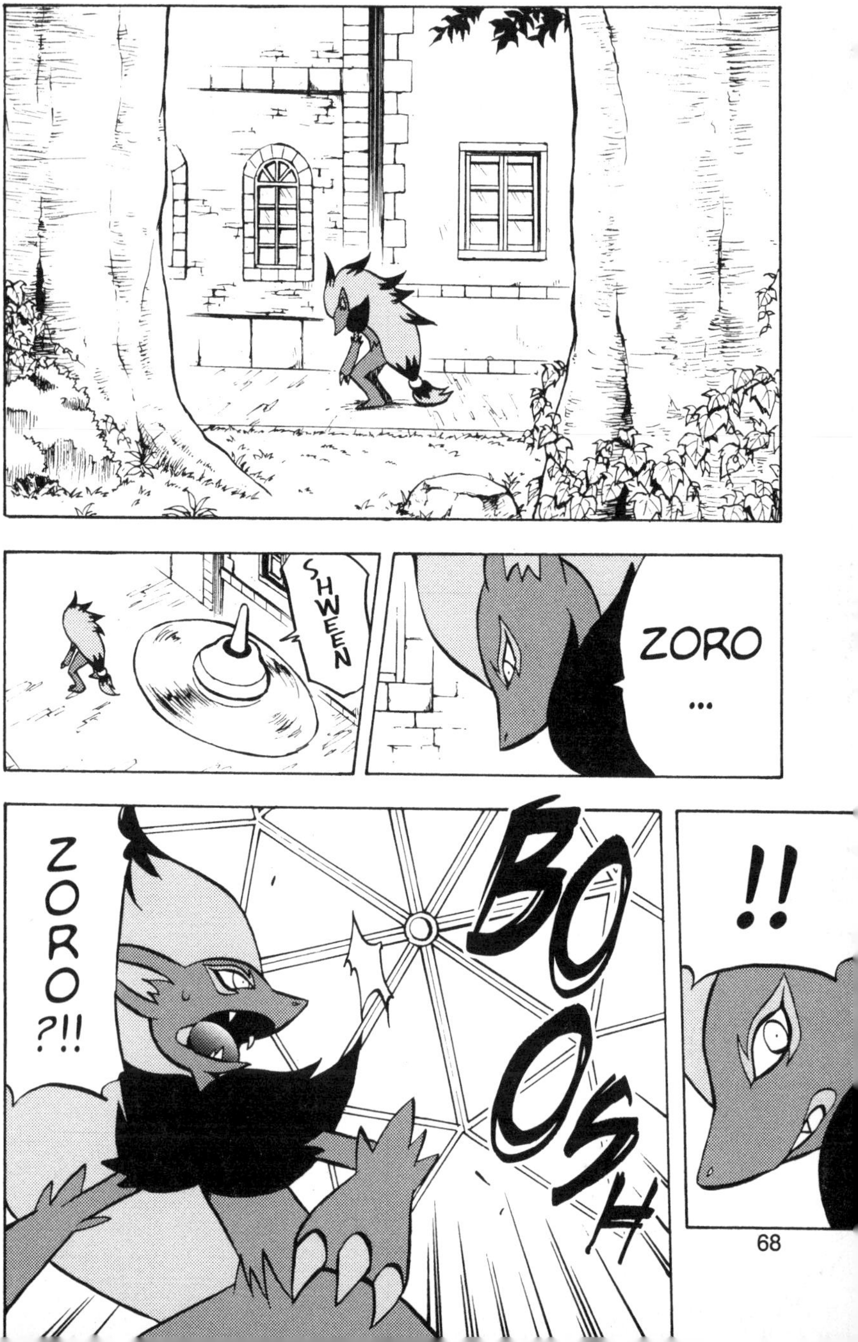
ZORO
...
SHWEEN
!!
BOOSH
ZORO?!!

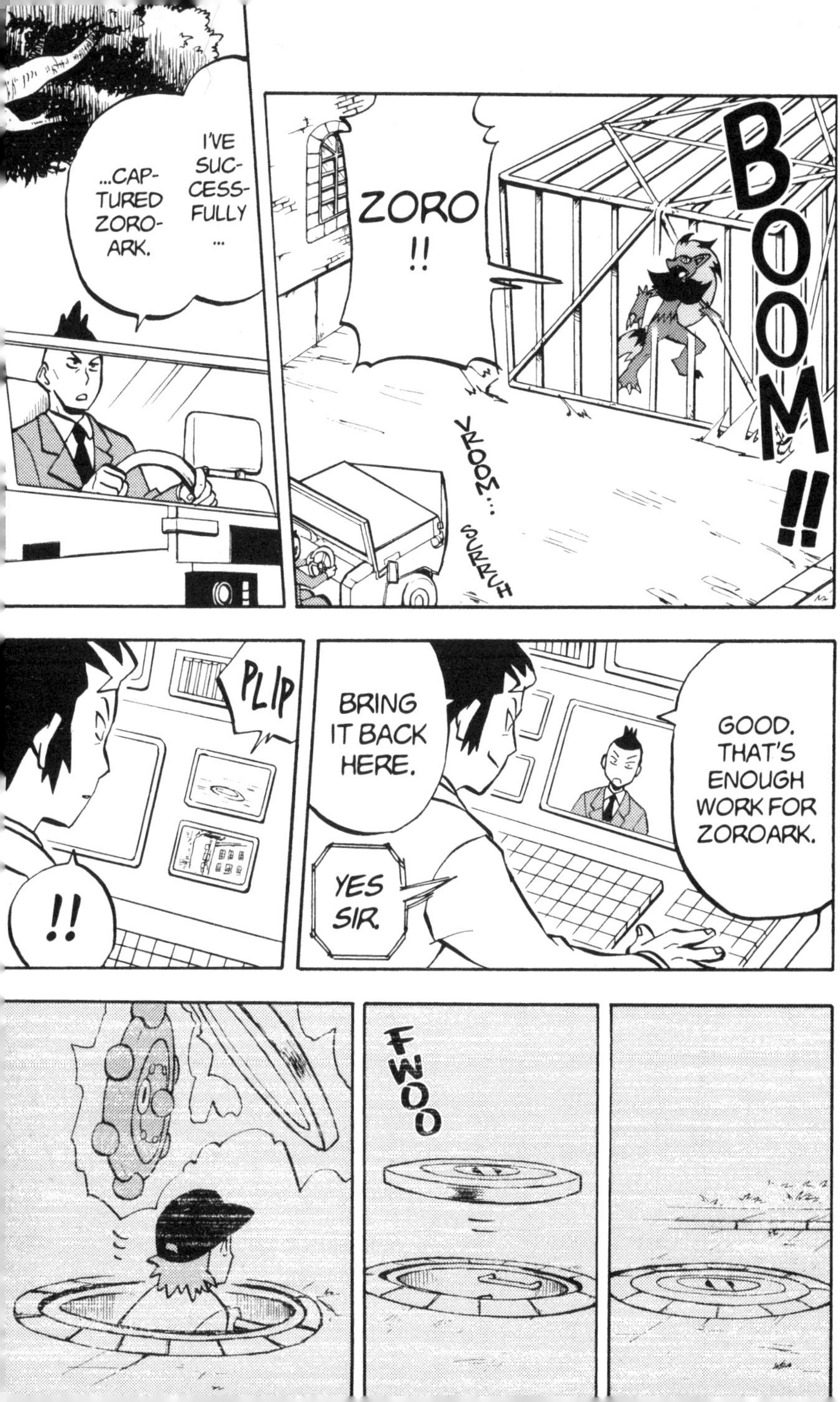
BOOM!!
ZORO!!
VROOM...
SCRRUH
I'VE SUCCESSFULLY...
...CAPTURED ZOROARK.
GOOD. THAT'S ENOUGH WORK FOR ZOROARK.
BRING IT BACK HERE.
YES SIR.
PLIP
!!
FWOO

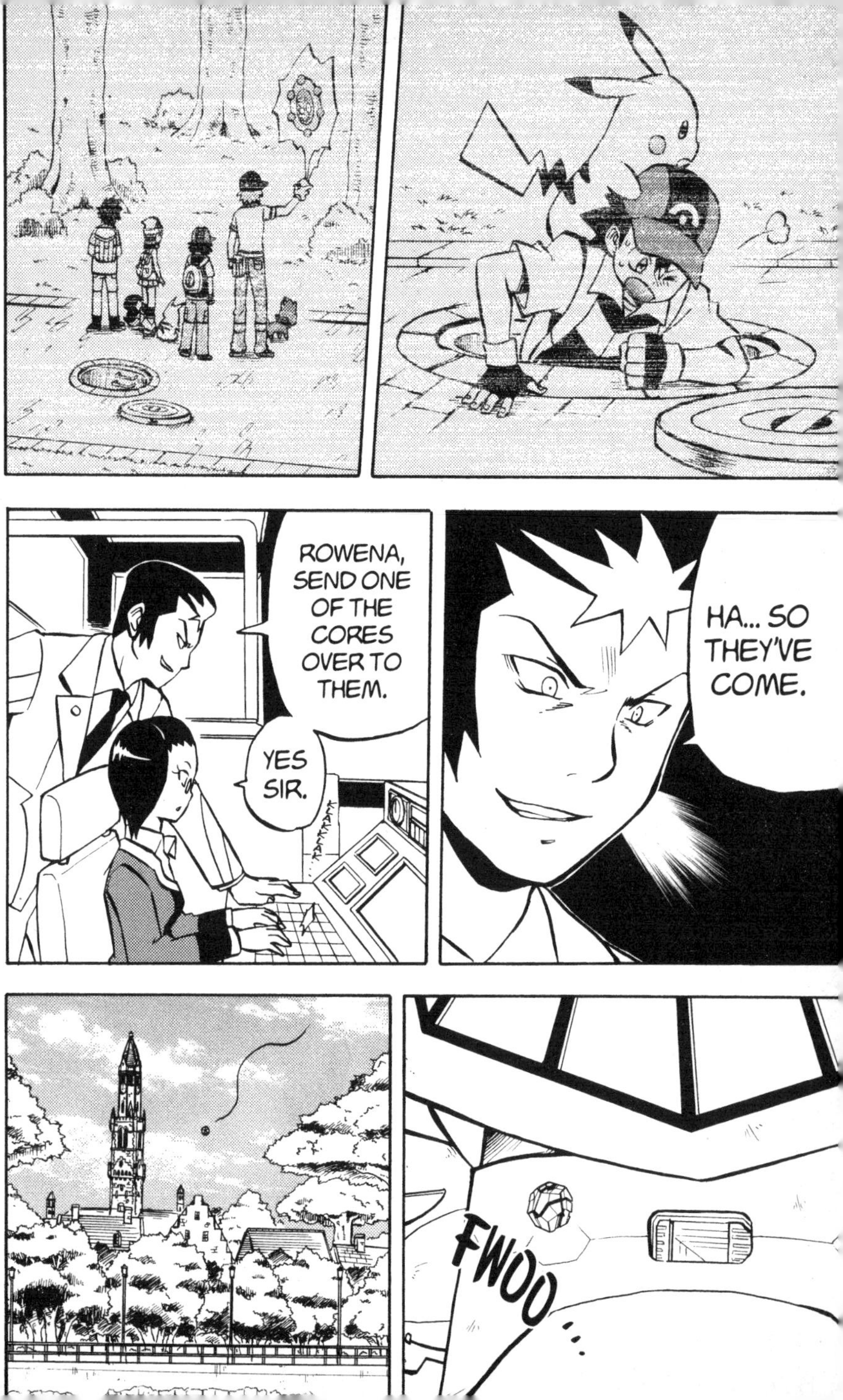
HA... SO THEY'VE COME.
ROWENA, SEND ONE OF THE CORES OVER TO THEM.
YES SIR.
FWOO...

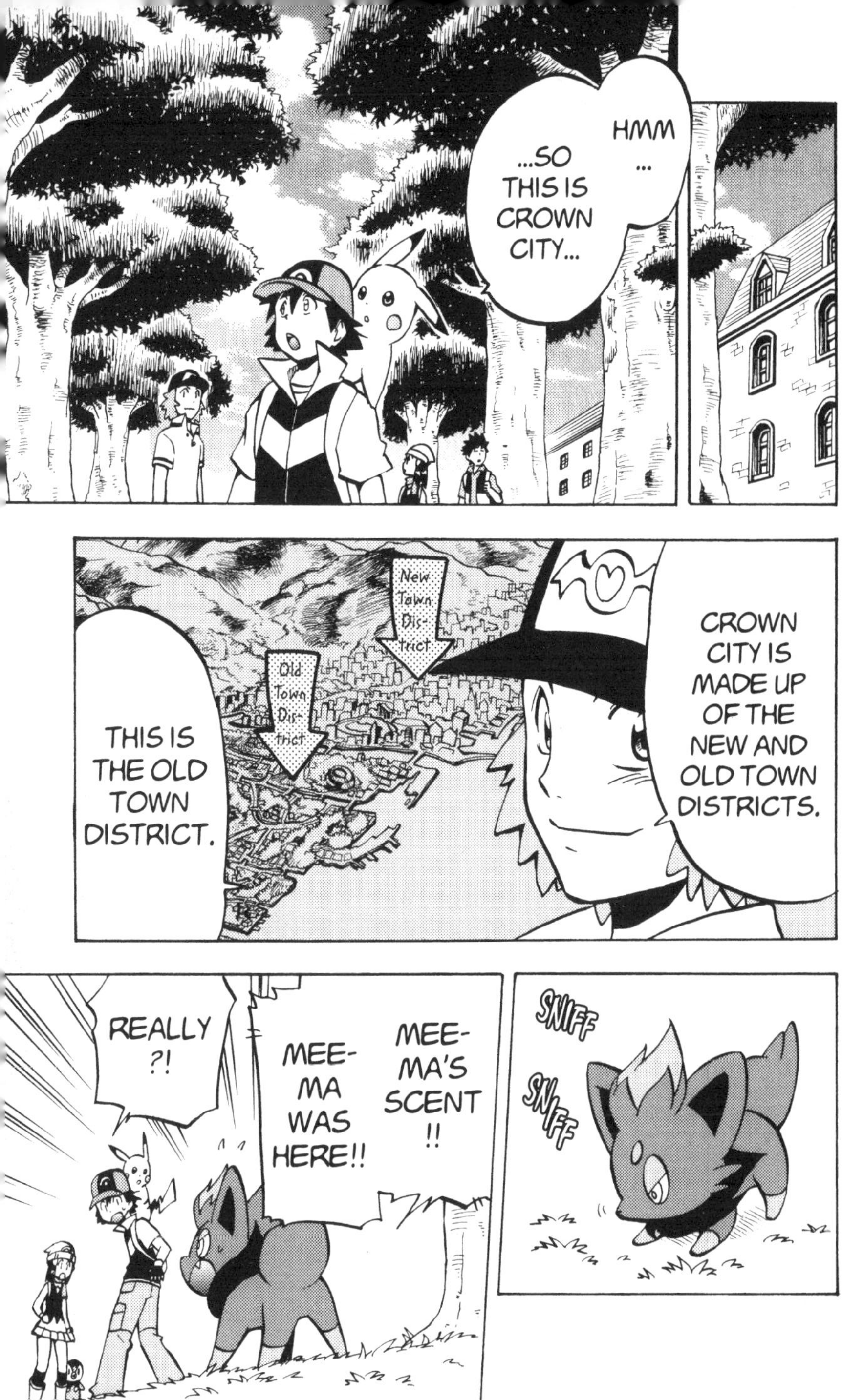
HMM ...
...SO THIS IS CROWN CITY...
CROWN CITY IS MADE UP OF THE NEW AND OLD TOWN DISTRICTS.
New Town District
Old Town District
THIS IS THE OLD TOWN DISTRICT.
SNIFF
SNIFF
MEE-MA'S SCENT!!
MEE-MA WAS HERE!!
REALLY?!

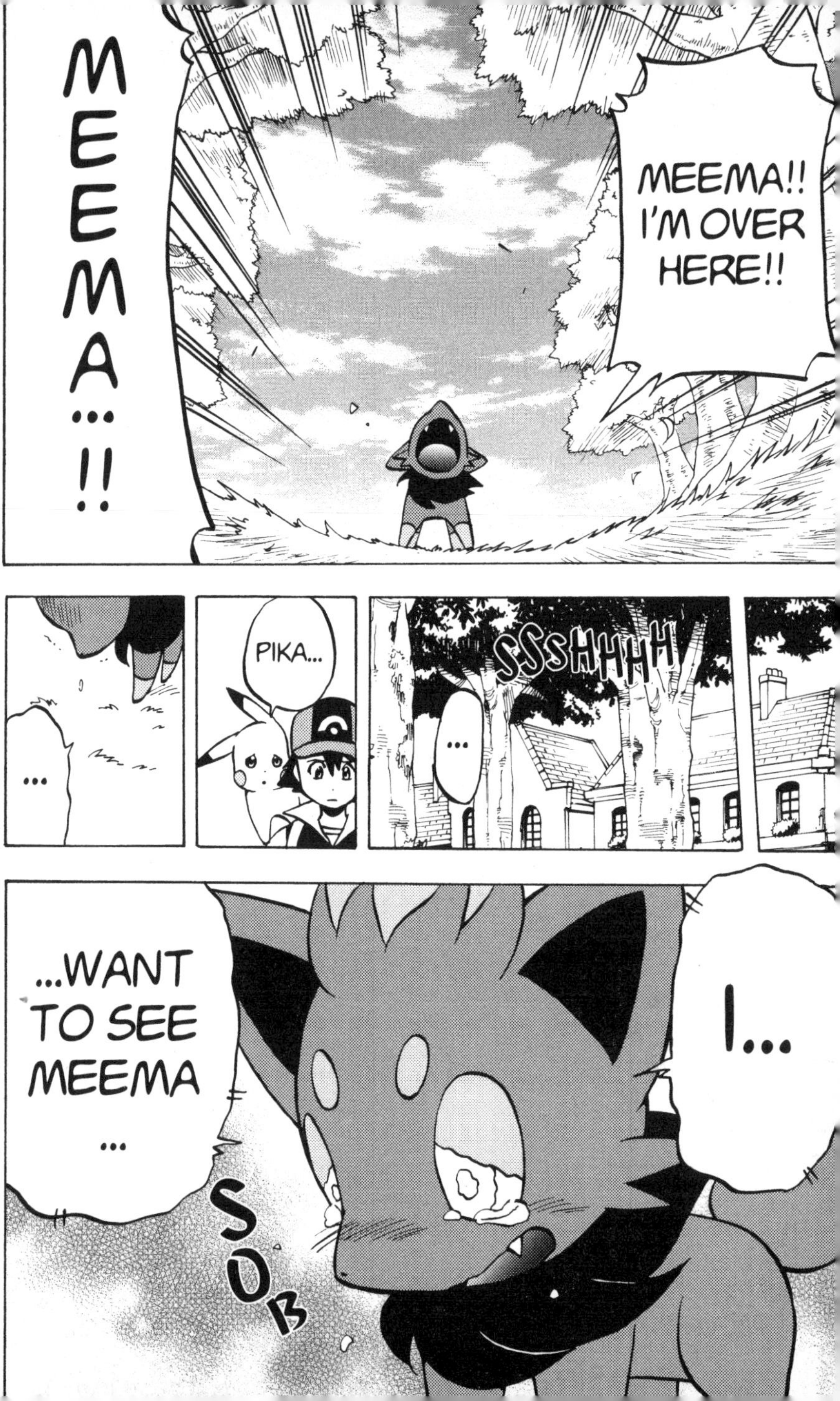
MEEMA!! I'M OVER HERE!!
MEEMA...!!
SSSHHHH
...
PIKA...
...
I...
...WANT TO SEE MEEMA ...
SOB

READ THIS WAY

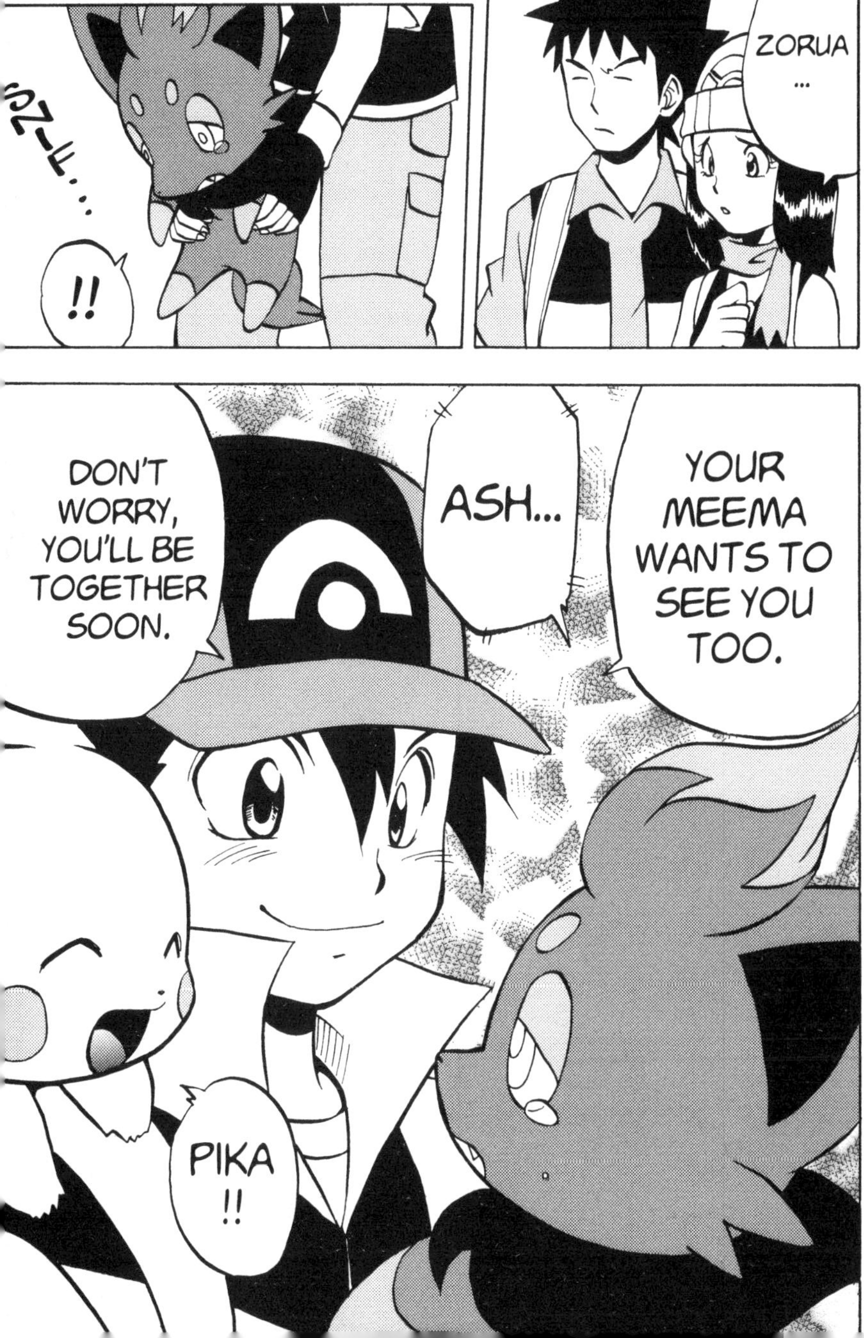
ZORUA ...
!!
YOUR MEEMA WANTS TO SEE YOU TOO.
ASH...
DON'T WORRY, YOU'LL BE TOGETHER SOON.
PIKA !!

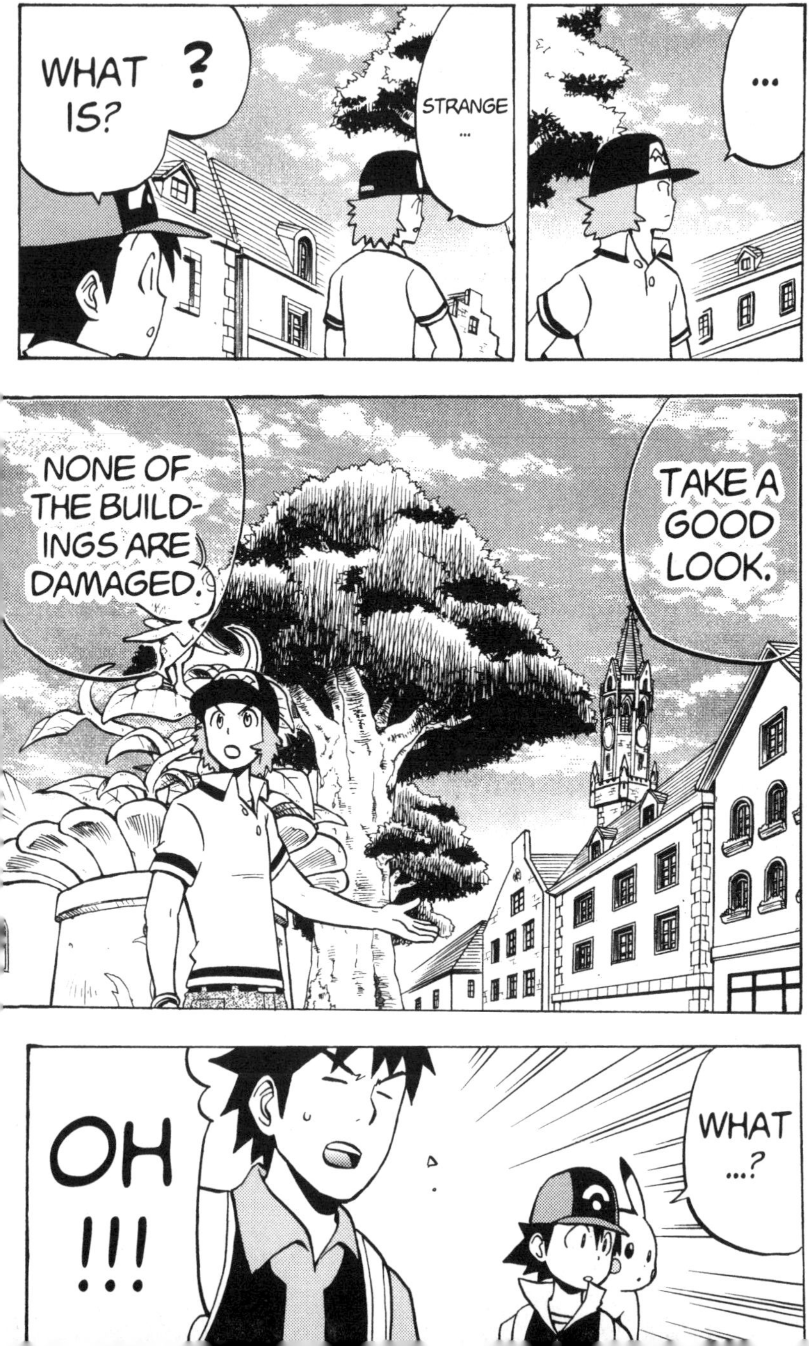
...
STRANGE ...
WHAT IS?
?
TAKE A GOOD LOOK.
NONE OF THE BUILDINGS ARE DAMAGED.
WHAT ...?
OH !!!

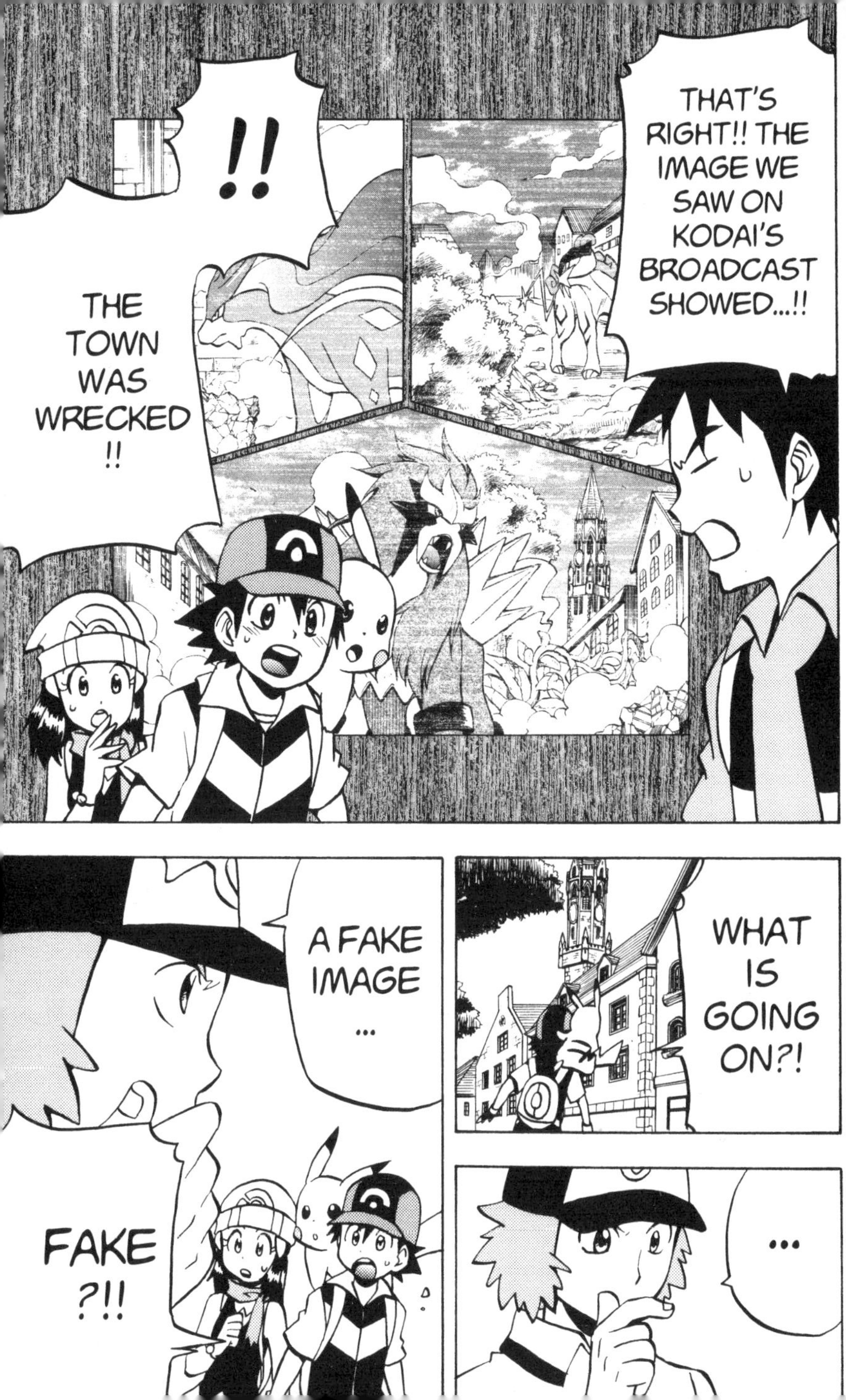
THAT'S RIGHT!! THE IMAGE WE SAW ON KODAI'S BROADCAST SHOWED...!!
!!
THE TOWN WAS WRECKED !!
WHAT IS GOING ON?!
...
A FAKE IMAGE ...
FAKE ?!!

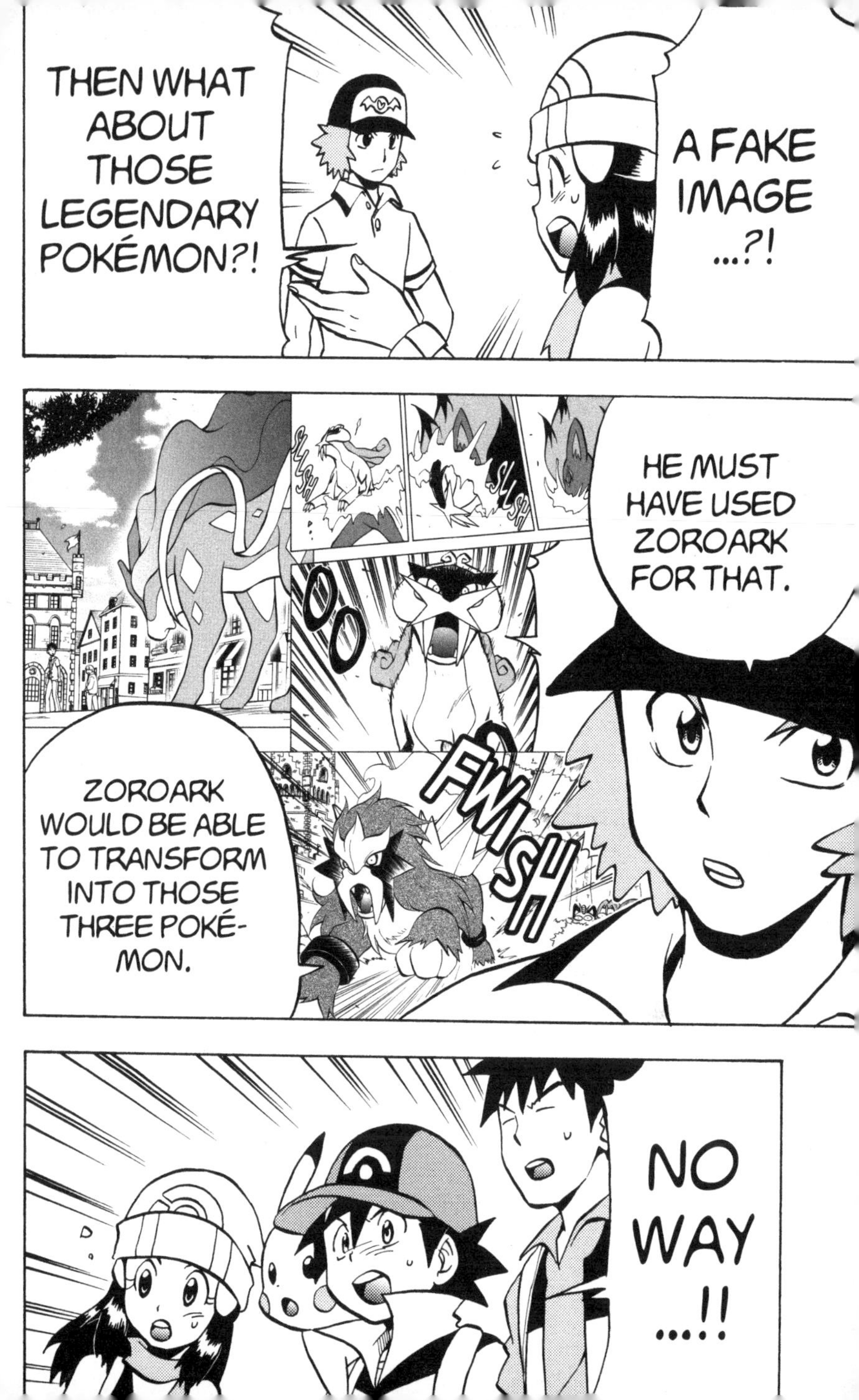

A FAKE IMAGE ...?!
THEN WHAT ABOUT THOSE LEGENDARY POKÉMON?!
HE MUST HAVE USED ZOROARK FOR THAT.
FWISH
ZOROARK WOULD BE ABLE TO TRANSFORM INTO THOSE THREE POKÉ-MON.
NO WAY ...!!

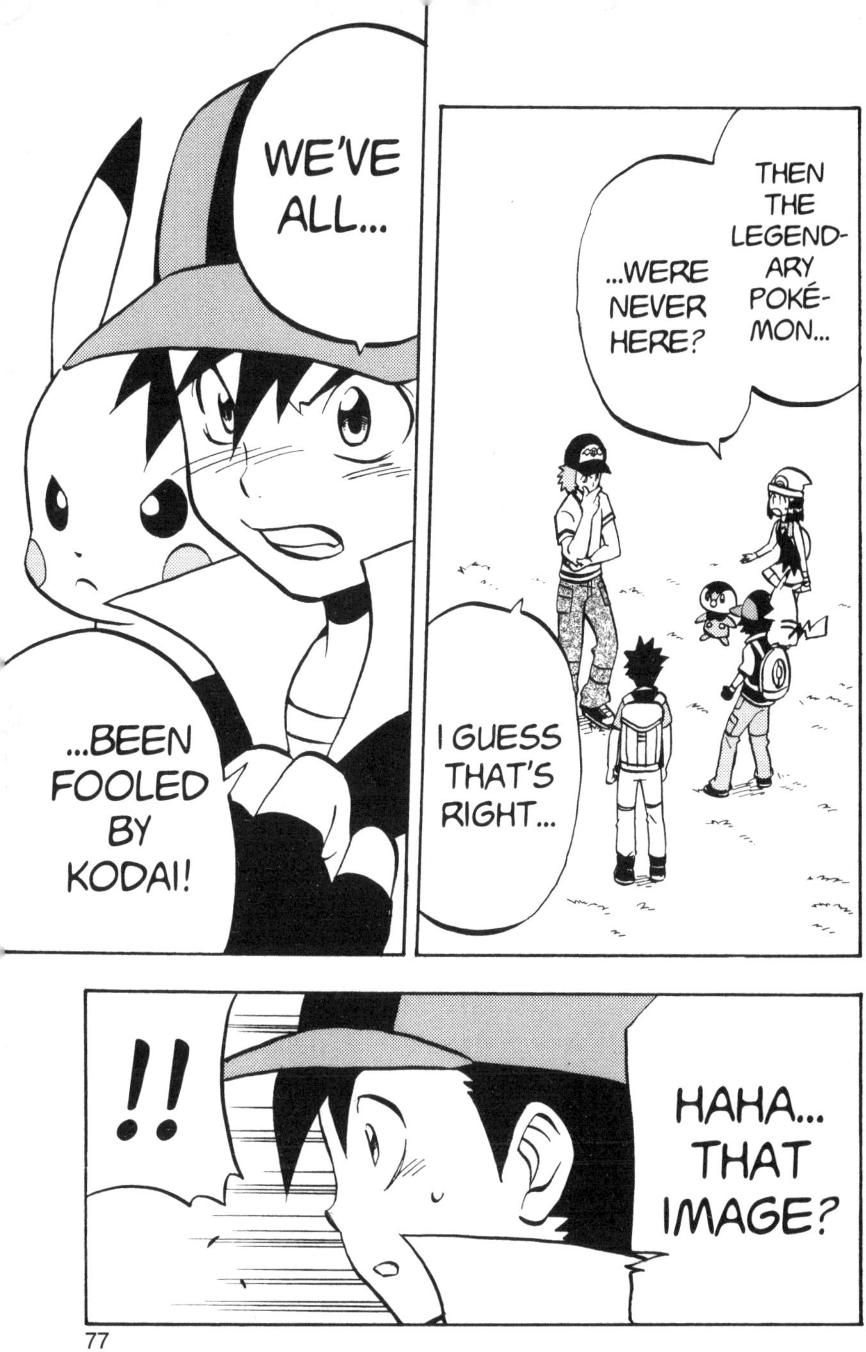
THEN THE LEGENDARY POKÉMON...
...WERE NEVER HERE?
I GUESS THAT'S RIGHT...
WE'VE ALL...
...BEEN FOOLED BY KODAI!
HAHA... THAT IMAGE?
!!

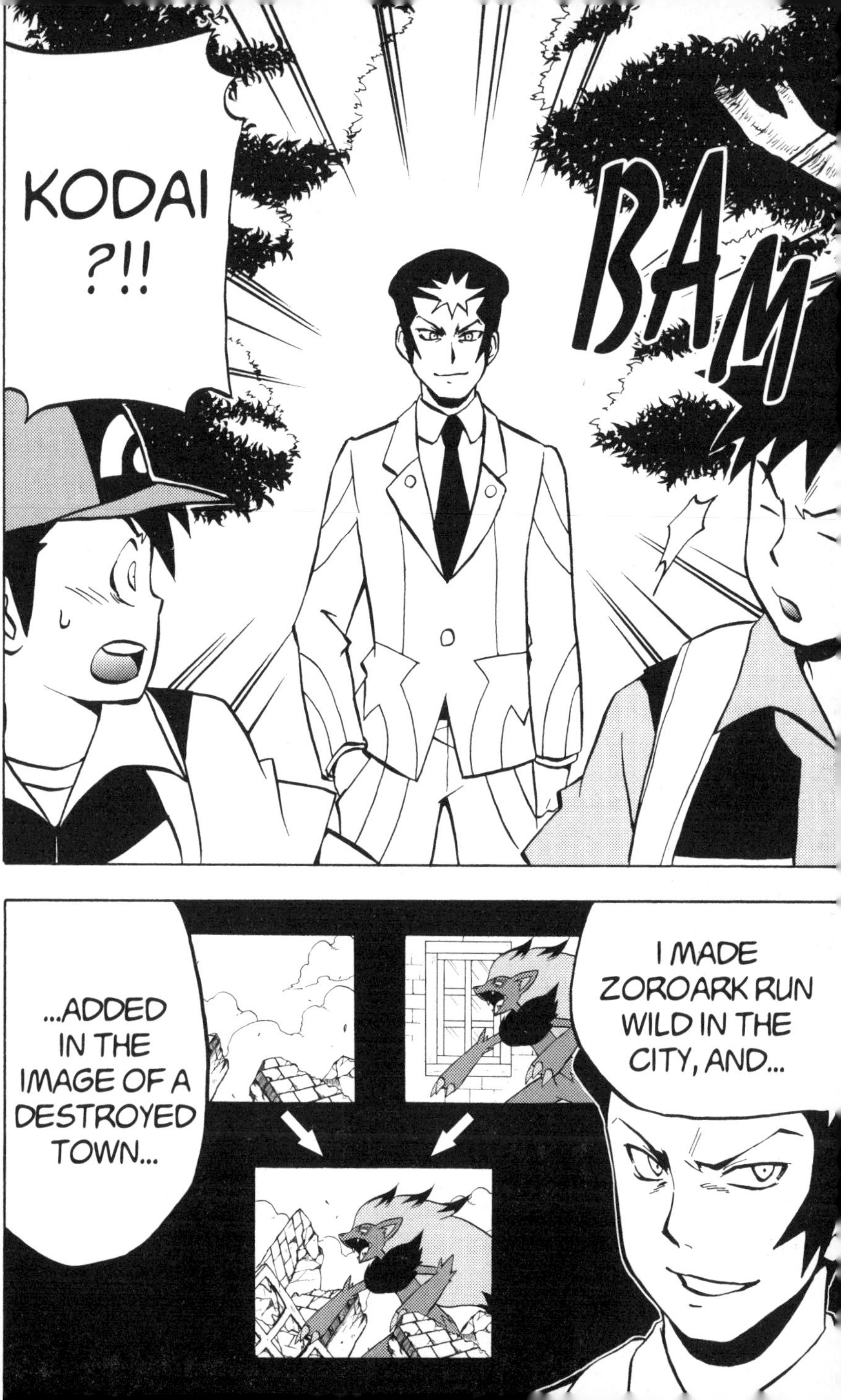
BAM
KODAI ?!!
I MADE ZOROARK RUN WILD IN THE CITY, AND...
...ADDED IN THE IMAGE OF A DESTROYED TOWN...

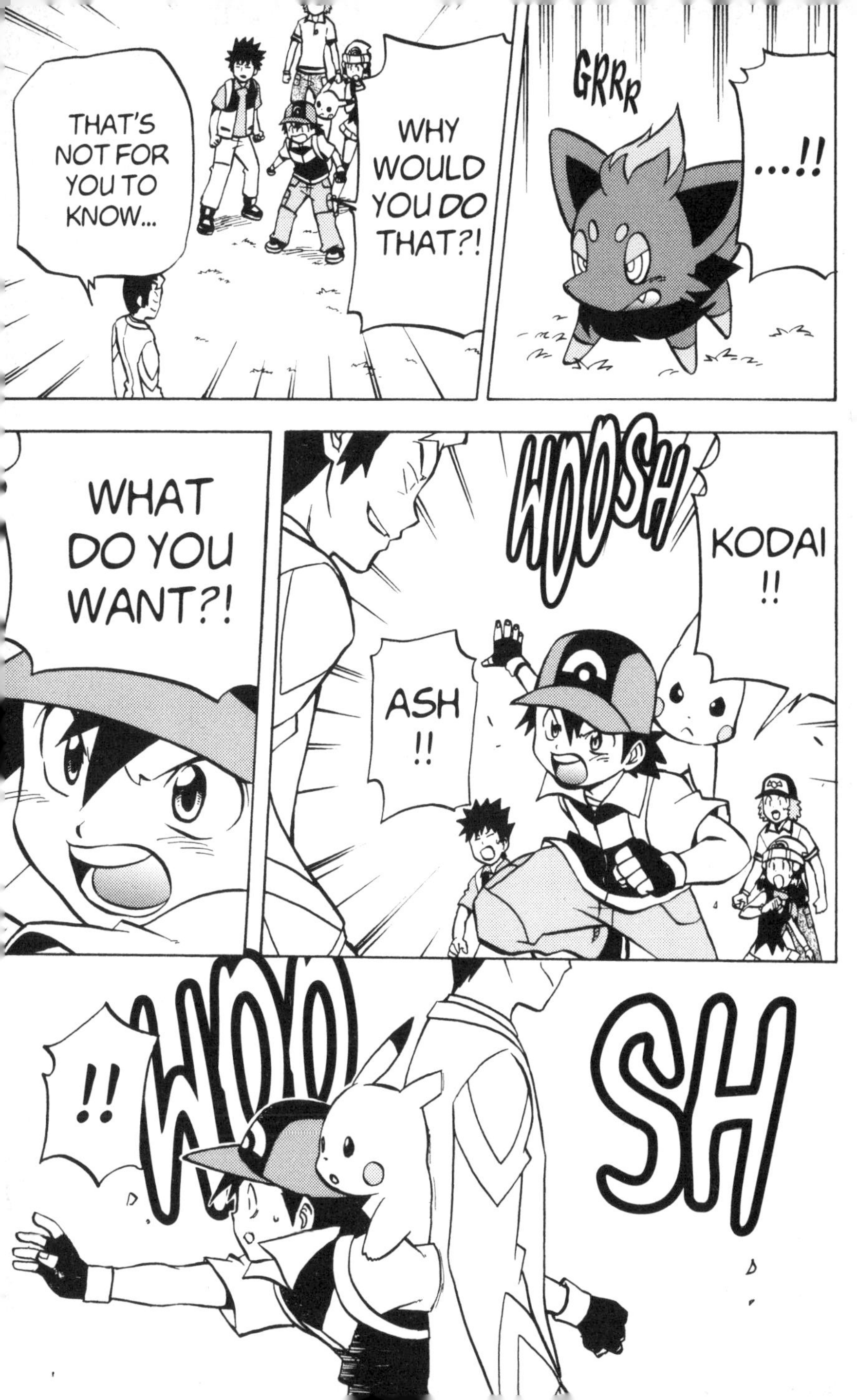
GRRR
...!!
WHY WOULD YOU DO THAT?!
THAT'S NOT FOR YOU TO KNOW...
WHOOSH
KODAI !!
ASH !!
WHAT DO YOU WANT?!
WHOOSH
!!

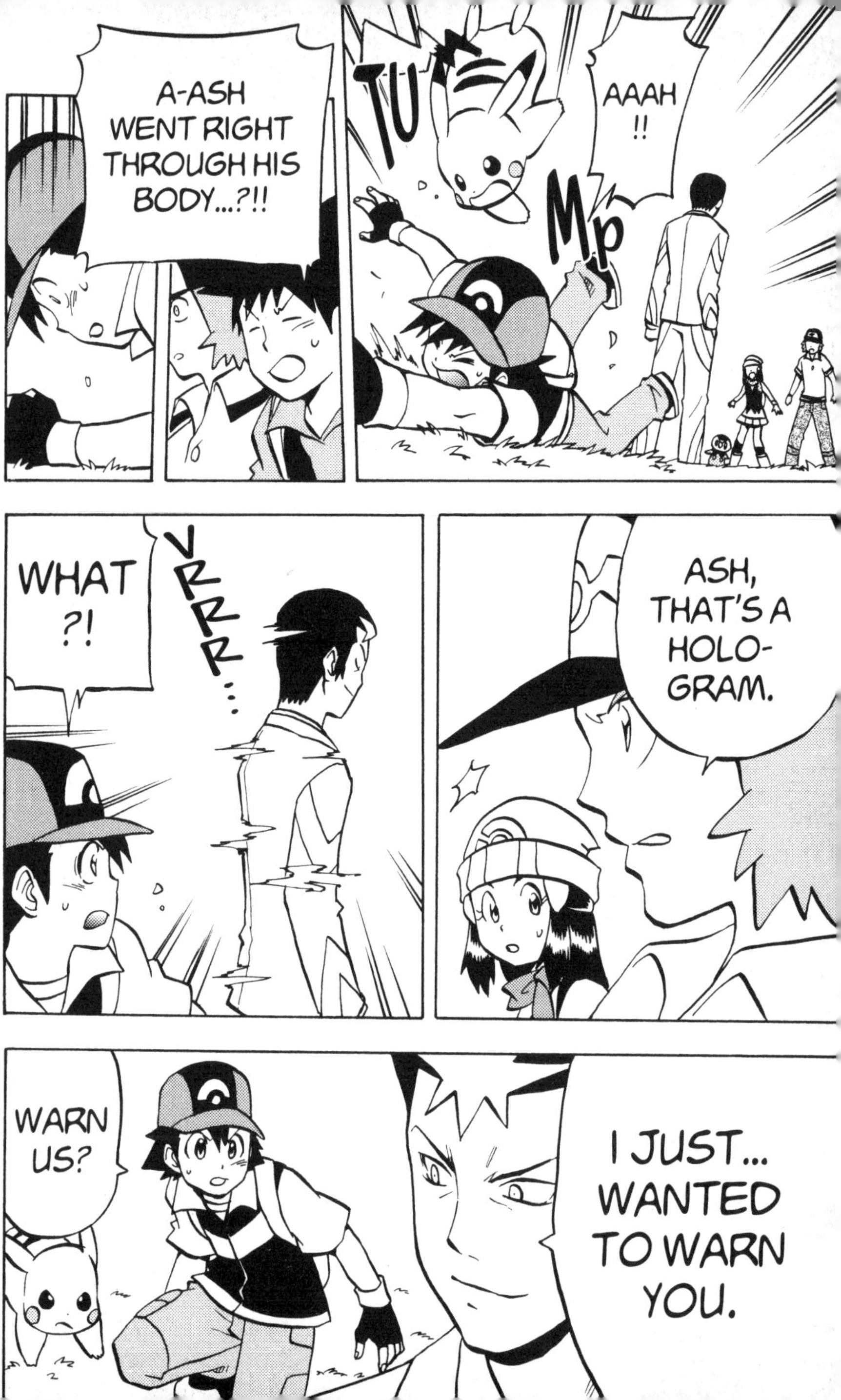

AAAH!!
TU
Mp
A-ASH WENT RIGHT THROUGH HIS BODY...?!!
ASH, THAT'S A HOLO-GRAM.
VRRR...
WHAT?!
I JUST... WANTED TO WARN YOU.
WARN US?

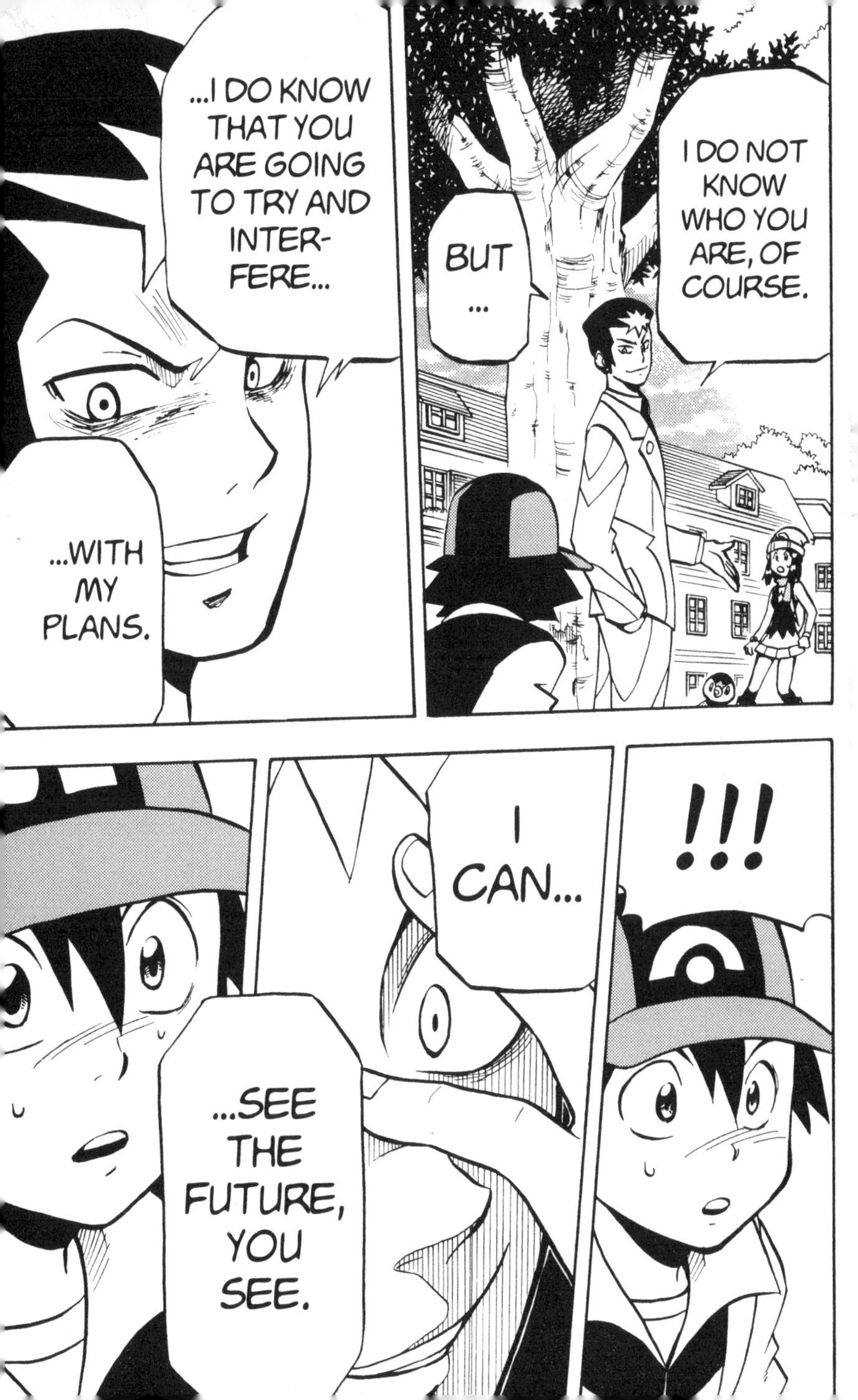
I DO NOT KNOW WHO YOU ARE, OF COURSE.
BUT ...
...I DO KNOW THAT YOU ARE GOING TO TRY AND INTER-FERE...
...WITH MY PLANS.
!!!
I CAN...
...SEE THE FUTURE, YOU SEE.

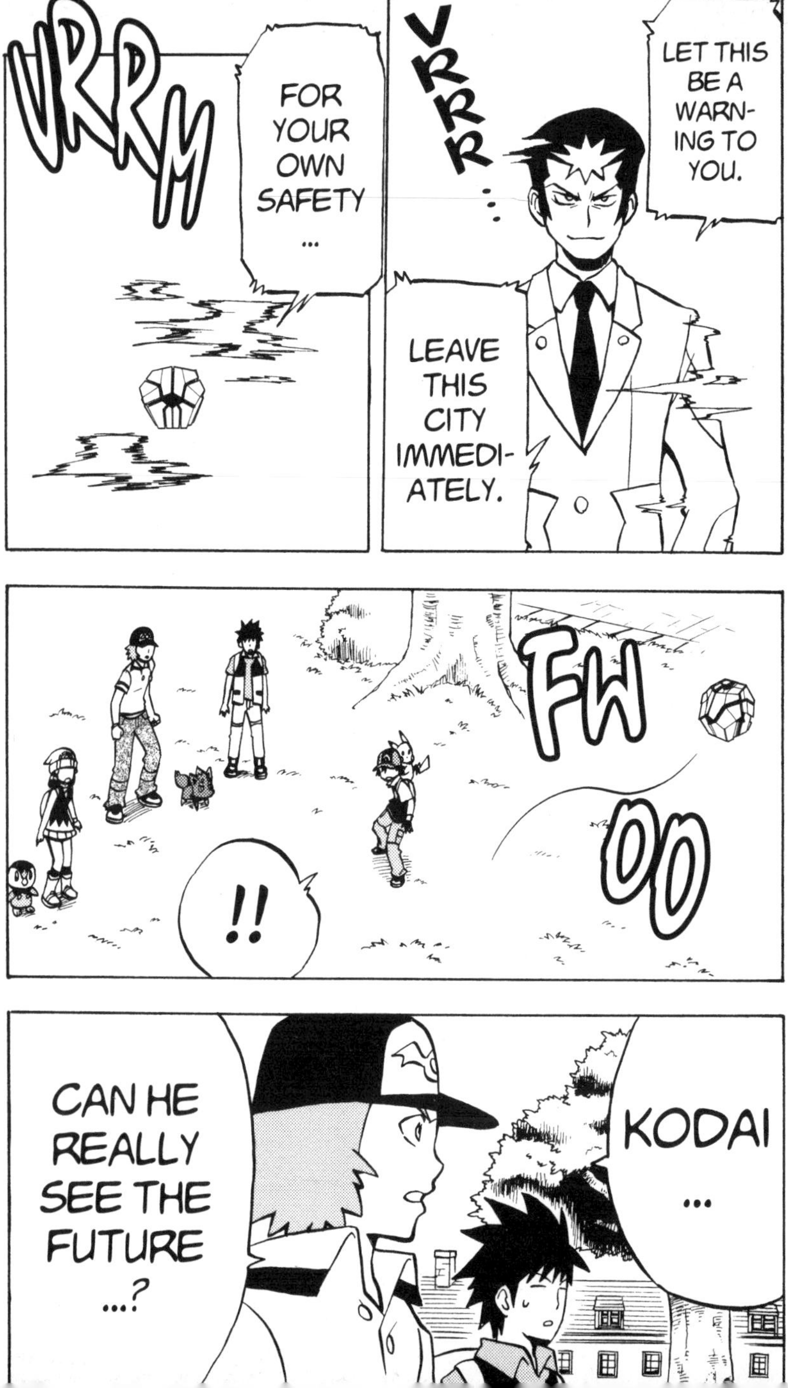
VRRR
LET THIS BE A WARNING TO YOU.
LEAVE THIS CITY IMMEDIATELY.
VRRM
FOR YOUR OWN SAFETY ...
FWOO
!!
KODAI ...
CAN HE REALLY SEE THE FUTURE ...?

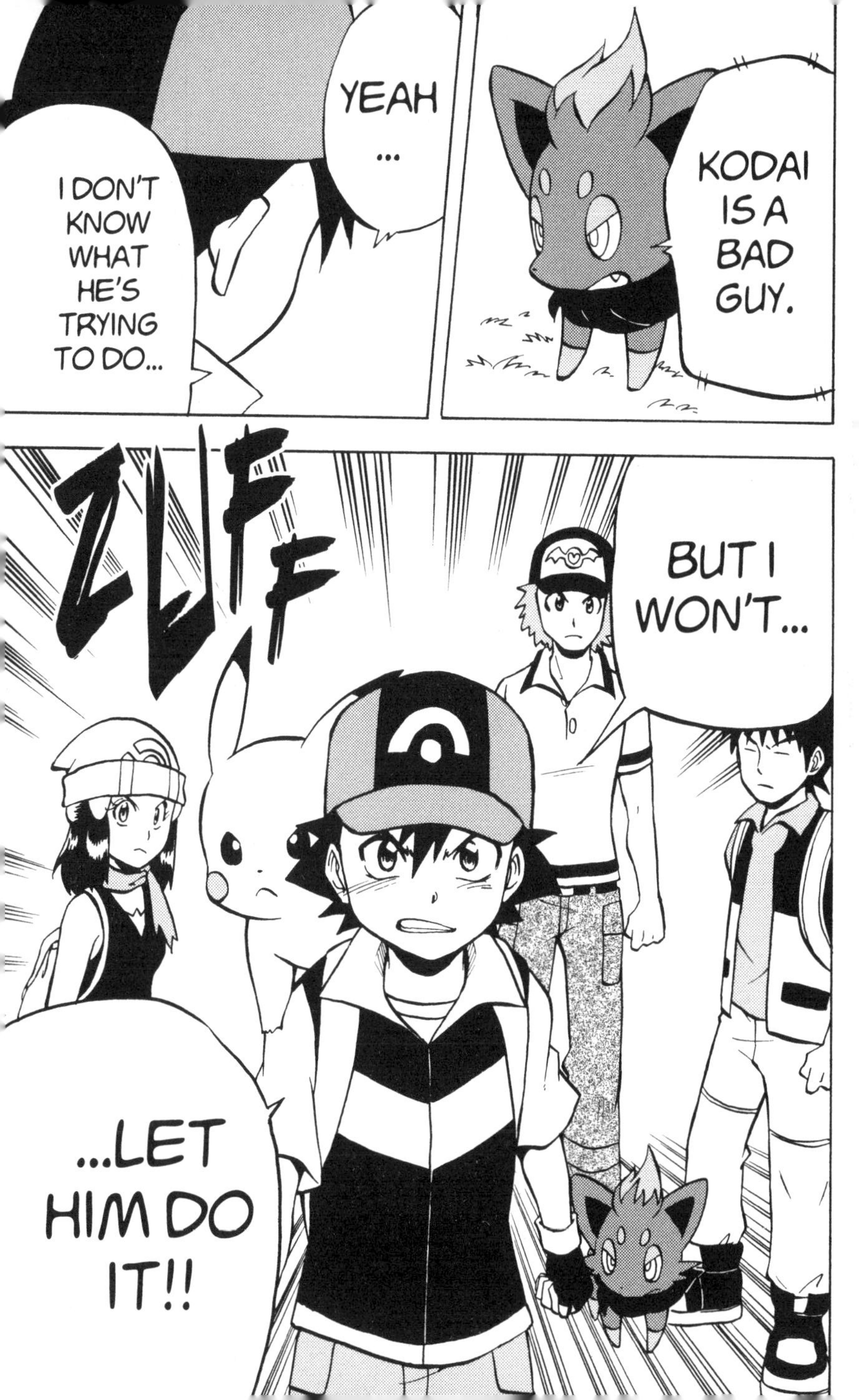
KODAI IS A BAD GUY.
YEAH ...
I DON'T KNOW WHAT HE'S TRYING TO DO...
ZUFF
BUT I WON'T...
...LET HIM DO IT!!

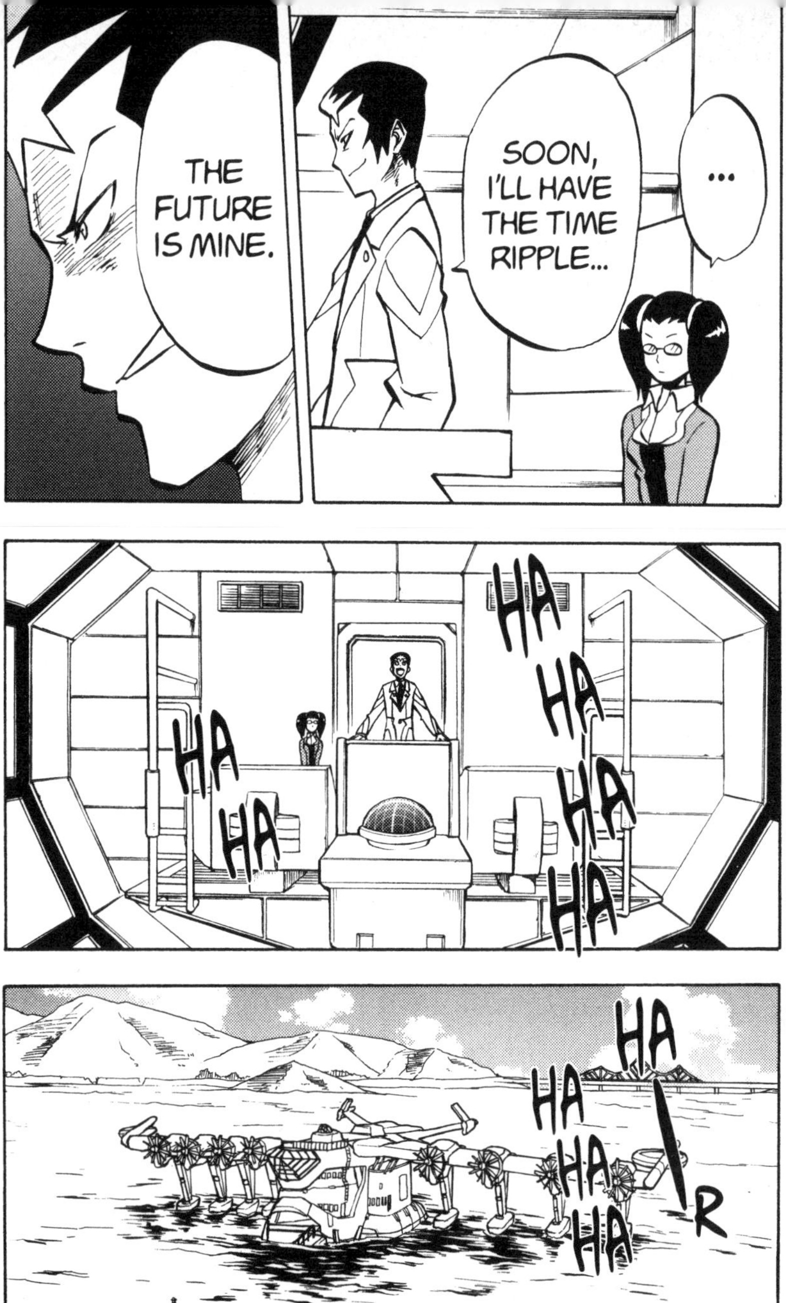
...
SOON, I'LL HAVE THE TIME RIPPLE...
THE FUTURE IS MINE.
HA HA HA HA
HA HA
HA HA HA HA HA
R

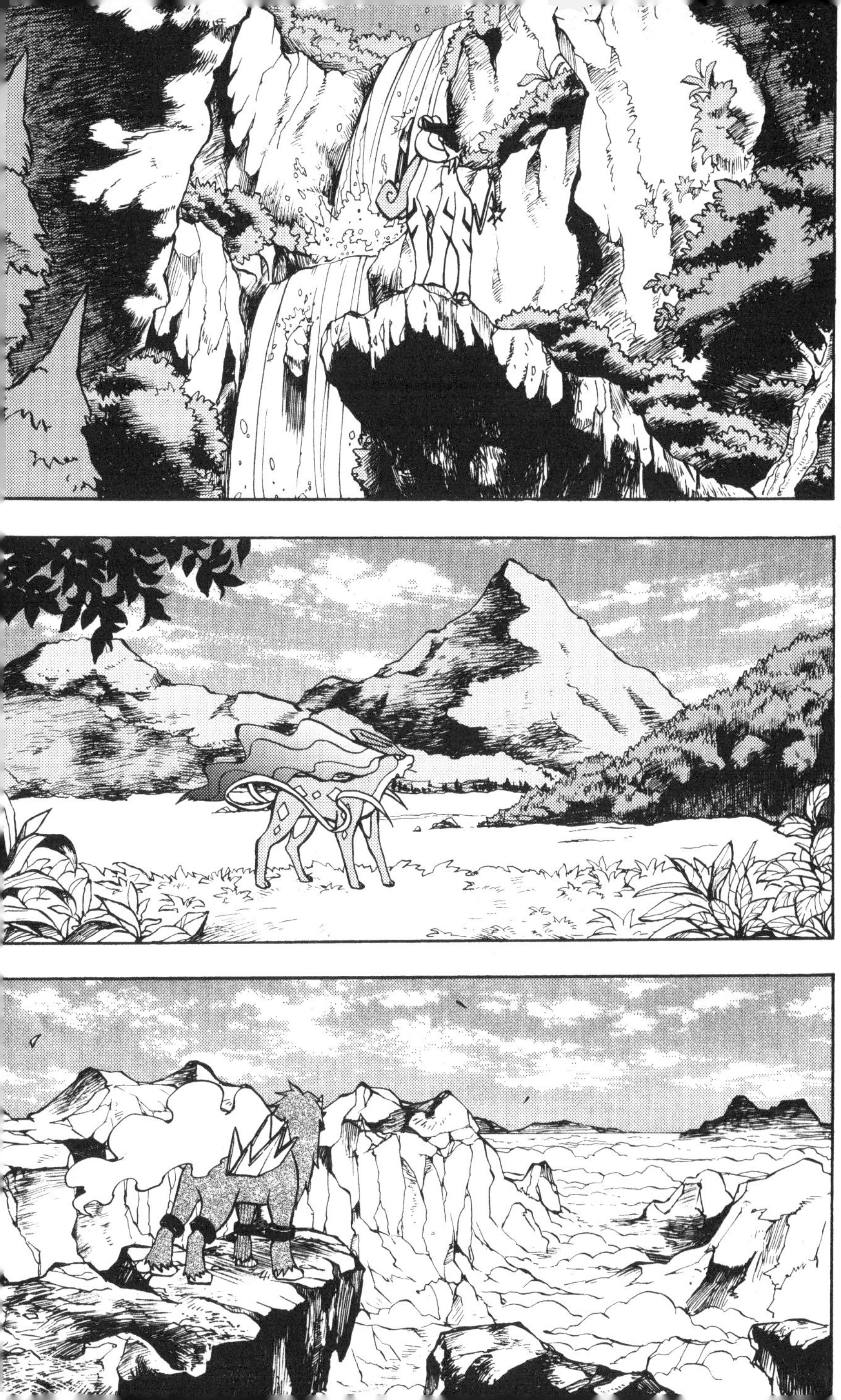

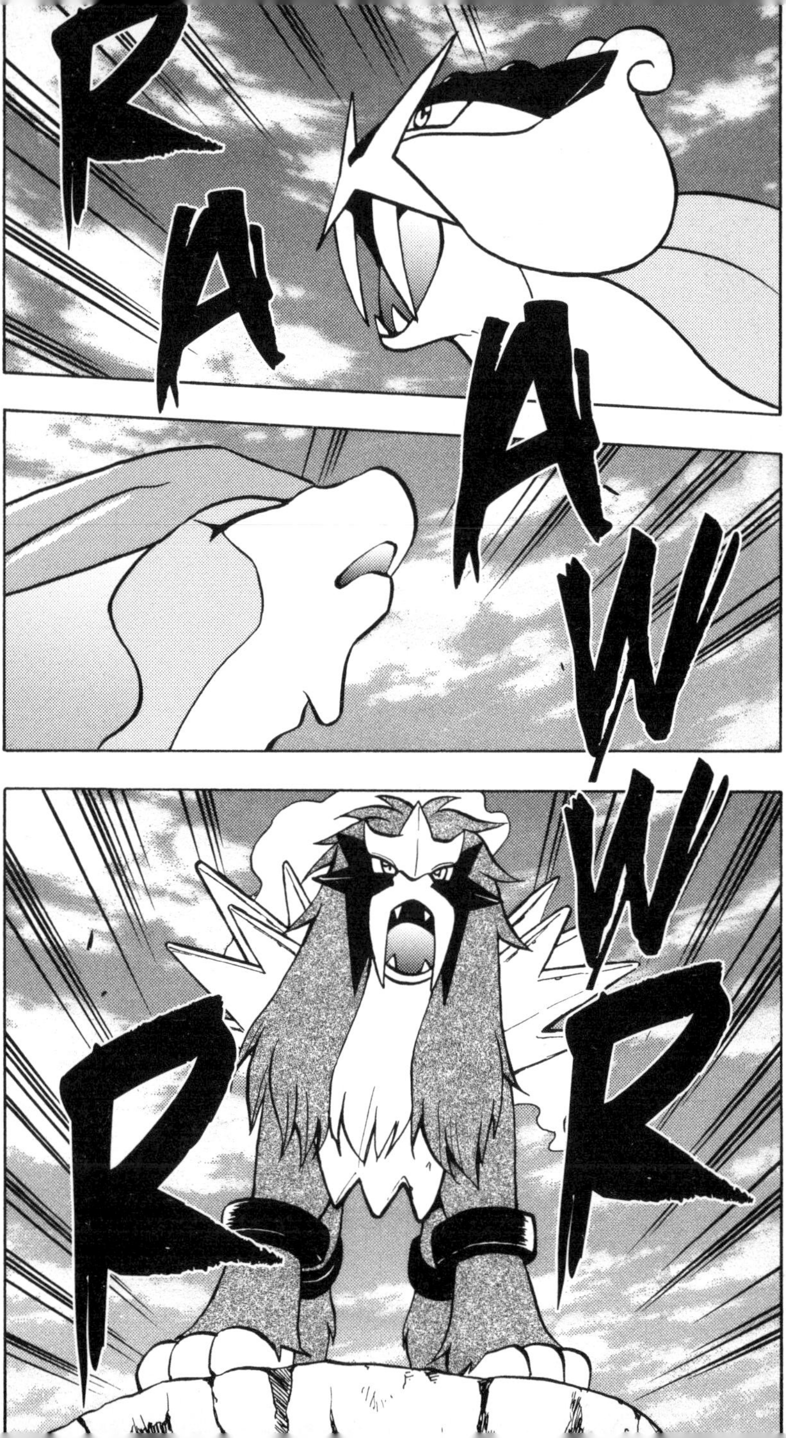
RAAWWRR

ZORUA MEETS CELEBI

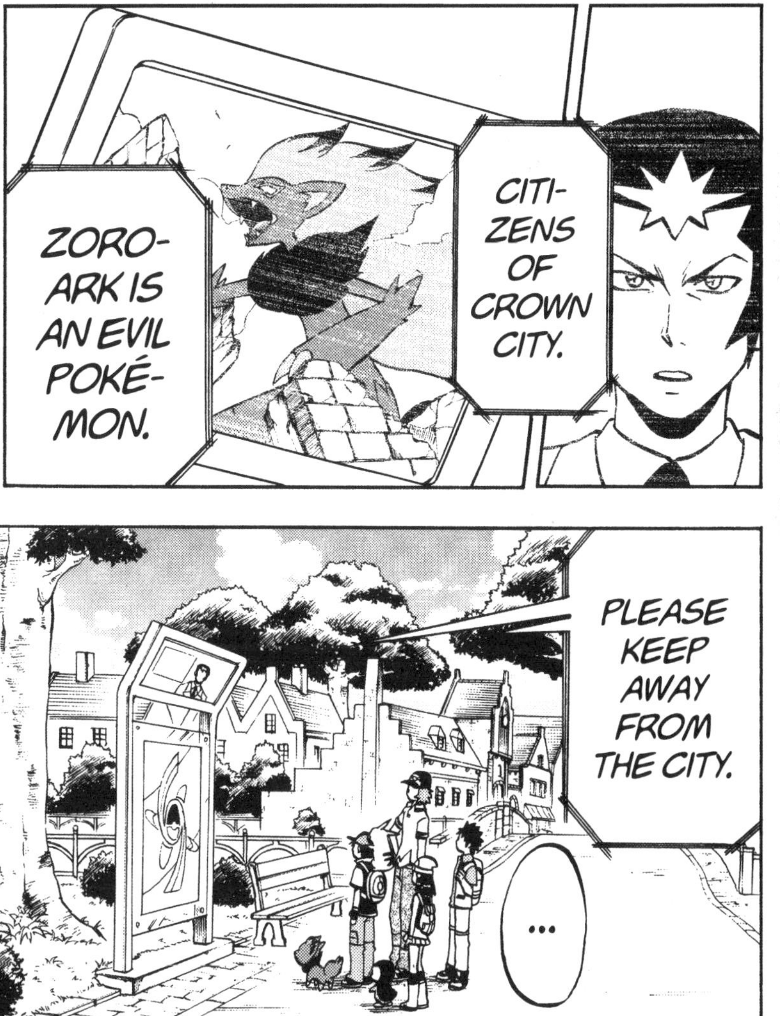
CITIZENS OF CROWN CITY.
ZOROARK IS AN EVIL POKÉMON.
PLEASE KEEP AWAY FROM THE CITY.
...

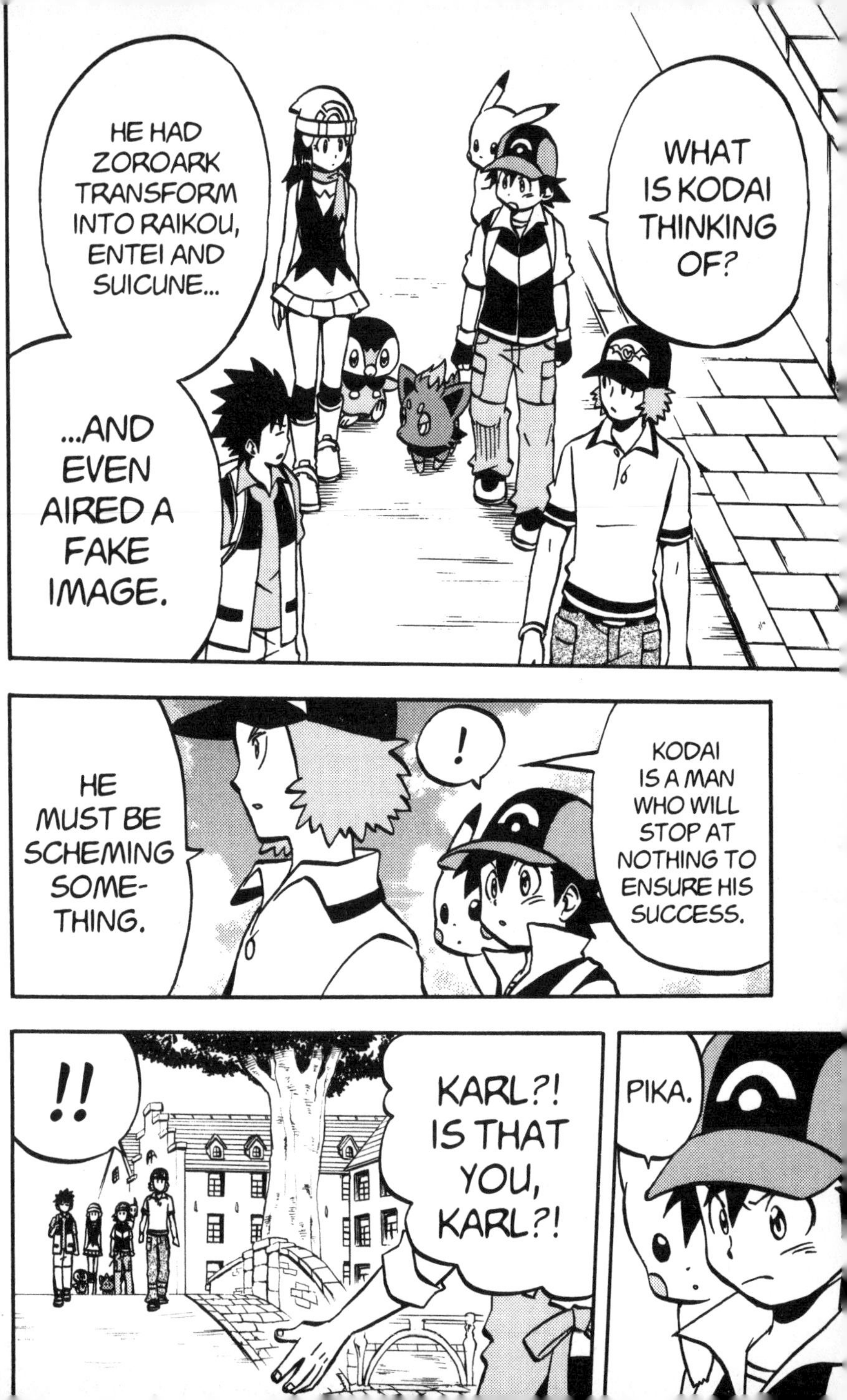
WHAT IS KODAI THINKING OF?
HE HAD ZOROARK TRANSFORM INTO RAIKOU, ENTEI AND SUICUNE...
...AND EVEN AIRED A FAKE IMAGE.
KODAI IS A MAN WHO WILL STOP AT NOTHING TO ENSURE HIS SUCCESS.
!
HE MUST BE SCHEMING SOME-THING.
PIKA.
KARL?! IS THAT YOU, KARL?!
!!

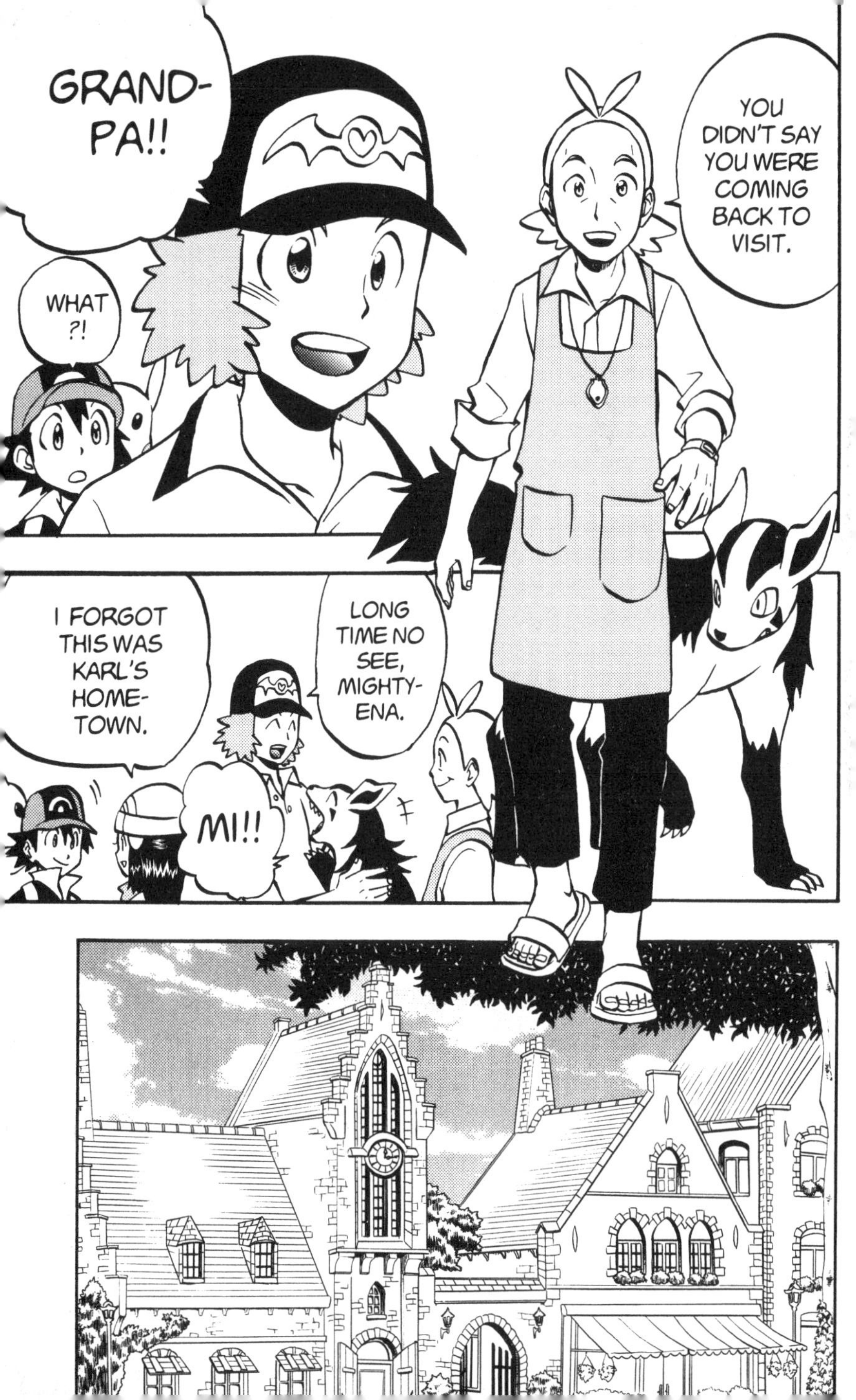
GRAND-PA!!
WHAT?!
YOU DIDN'T SAY YOU WERE COMING BACK TO VISIT.
I FORGOT THIS WAS KARL'S HOME-TOWN.
LONG TIME NO SEE, MIGHTY-ENA.
MI!!

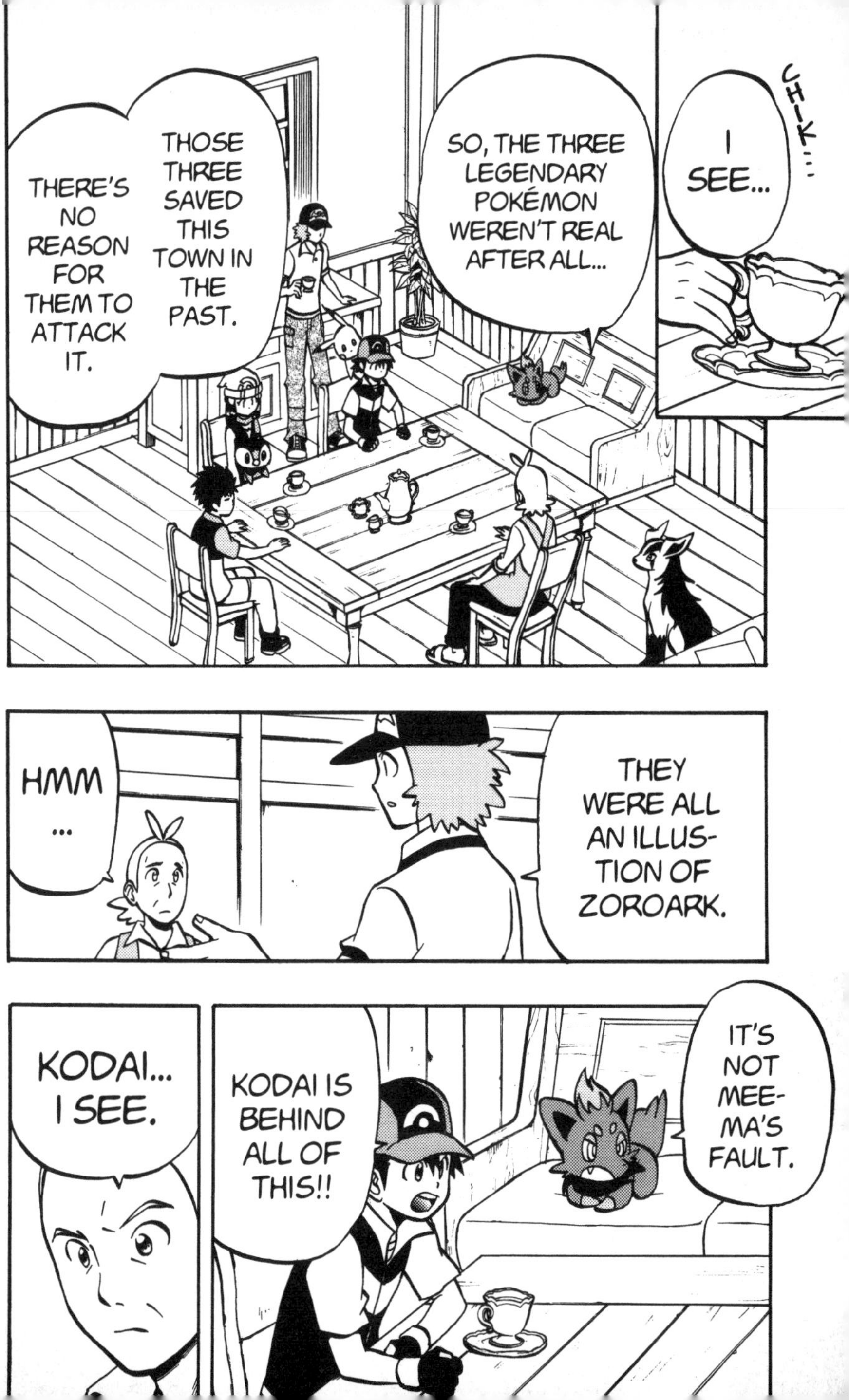
CHIK...
I SEE...
SO, THE THREE LEGENDARY POKÉMON WEREN'T REAL AFTER ALL...
THOSE THREE SAVED THIS TOWN IN THE PAST.
THERE'S NO REASON FOR THEM TO ATTACK IT.
THEY WERE ALL AN ILLUSION OF ZOROARK.
HMM...
IT'S NOT MEE-MA'S FAULT.
KODAI IS BEHIND ALL OF THIS!!
KODAI... I SEE.

READ THIS WAY

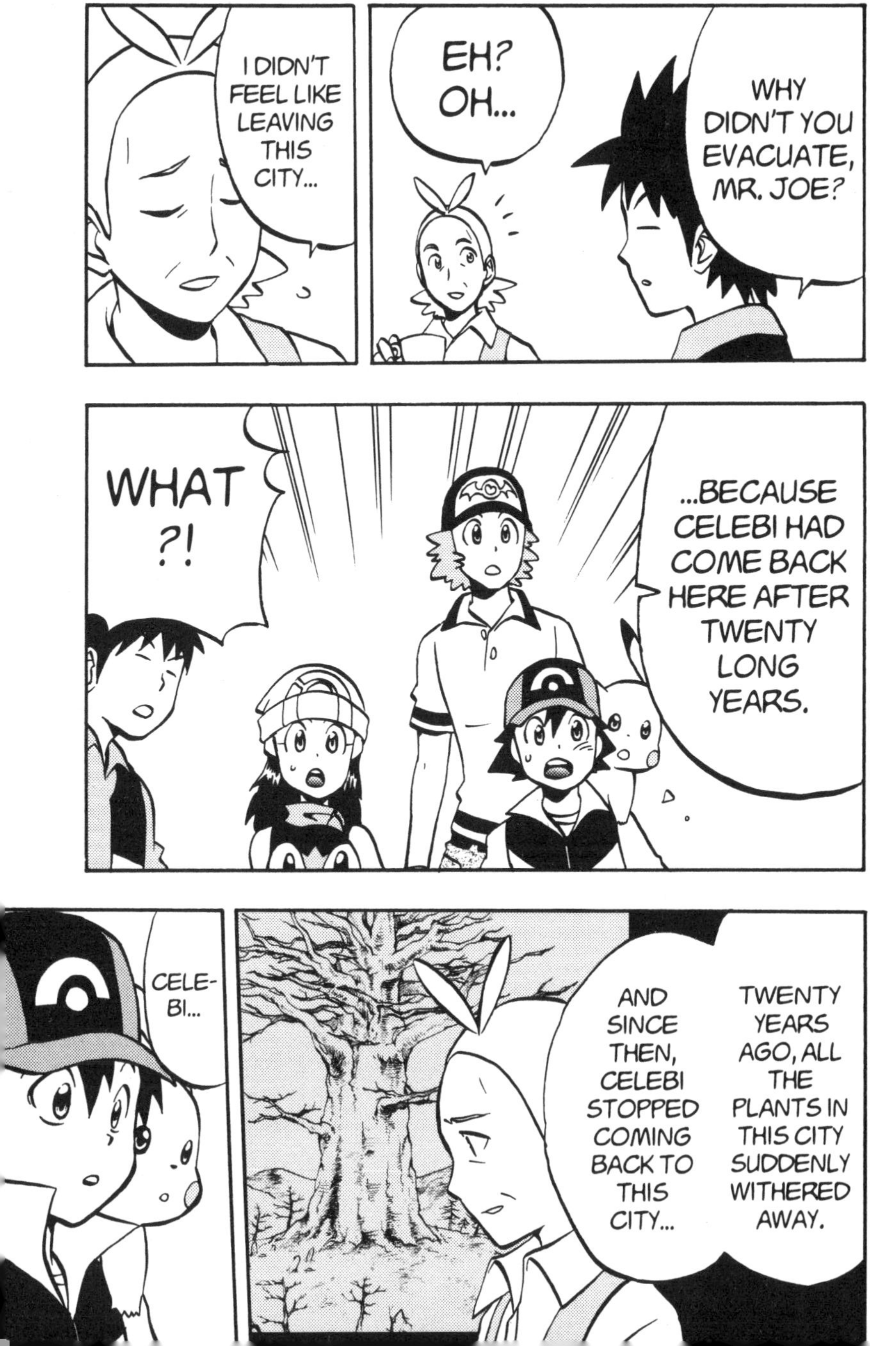
WHY DIDN'T YOU EVACUATE, MR. JOE?
EH? OH...
I DIDN'T FEEL LIKE LEAVING THIS CITY...
...BECAUSE CELEBI HAD COME BACK HERE AFTER TWENTY LONG YEARS.
WHAT?!
TWENTY YEARS AGO, ALL THE PLANTS IN THIS CITY SUDDENLY WITHERED AWAY.
AND SINCE THEN, CELEBI STOPPED COMING BACK TO THIS CITY...
CELE-BI...

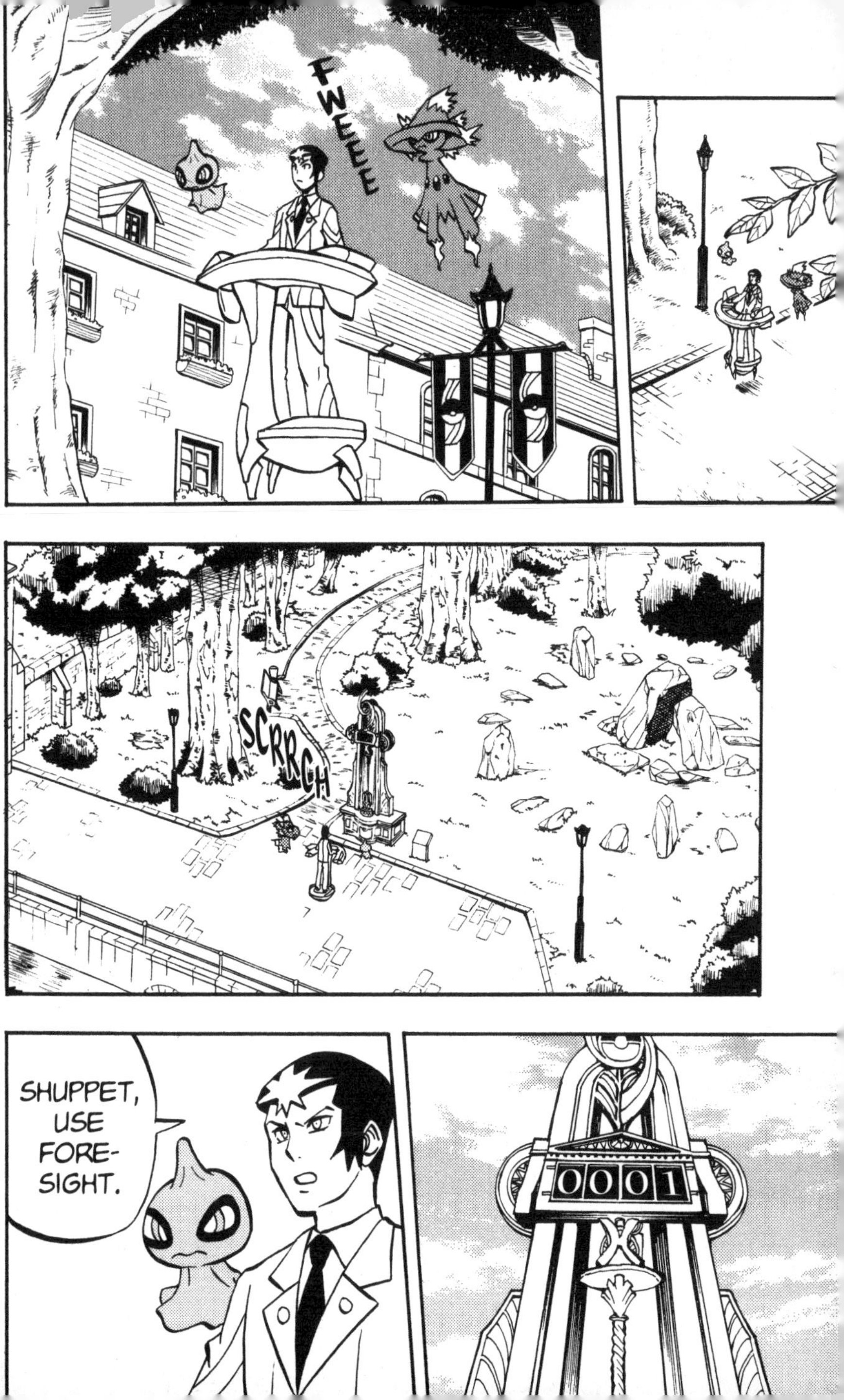
FWEEEE
SCRRRCH
0001
SHUPPET, USE FORE-SIGHT.

READ THIS WAY

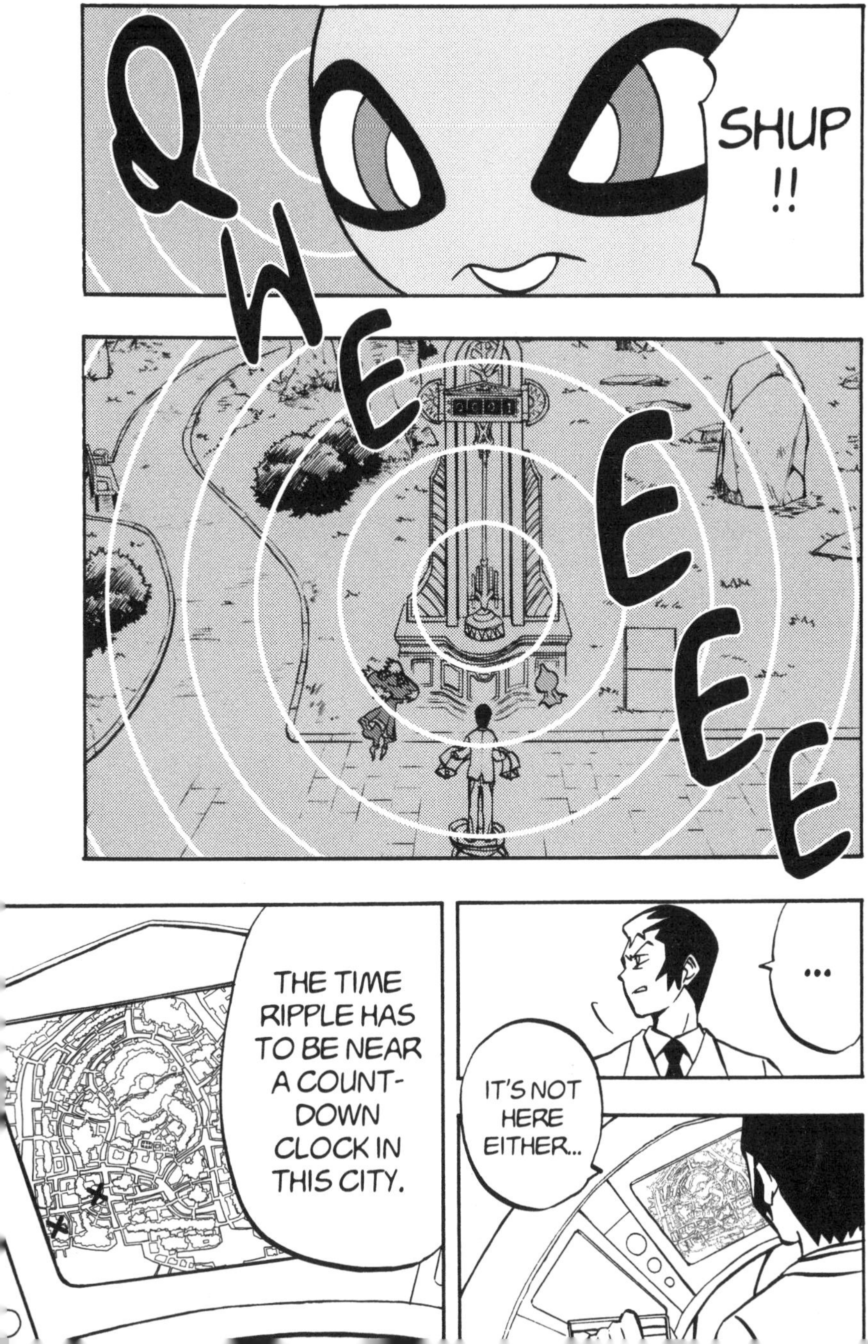
SHUP !!
QWEEEEE
...
IT'S NOT HERE EITHER...
THE TIME RIPPLE HAS TO BE NEAR A COUNT-DOWN CLOCK IN THIS CITY.

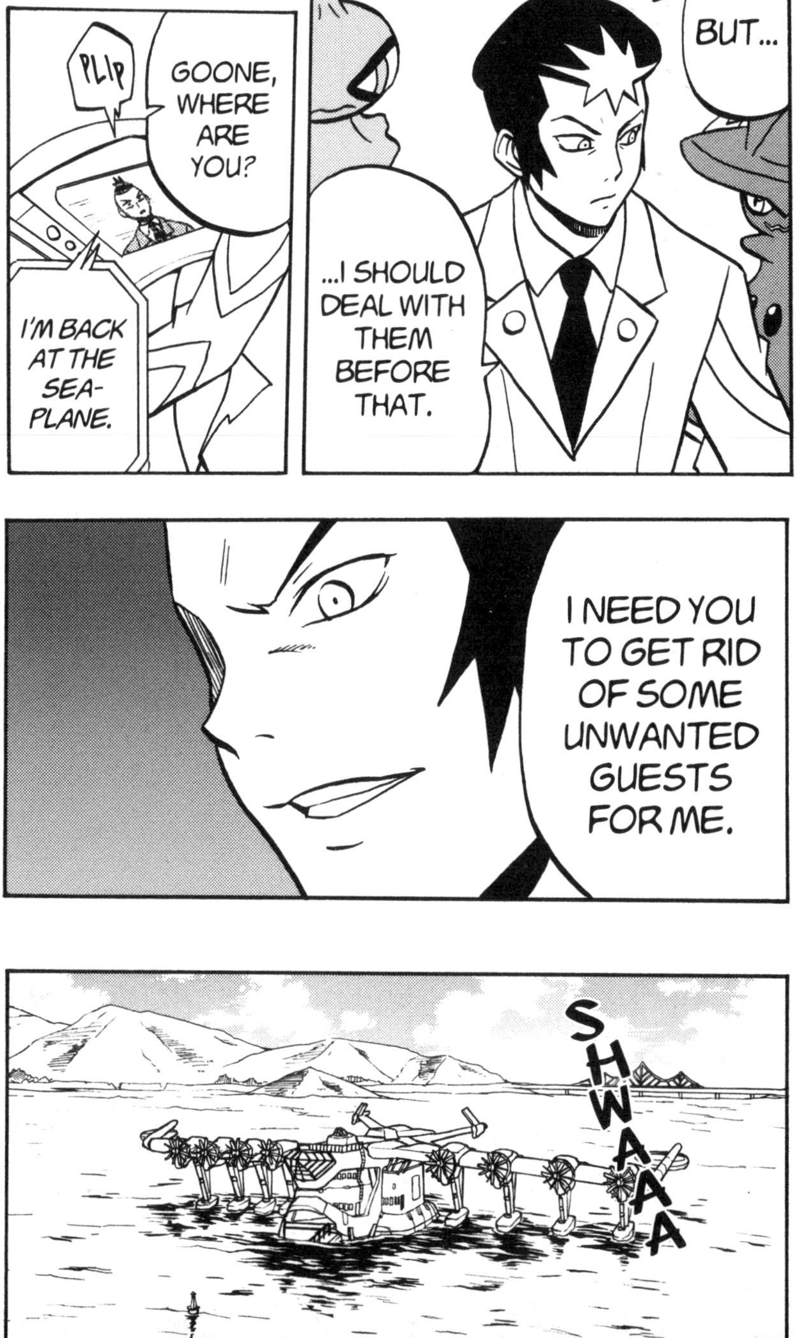
BUT...
...I SHOULD DEAL WITH THEM BEFORE THAT.
PLIP
GOONE, WHERE ARE YOU?
I'M BACK AT THE SEA-PLANE.
I NEED YOU TO GET RID OF SOME UNWANTED GUESTS FOR ME.
SHWAAA

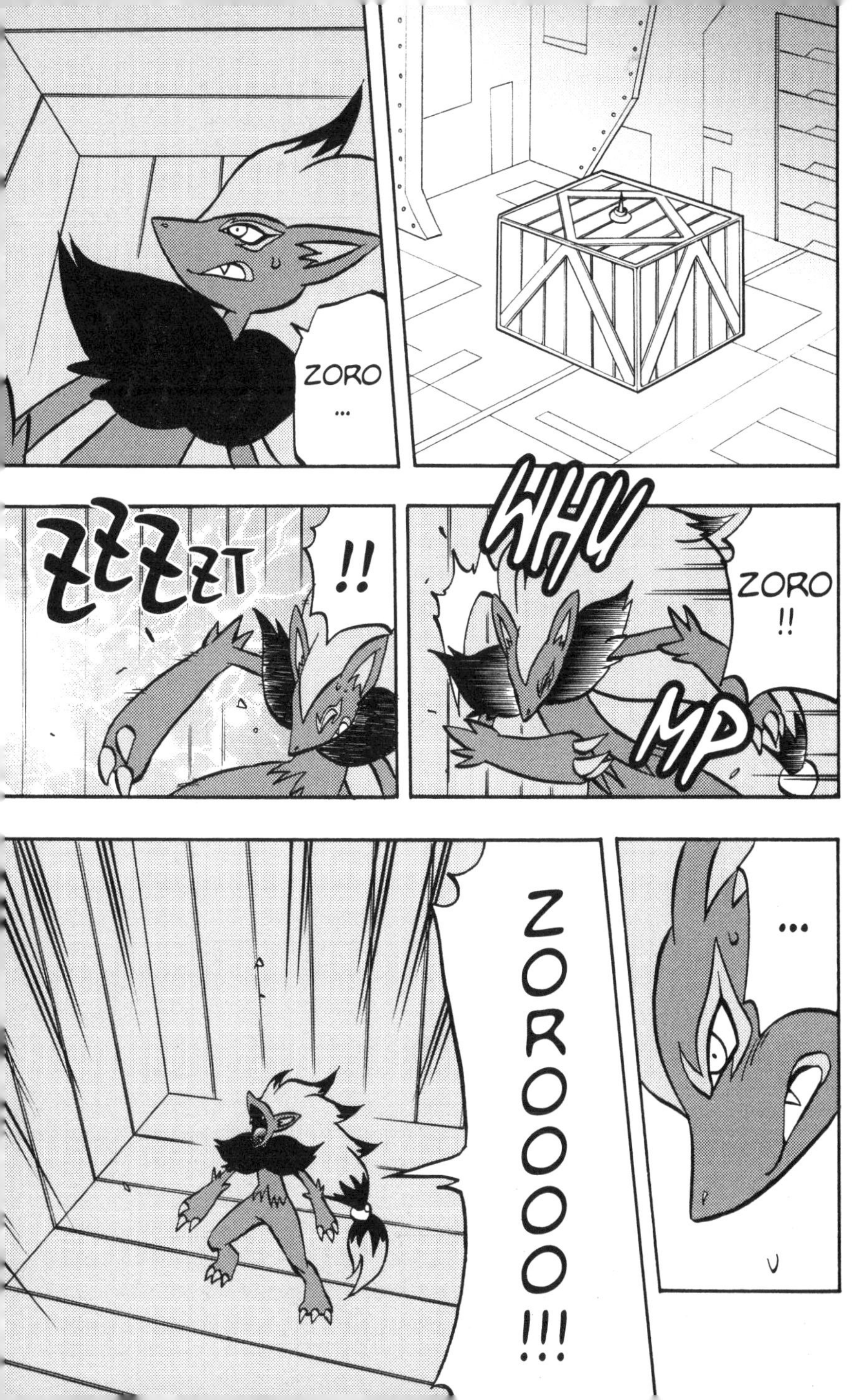

ZORO
...
WHU
MP
ZORO
!!
ZZZZZT
!!
...
ZOROOOOOO
!!!

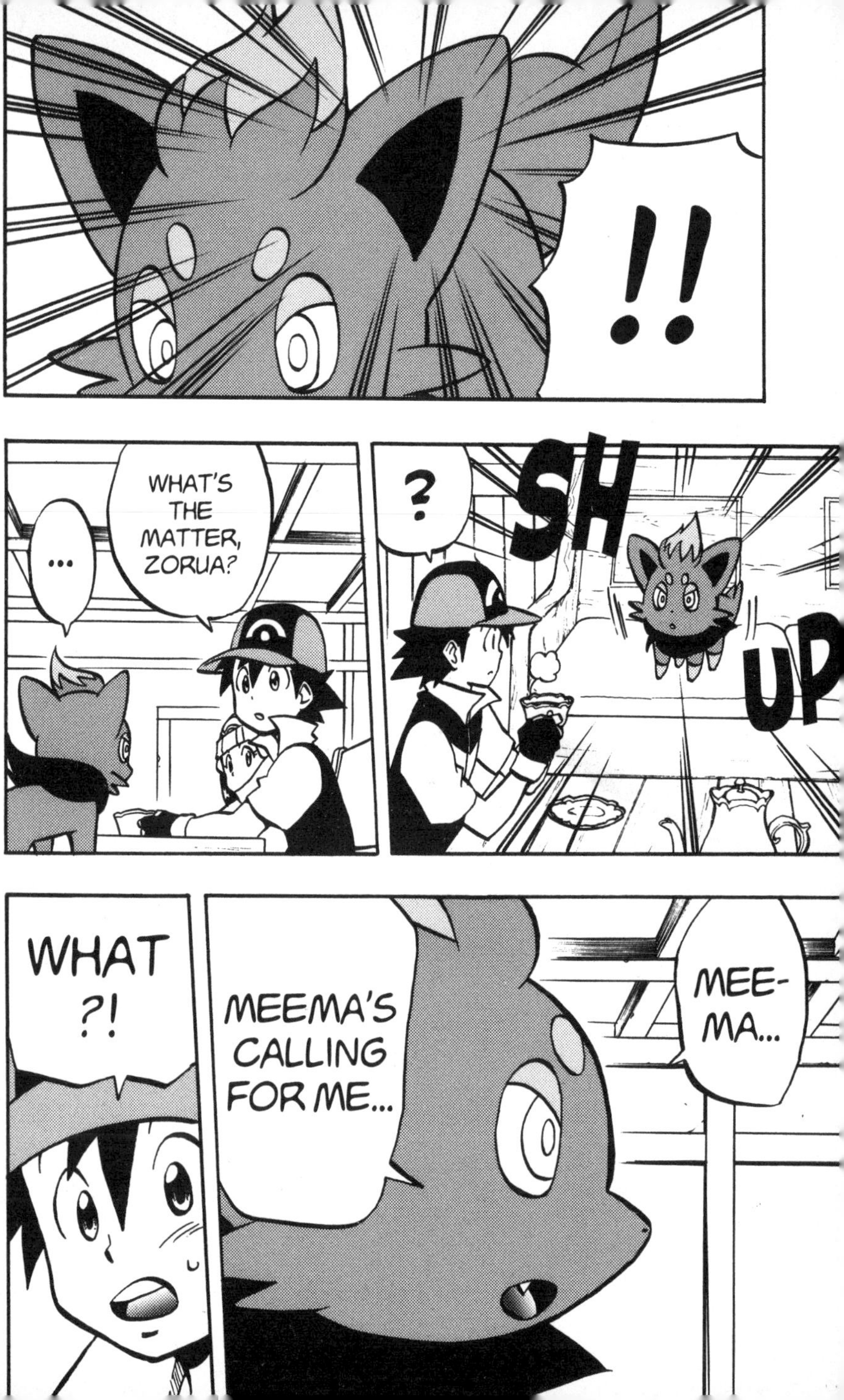
!!
SH
UP
?
WHAT'S THE MATTER, ZORUA?
...
MEE-MA...
MEEMA'S CALLING FOR ME...
WHAT?!

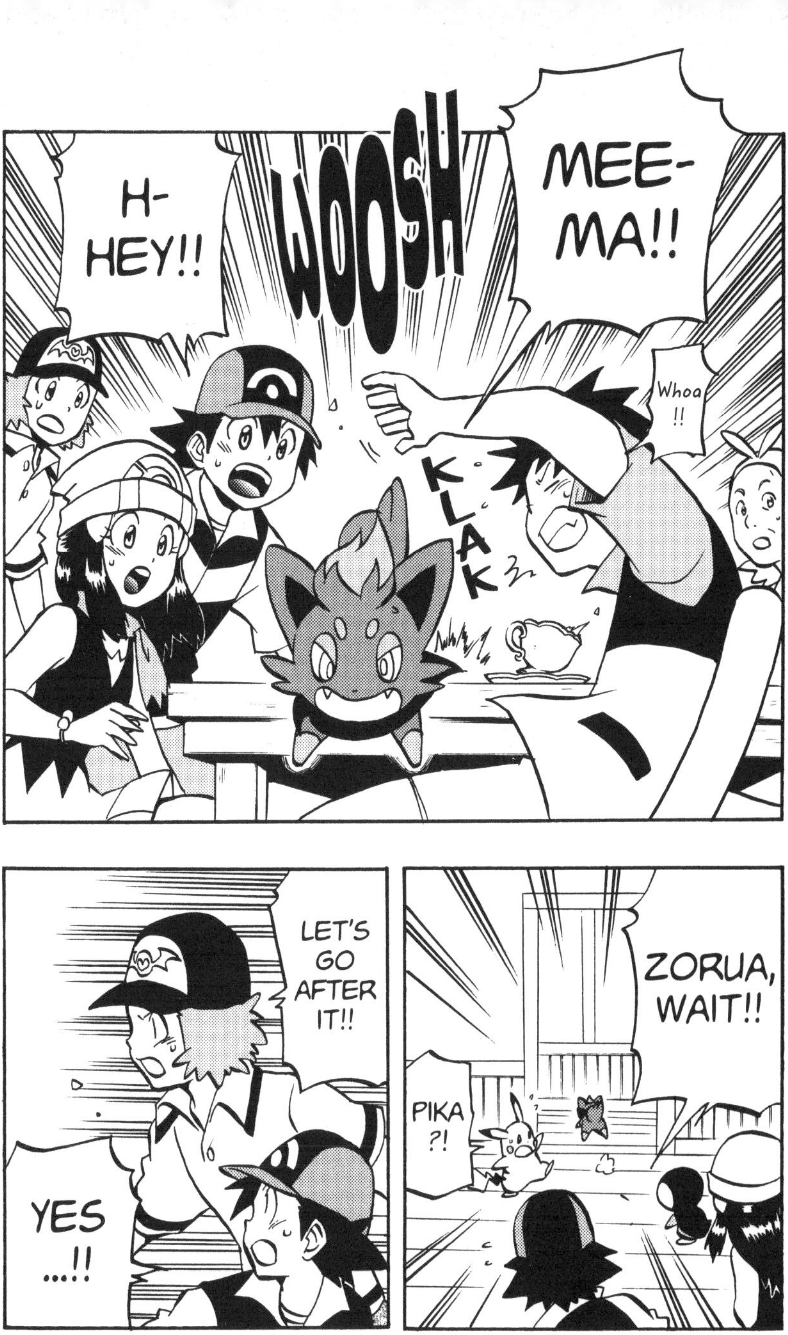
MEE-MA!!
WOOSH
H-HEY!!
Whoa!!
KLAK
ZORUA, WAIT!!
PIKA?!
LET'S GO AFTER IT!!
YES ...!!

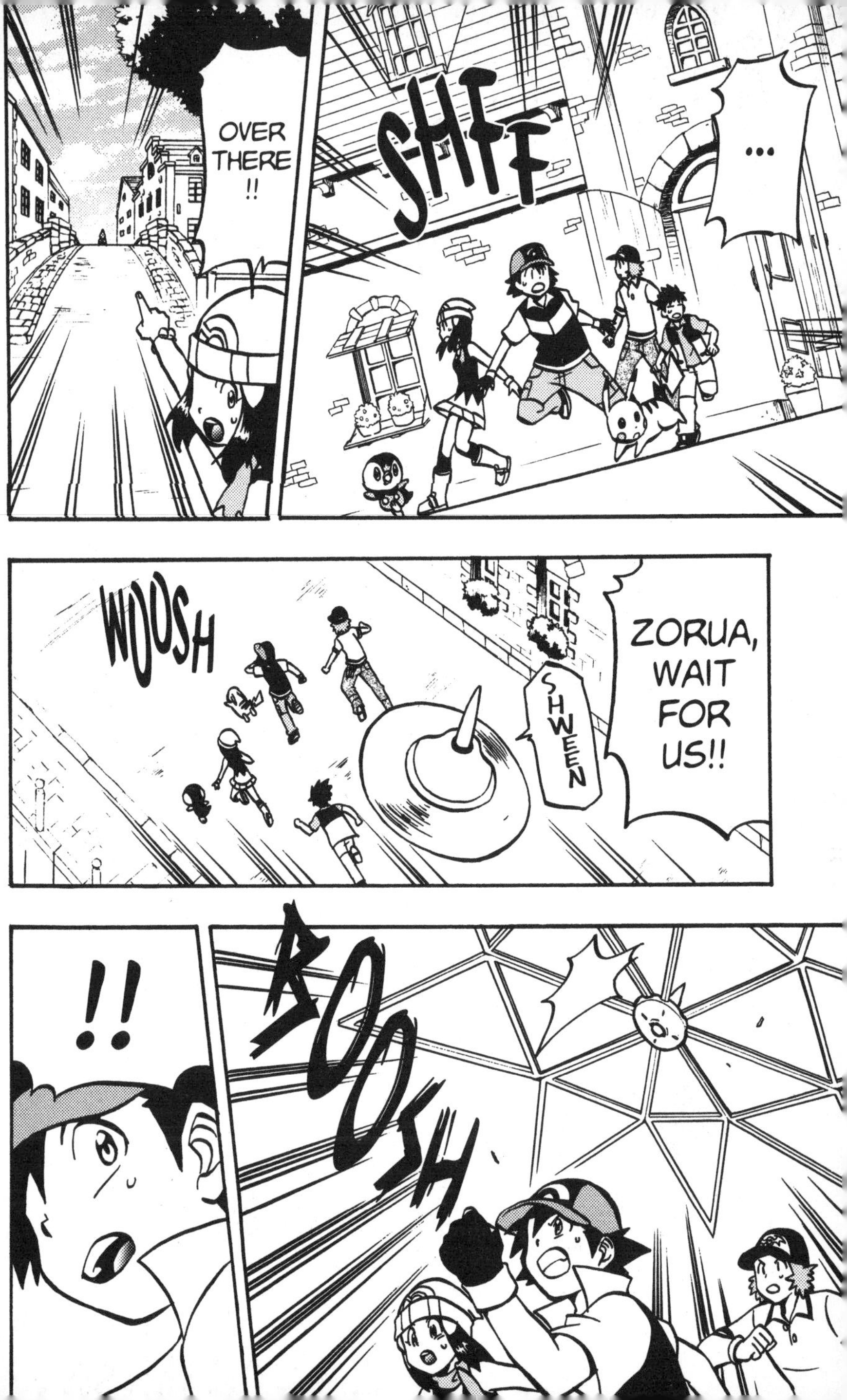
...
SHFF
OVER THERE !!
ZORUA, WAIT FOR US!!
SHWEEN
WOOSH
BOOSH
!!

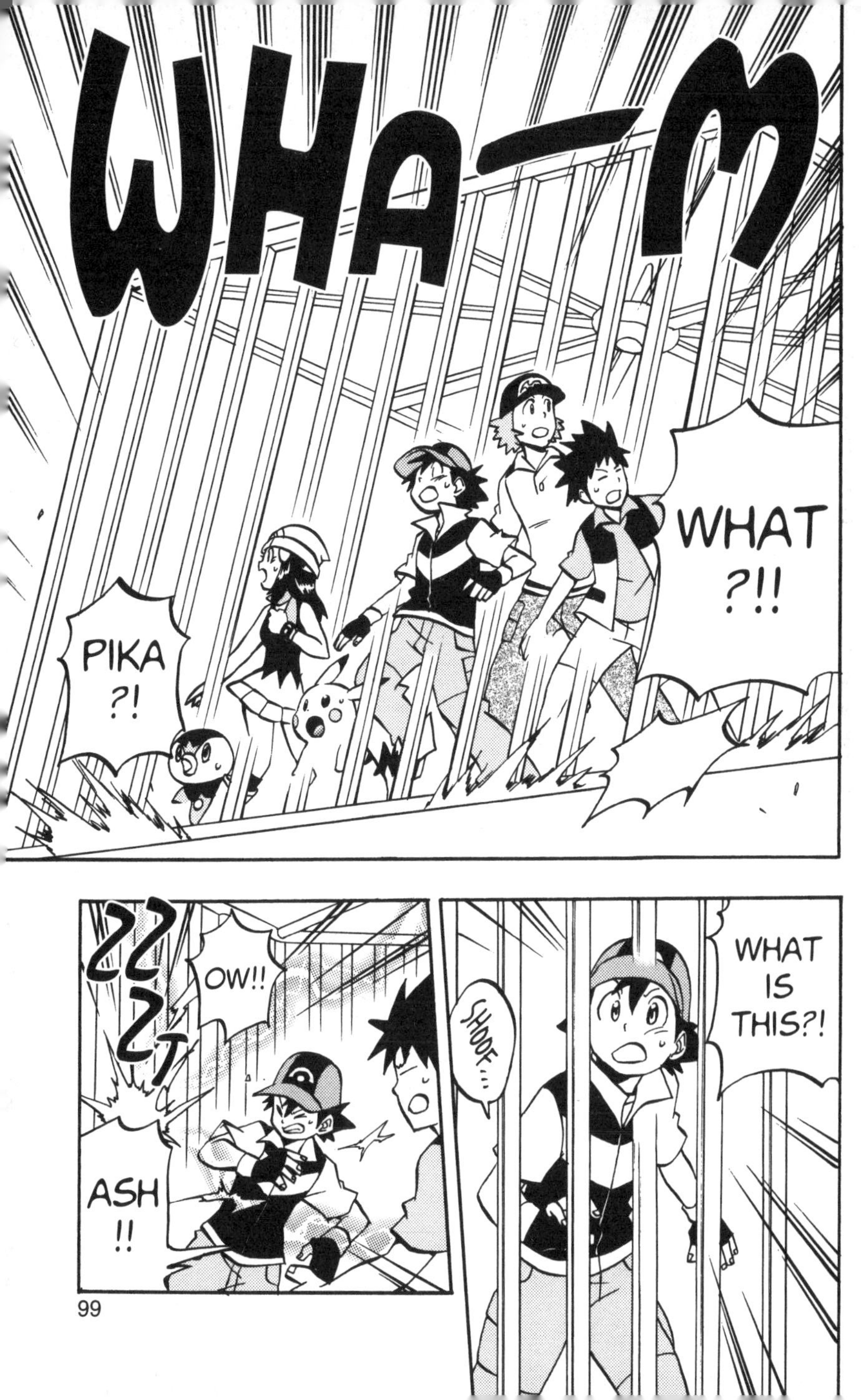
WHA-M
WHAT ?!!
PIKA ?!
WHAT IS THIS?!
SHOOF...
ZZZT
OW!!
ASH !!

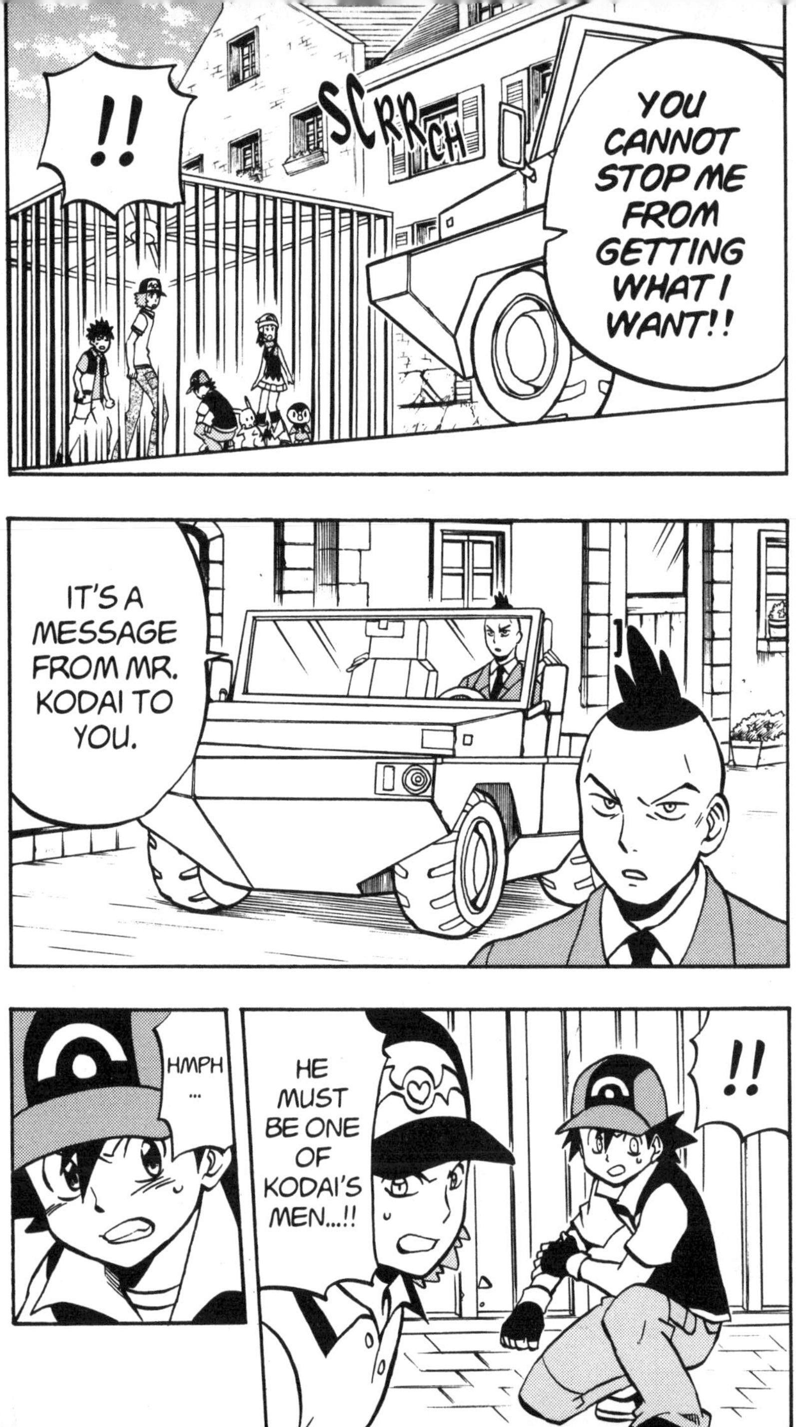
YOU CANNOT STOP ME FROM GETTING WHAT I WANT!!
SCRRRCH
!!
IT'S A MESSAGE FROM MR. KODAI TO YOU.
!!
HE MUST BE ONE OF KODAI'S MEN...!!
HMPH ...

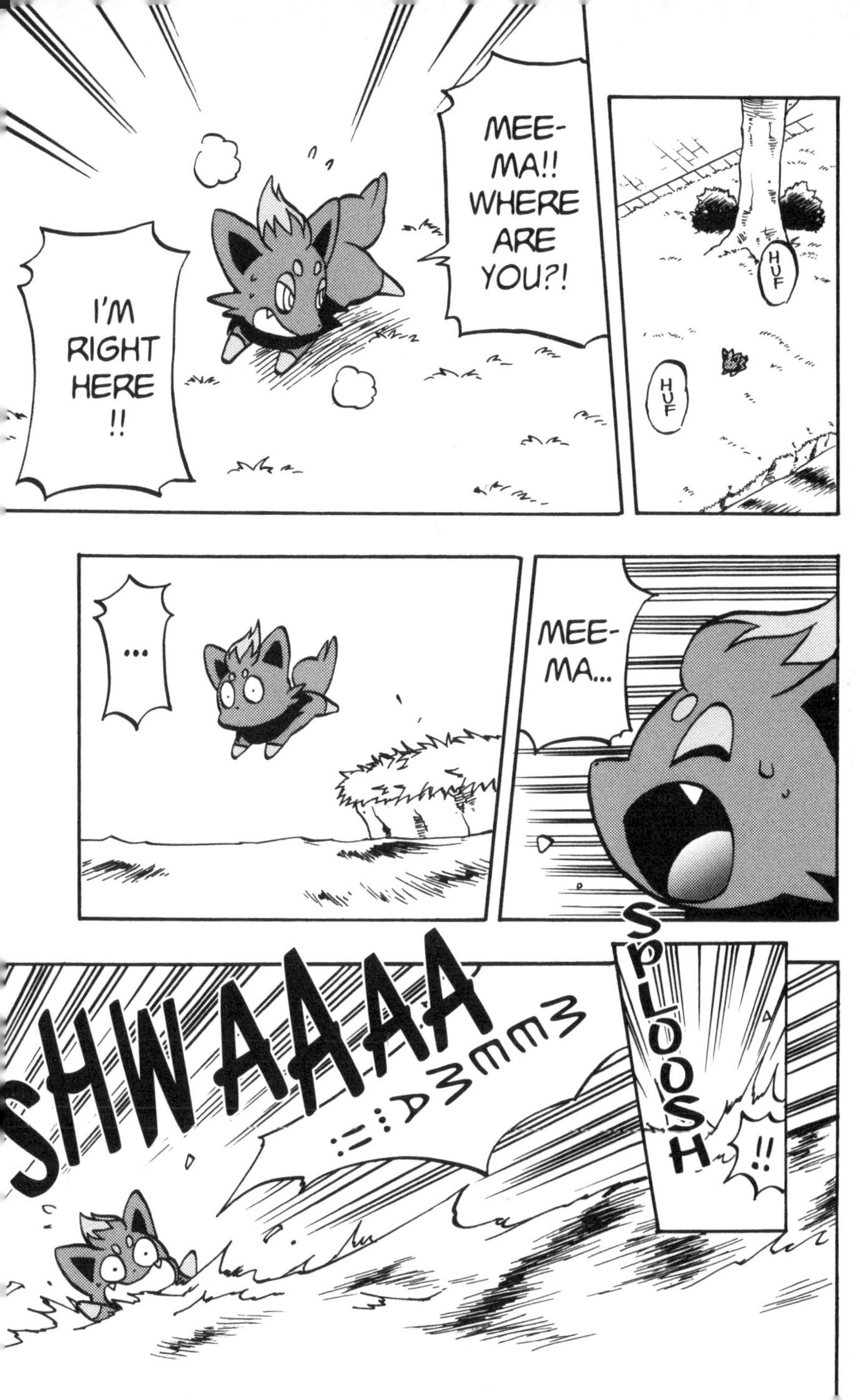
HUF
HUF
MEE-MA!! WHERE ARE YOU?!
I'M RIGHT HERE!!
MEE-MA...
...
SPLOOSH
!!
SHWAAAA

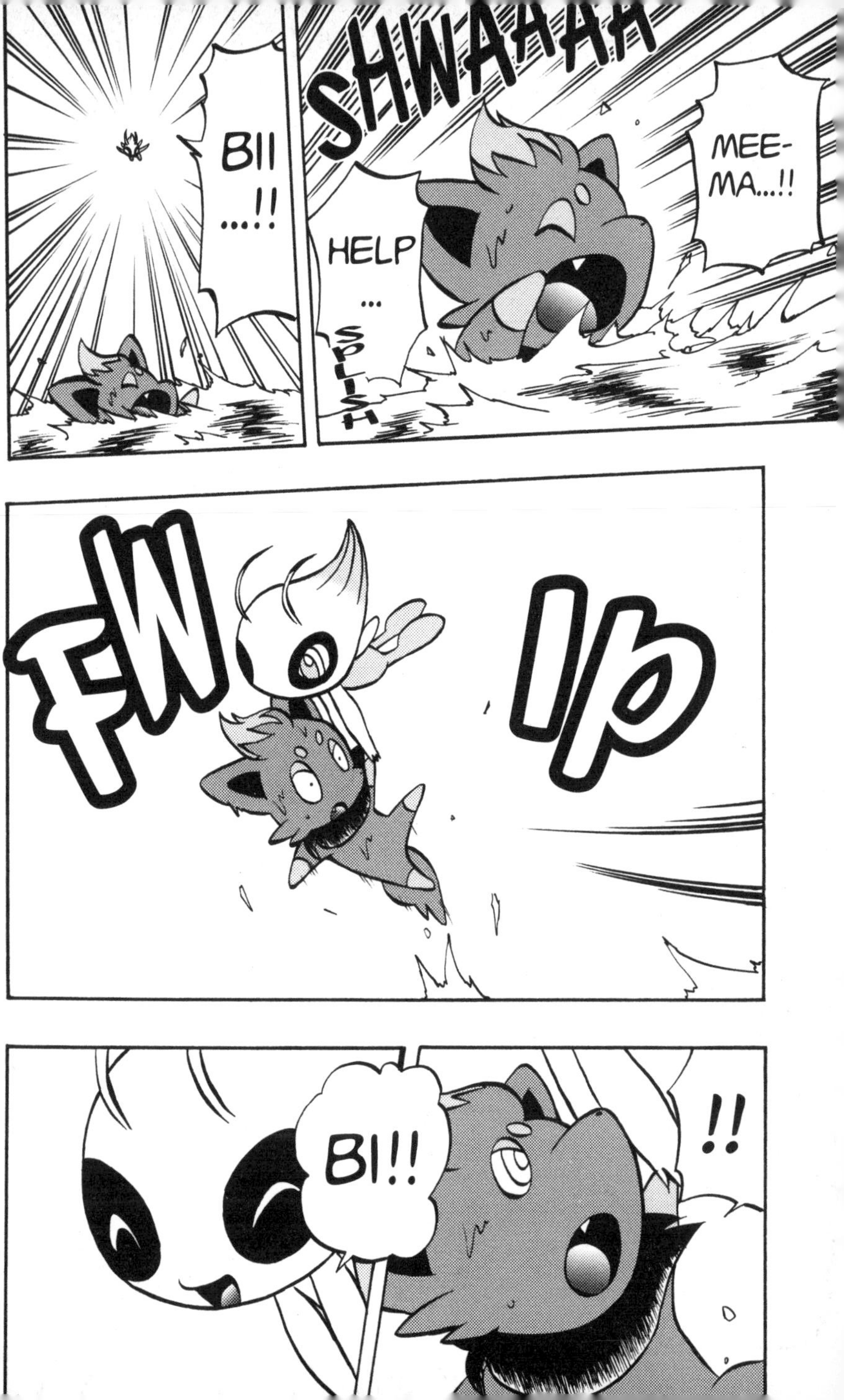
SHWAAAA
MEE-MA...!!
HELP ...
SPLISH
BII ...!!
FWIP
!!
BI!!

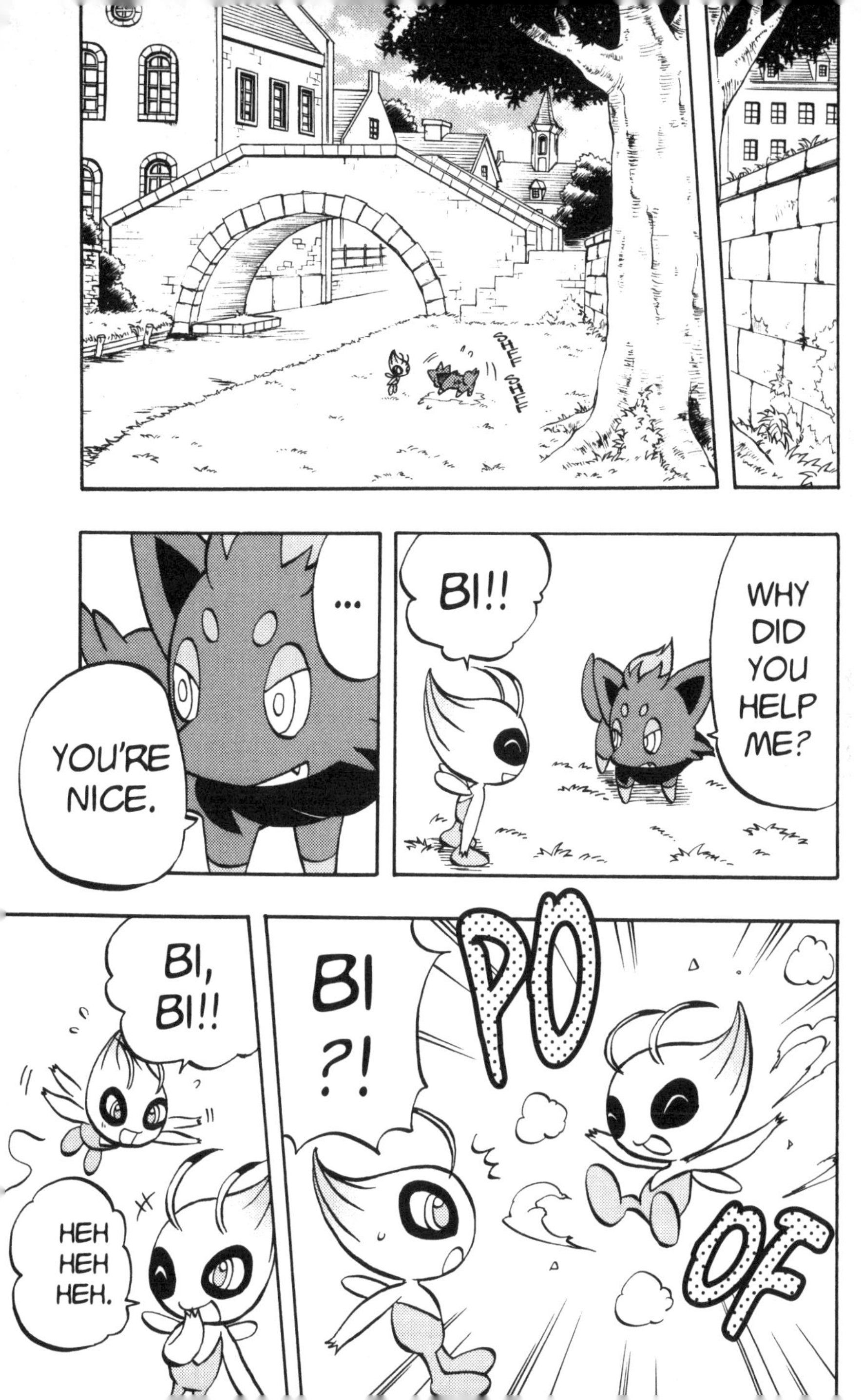
SHFF SHFF
WHY DID YOU HELP ME?
BI!!
...
YOU'RE NICE.
PO OF
BI ?!
BI, BI!!
HEH HEH HEH.

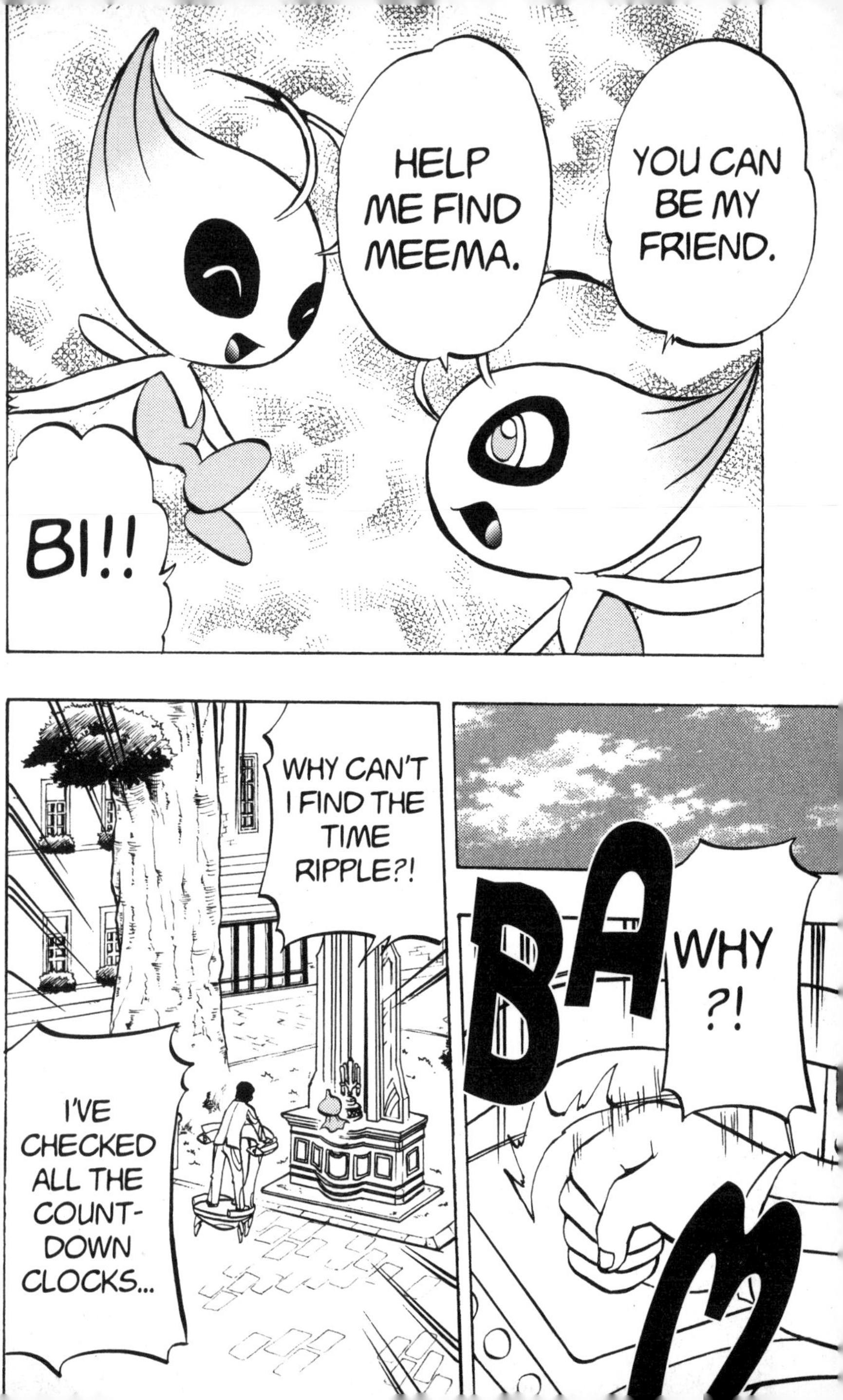
YOU CAN BE MY FRIEND.
HELP ME FIND MEEMA.
BI!!
WHY ?!
BAM
WHY CAN'T I FIND THE TIME RIPPLE?!
I'VE CHECKED ALL THE COUNT-DOWN CLOCKS...

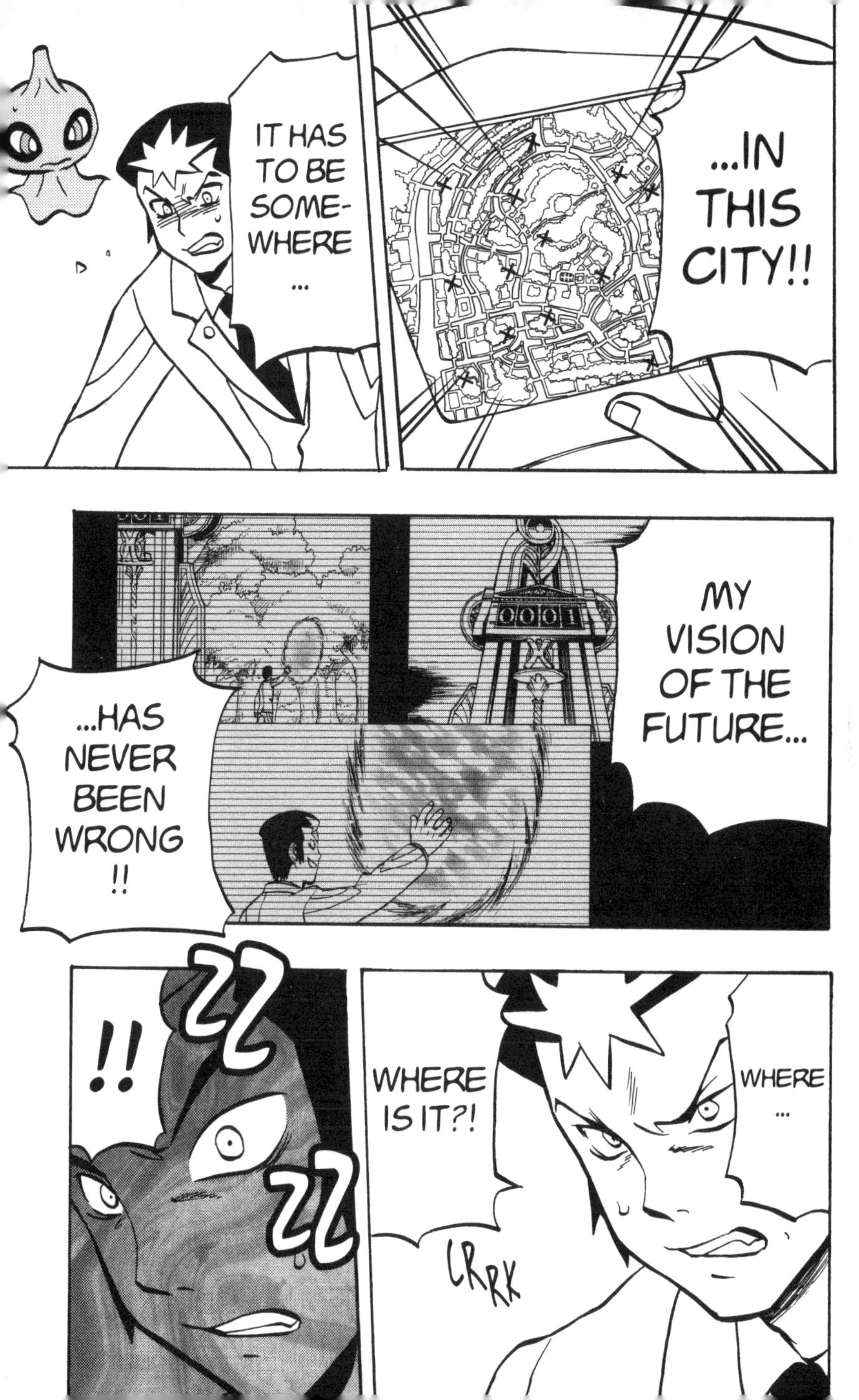
IT HAS TO BE SOME-WHERE ...
...IN THIS CITY!!
MY VISION OF THE FUTURE...
...HAS NEVER BEEN WRONG !!
WHERE ...
WHERE IS IT?!
CRRK
!!

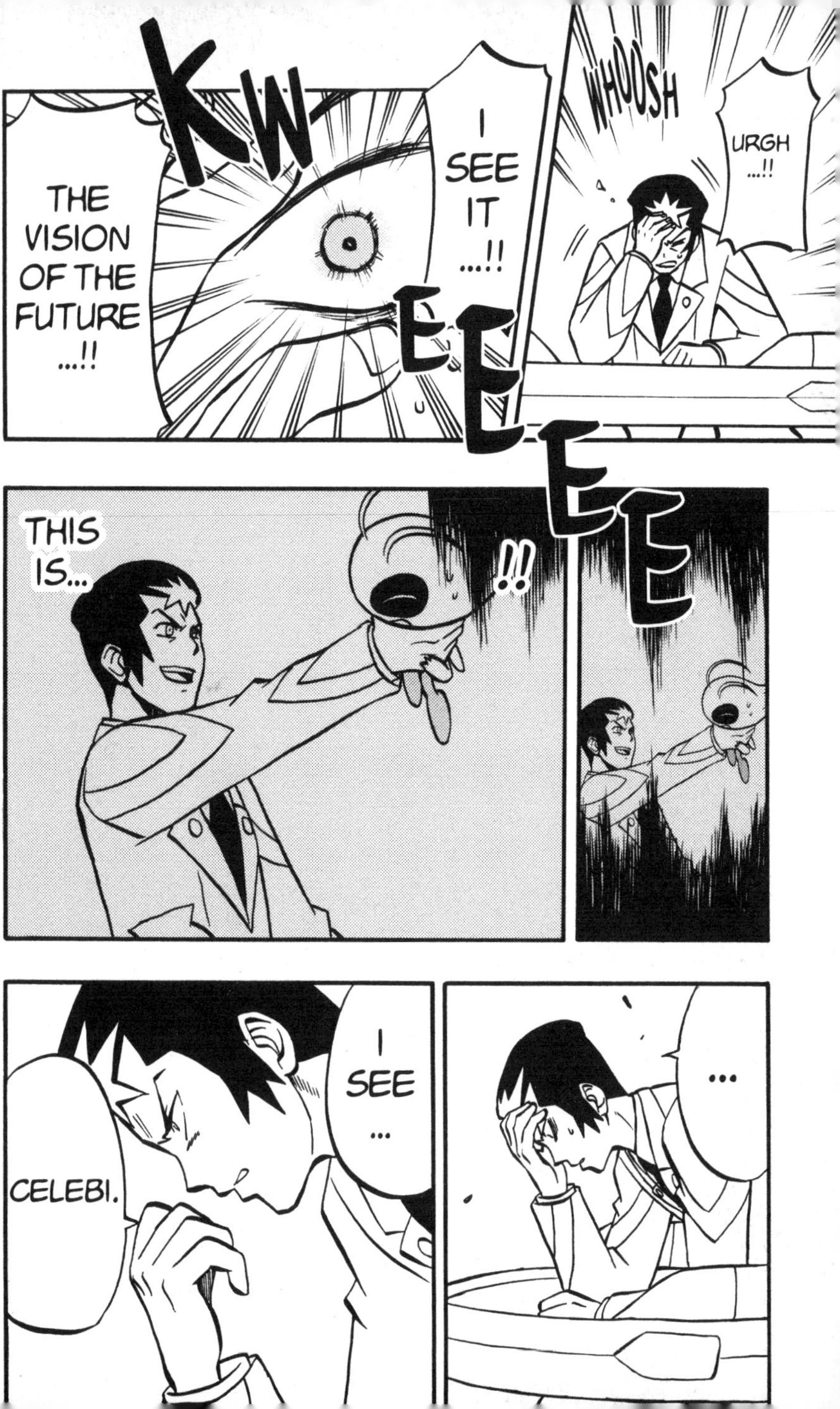
WHOOSH
URGH ...!!
I SEE IT ...!!
THE VISION OF THE FUTURE ...!!
KWEEEEE!!
THIS IS...
...
I SEE ...
CELEBI.

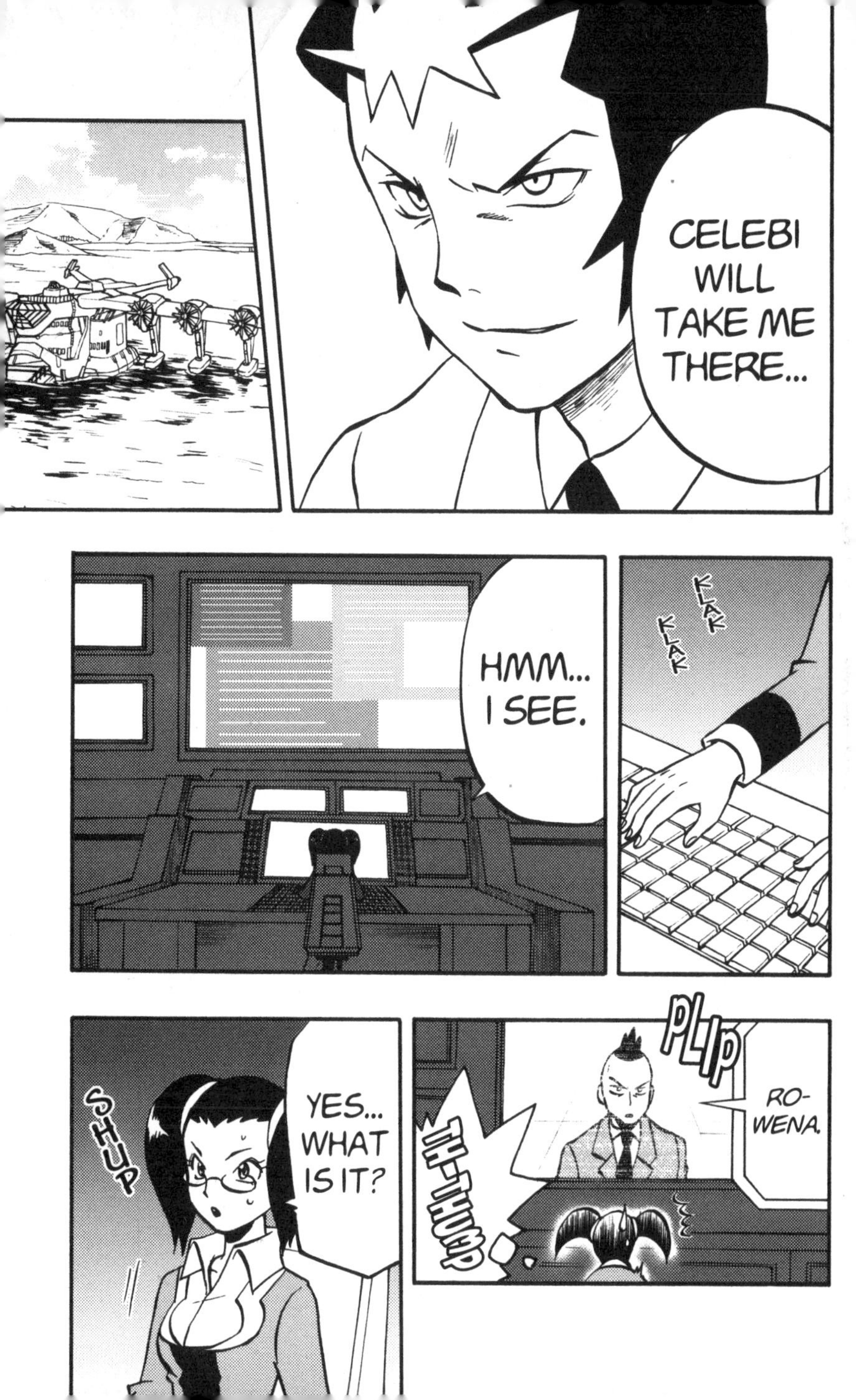
CELEBI WILL TAKE ME THERE...
KLAK KLAK
HMM... I SEE.
PLIP
RO-WENA.
TH-THUMP
SHUP
YES... WHAT IS IT?

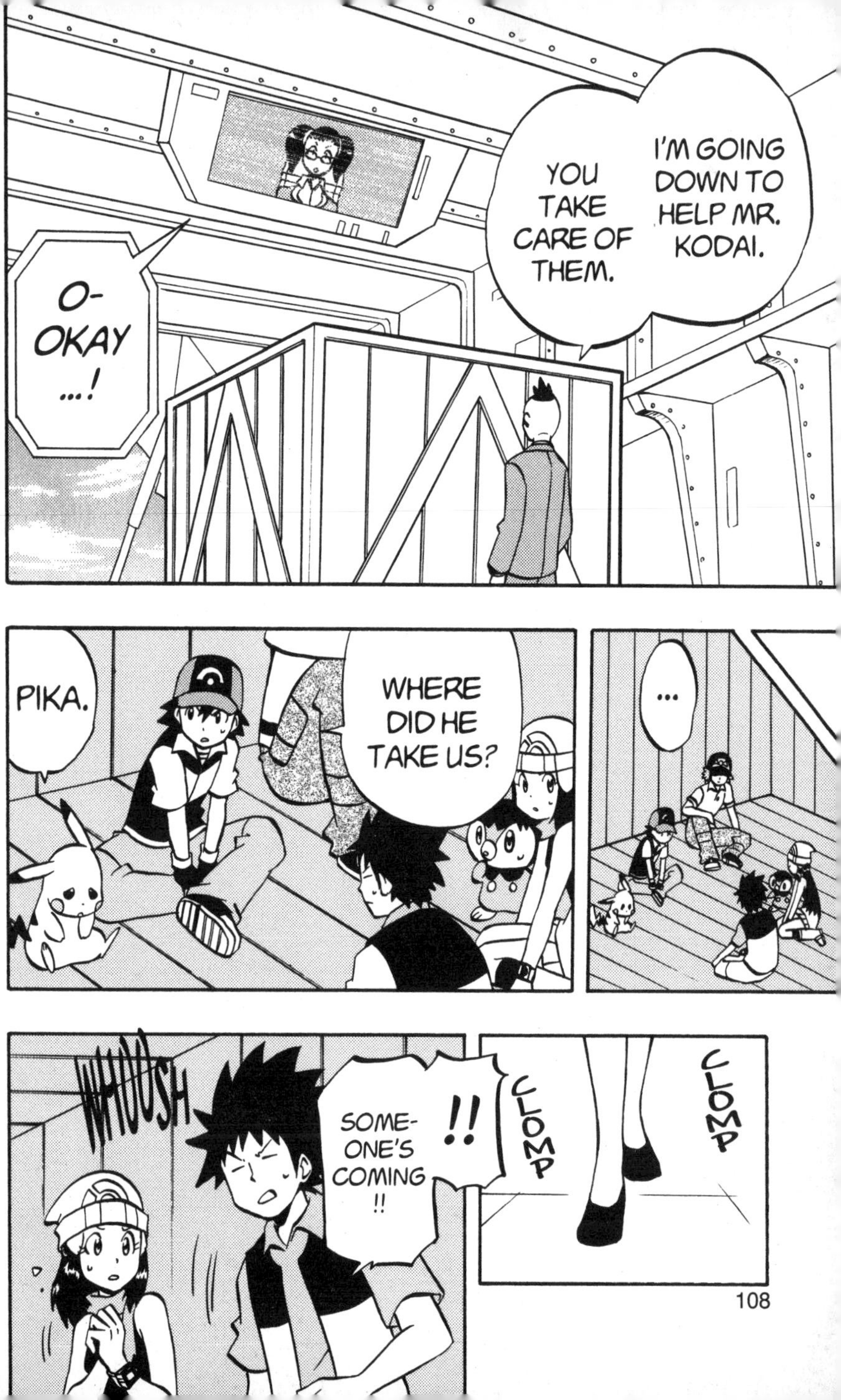
I'M GOING DOWN TO HELP MR. KODAI.
YOU TAKE CARE OF THEM.
O-OKAY ...!
...
WHERE DID HE TAKE US?
PIKA.
CLOMP
CLOMP
!!
SOME-ONE'S COMING !!
WHOOSH

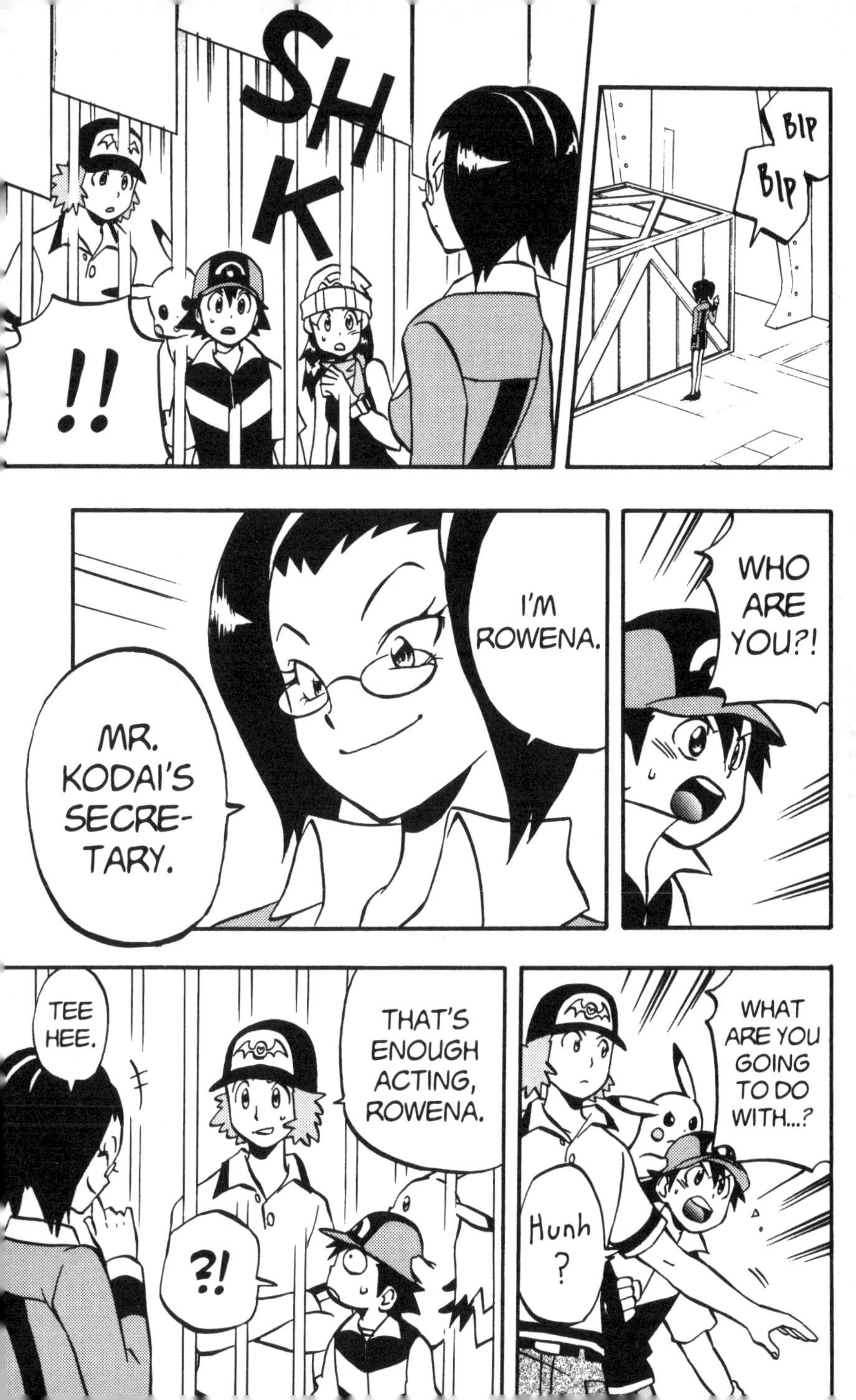
BIP
BIP
SHK
!!
WHO ARE YOU?!
I'M ROWENA.
MR. KODAI'S SECRETARY.
WHAT ARE YOU GOING TO DO WITH...?
Hunh ?
THAT'S ENOUGH ACTING, ROWENA.
TEE HEE.
?!

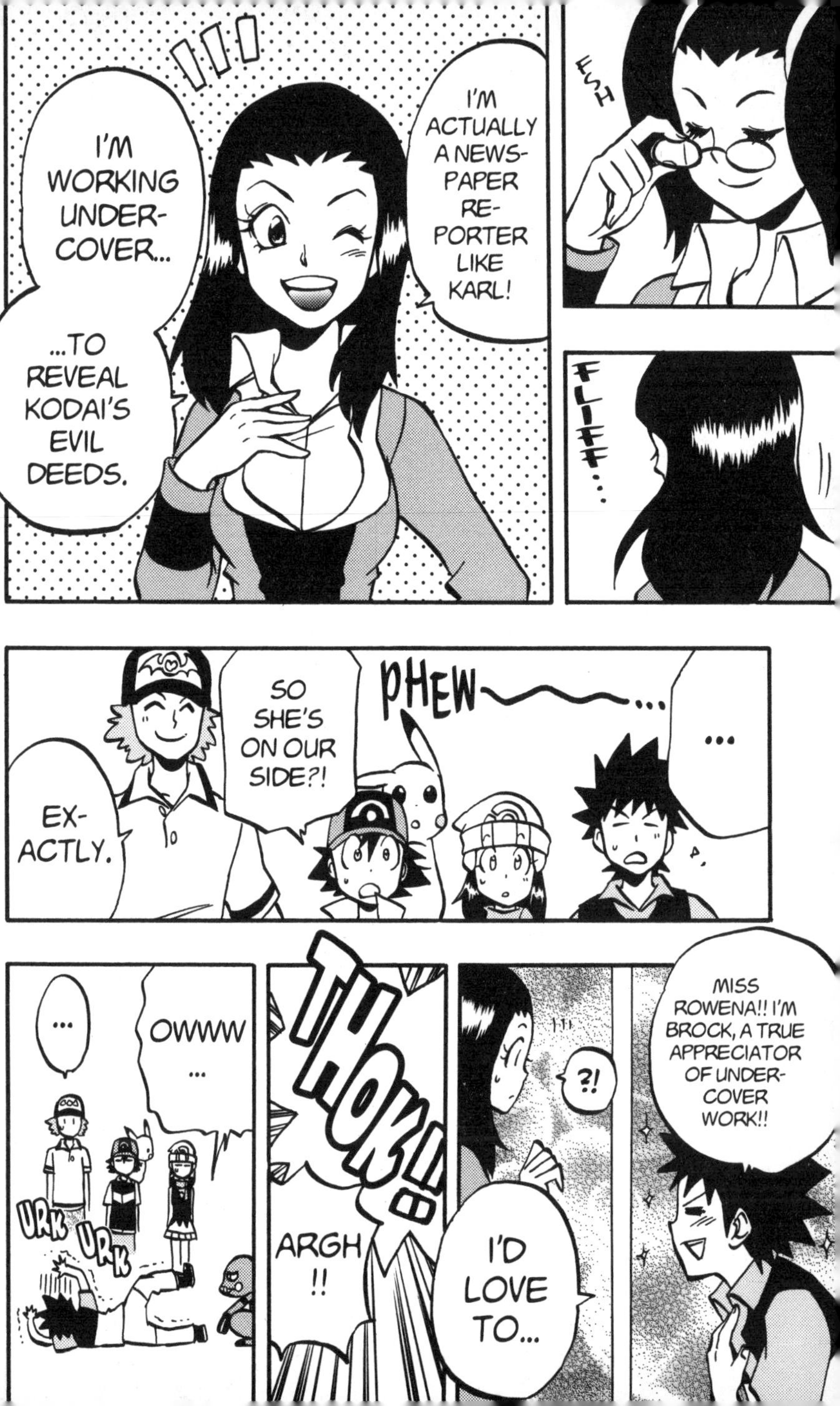
FSH
FLIFFF...
I'M ACTUALLY A NEWSPAPER REPORTER LIKE KARL!
!!!
I'M WORKING UNDERCOVER...
...TO REVEAL KODAI'S EVIL DEEDS.
...
PHEW~...
SO SHE'S ON OUR SIDE?!
EXACTLY.
MISS ROWENA!! I'M BROCK, A TRUE APPRECIATOR OF UNDERCOVER WORK!!
?!
I'D LOVE TO...
THOK!!
ARGH!!
OWWW...
...
URK URK

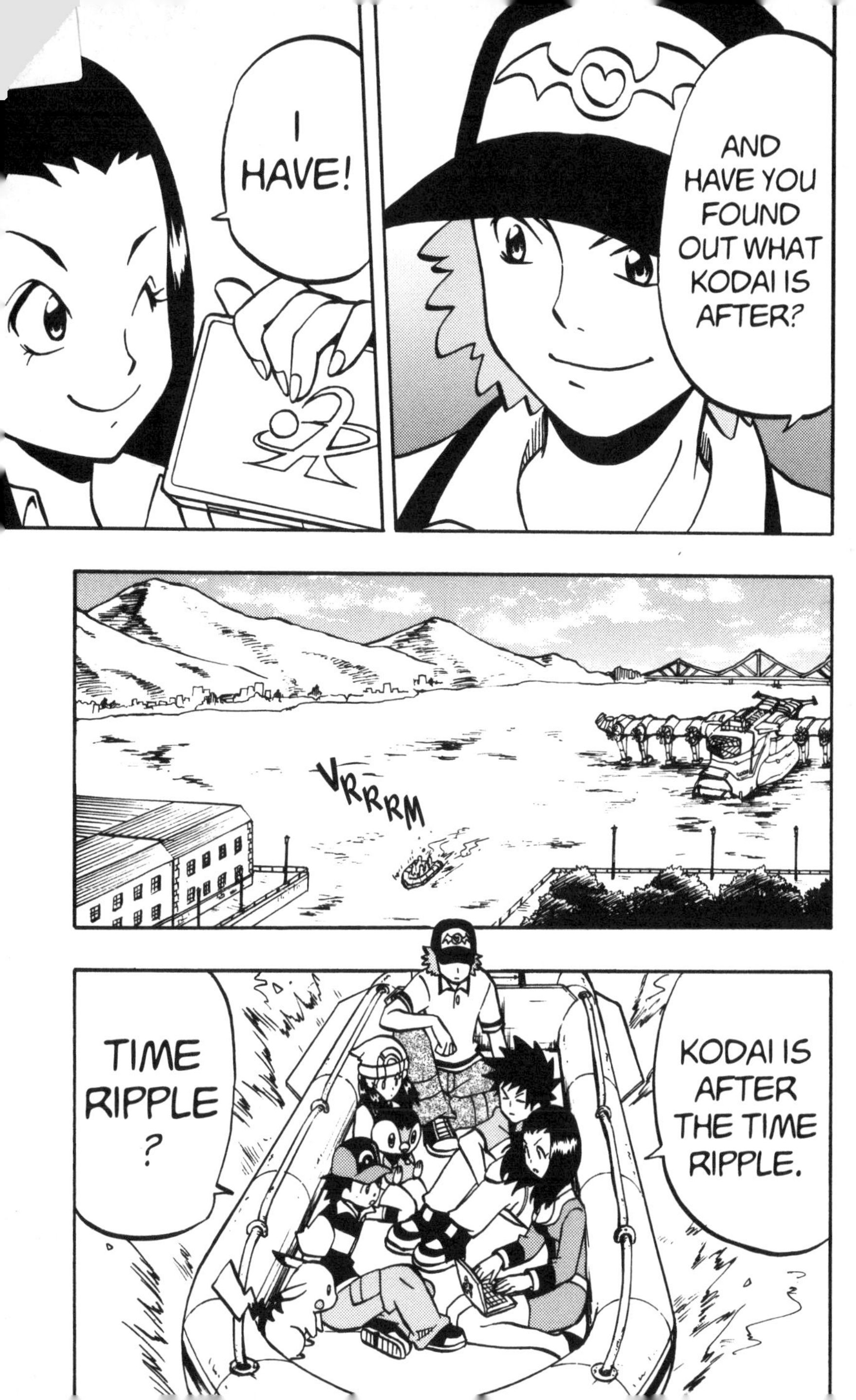
AND HAVE YOU FOUND OUT WHAT KODAI IS AFTER?
I HAVE!
VRRRM
KODAI IS AFTER THE TIME RIPPLE.
TIME RIPPLE?

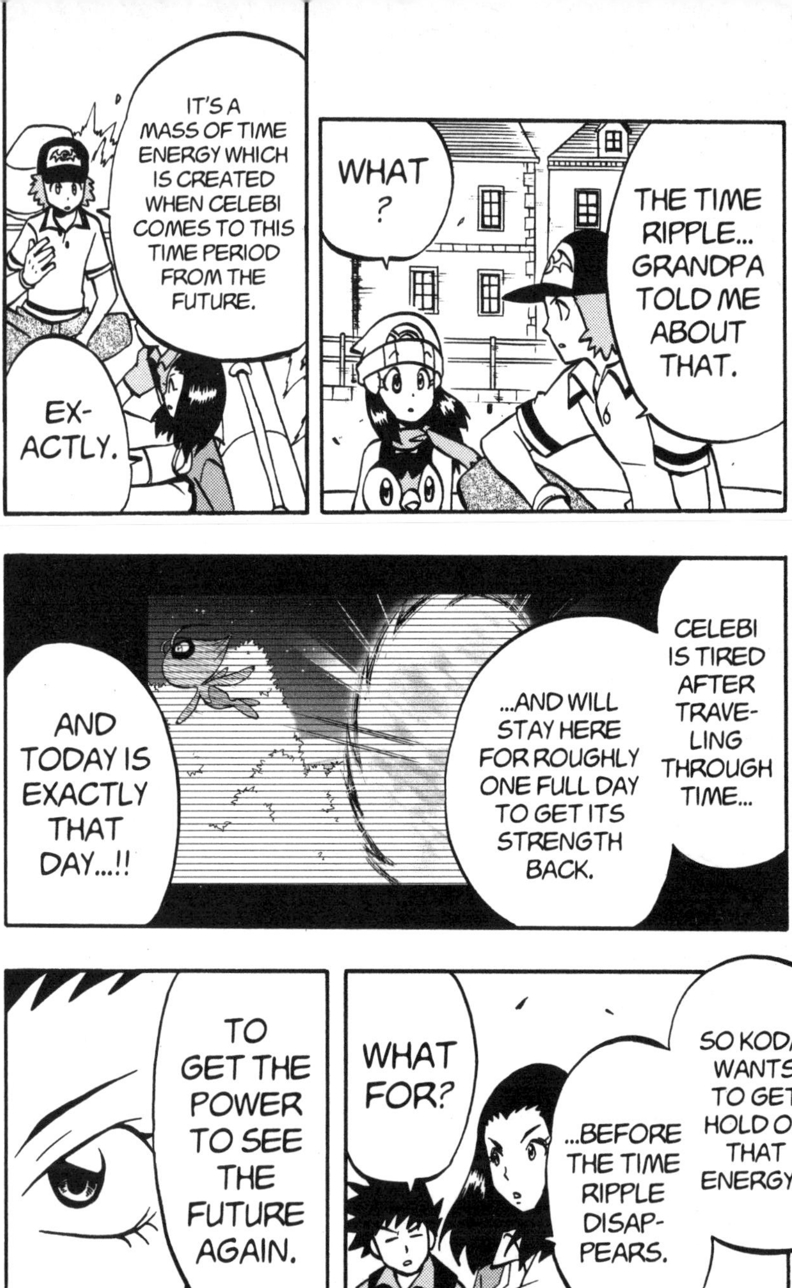
THE TIME RIPPLE... GRANDPA TOLD ME ABOUT THAT.
WHAT ?
IT'S A MASS OF TIME ENERGY WHICH IS CREATED WHEN CELEBI COMES TO THIS TIME PERIOD FROM THE FUTURE.
EX-ACTLY.
CELEBI IS TIRED AFTER TRAVE-LING THROUGH TIME...
...AND WILL STAY HERE FOR ROUGHLY ONE FULL DAY TO GET ITS STRENGTH BACK.
AND TODAY IS EXACTLY THAT DAY...!!
SO KODAI WANTS TO GET HOLD OF THAT ENERGY...
...BEFORE THE TIME RIPPLE DISAP-PEARS.
WHAT FOR?
TO GET THE POWER TO SEE THE FUTURE AGAIN.

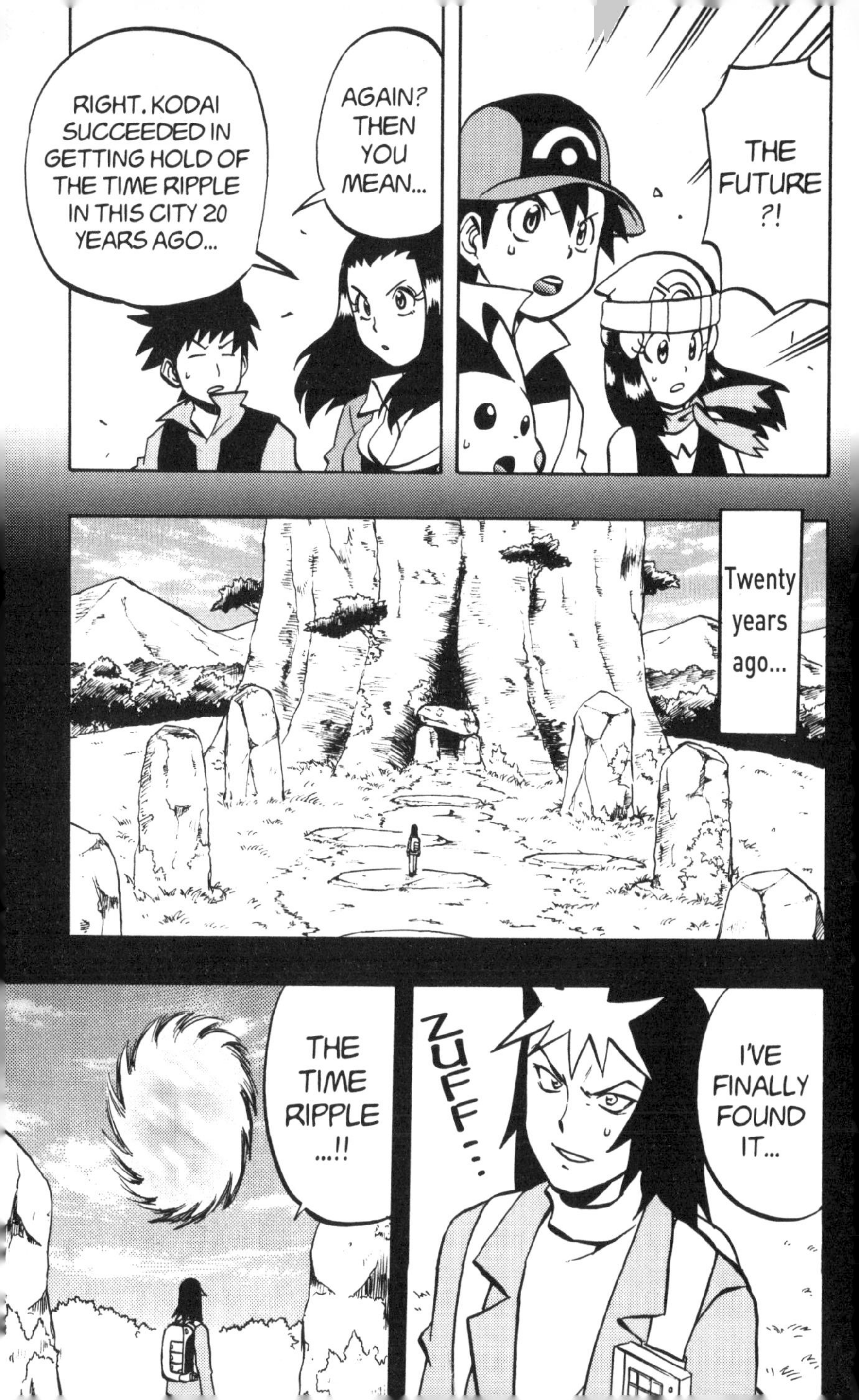
RIGHT. KODAI SUCCEEDED IN GETTING HOLD OF THE TIME RIPPLE IN THIS CITY 20 YEARS AGO...
AGAIN? THEN YOU MEAN...
THE FUTURE ?!
Twenty years ago...
THE TIME RIPPLE ...!!
ZUFF...
I'VE FINALLY FOUND IT...

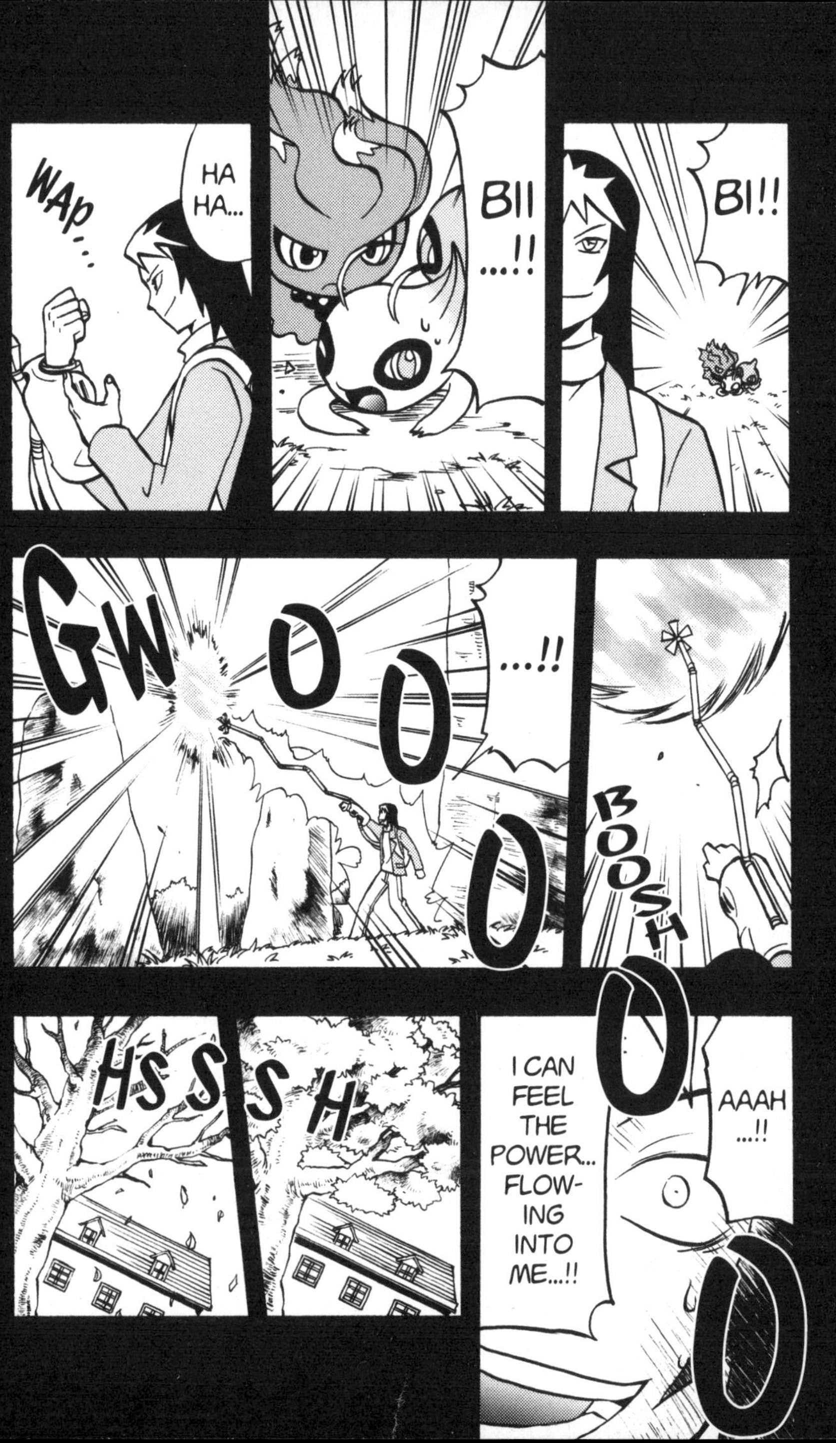
BI!!
BII ...!!
HA HA...
WAP...
BOOSH
...!!
GWOOOOOO
AAAH ...!!
I CAN FEEL THE POWER... FLOWING INTO ME...!!
HSSSH

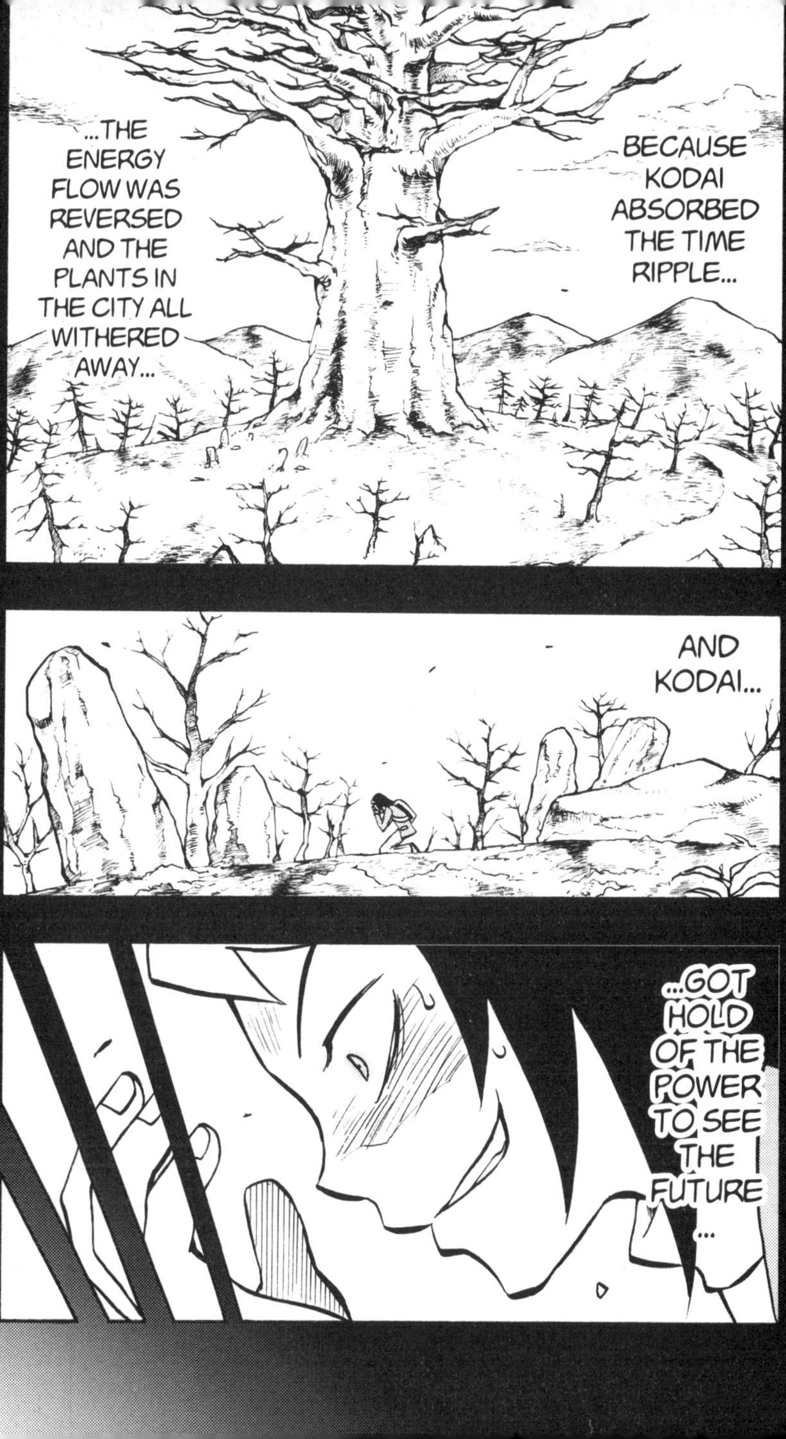
BECAUSE KODAI ABSORBED THE TIME RIPPLE...
...THE ENERGY FLOW WAS REVERSED AND THE PLANTS IN THE CITY ALL WITHERED AWAY...
AND KODAI...
...GOT HOLD OF THE POWER TO SEE THE FUTURE...

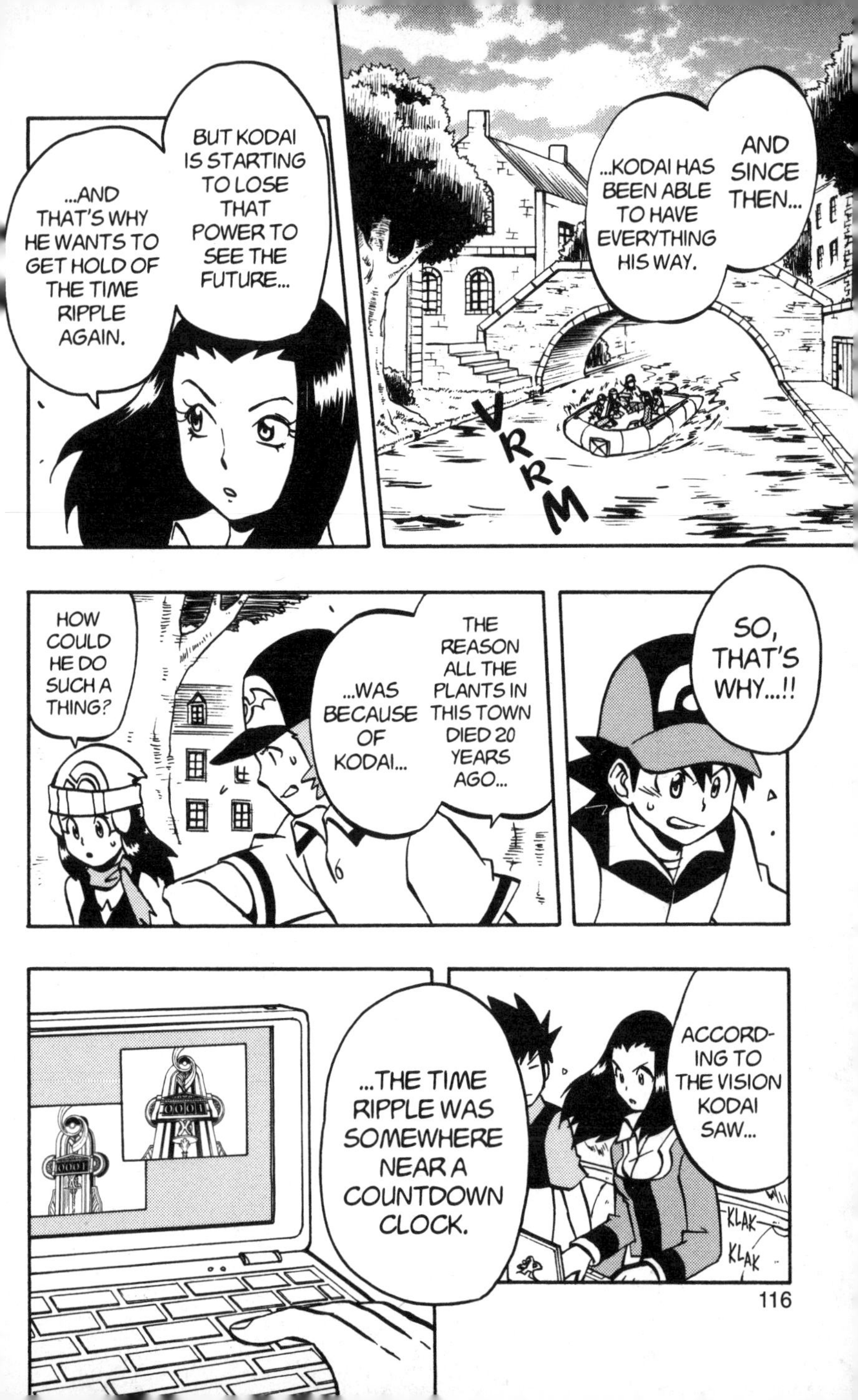
AND SINCE THEN...
...KODAI HAS BEEN ABLE TO HAVE EVERYTHING HIS WAY.
VRRM
BUT KODAI IS STARTING TO LOSE THAT POWER TO SEE THE FUTURE...
...AND THAT'S WHY HE WANTS TO GET HOLD OF THE TIME RIPPLE AGAIN.
SO, THAT'S WHY...!!
THE REASON ALL THE PLANTS IN THIS TOWN DIED 20 YEARS AGO...
...WAS BECAUSE OF KODAI...
HOW COULD HE DO SUCH A THING?
ACCORD-ING TO THE VISION KODAI SAW...
...THE TIME RIPPLE WAS SOMEWHERE NEAR A COUNTDOWN CLOCK.
KLAK
KLAK

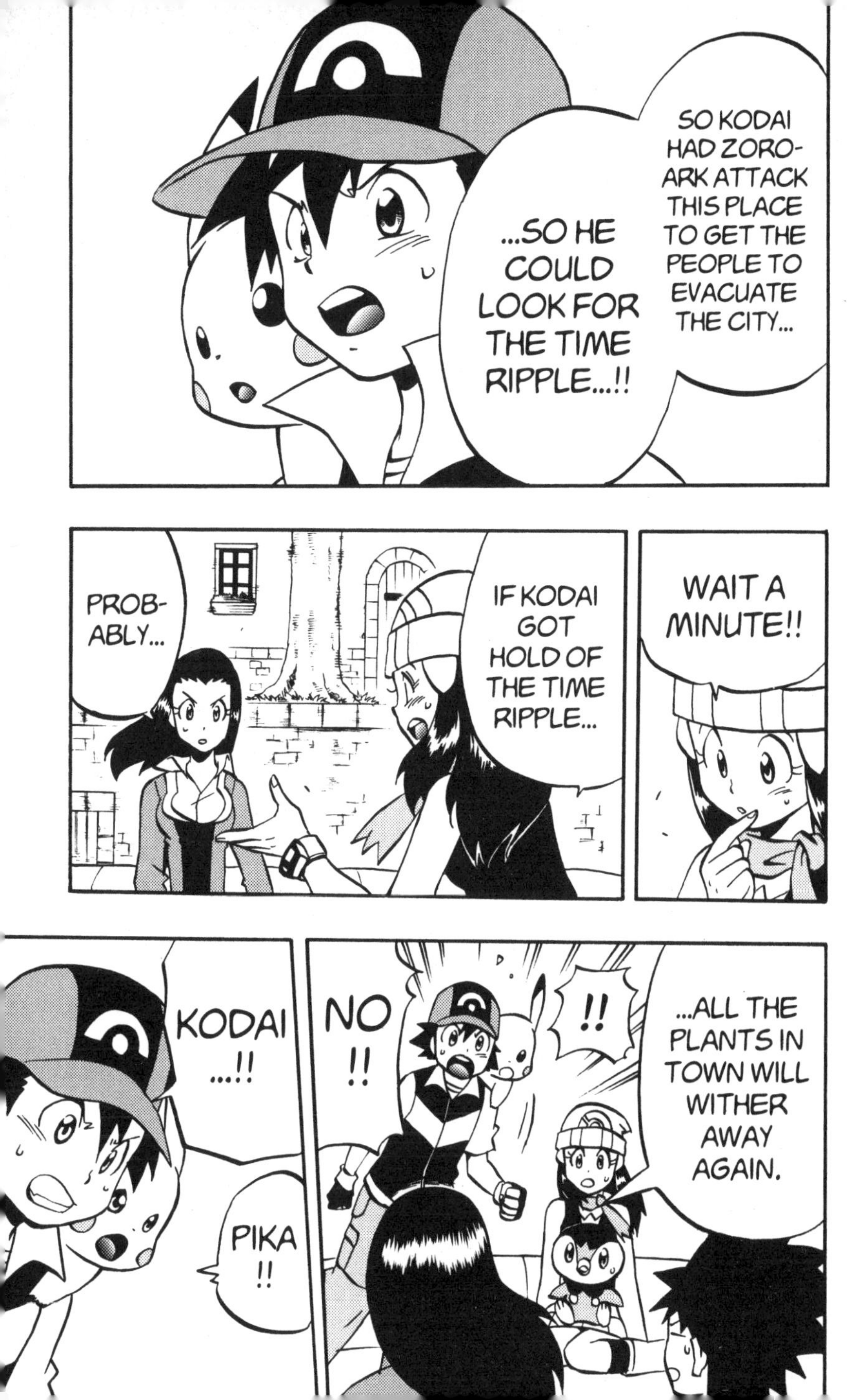
SO KODAI HAD ZORO-ARK ATTACK THIS PLACE TO GET THE PEOPLE TO EVACUATE THE CITY...
...SO HE COULD LOOK FOR THE TIME RIPPLE...!!
PROB-ABLY...
WAIT A MINUTE!!
IF KODAI GOT HOLD OF THE TIME RIPPLE...
...ALL THE PLANTS IN TOWN WILL WITHER AWAY AGAIN.
!!
NO !!
KODAI ...!!
PIKA !!

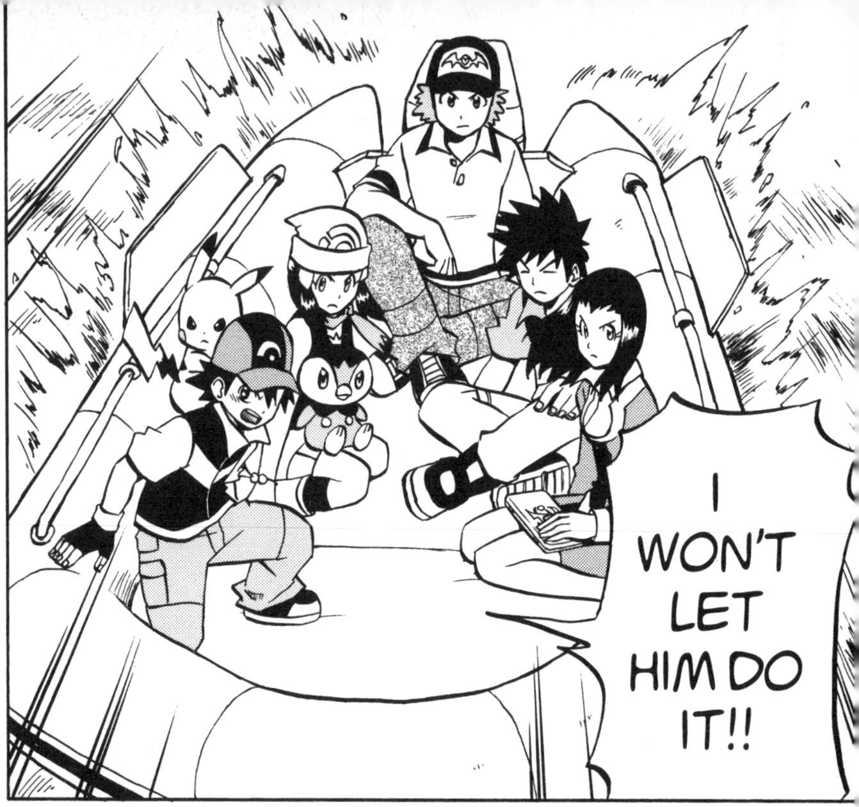
I WON'T LET HIM DO IT!!
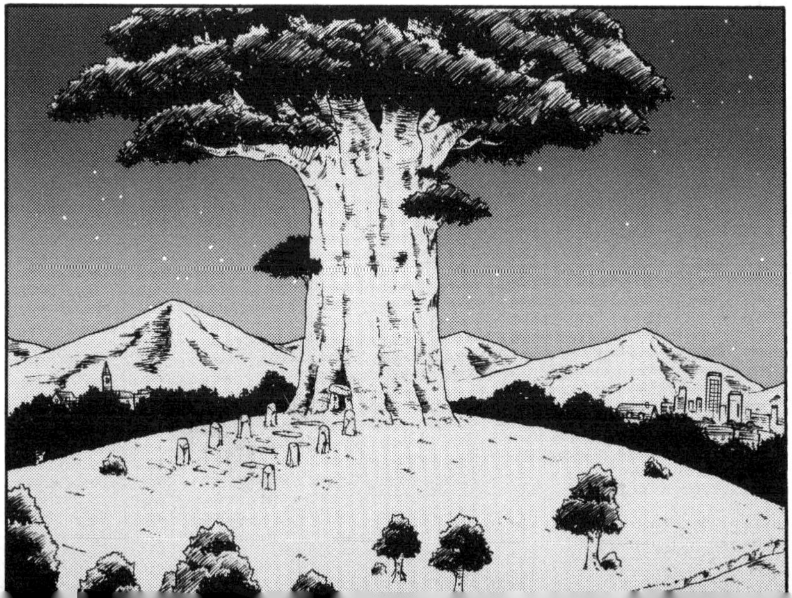

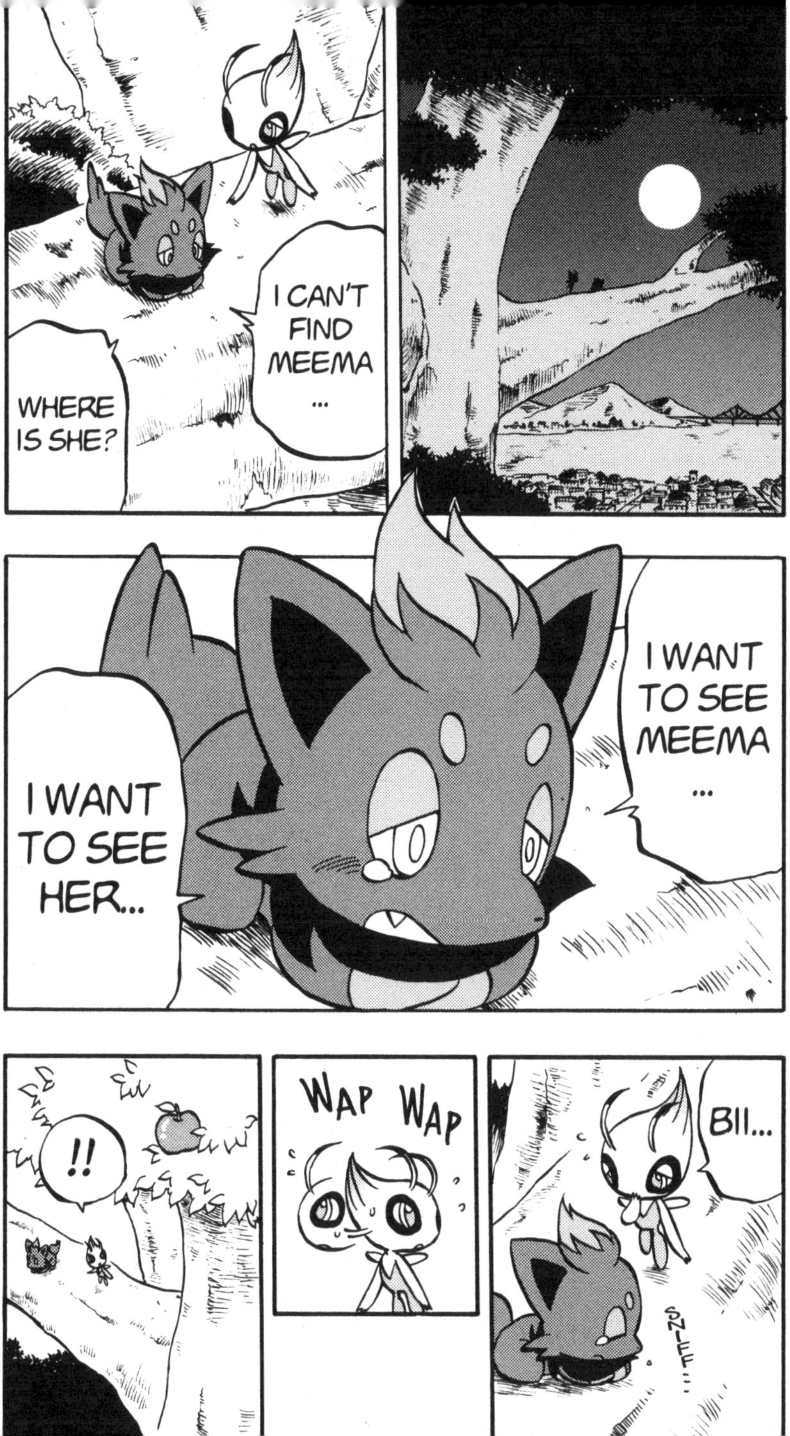

I CAN'T FIND MEEMA ...
WHERE IS SHE?
I WANT TO SEE MEEMA ...
I WANT TO SEE HER...
BII...
SNIFF...
WAP WAP
!!

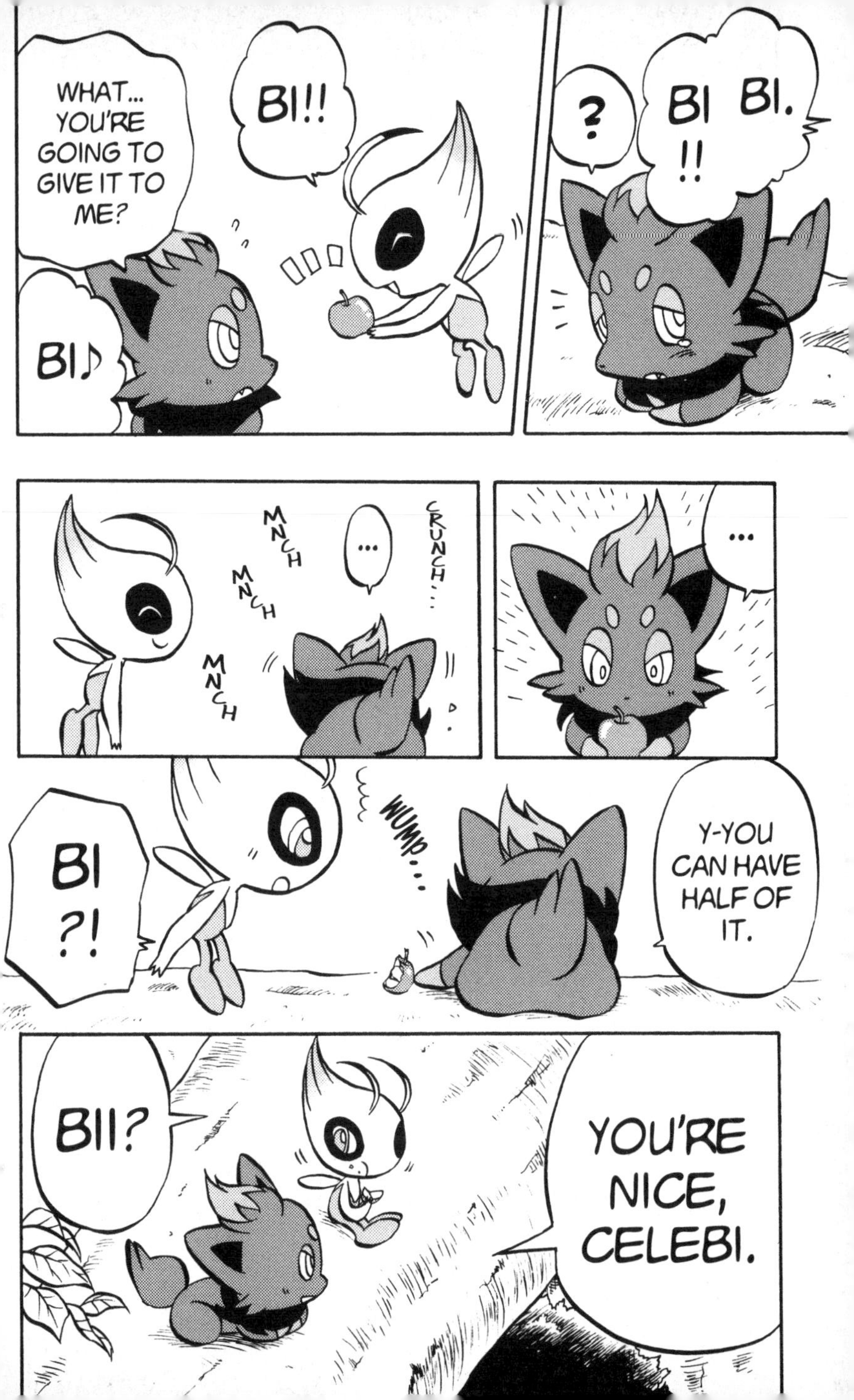

BI. BI !!
?
BI!!
WHAT... YOU'RE GOING TO GIVE IT TO ME?
BI♪
...
CRUNCH...
...
MNCH
MNCH
MNCH
Y-YOU CAN HAVE HALF OF IT.
WUMP...
BI ?!
YOU'RE NICE, CELEBI.
BII?

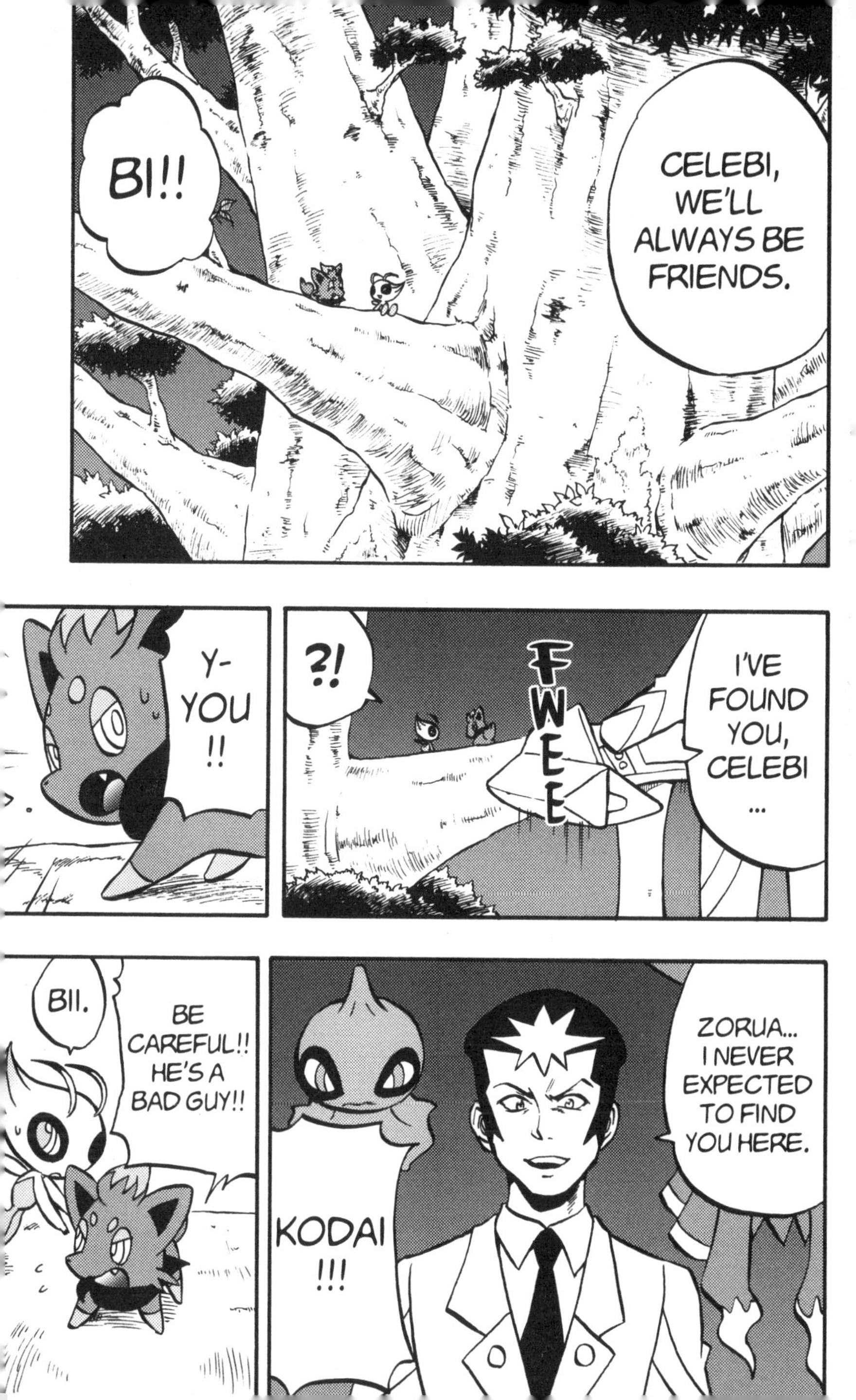
CELEBI, WE'LL ALWAYS BE FRIENDS.
BI!!
I'VE FOUND YOU, CELEBI ...
FWEE
?!
Y-YOU !!
ZORUA... I NEVER EXPECTED TO FIND YOU HERE.
KODAI !!!
BE CAREFUL!! HE'S A BAD GUY!!
BII.

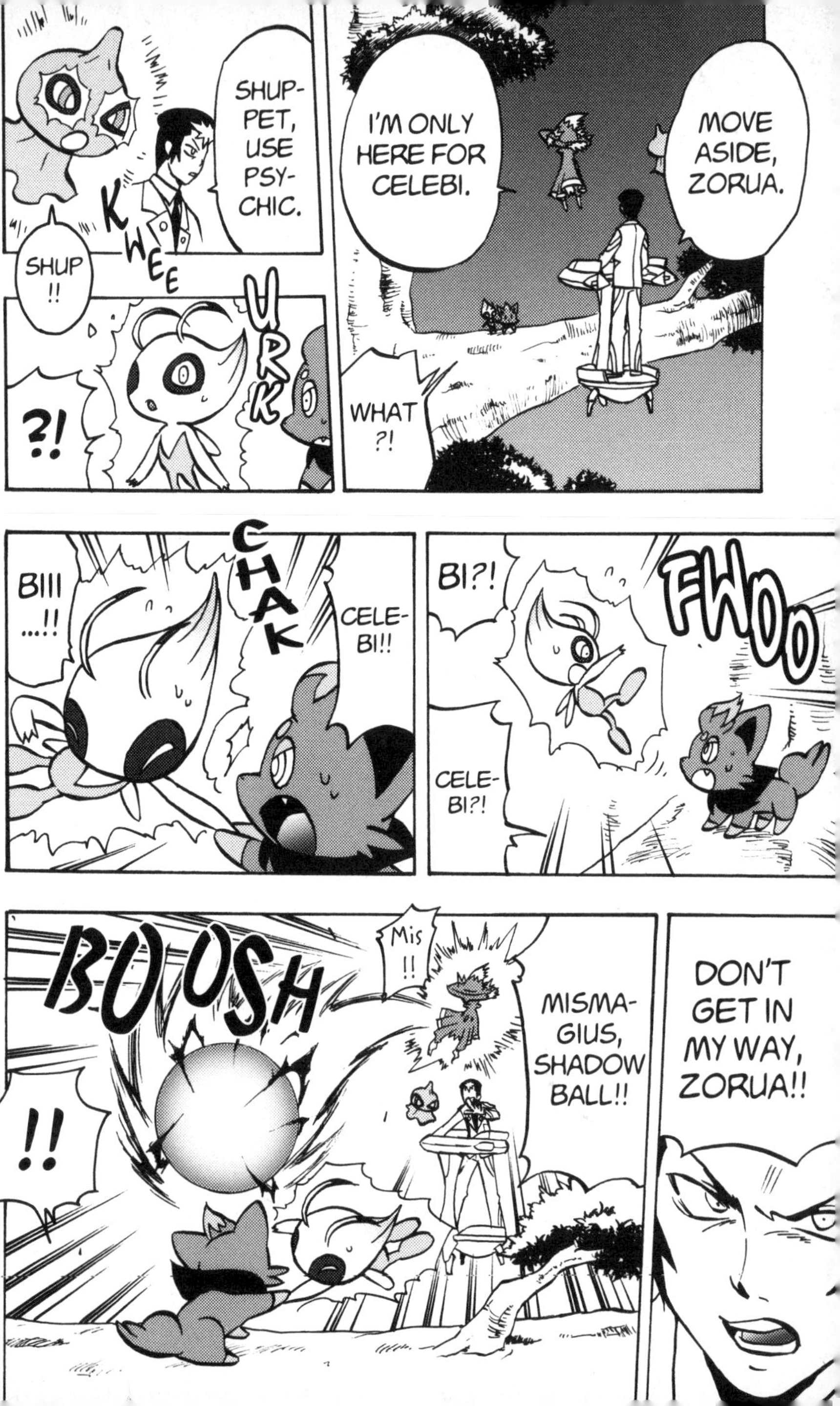
MOVE ASIDE, ZORUA.
I'M ONLY HERE FOR CELEBI.
WHAT ?!
SHUP-PET, USE PSY-CHIC.
KWEE
SHUP !!
URK
?!
FWOO
BI?!
CELE-BI?!
CHAK
CELE-BI!!
BIII ....!!
DON'T GET IN MY WAY, ZORUA!!
MISMA-GIUS, SHADOW BALL!!
Mis !!
BOOSH
!!

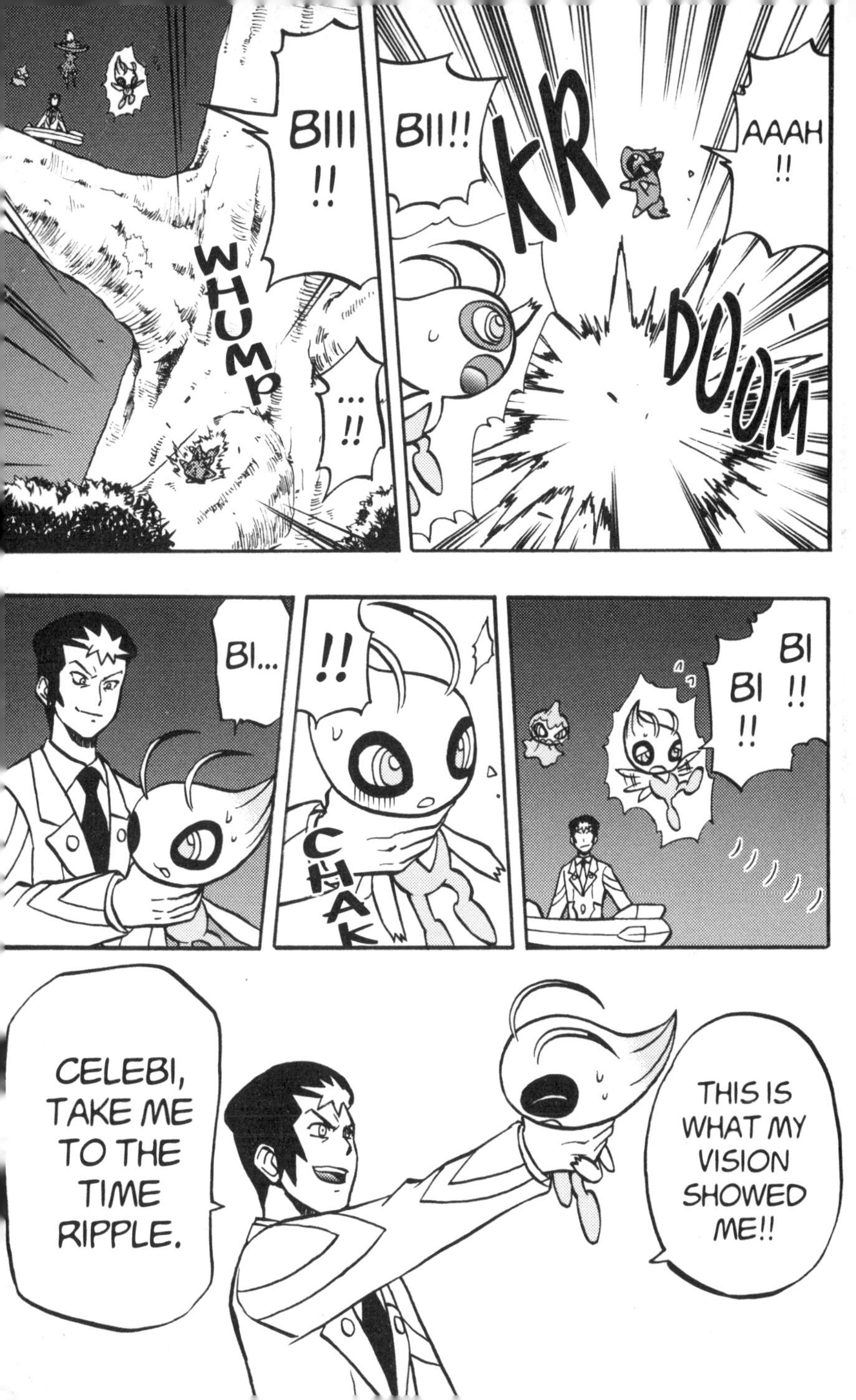
AAAH!!
BII!!
KR
DOOM
BIII!!
WHUMP
...!!
BI BI!!
BI!!
!!
CHAK
BI...
THIS IS WHAT MY VISION SHOWED ME!!
CELEBI, TAKE ME TO THE TIME RIPPLE.

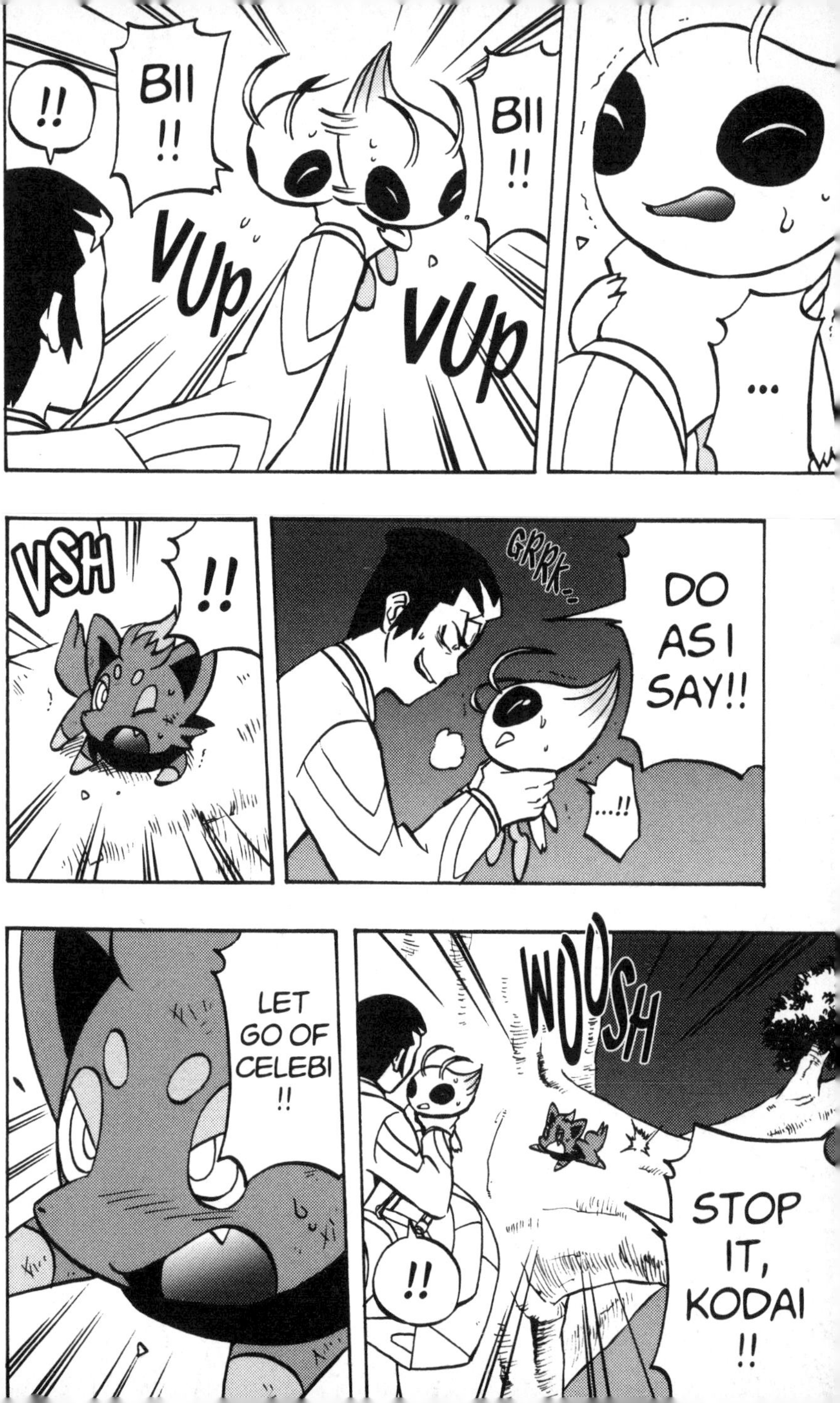
...
BII !!
VUp
BII !!
!!
VUp
GRRK..
DO AS I SAY!!
...!!
!!
VSH
WOOSH
STOP IT, KODAI !!
!!
LET GO OF CELEBI !!

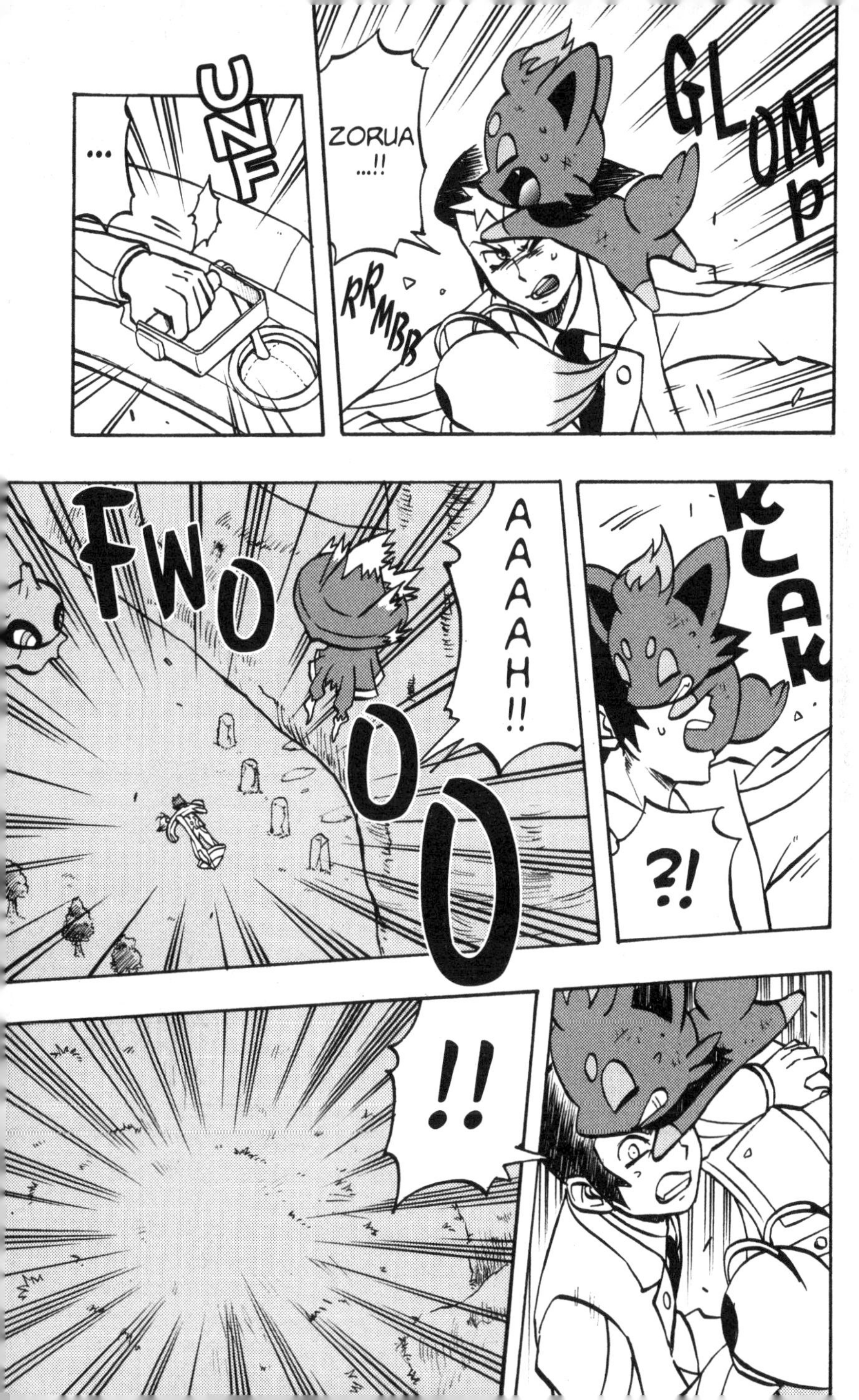
GLOMP
ZORUA ...!!
RRMBB
UNF
...
KLAK
?!
AAAAAH!!
FWOOOO
!!

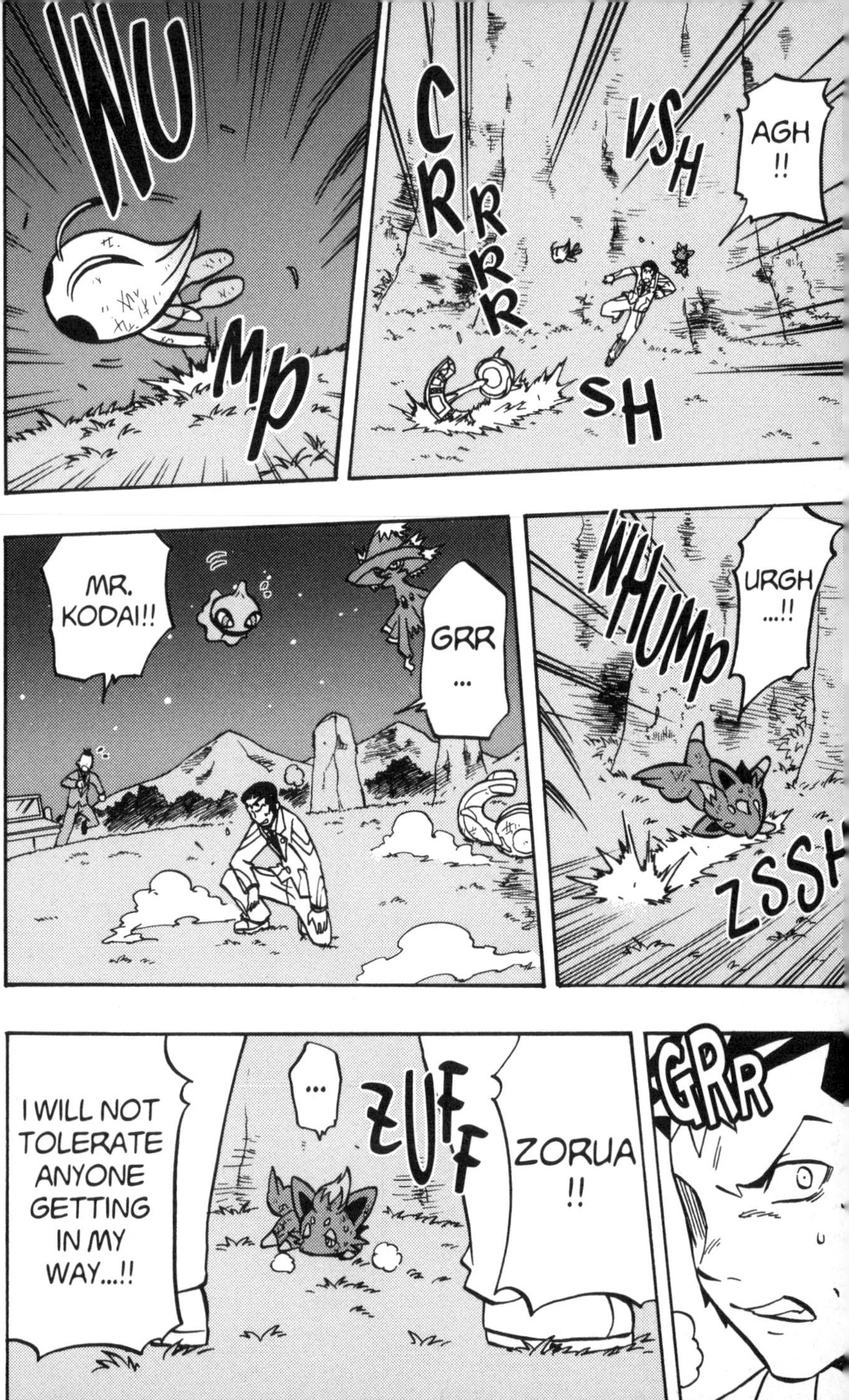
AGH!!
VSH
CRRRR
SH
WU
MP
URGH...!!
WHUMP
ZSSH
GRR...
MR. KODAI!!
GRR
ZORUA!!
ZUFF
...
I WILL NOT TOLERATE ANYONE GETTING IN MY WAY...!!

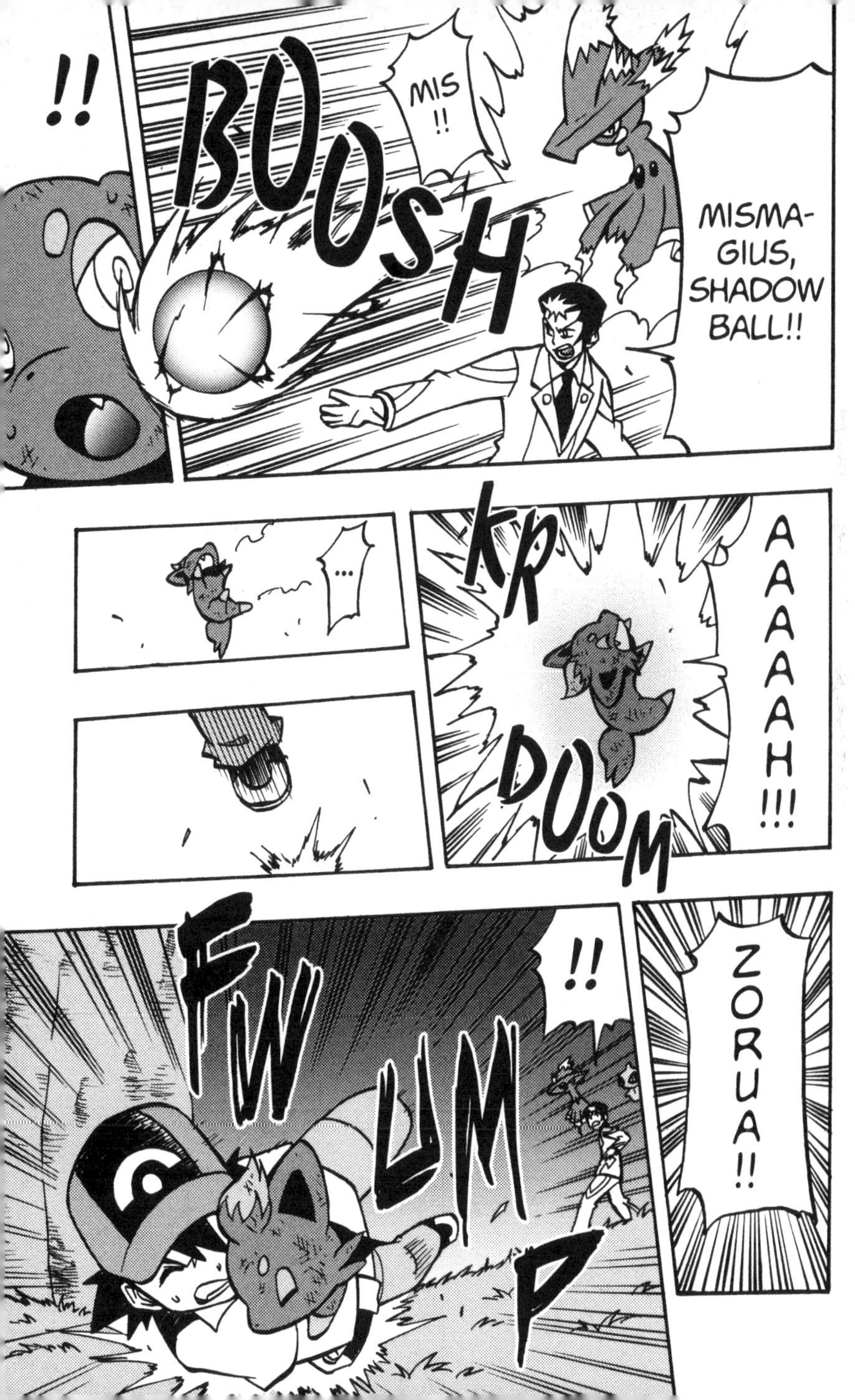
MISMAGIUS, SHADOW BALL!!
MIS !!
BOOSH
!!
AAAAAAH!!!
KR
DOOOM
...
ZORUA!!
!!
FWUMP

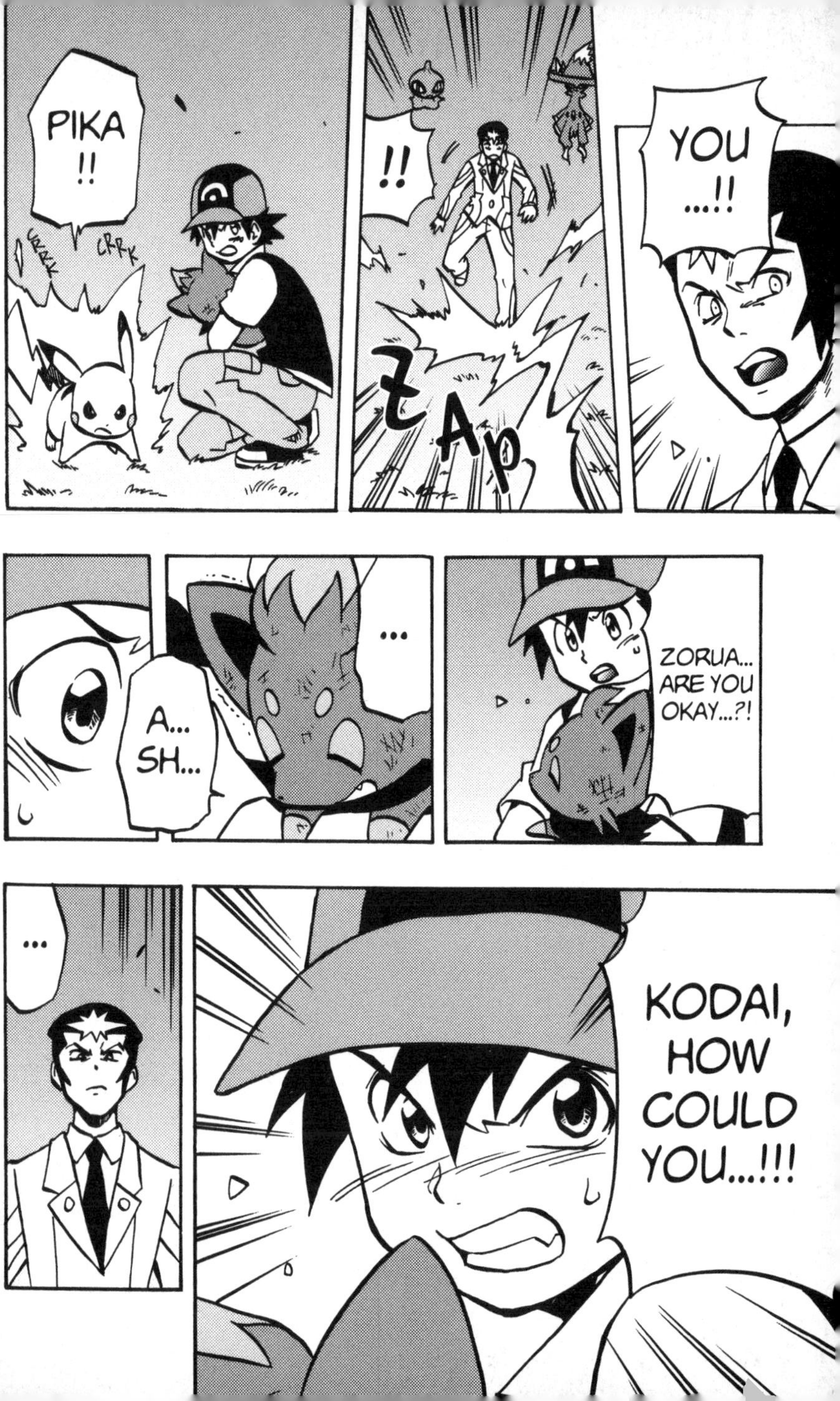
YOU ...!!
!!
ZAP
PIKA !!
CRRK
CRRK
ZORUA... ARE YOU OKAY...?!
...
A... SH...
KODAI, HOW COULD YOU...!!!
...

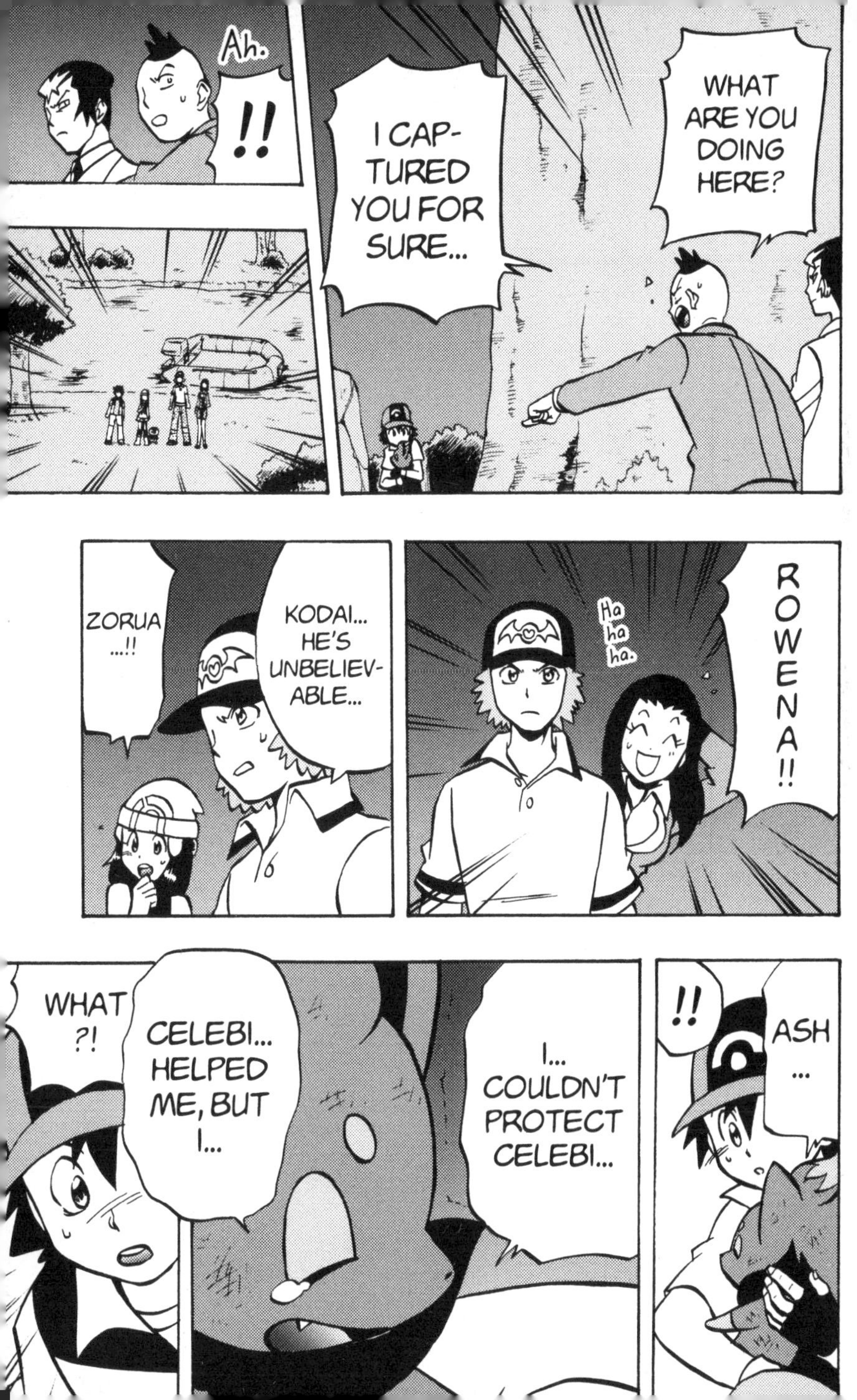

WHAT ARE YOU DOING HERE?
I CAPTURED YOU FOR SURE...
Ah.
!!
ROWENA!!
Ha ha ha.
KODAI... HE'S UNBELIEVABLE...
ZORUA ...!!
ASH ...
!!
I... COULDN'T PROTECT CELEBI...
CELEBI... HELPED ME, BUT I...
WHAT ?!

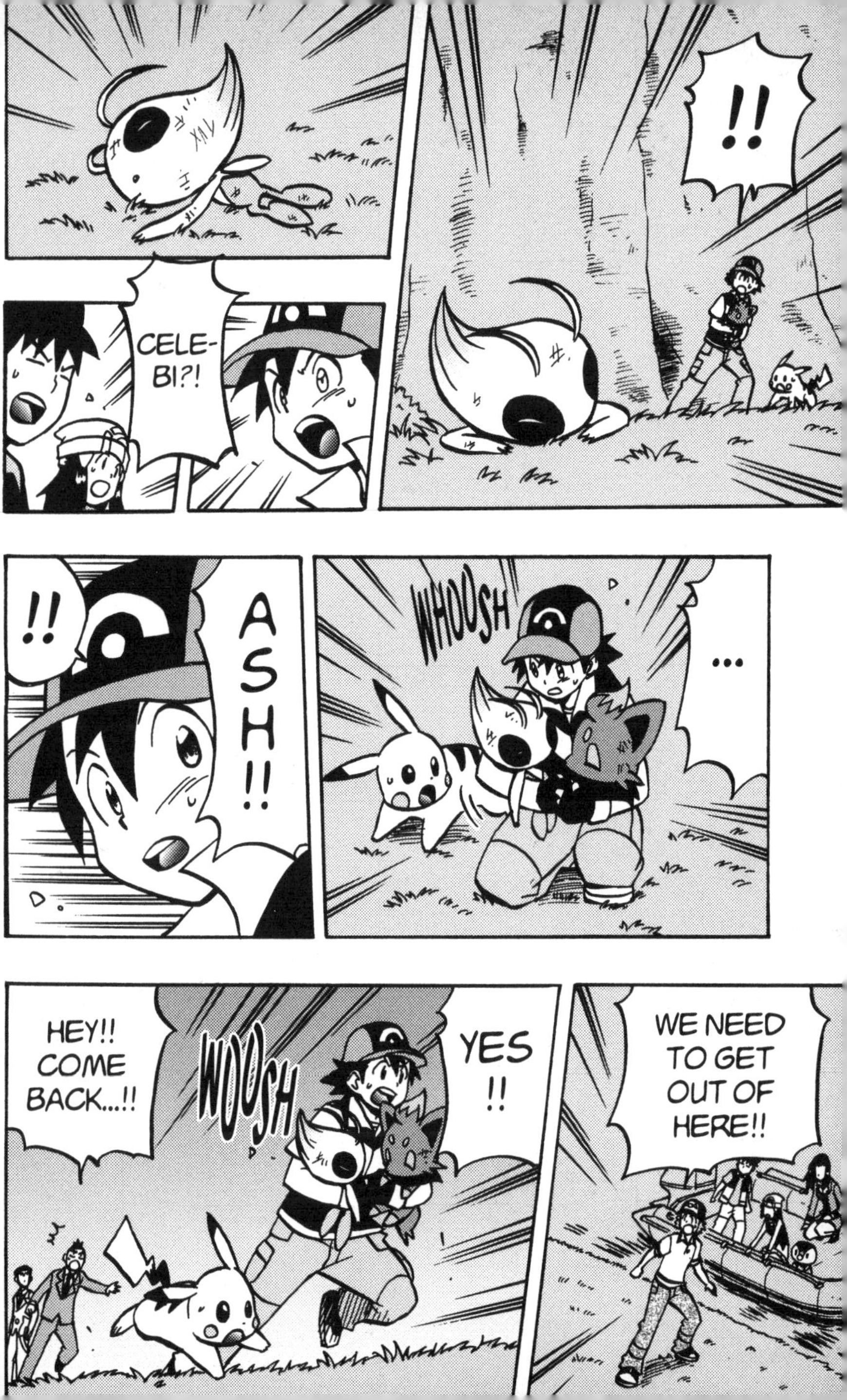
!!
CELE-BI?!
...
WHOOSH
!!
ASH!!
WE NEED TO GET OUT OF HERE!!
YES!!
WOOSH
HEY!! COME BACK...!!

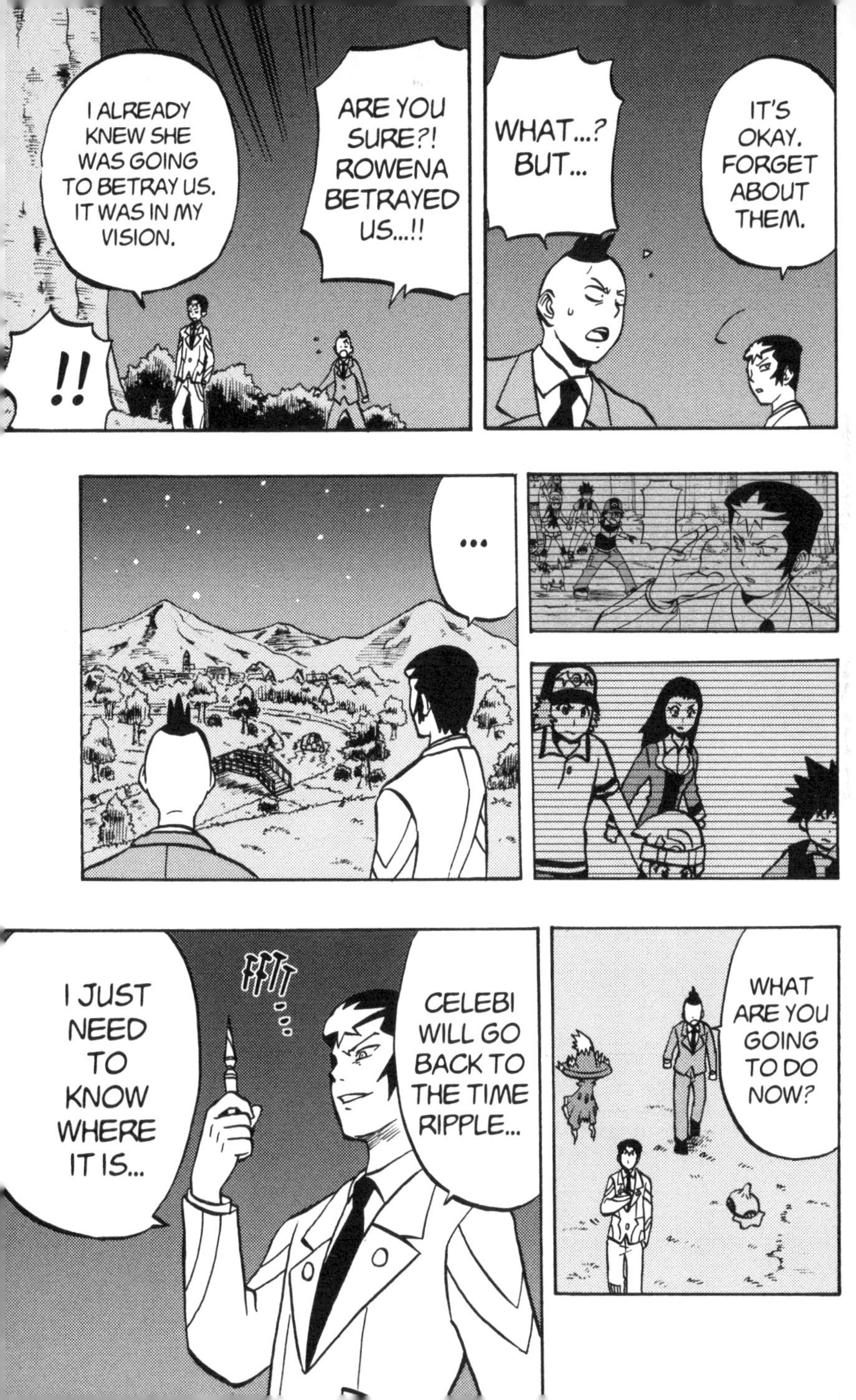
IT'S OKAY. FORGET ABOUT THEM.
WHAT...? BUT...
ARE YOU SURE?! ROWENA BETRAYED US...!!
I ALREADY KNEW SHE WAS GOING TO BETRAY US. IT WAS IN MY VISION.
!!
...
WHAT ARE YOU GOING TO DO NOW?
FFTT
CELEBI WILL GO BACK TO THE TIME RIPPLE...
I JUST NEED TO KNOW WHERE IT IS...

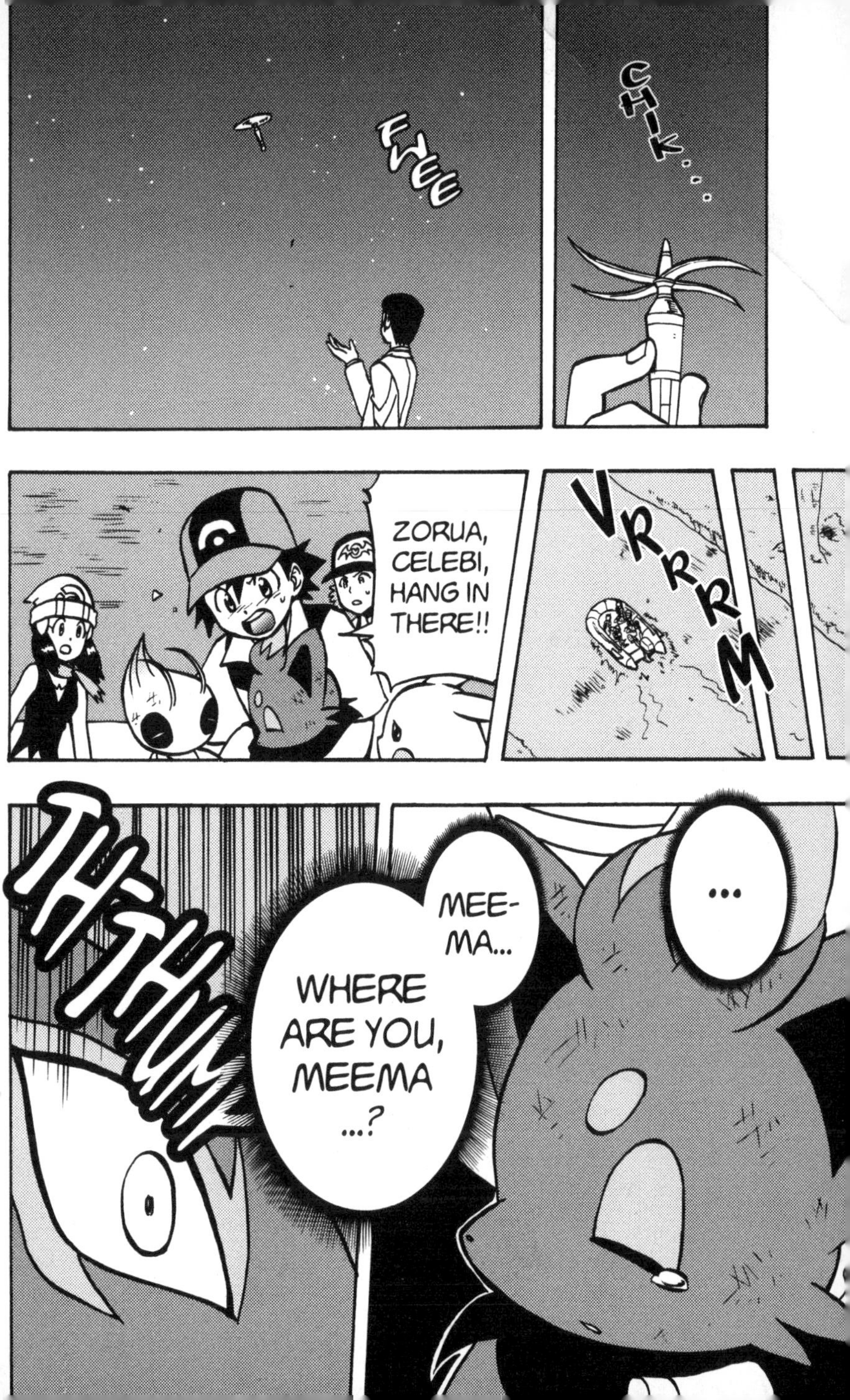
CHIK...
FWEE
VRRRRM
ZORUA, CELEBI, HANG IN THERE!!
...
MEE-MA...
WHERE ARE YOU, MEEMA ...?
THTHUMM

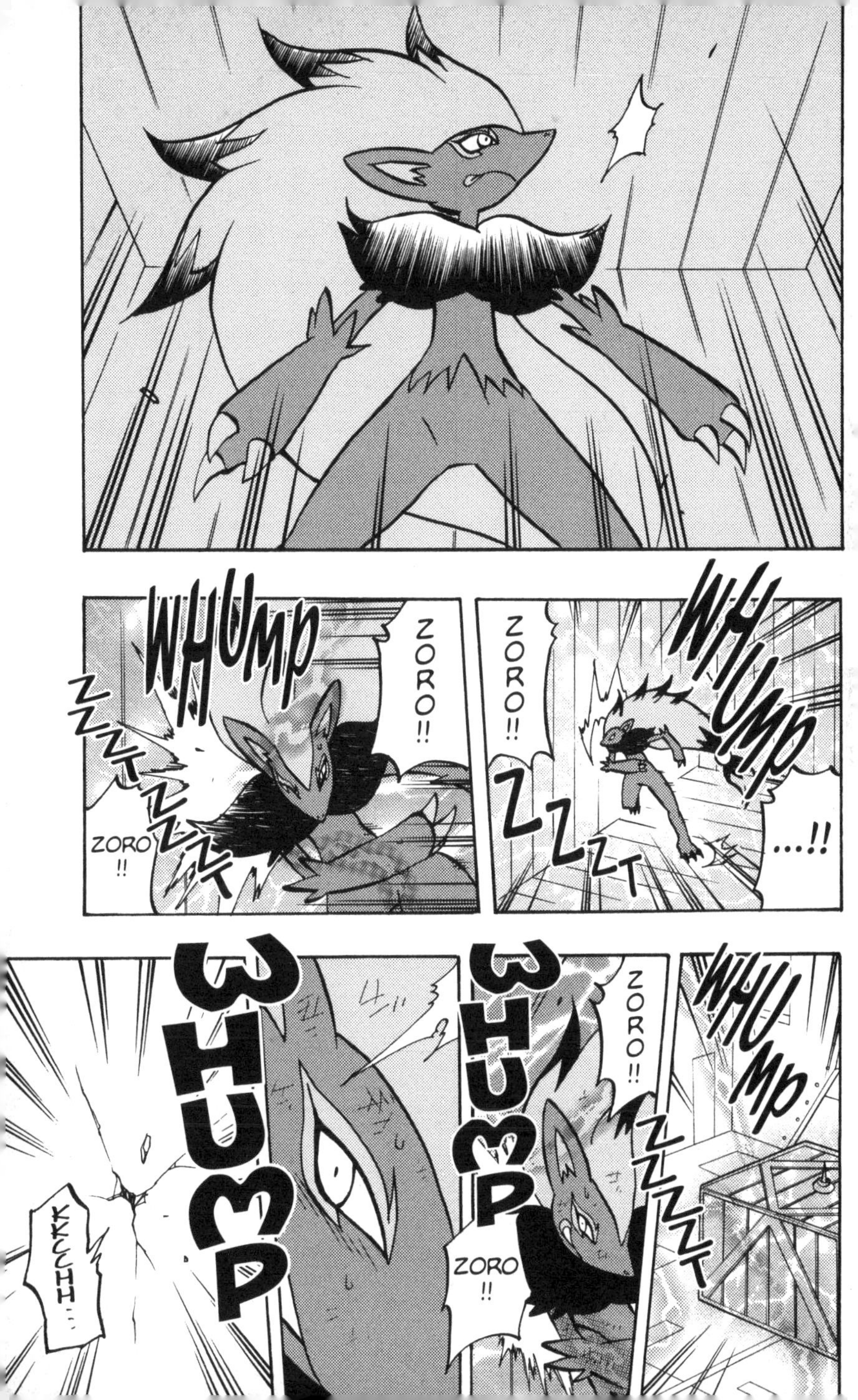
ZORO!!
WHUMP
ZZZZT
...!!
WHUMP
ZORO!!
ZZZZT
ZZZZT
ZORO!!
WHUMP
ZORO!!
ZZZZZT
ZORO!!
THUMP
THUMP
KKCCHH...

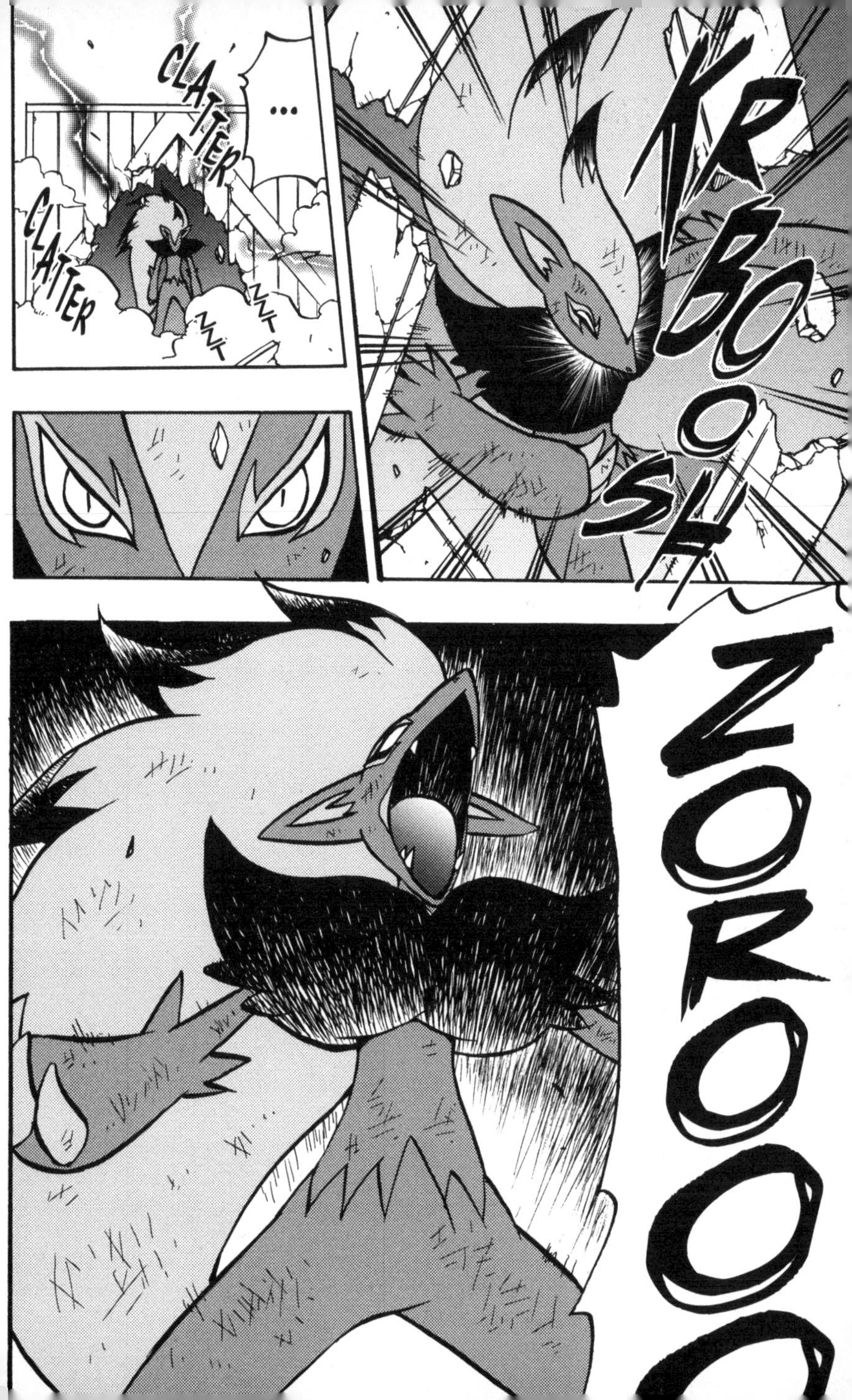
KRBOOSH
...
CLATTER
ZZZT
CLATTER
ZZZT
ZOROOO

BATTLE FOR THE FUTURE!!

PIKA-PII.

ZORUA, CELEBI, HANG IN THERE!!

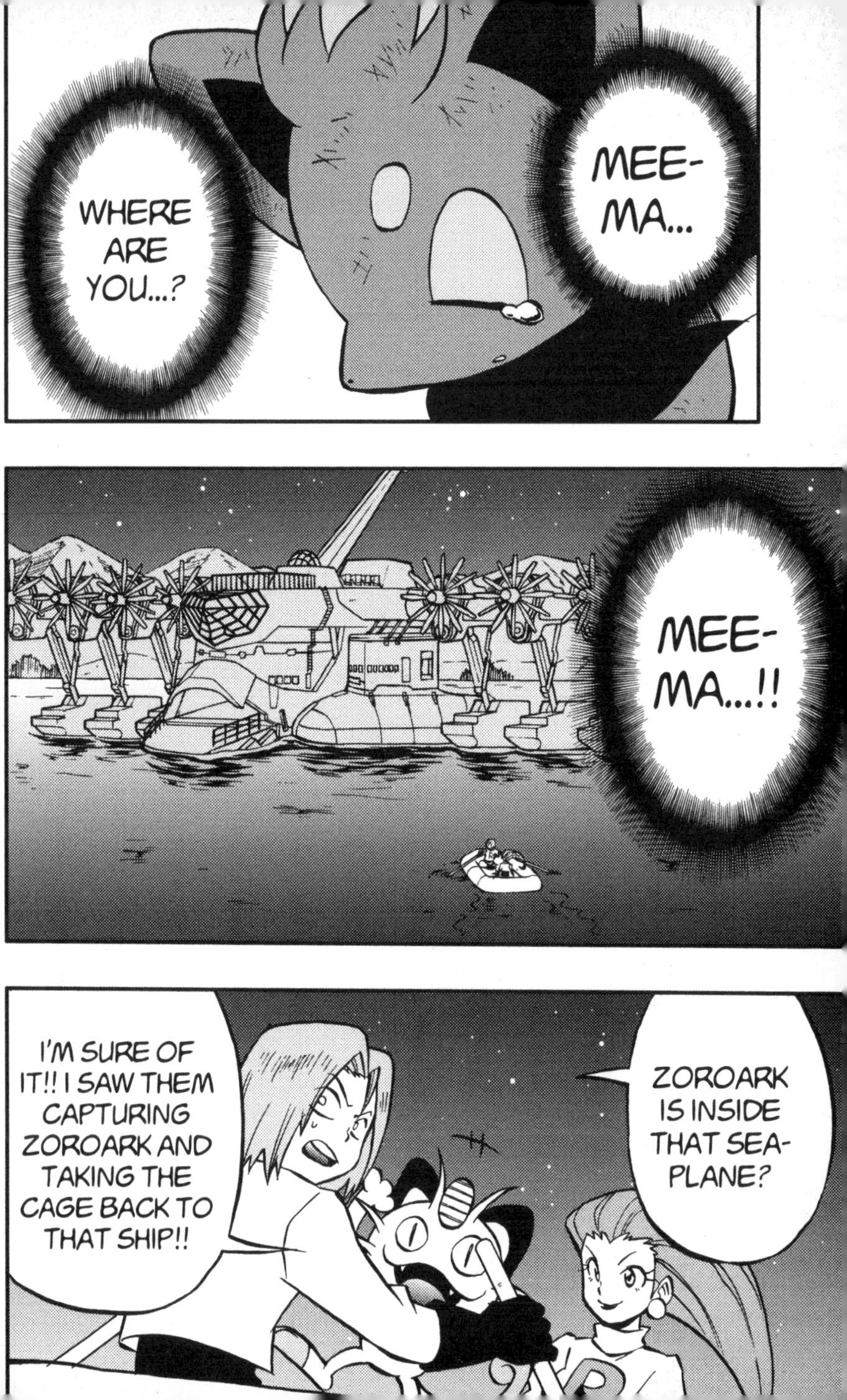
MEE-MA...
WHERE ARE YOU...?
MEE-MA...!!
ZOROARK IS INSIDE THAT SEA-PLANE?
I'M SURE OF IT!! I SAW THEM CAPTURING ZOROARK AND TAKING THE CAGE BACK TO THAT SHIP!!

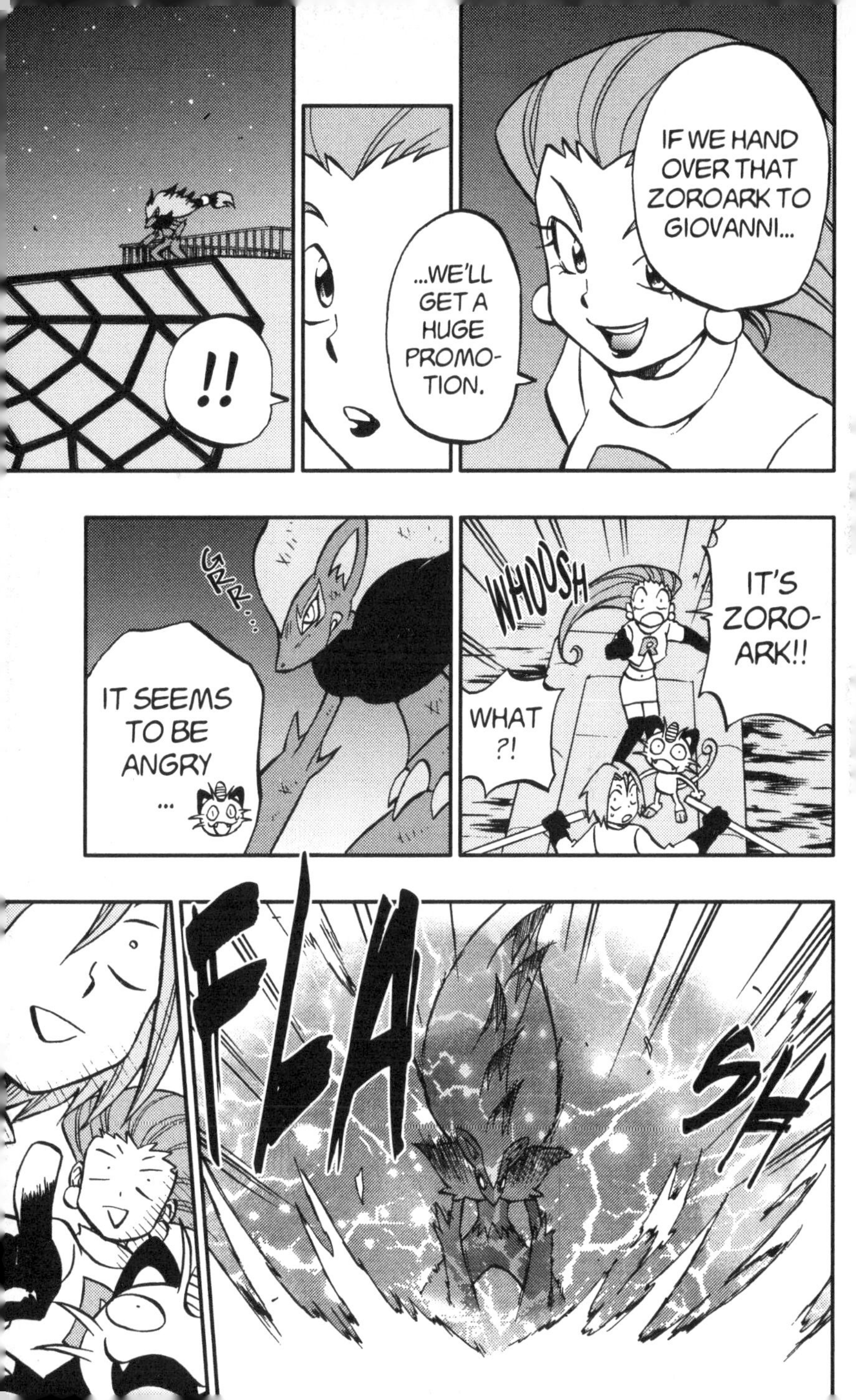

IF WE HAND OVER THAT ZOROARK TO GIOVANNI...
...WE'LL GET A HUGE PROMOTION.
!!
IT'S ZORO-ARK!!
WHOOSH
WHAT ?!
GRR...
IT SEEMS TO BE ANGRY ...
FLASH

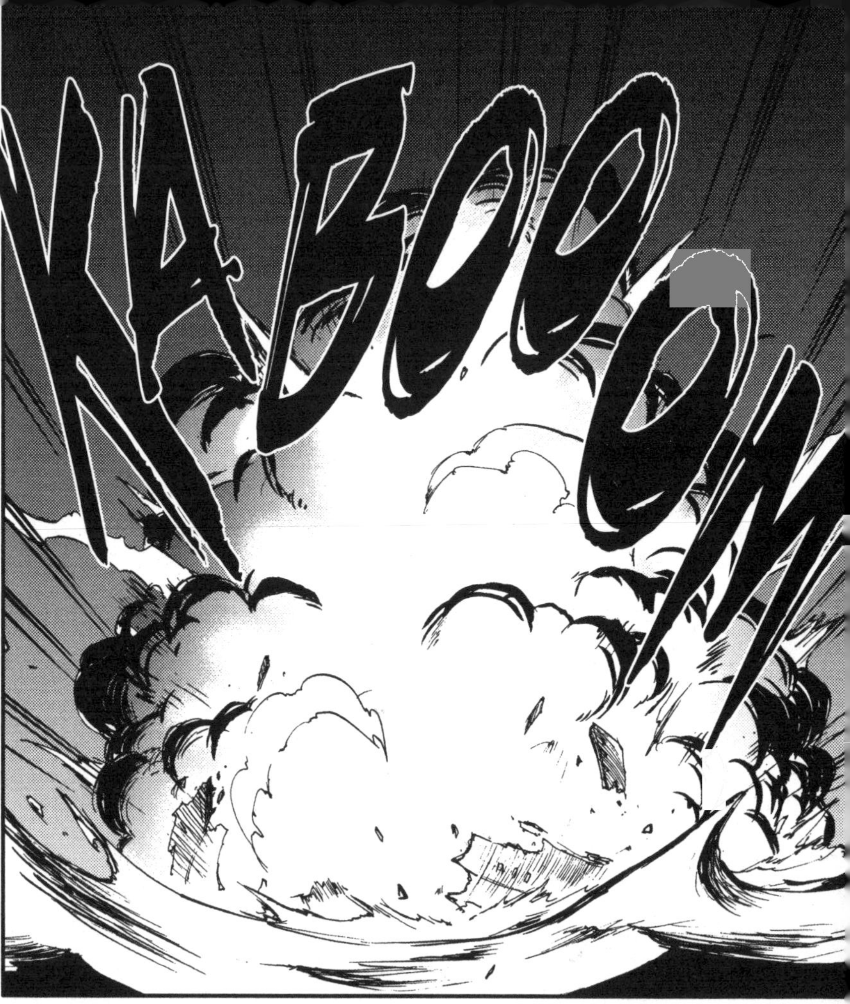
KABOOOM

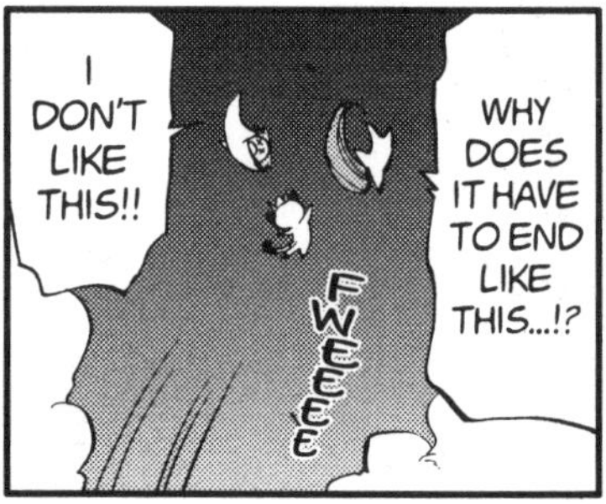
WHY DOES IT HAVE TO END LIKE THIS...!?
I DON'T LIKE THIS!!
FWEEEE

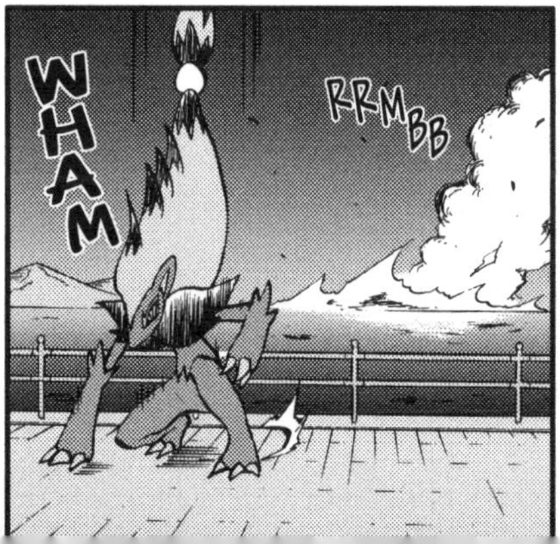
WHAM
RRMBB

READ THIS WAY

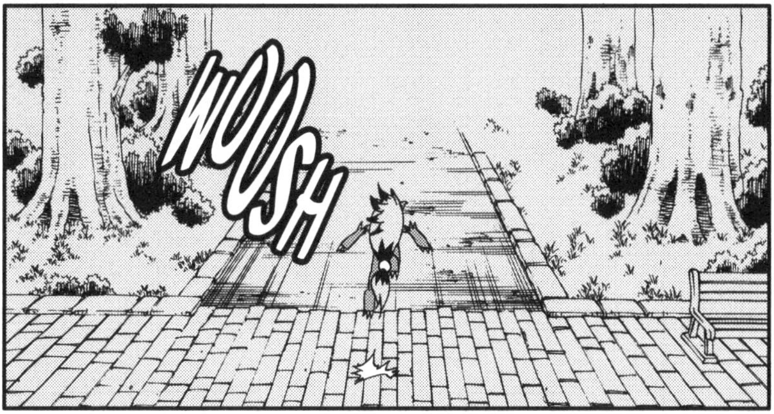
WOOSH

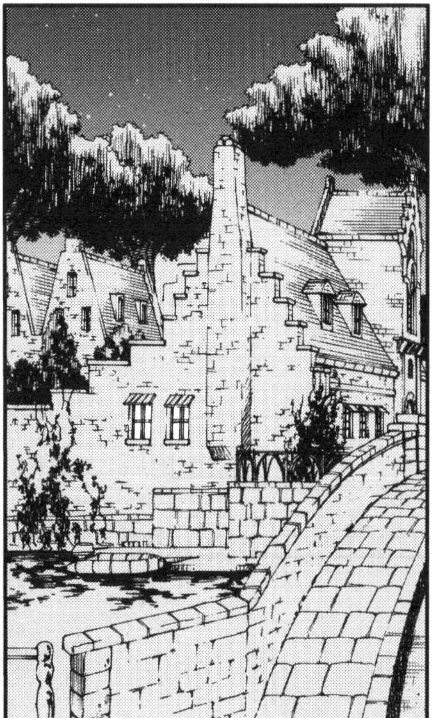

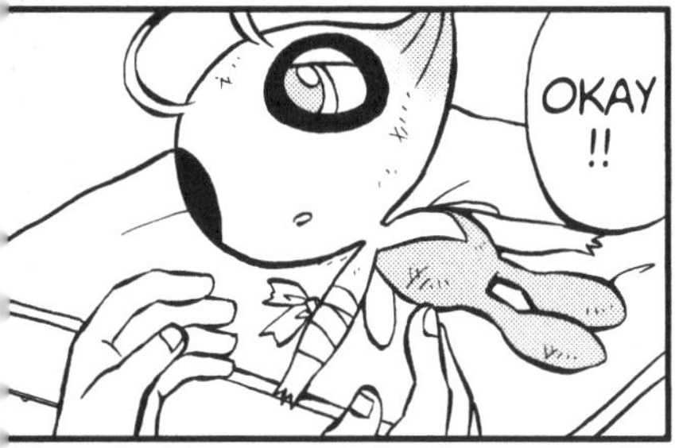
OKAY !!

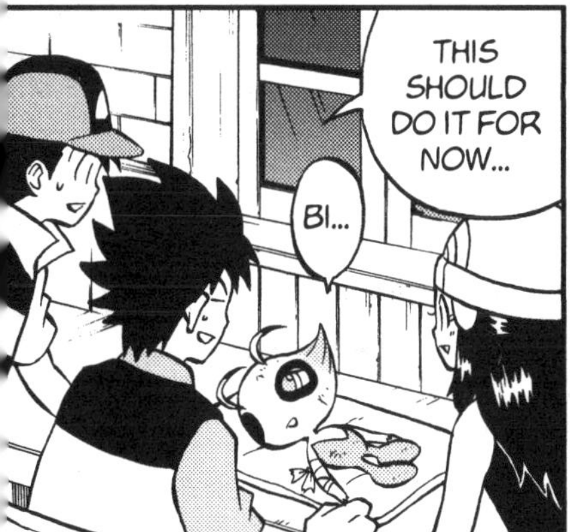
THIS SHOULD DO IT FOR NOW...
BI...

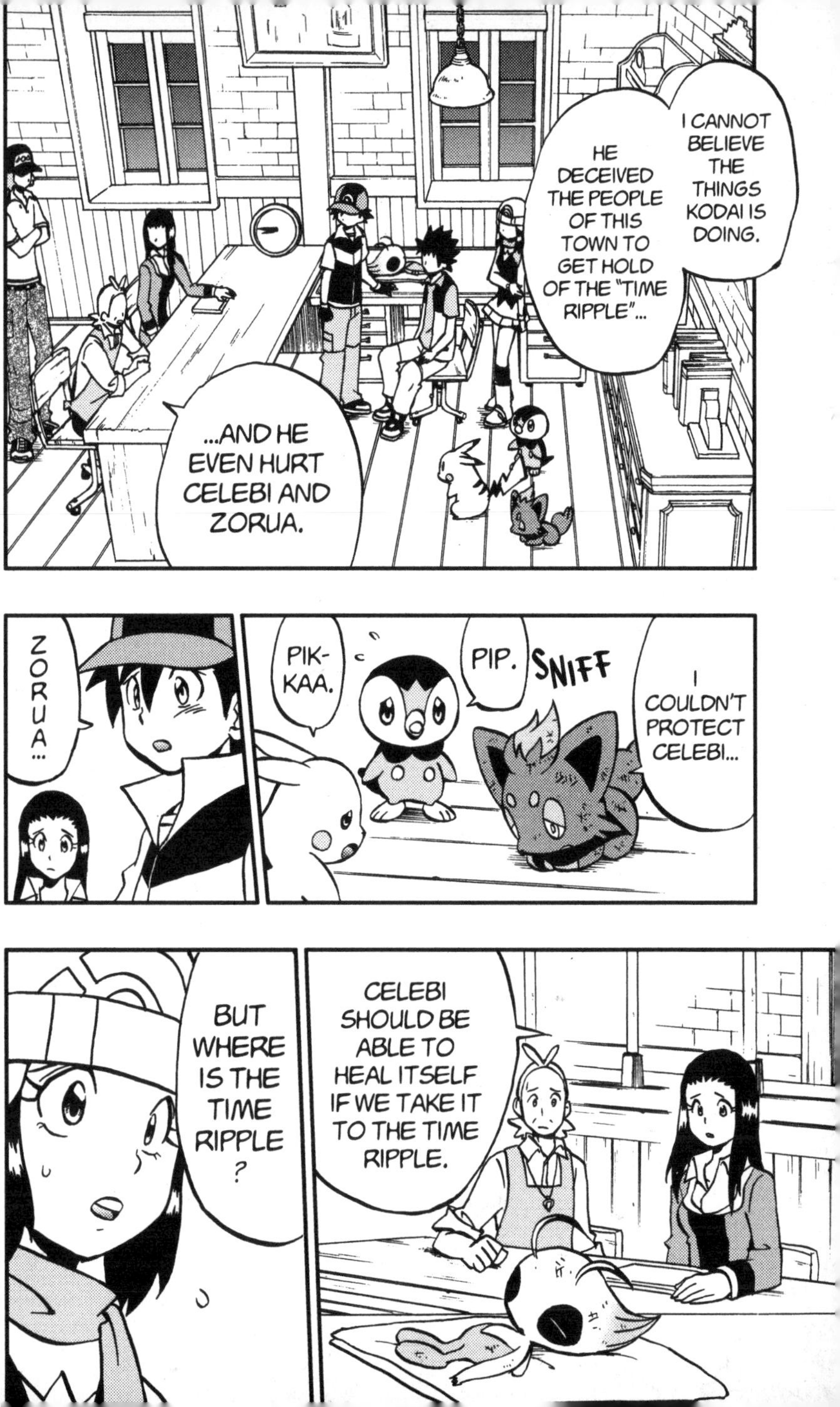
I CANNOT BELIEVE THE THINGS KODAI IS DOING.
HE DECEIVED THE PEOPLE OF THIS TOWN TO GET HOLD OF THE "TIME RIPPLE"...
...AND HE EVEN HURT CELEBI AND ZORUA.
I COULDN'T PROTECT CELEBI...
SNIFF
PIP.
PIK-KAA.
ZORUA...
CELEBI SHOULD BE ABLE TO HEAL ITSELF IF WE TAKE IT TO THE TIME RIPPLE.
BUT WHERE IS THE TIME RIPPLE?

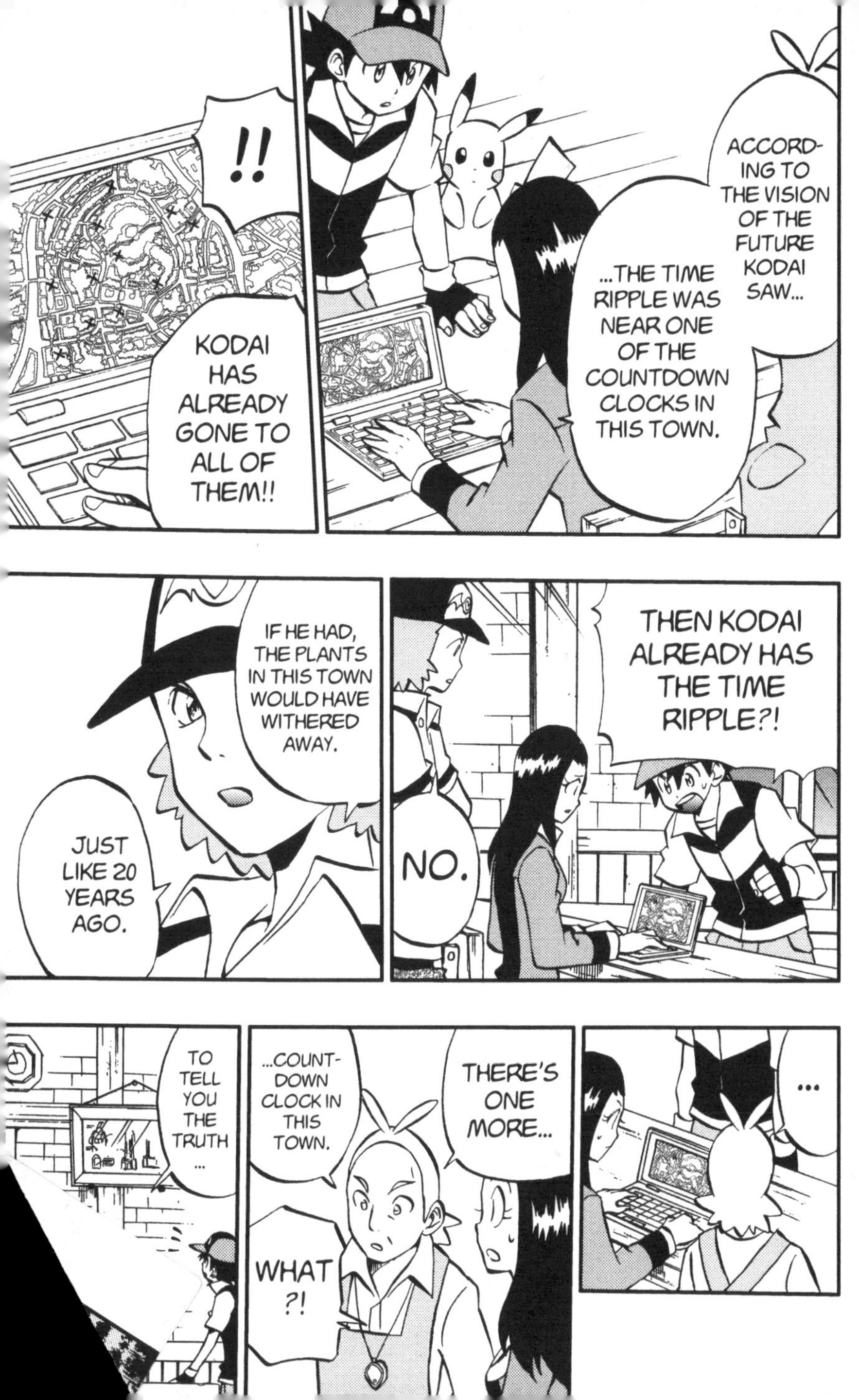
ACCORDING TO THE VISION OF THE FUTURE KODAI SAW...
...THE TIME RIPPLE WAS NEAR ONE OF THE COUNTDOWN CLOCKS IN THIS TOWN.
!!
KODAI HAS ALREADY GONE TO ALL OF THEM!!
THEN KODAI ALREADY HAS THE TIME RIPPLE?!
NO.
IF HE HAD, THE PLANTS IN THIS TOWN WOULD HAVE WITHERED AWAY.
JUST LIKE 20 YEARS AGO.
...
THERE'S ONE MORE...
...COUNTDOWN CLOCK IN THIS TOWN.
WHAT?!
TO TELL YOU THE TRUTH...

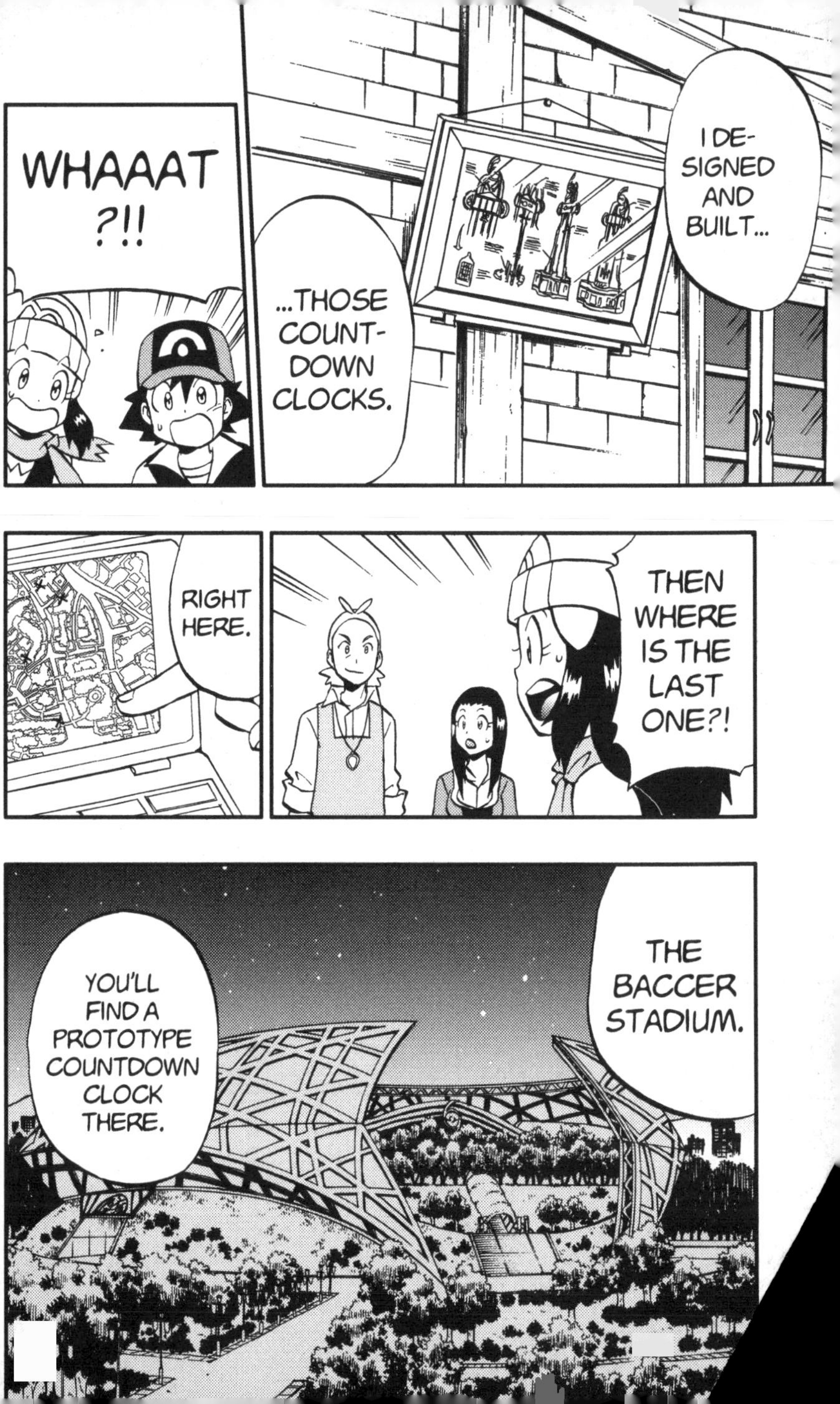
I DE-SIGNED AND BUILT...
...THOSE COUNT-DOWN CLOCKS.
WHAAAT?!!
THEN WHERE IS THE LAST ONE?!
RIGHT HERE.
THE BACCER STADIUM.
YOU'LL FIND A PROTOTYPE COUNTDOWN CLOCK THERE.

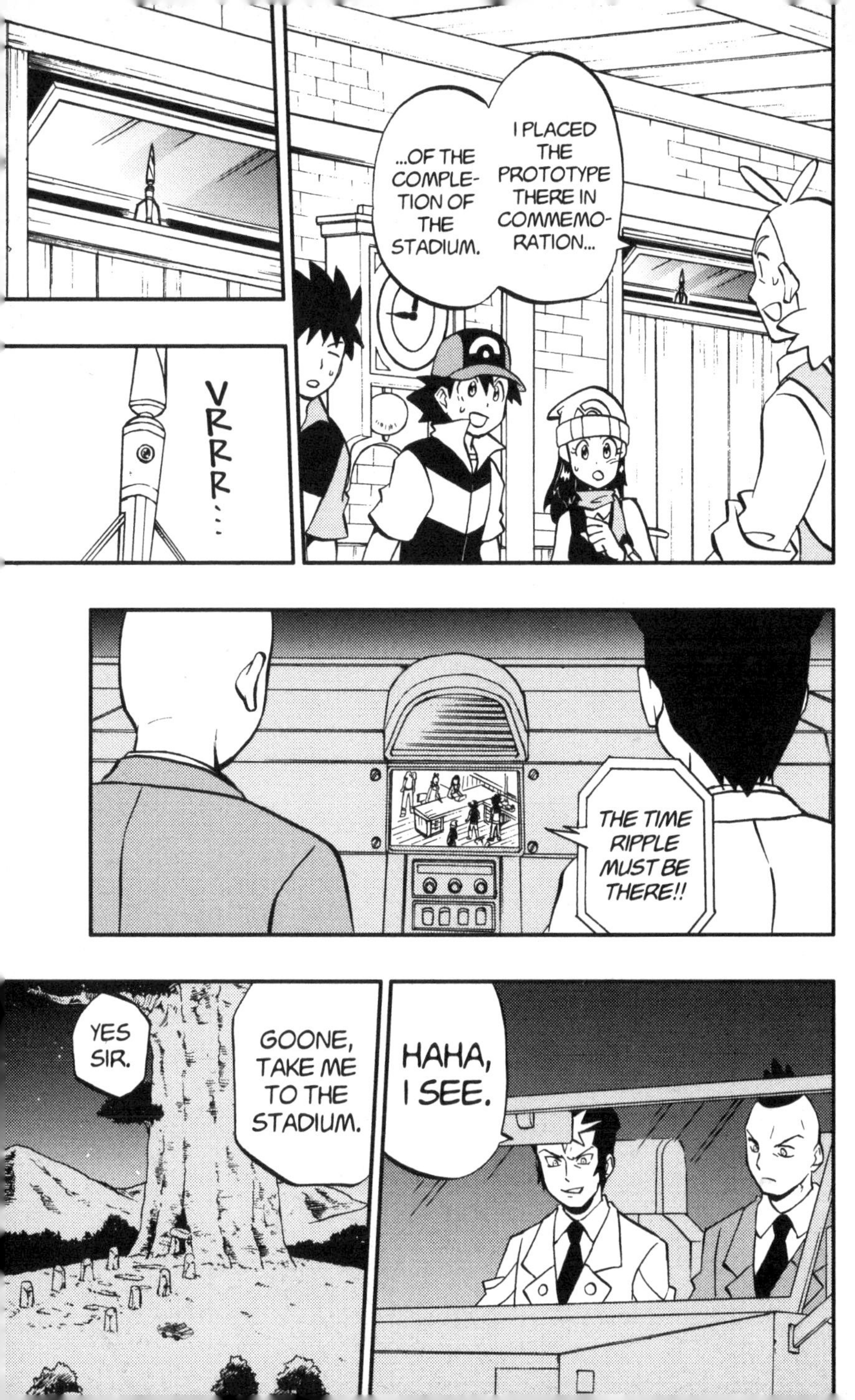
I PLACED THE PROTOTYPE THERE IN COMMEMO-RATION...
...OF THE COMPLE-TION OF THE STADIUM.
VRRR...
THE TIME RIPPLE MUST BE THERE!!
HAHA, I SEE.
GOONE, TAKE ME TO THE STADIUM.
YES SIR.

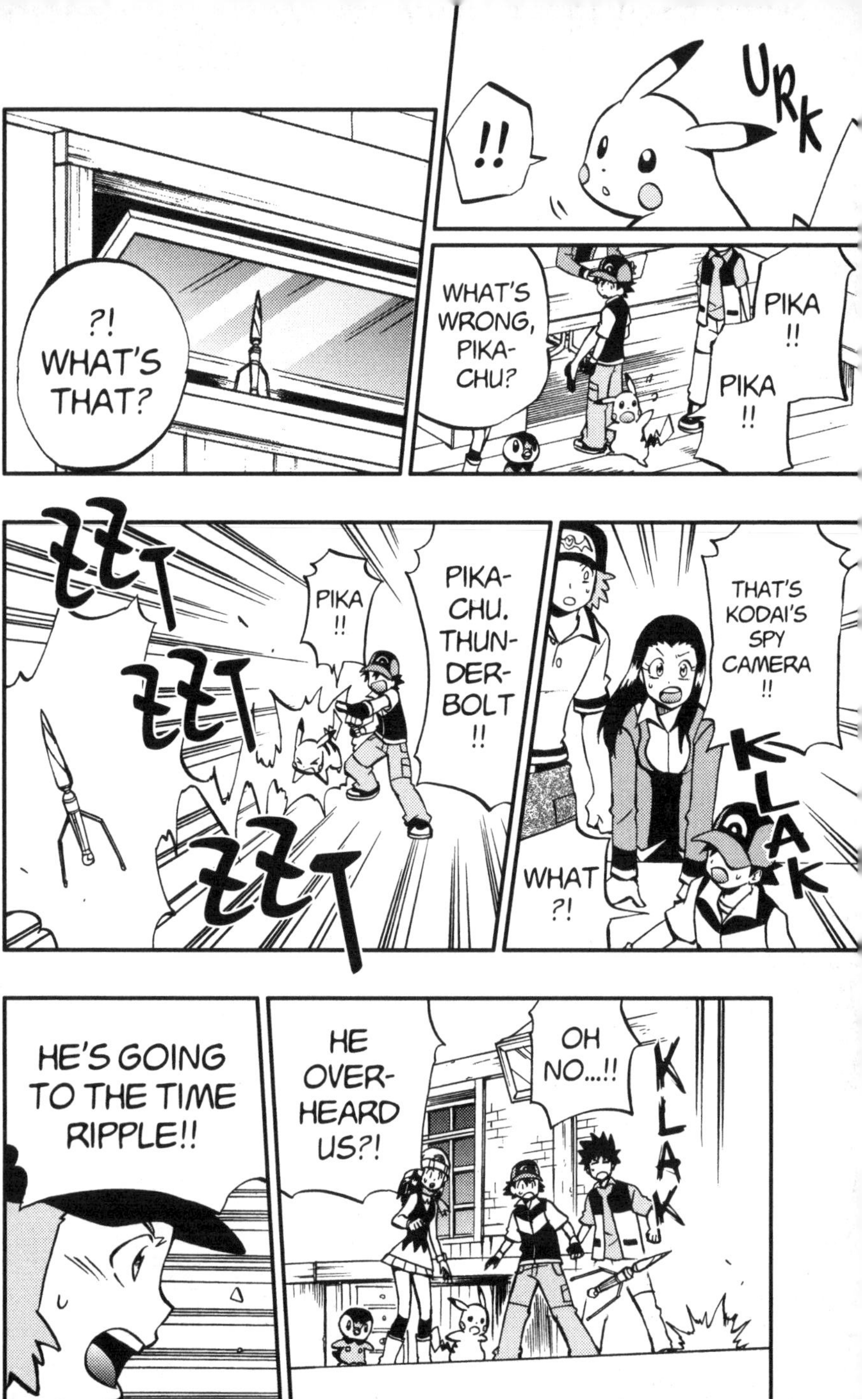
URK
!!
PIKA!!
PIKA!!
WHAT'S WRONG, PIKA-CHU?
?! WHAT'S THAT?
THAT'S KODAI'S SPY CAMERA!!
KLAK
WHAT?!
PIKA-CHU. THUN-DER-BOLT!!
PIKA!!
ZZT
ZZT
ZZT
OH NO...!!
KLAK
HE OVER-HEARD US?!
HE'S GOING TO THE TIME RIPPLE!!

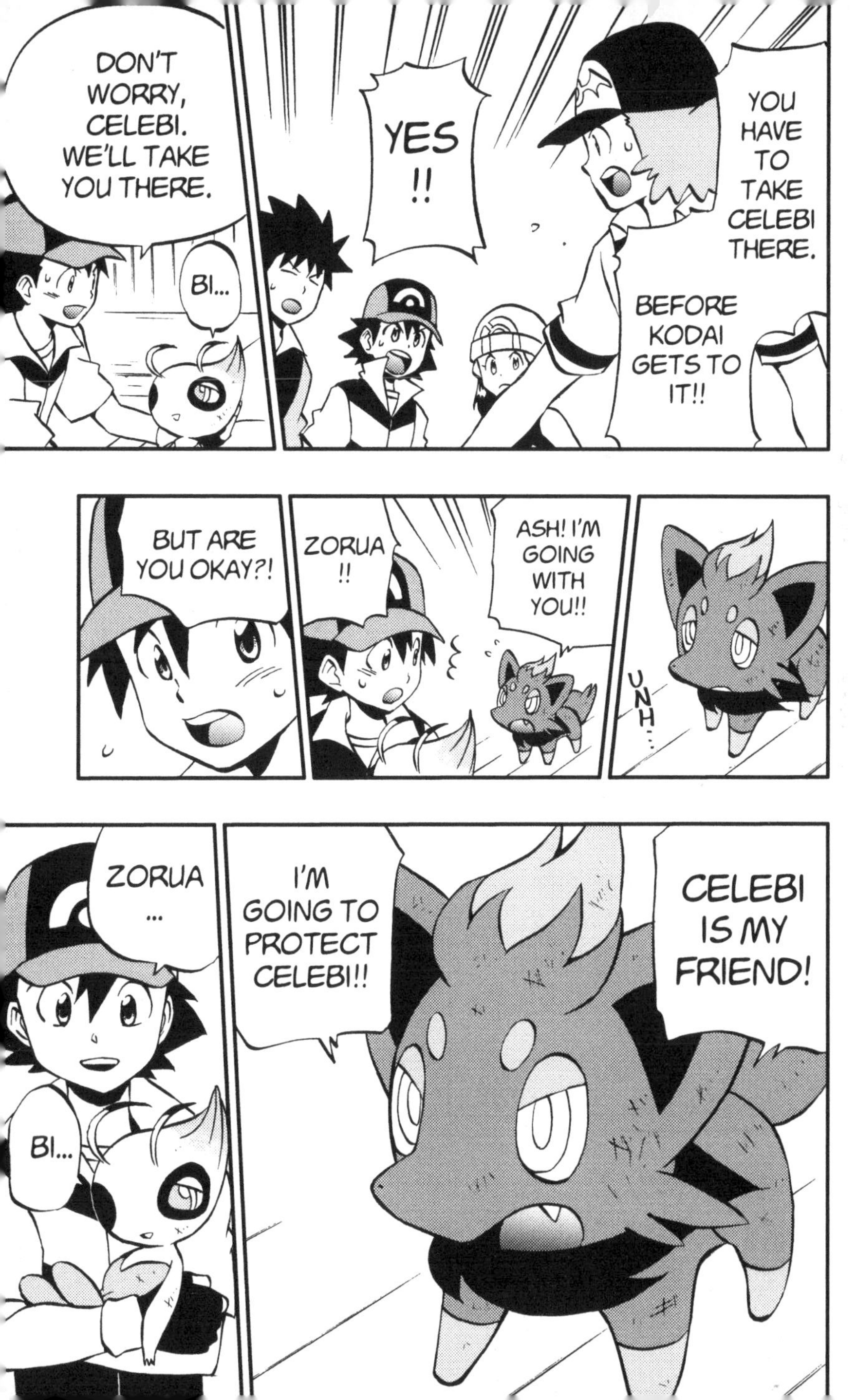
YOU HAVE TO TAKE CELEBI THERE.
BEFORE KODAI GETS TO IT!!
YES !!
DON'T WORRY, CELEBI. WE'LL TAKE YOU THERE.
BI...
UNH...
ASH! I'M GOING WITH YOU!!
ZORUA !!
BUT ARE YOU OKAY?!
CELEBI IS MY FRIEND!
I'M GOING TO PROTECT CELEBI!!
ZORUA ...
BI...

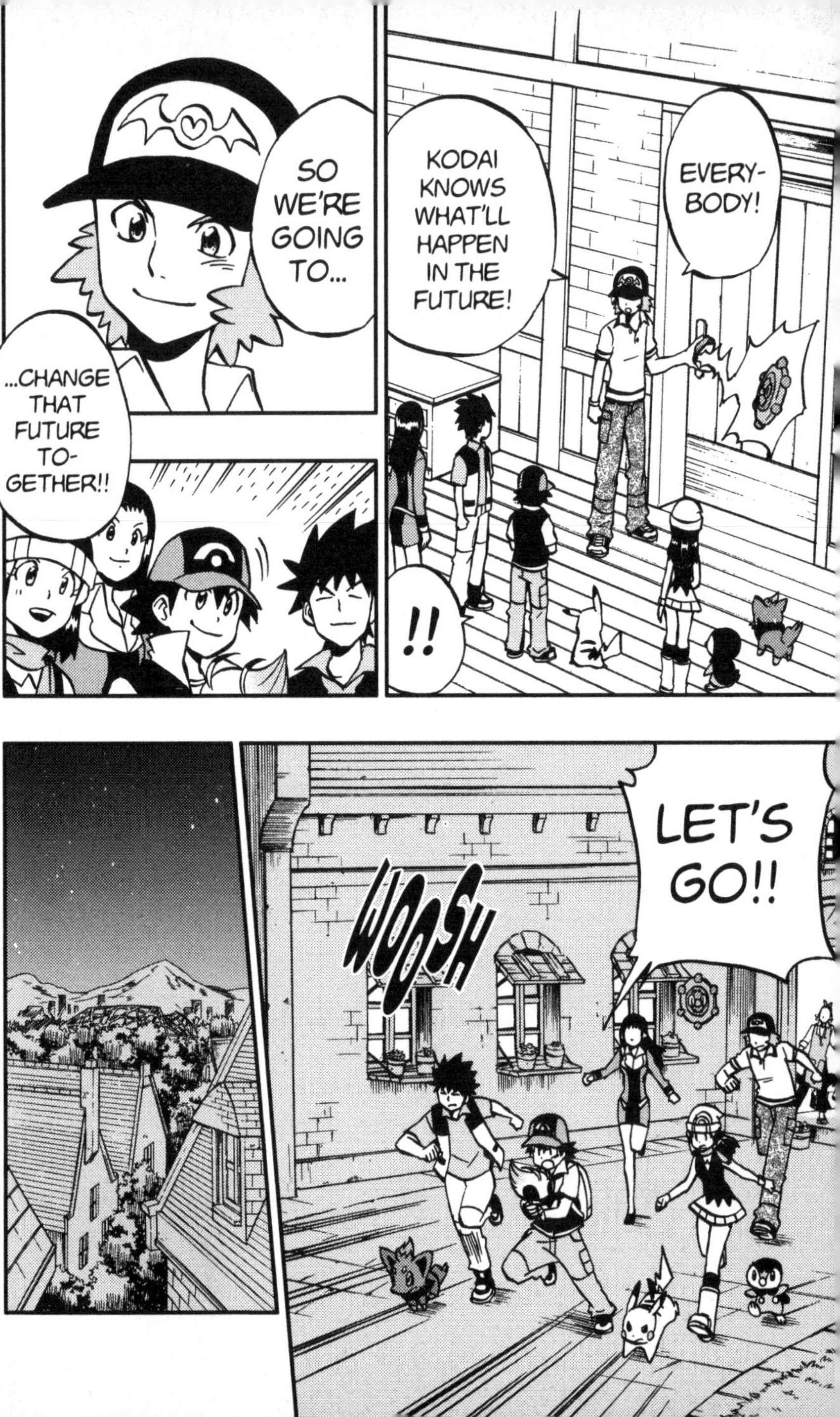
EVERY-BODY!
KODAI KNOWS WHAT'LL HAPPEN IN THE FUTURE!
!!
SO WE'RE GOING TO...
...CHANGE THAT FUTURE TO-GETHER!!
LET'S GO!!
WOOSH

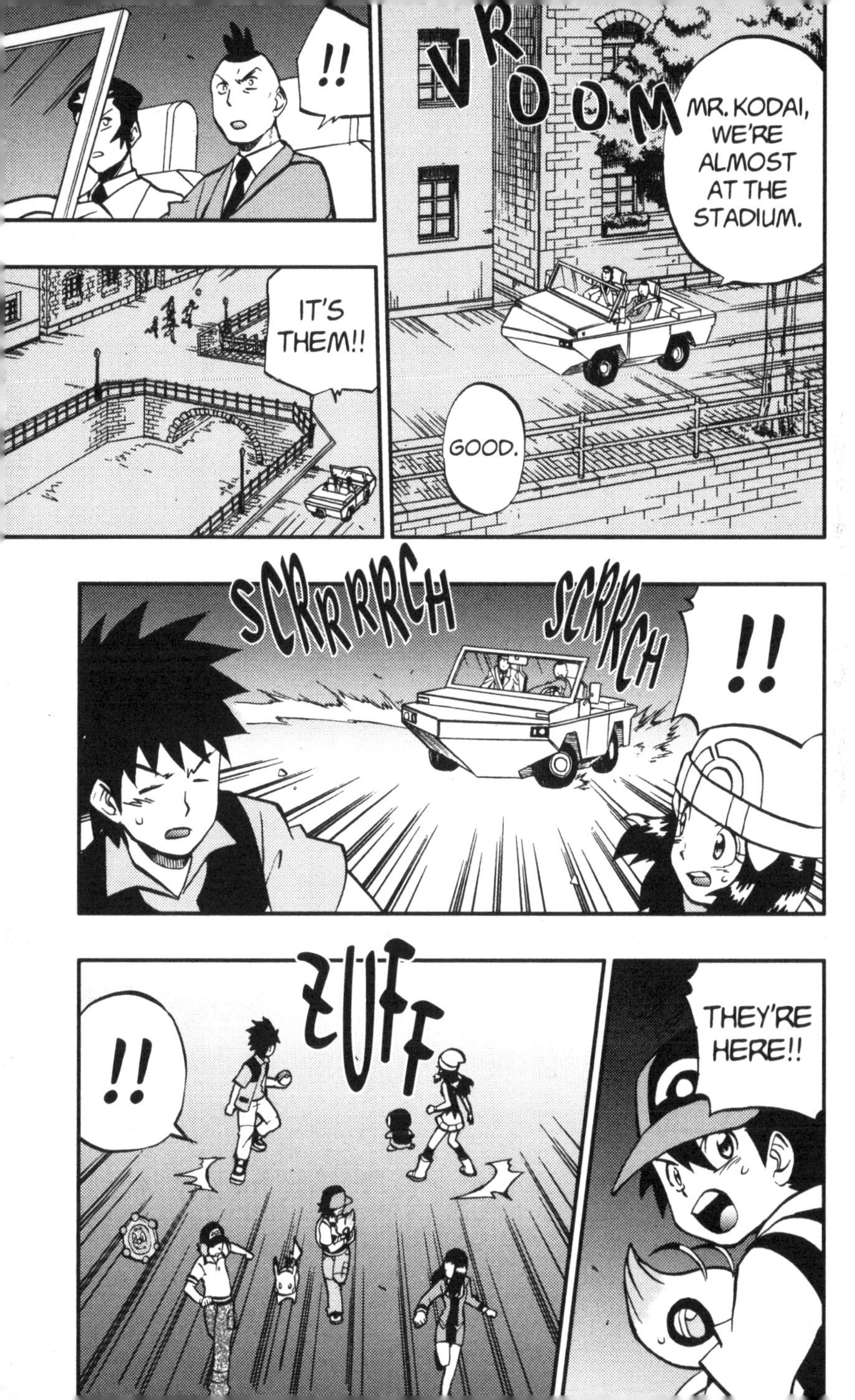
VROOM
MR. KODAI, WE'RE ALMOST AT THE STADIUM.
GOOD.
!!
IT'S THEM!!
!!
SCRRCH
SCRRRRCH
THEY'RE HERE!!
ZUFF
!!

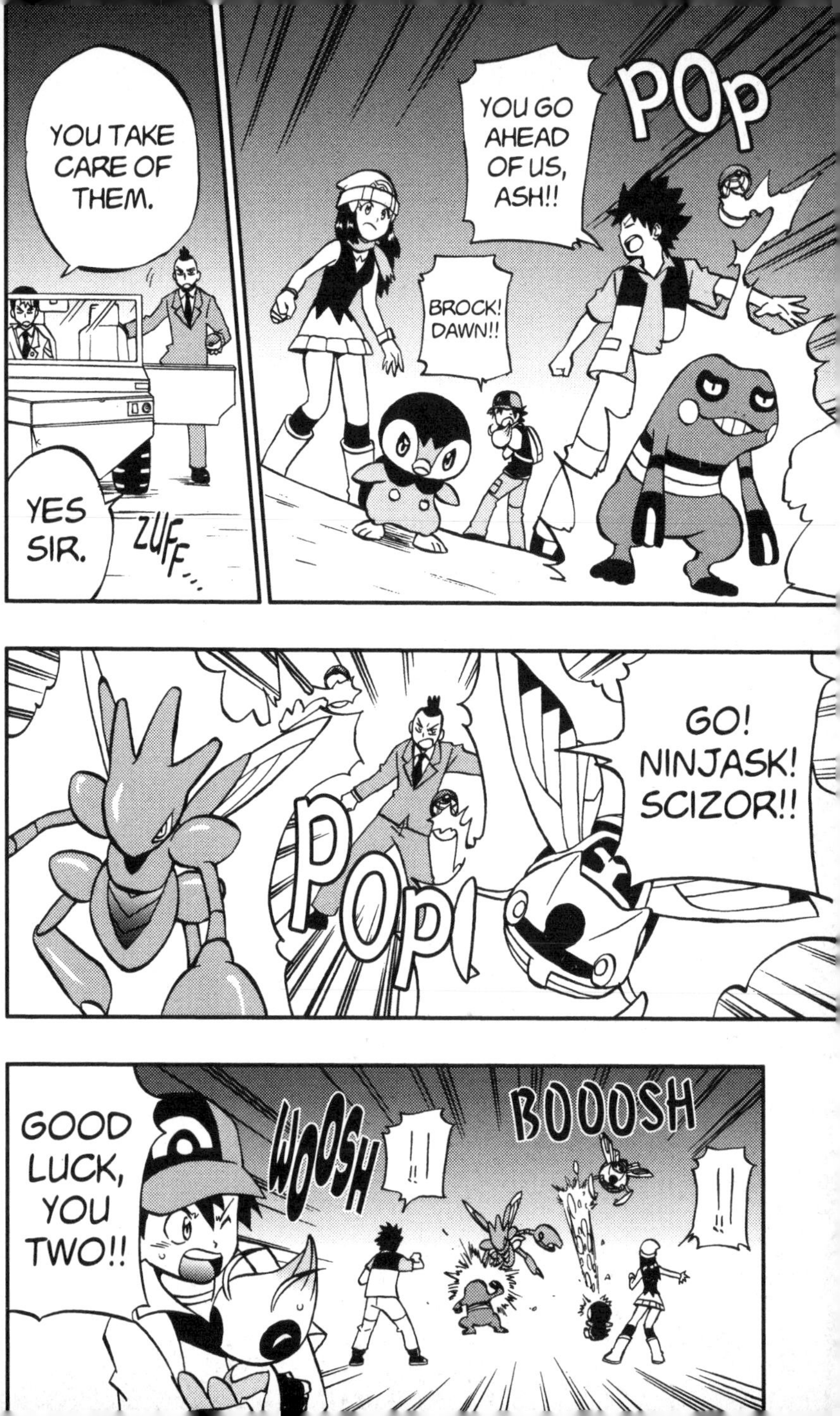
POP
YOU GO AHEAD OF US, ASH!!
BROCK! DAWN!!
YOU TAKE CARE OF THEM.
YES SIR.
ZUFF...
GO! NINJASK! SCIZOR!!
POP
!!
BOOOSH
!!
WOOSH
GOOD LUCK, YOU TWO!!

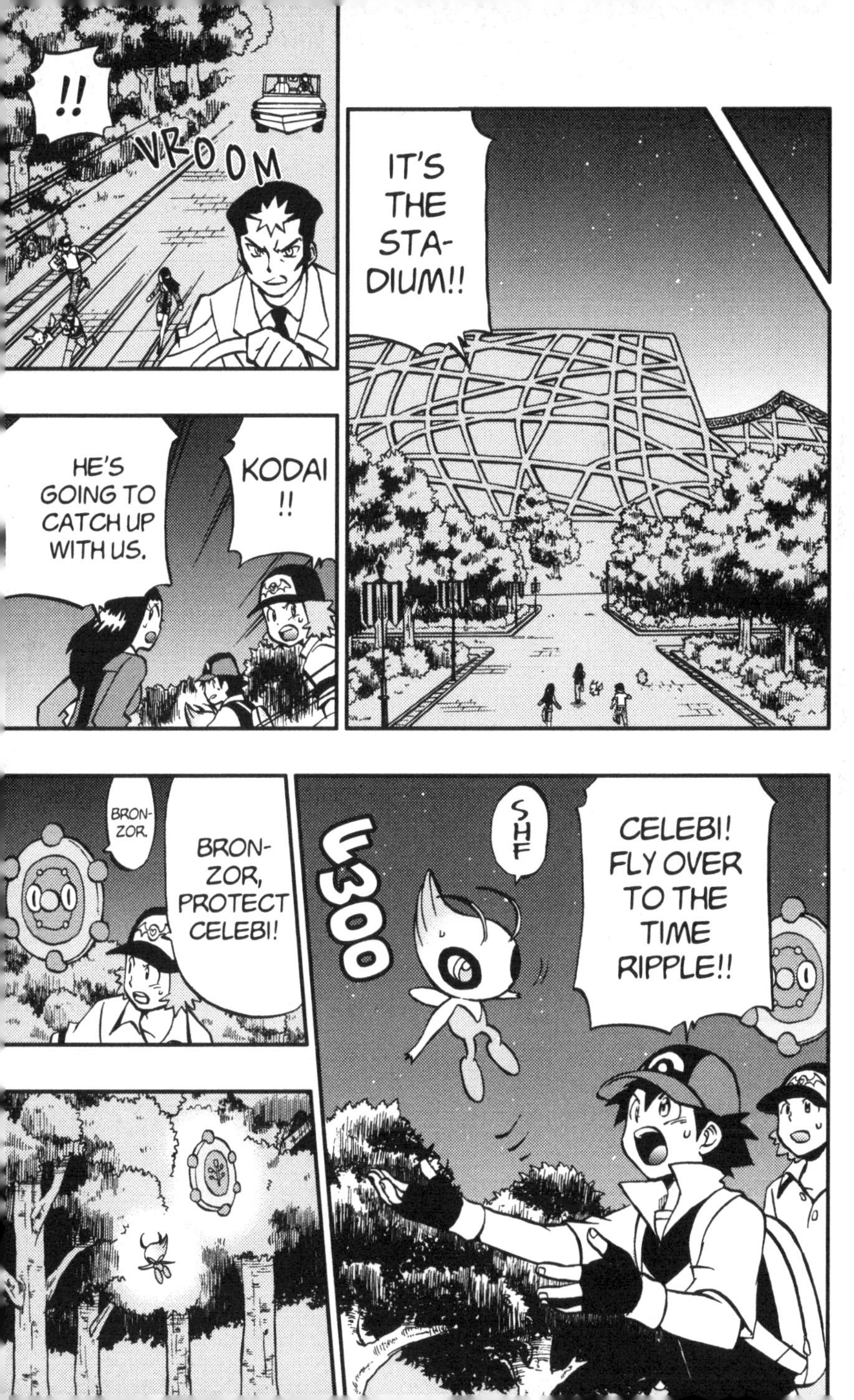
IT'S THE STA-DIUM!!
!!
VROOM
KODAI!!
HE'S GOING TO CATCH UP WITH US.
CELEBI! FLY OVER TO THE TIME RIPPLE!!
SHF
FWOO
BRON-ZOR, PROTECT CELEBI!
BRON-ZOR.

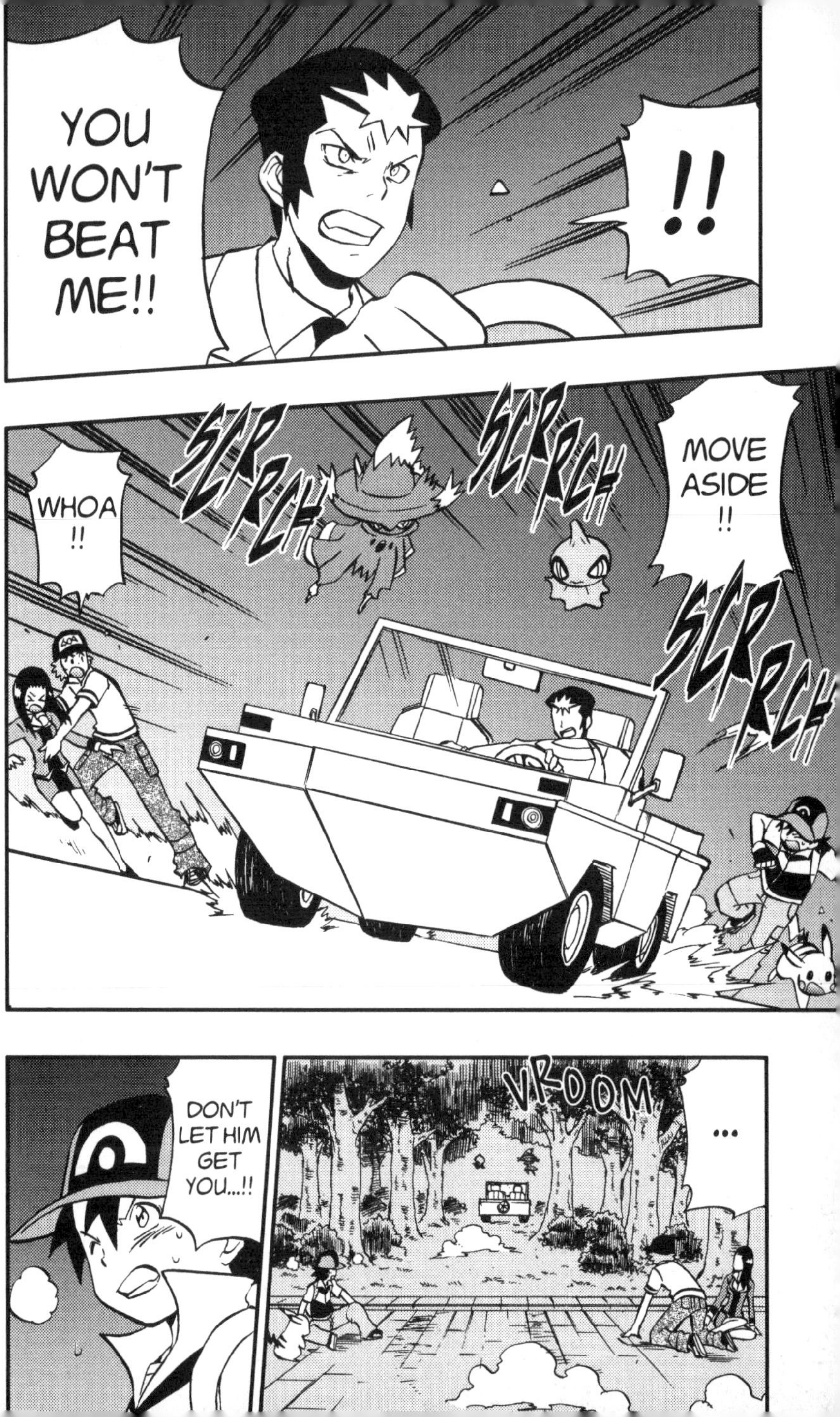
!!
YOU WON'T BEAT ME!!
MOVE ASIDE !!
SCRRCH
SCRRCH
SCRRCH
WHOA !!
VROOM
...
DON'T LET HIM GET YOU...!!

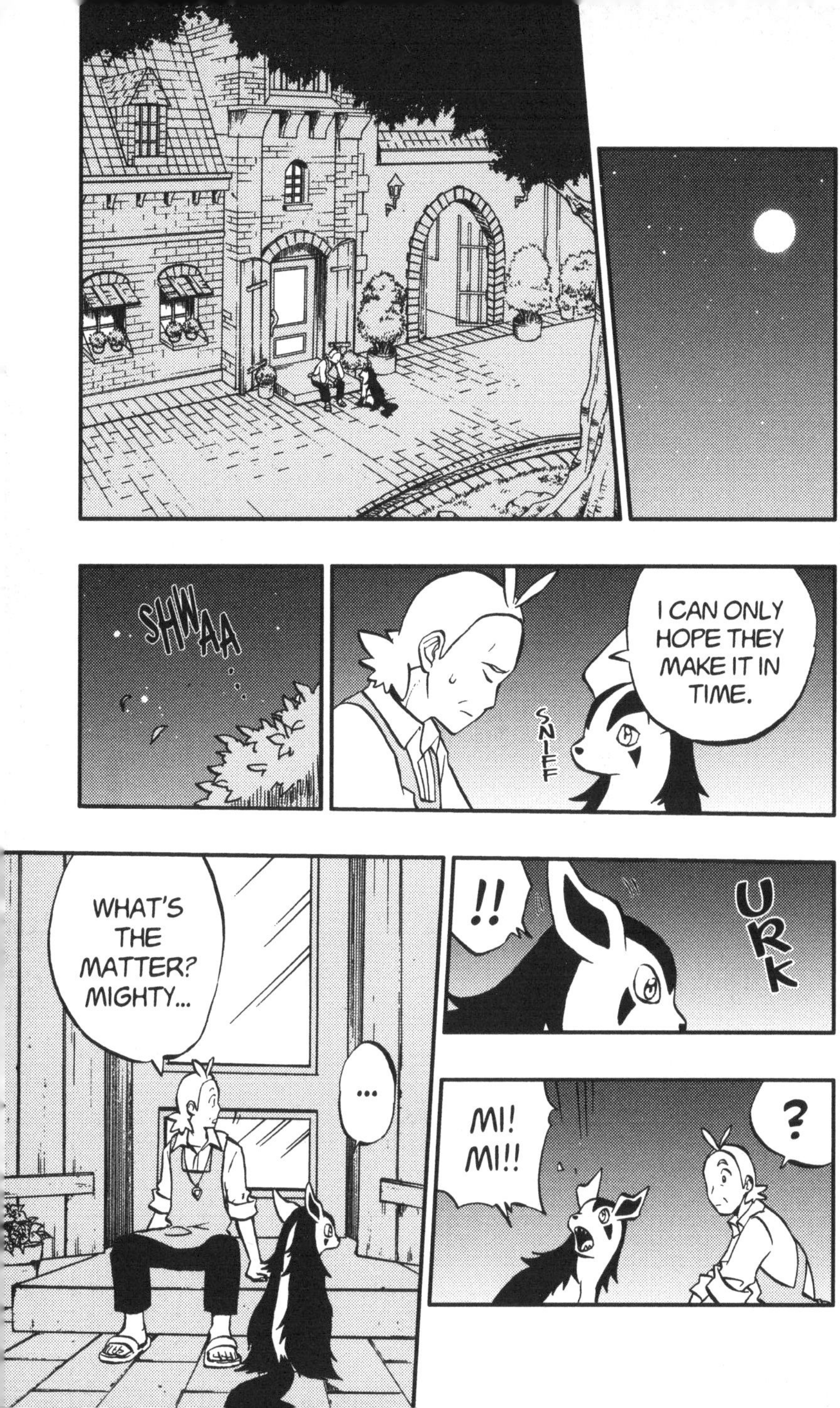
I CAN ONLY HOPE THEY MAKE IT IN TIME.
SNIFF
SHWAA
URK
!!
?
MI! MI!!
WHAT'S THE MATTER? MIGHTY...
...

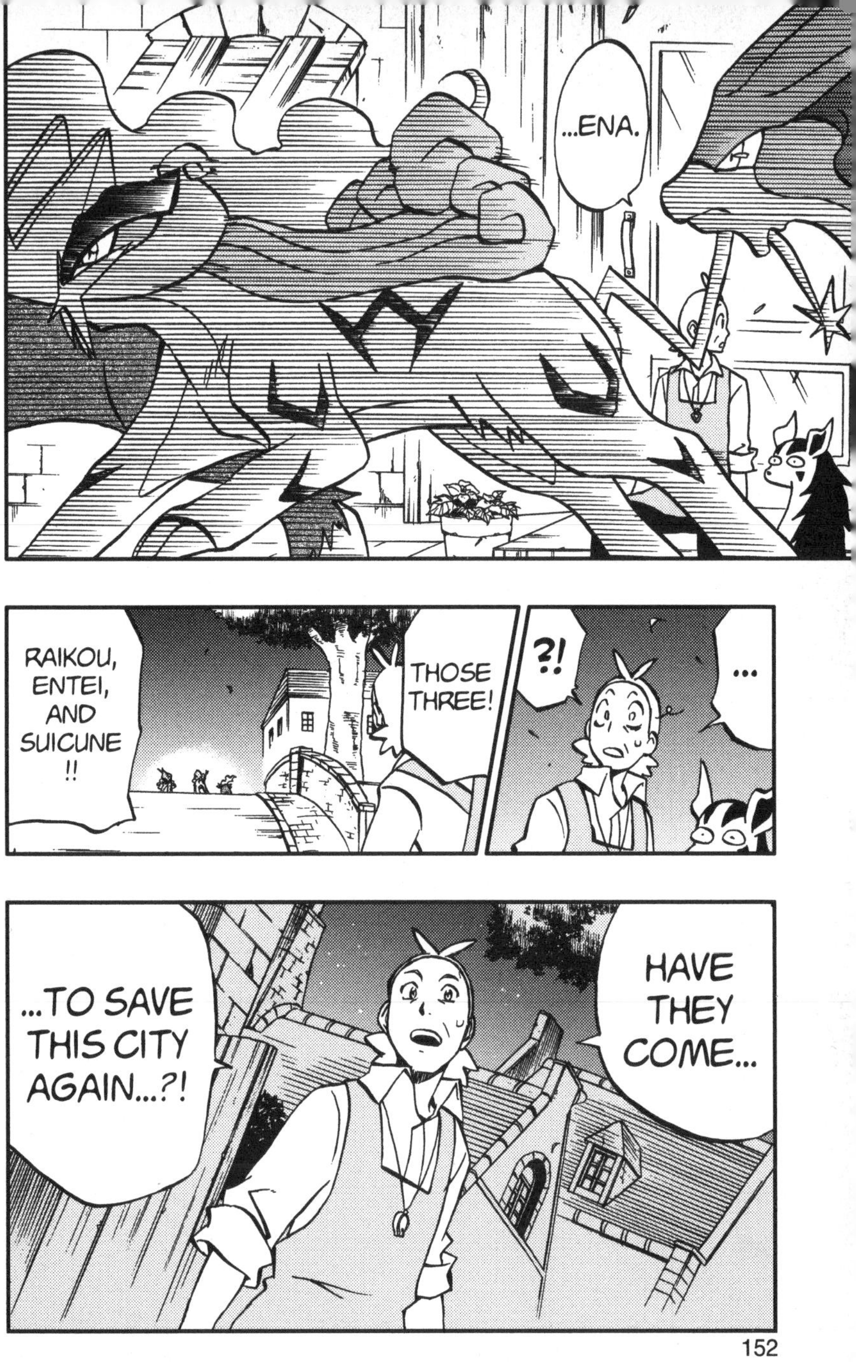
...ENA.
...
?!
THOSE THREE!
RAIKOU, ENTEI, AND SUICUNE !!
HAVE THEY COME...
...TO SAVE THIS CITY AGAIN...?!

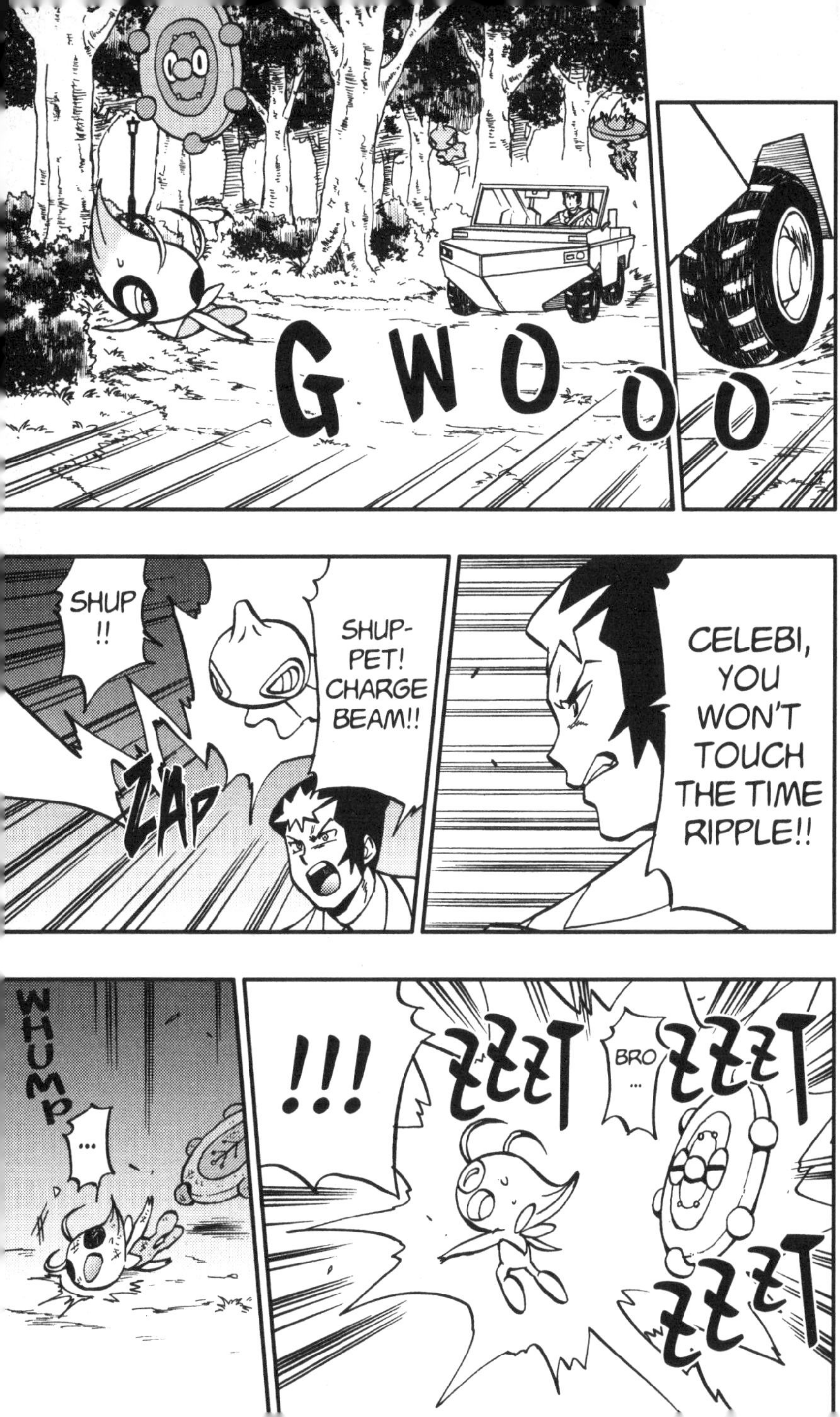
GWOOOO
CELEBI, YOU WON'T TOUCH THE TIME RIPPLE!!
SHUP-PET! CHARGE BEAM!!
SHUP !!
ZAP
ZZZT
BRO ...
ZZZT
!!!
ZZZT
WHUMP
...

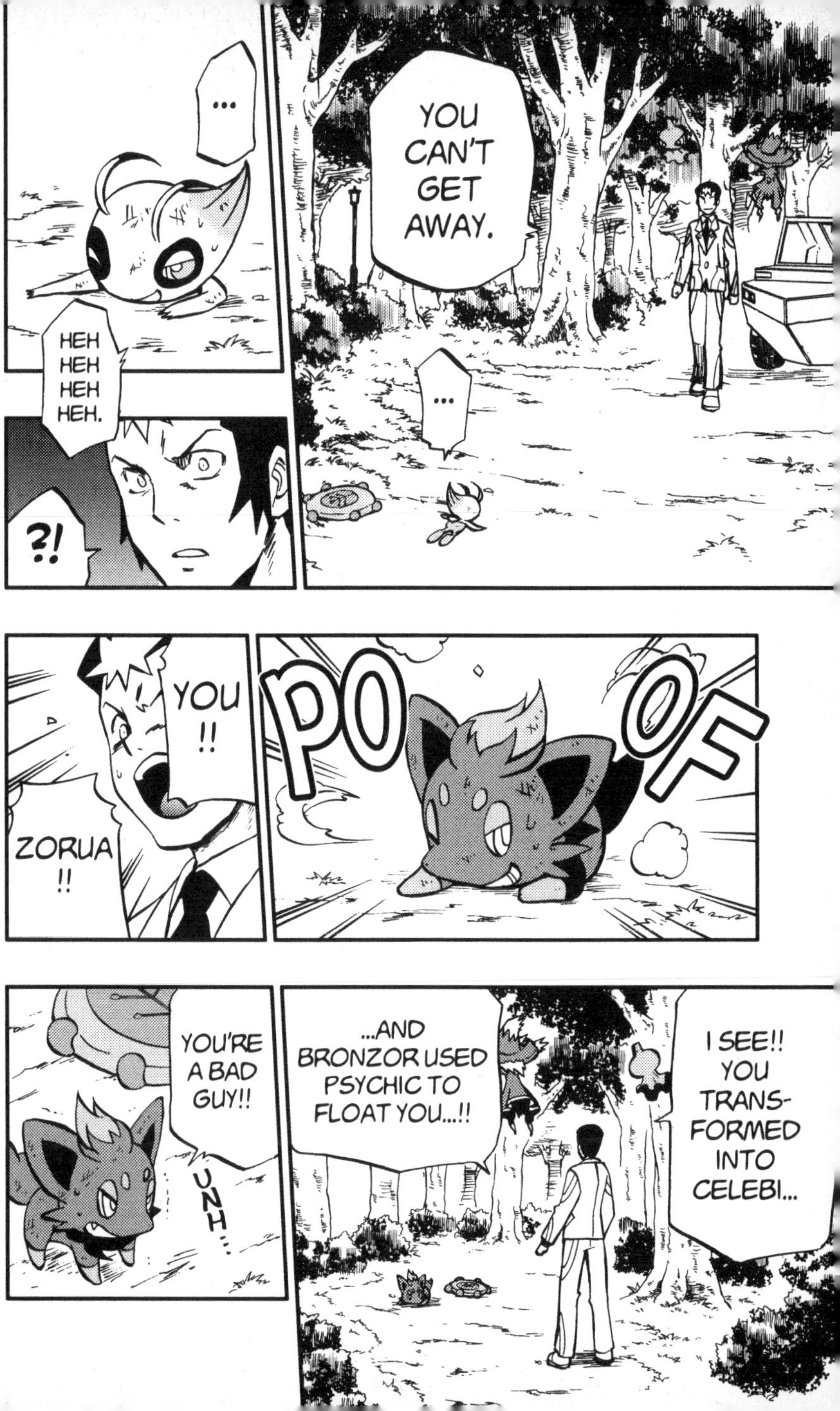
YOU CAN'T GET AWAY.
...
...
HEH HEH HEH HEH.
?!
POOF
YOU !!
ZORUA !!
I SEE!! YOU TRANS-FORMED INTO CELEBI...
...AND BRONZOR USED PSYCHIC TO FLOAT YOU...!!
YOU'RE A BAD GUY!!
UNH...

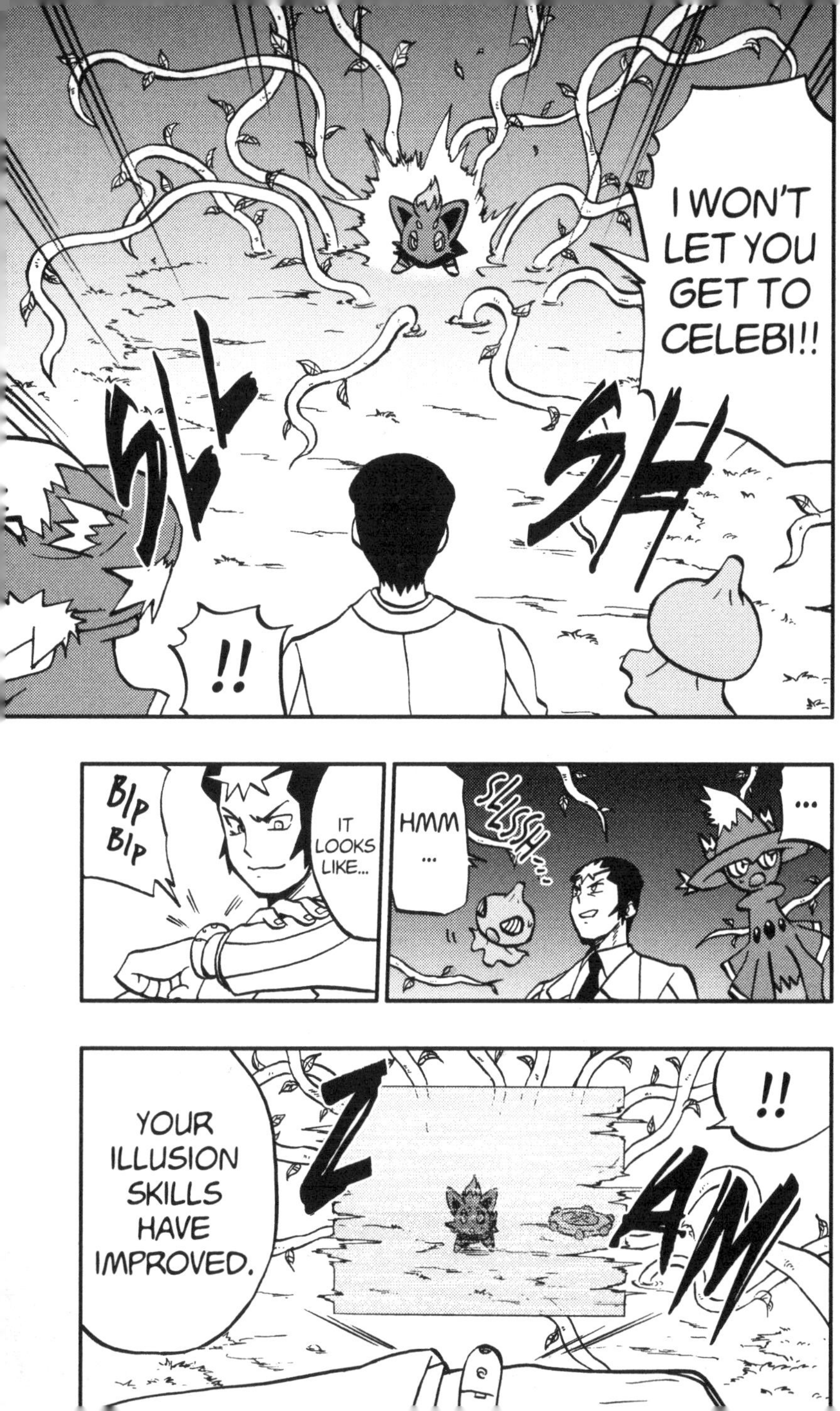
I WON'T LET YOU GET TO CELEBI!!
!!
HMM ...
SLISSSH...
...
IT LOOKS LIKE...
BIP BIP
!!
ZAM
YOUR ILLUSION SKILLS HAVE IMPROVED.

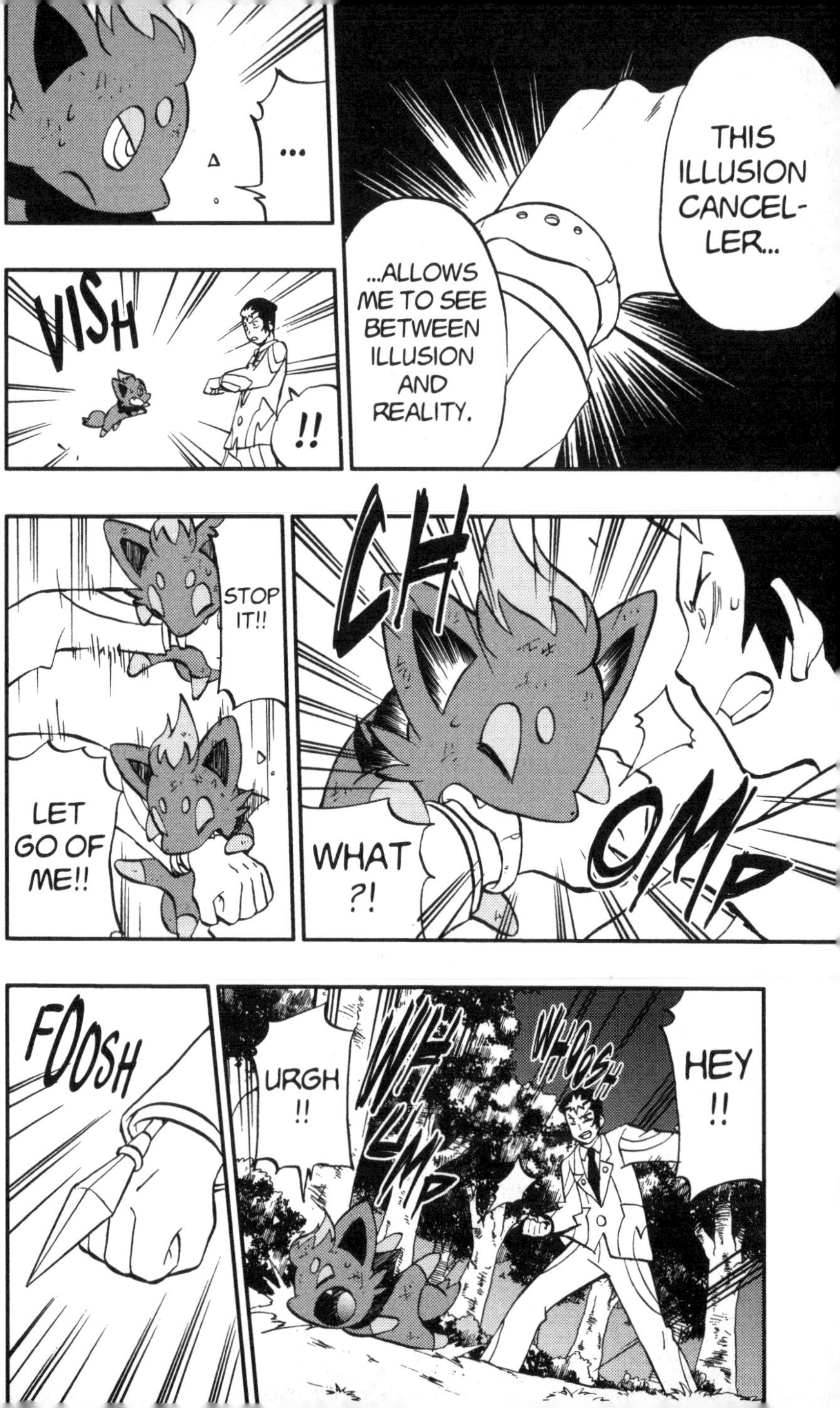
THIS ILLUSION CANCELLER...
...ALLOWS ME TO SEE BETWEEN ILLUSION AND REALITY.
...
VISH
!!
CHOMP
WHAT ?!
STOP IT!!
LET GO OF ME!!
HEY !!
WHOOSH
WHUMP
URGH !!
FOOSH

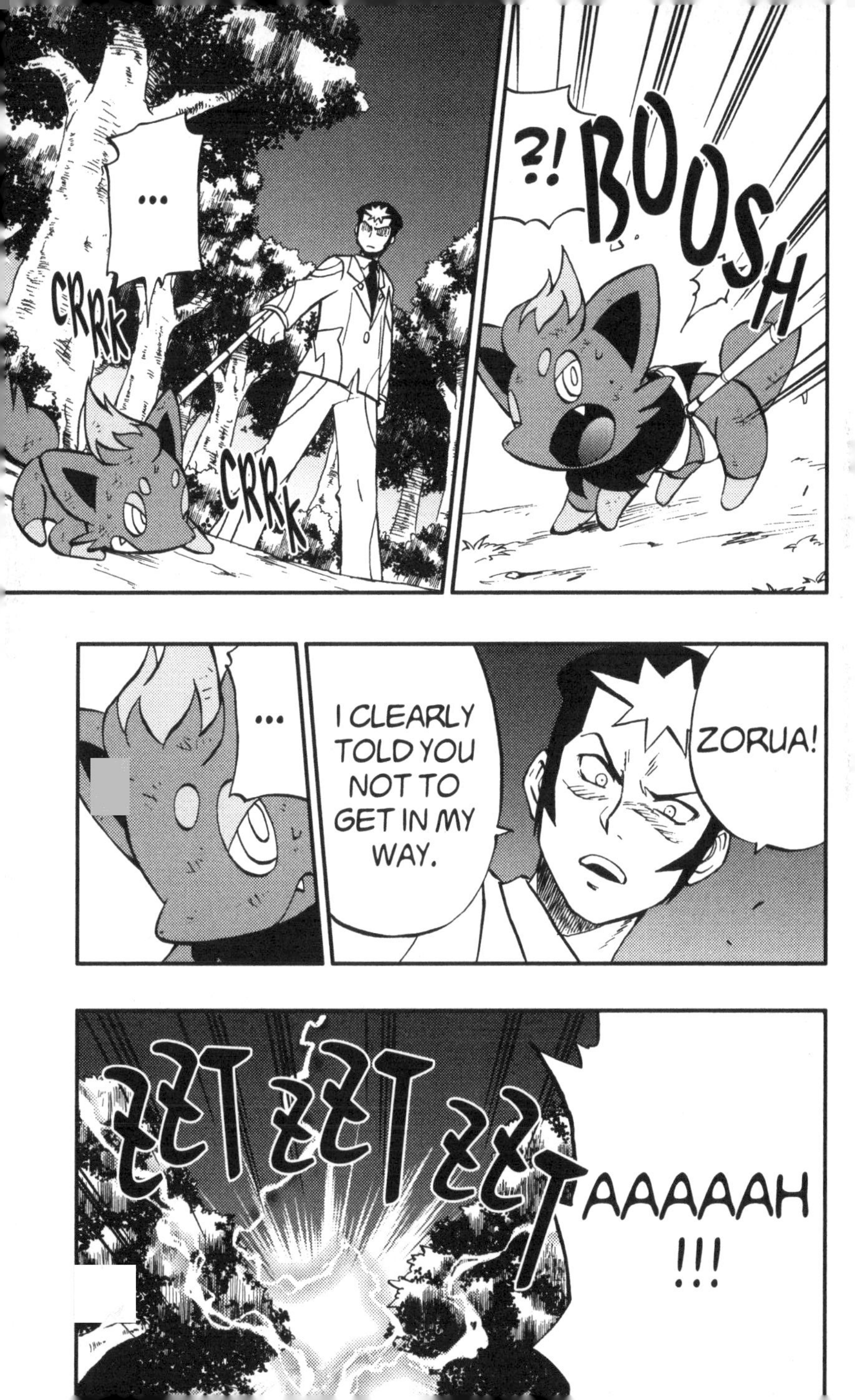
?!
BOOSH
...
CRRK
CRRK
ZORUA!
I CLEARLY TOLD YOU NOT TO GET IN MY WAY.
...
ZZT ZZT ZZT
TAAAAAH
!!!

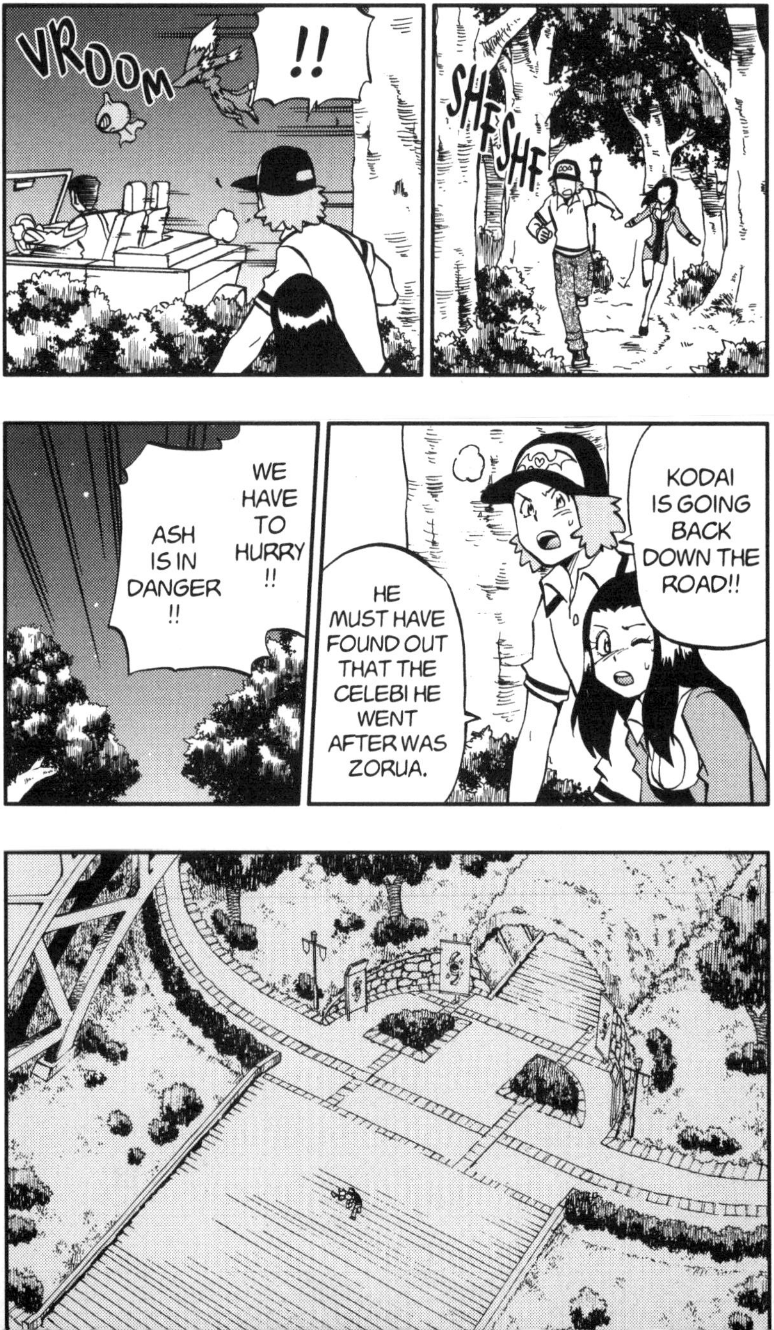
SHFSHF
VROOM
!!
KODAI IS GOING BACK DOWN THE ROAD!!
HE MUST HAVE FOUND OUT THAT THE CELEBI HE WENT AFTER WAS ZORUA.
WE HAVE TO HURRY!!
ASH IS IN DANGER!!

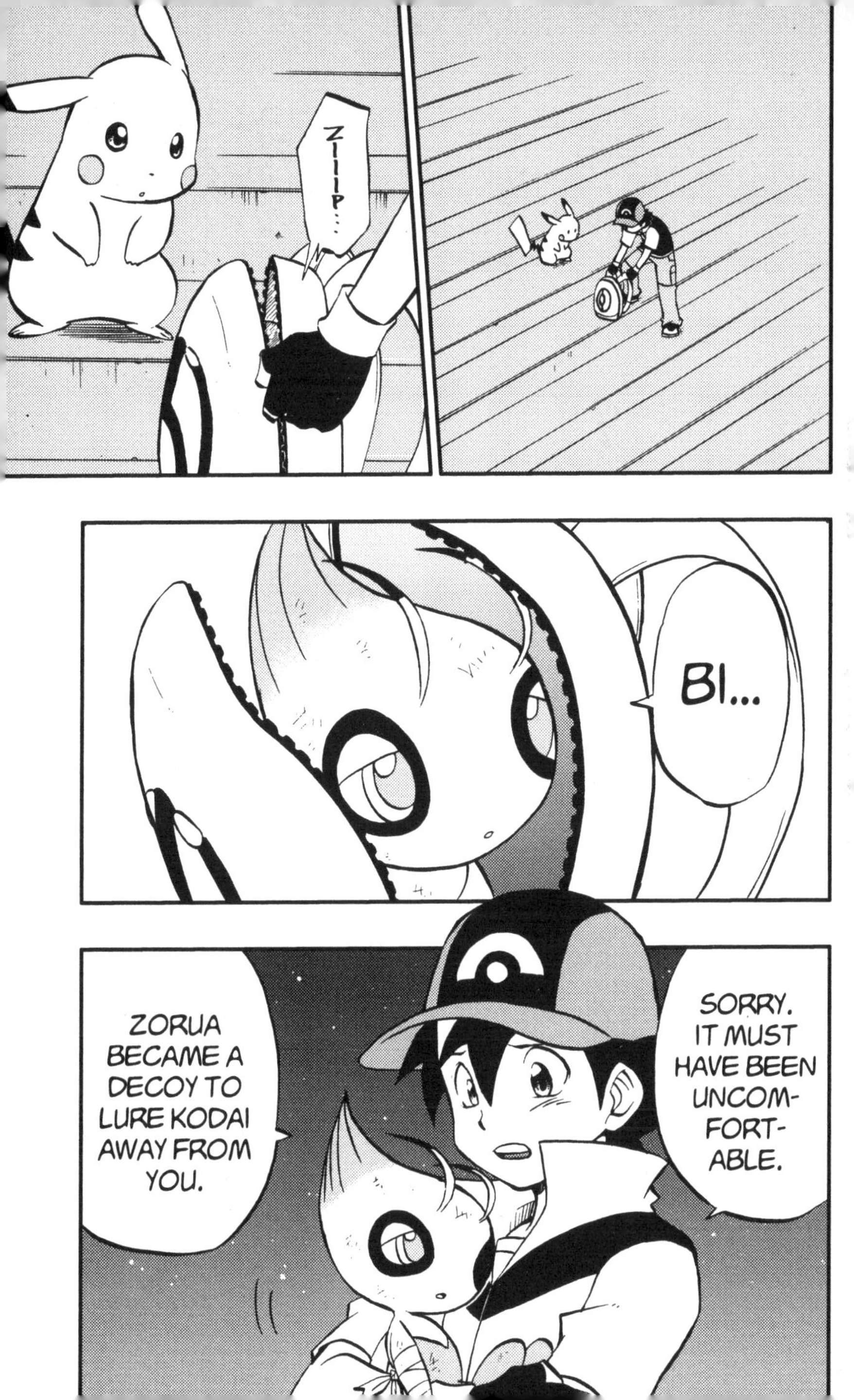
ZIIIP...
BI...
SORRY. IT MUST HAVE BEEN UNCOM- FORT- ABLE.
ZORUA BECAME A DECOY TO LURE KODAI AWAY FROM YOU.

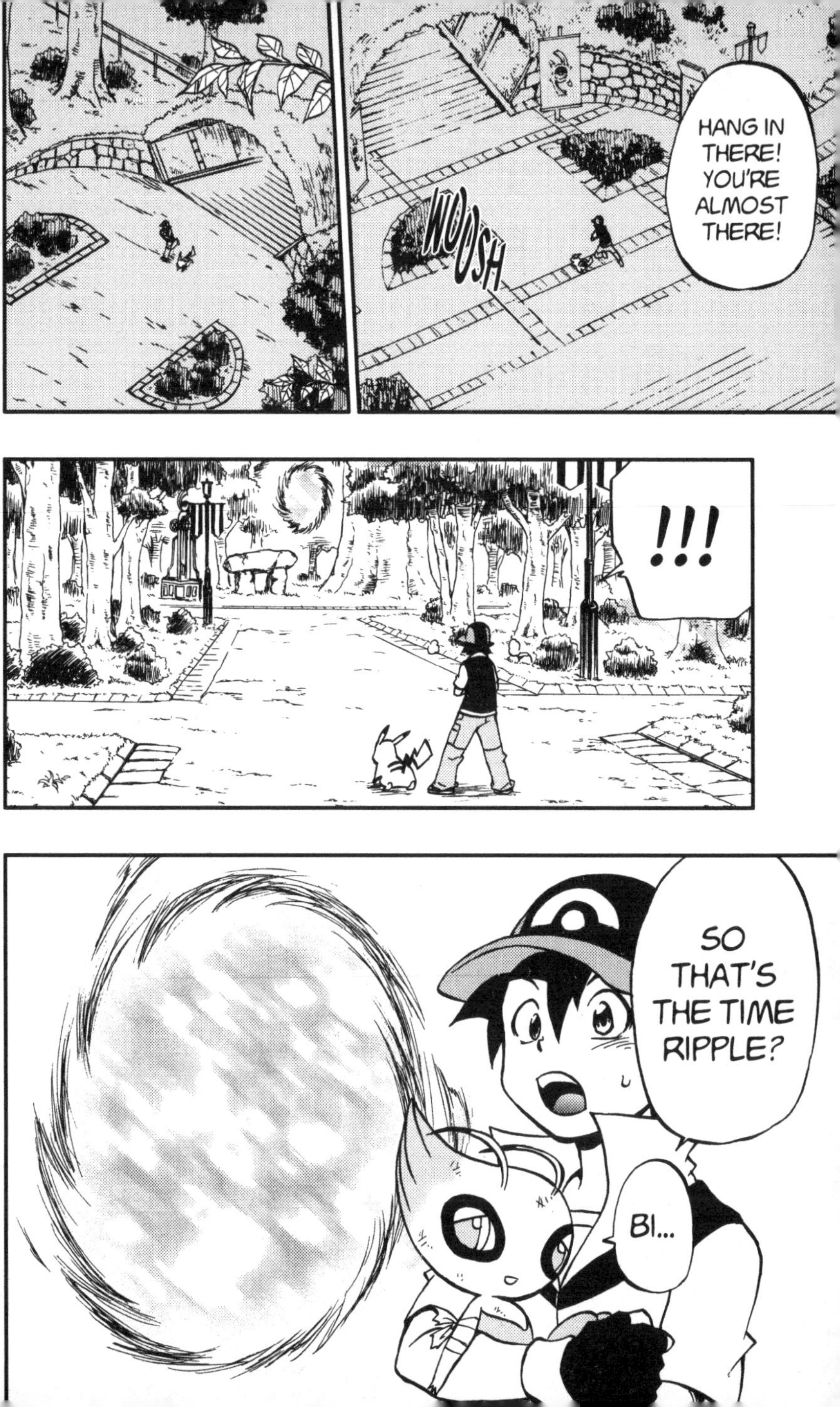
HANG IN THERE! YOU'RE ALMOST THERE!
WOOSH
!!!
SO THAT'S THE TIME RIPPLE?
BI...

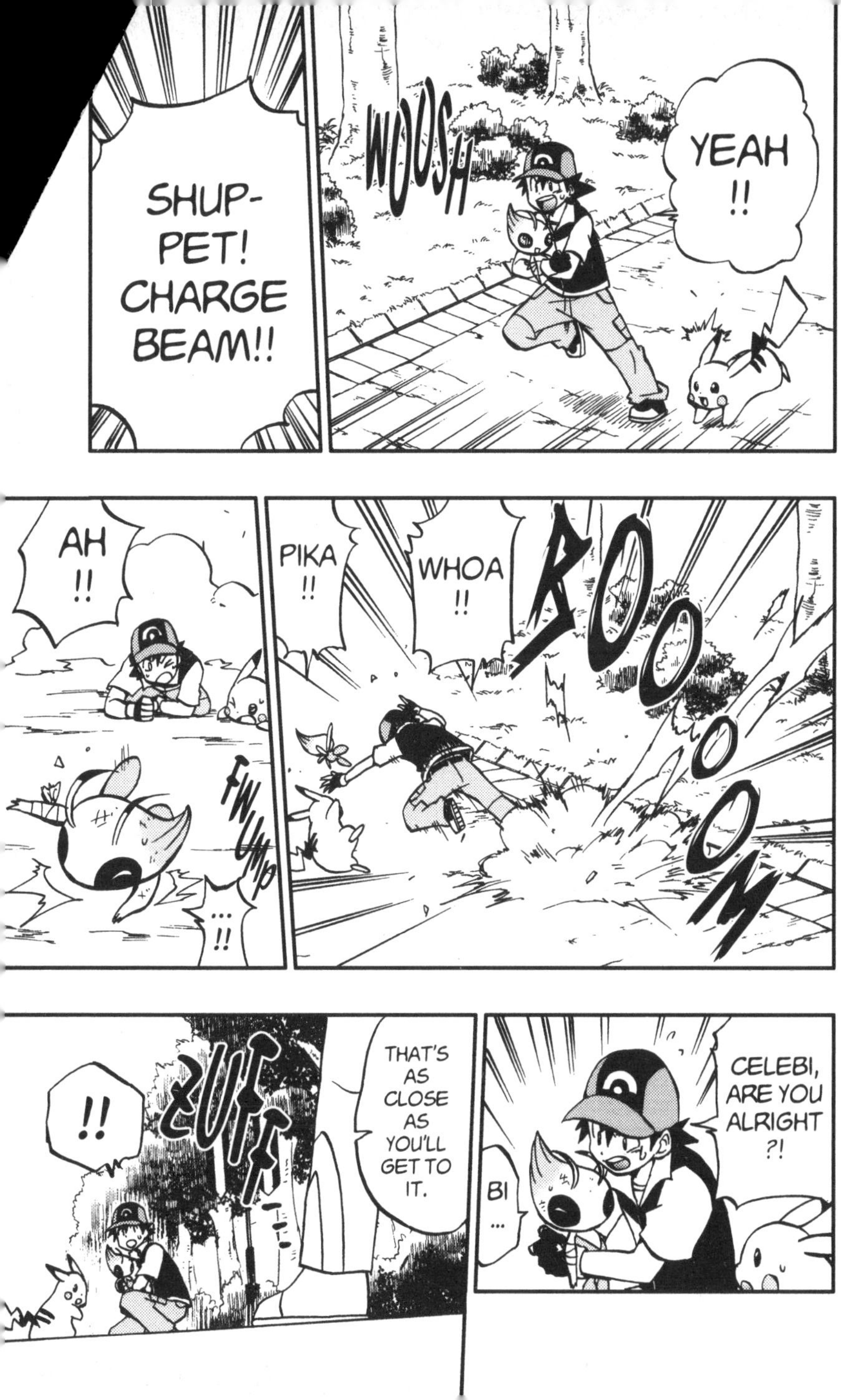
WOOSH
YEAH!!
SHUP-PET! CHARGE BEAM!!
BOOOOOM
WHOA!!
PIKA!!
AH!!
FWUMP
...!!
CELEBI, ARE YOU ALRIGHT?!
BI...
THAT'S AS CLOSE AS YOU'LL GET TO IT.
ZUFF
!!

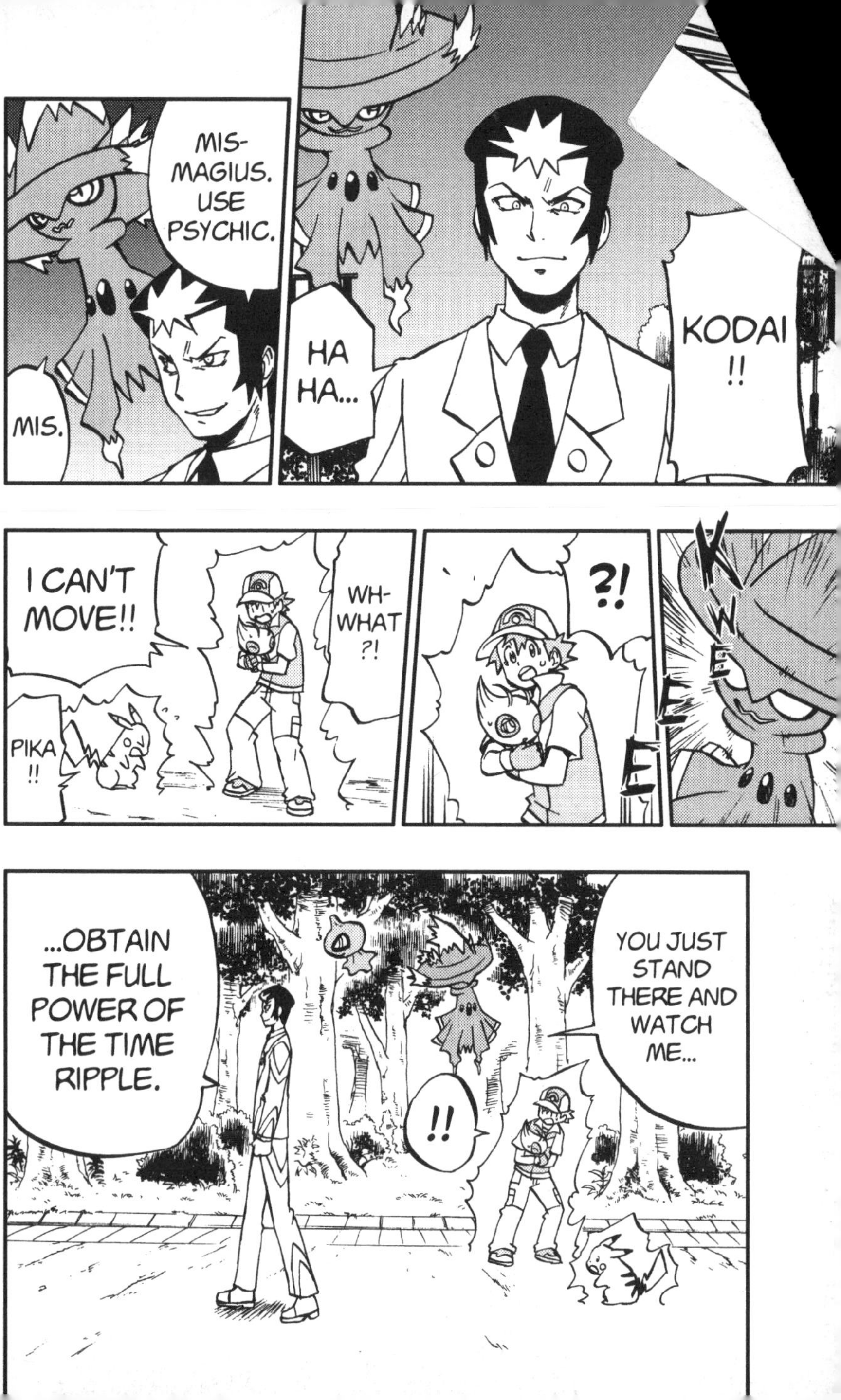
KODAI !!
HA HA...
MIS-MAGIUS. USE PSYCHIC.
MIS.
KWEEEE
?!
WH-WHAT ?!
I CAN'T MOVE!!
PIKA !!
YOU JUST STAND THERE AND WATCH ME...
!!
...OBTAIN THE FULL POWER OF THE TIME RIPPLE.

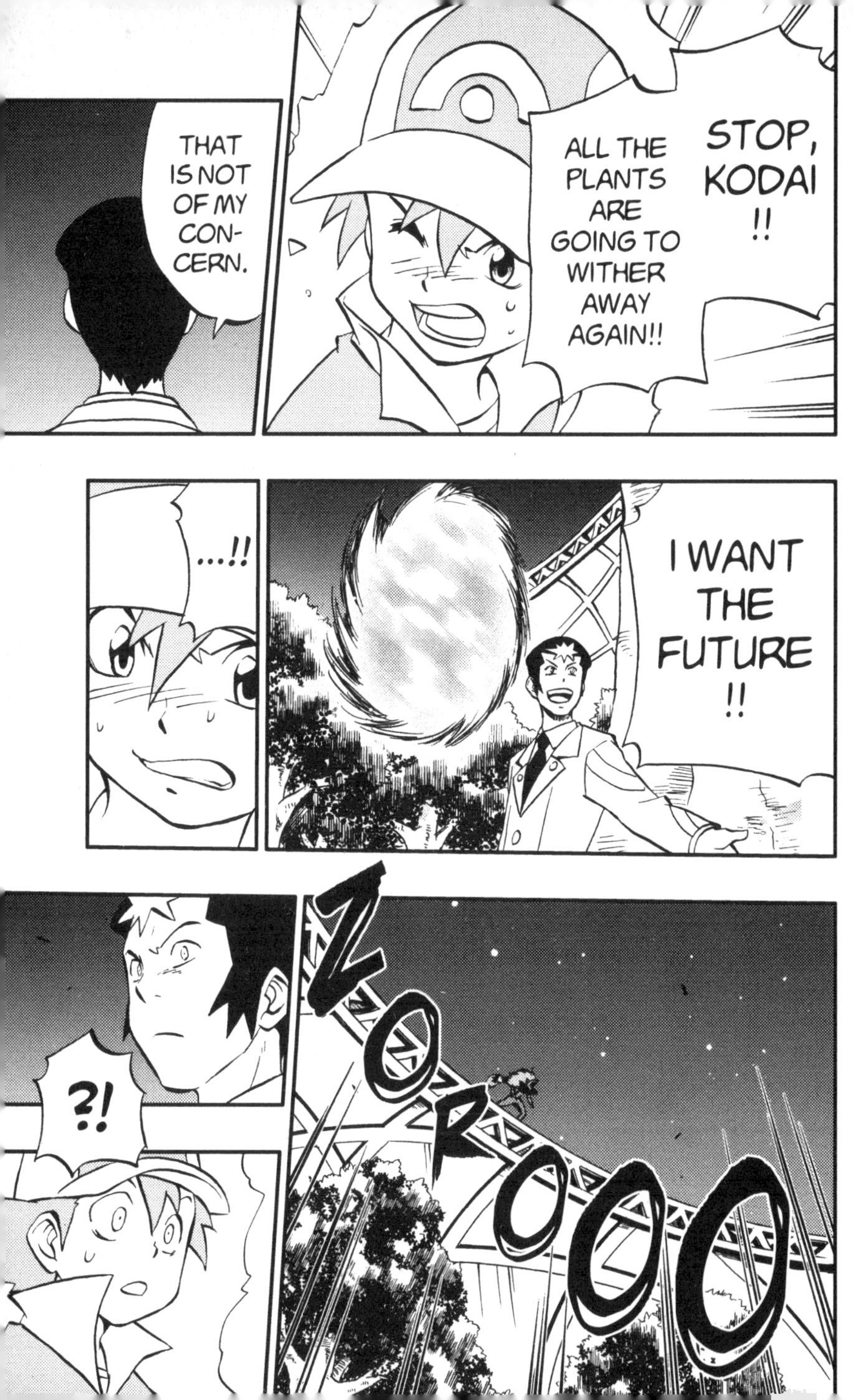
STOP, KODAI!!
ALL THE PLANTS ARE GOING TO WITHER AWAY AGAIN!!
THAT IS NOT OF MY CONCERN.
I WANT THE FUTURE!!
...!!
ZOROOOO
?!

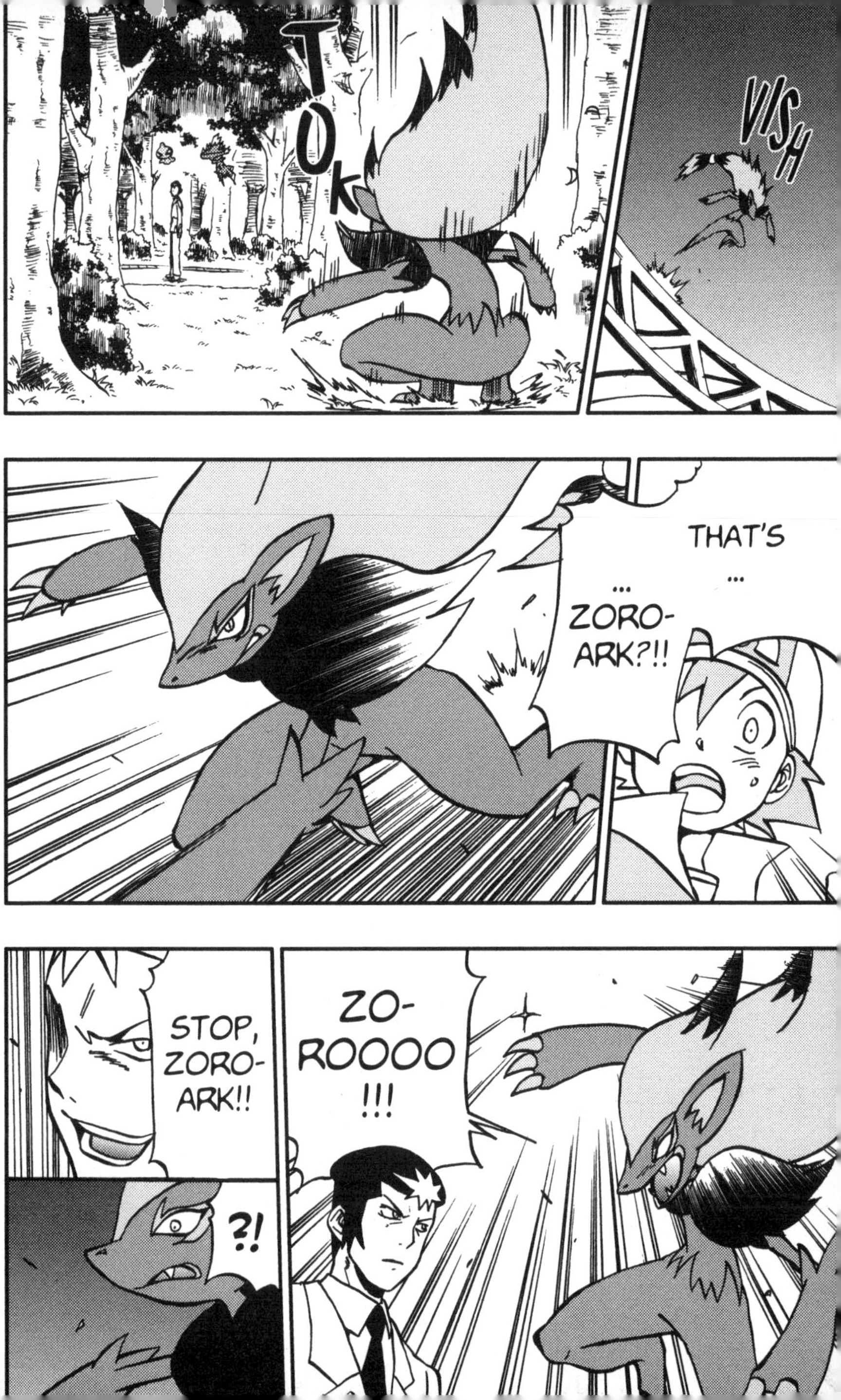
VISH
TOK
THAT'S ...
... ZORO-ARK?!!
ZO-ROOOOO !!!
STOP, ZORO-ARK!!
?!

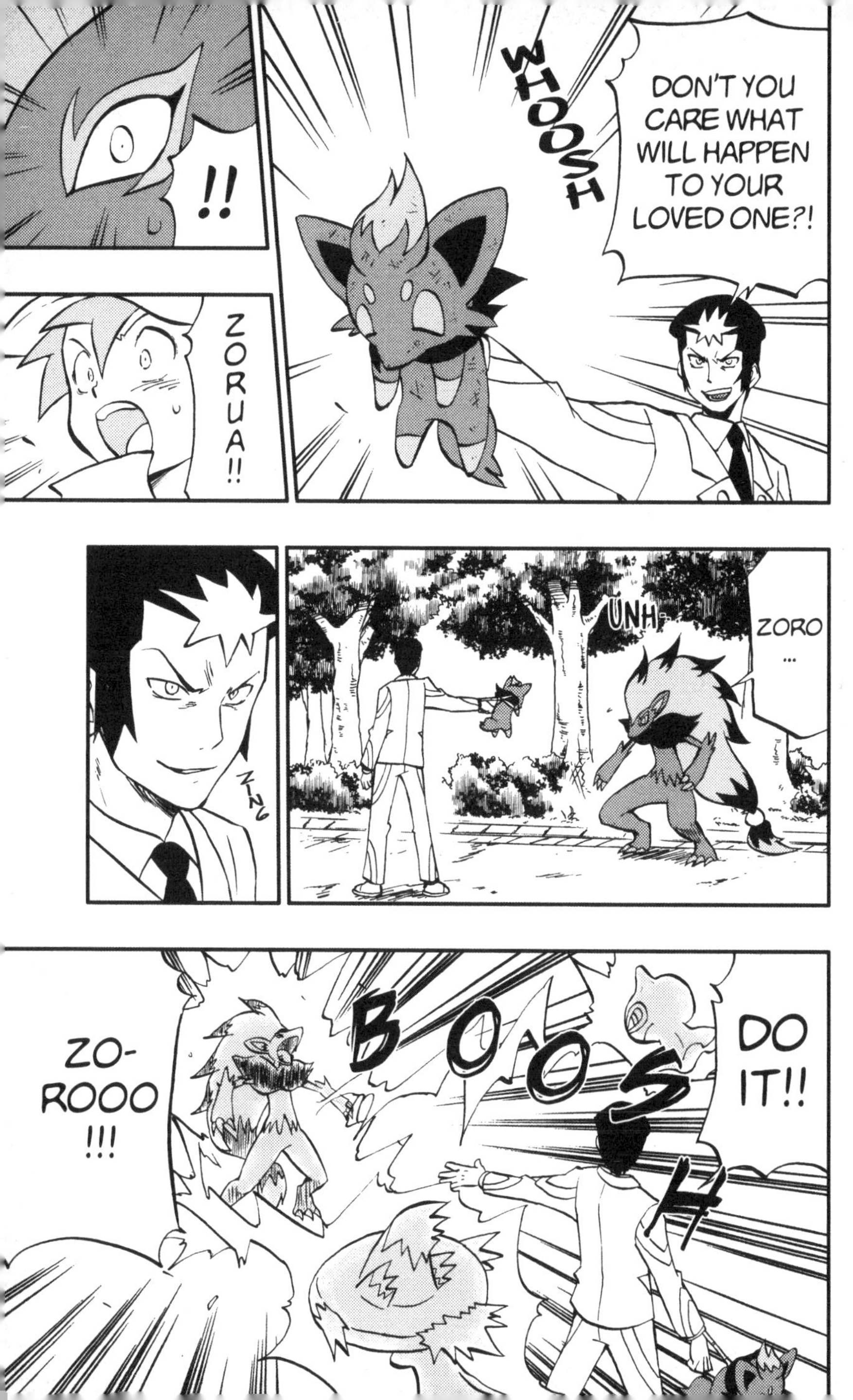
DON'T YOU CARE WHAT WILL HAPPEN TO YOUR LOVED ONE?!
WHOOSH
!!
ZORUA!!
ZORO ...
UNH-
ZING
DO IT!!
BOOOSH
ZO-ROOO!!!

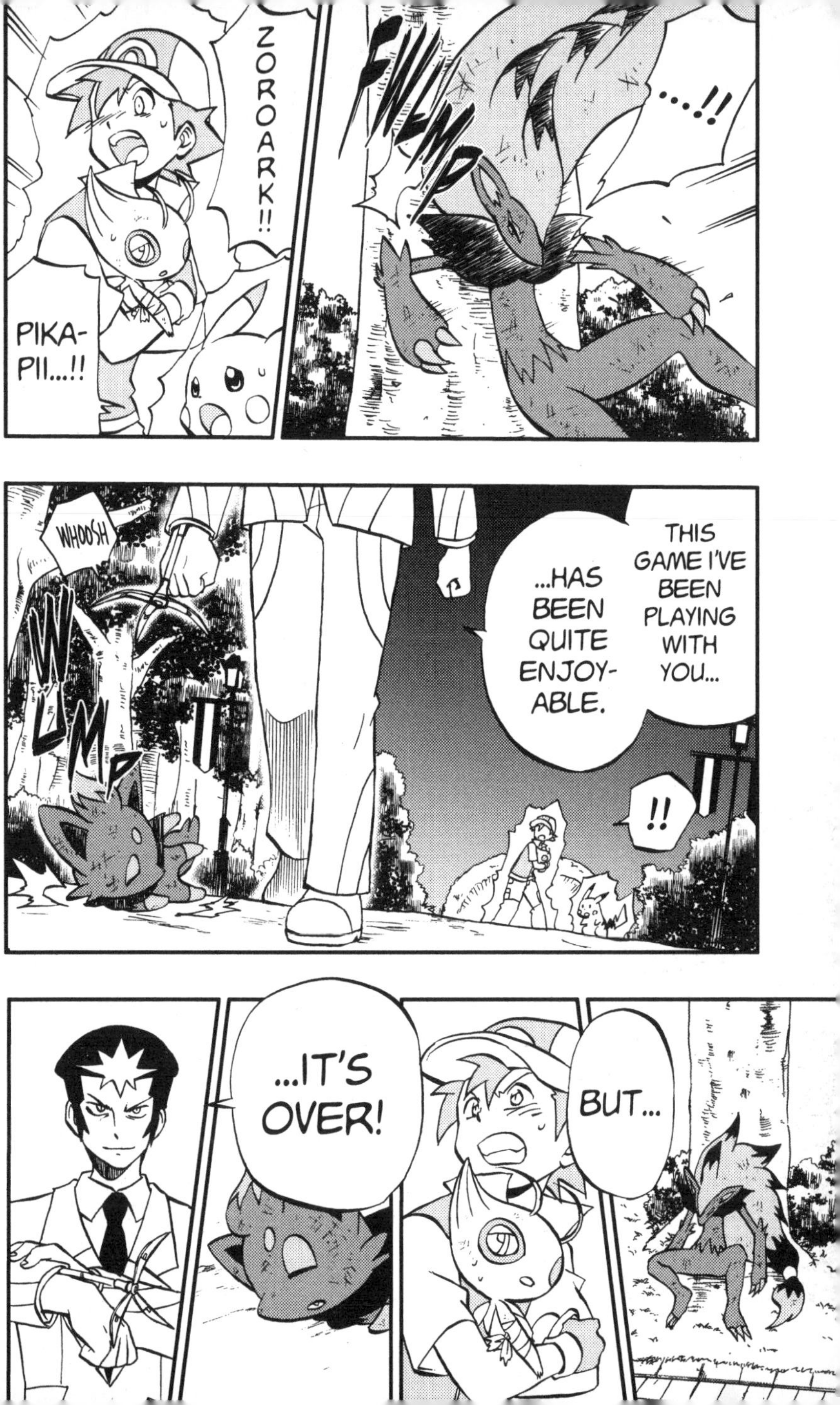
...!!
FWUMP
ZOROARK!!
PIKA-PII...!!
THIS GAME I'VE BEEN PLAYING WITH YOU...
...HAS BEEN QUITE ENJOY-ABLE.
WHOOSH
!!
WUMP
BUT...
...IT'S OVER!

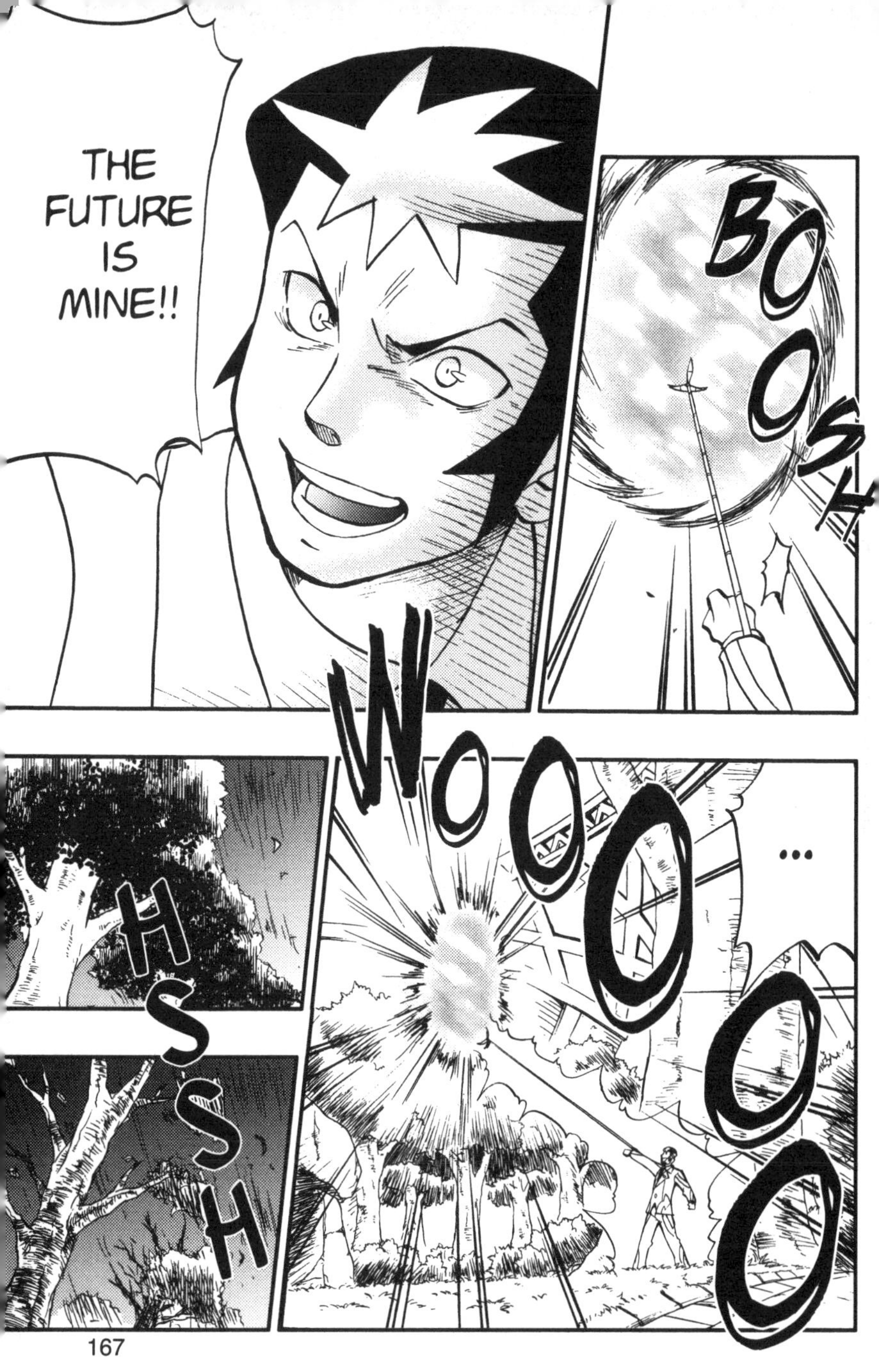
BOOSH
THE FUTURE IS MINE!!
WOOOOOOO
...
HSSH

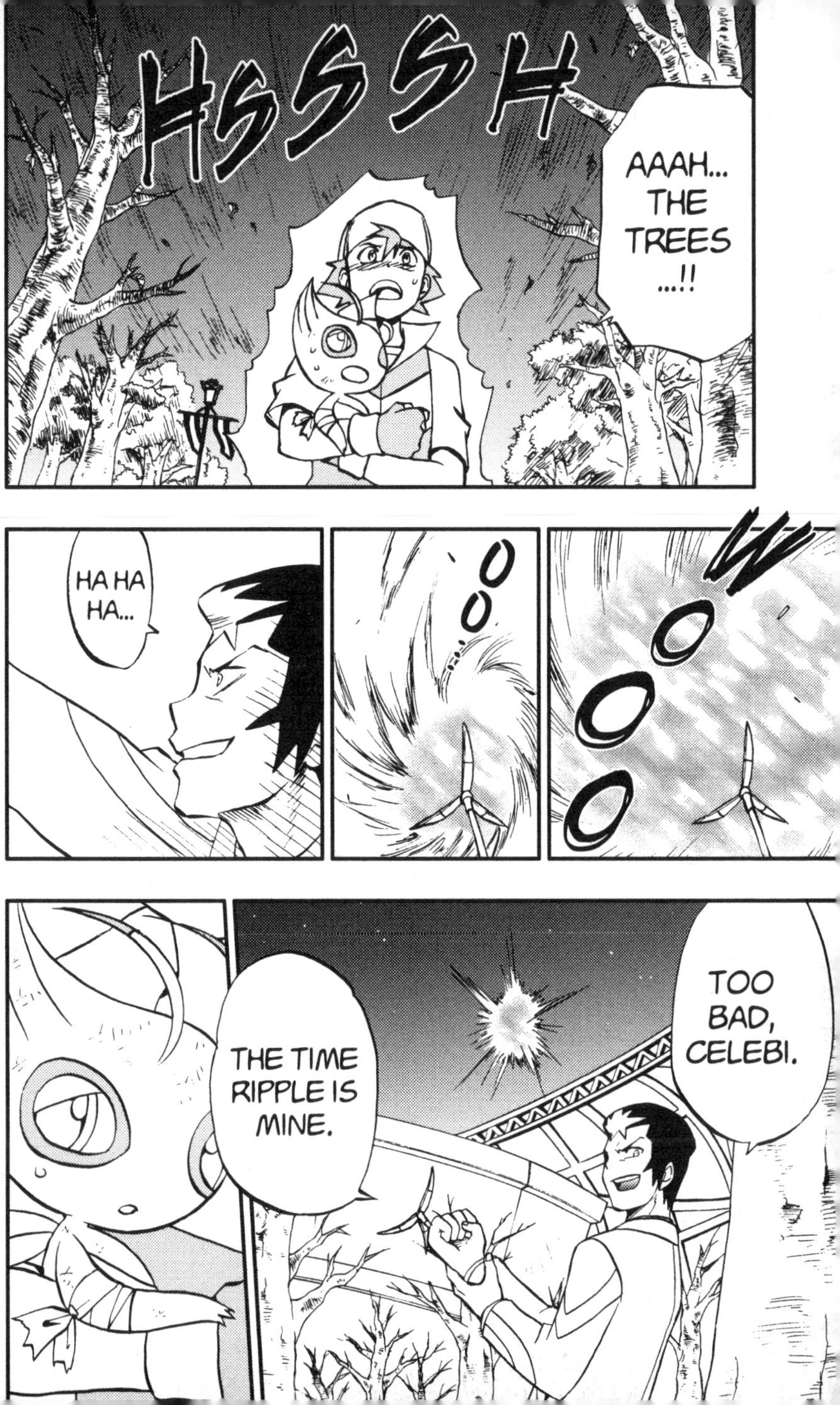
HSSSH
AAAH... THE TREES ...!!
WOOO
OOO...
HA HA HA...
TOO BAD, CELEBI.
THE TIME RIPPLE IS MINE.

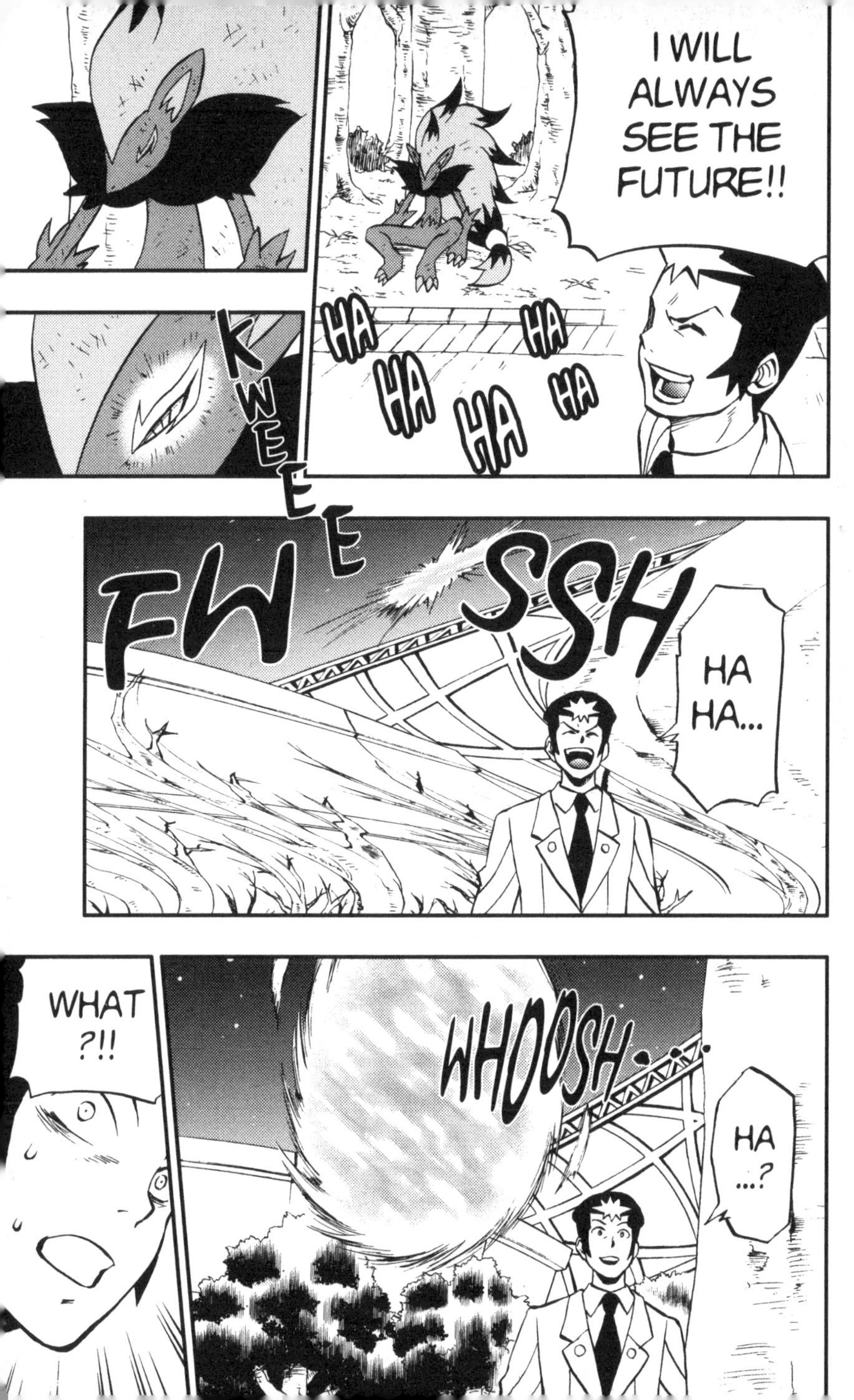
I WILL ALWAYS SEE THE FUTURE!!
HA HA HA HA HA
KWEEEE
FWSSH
HA HA...
HA ...?
WHOOSH...
WHAT ?!!

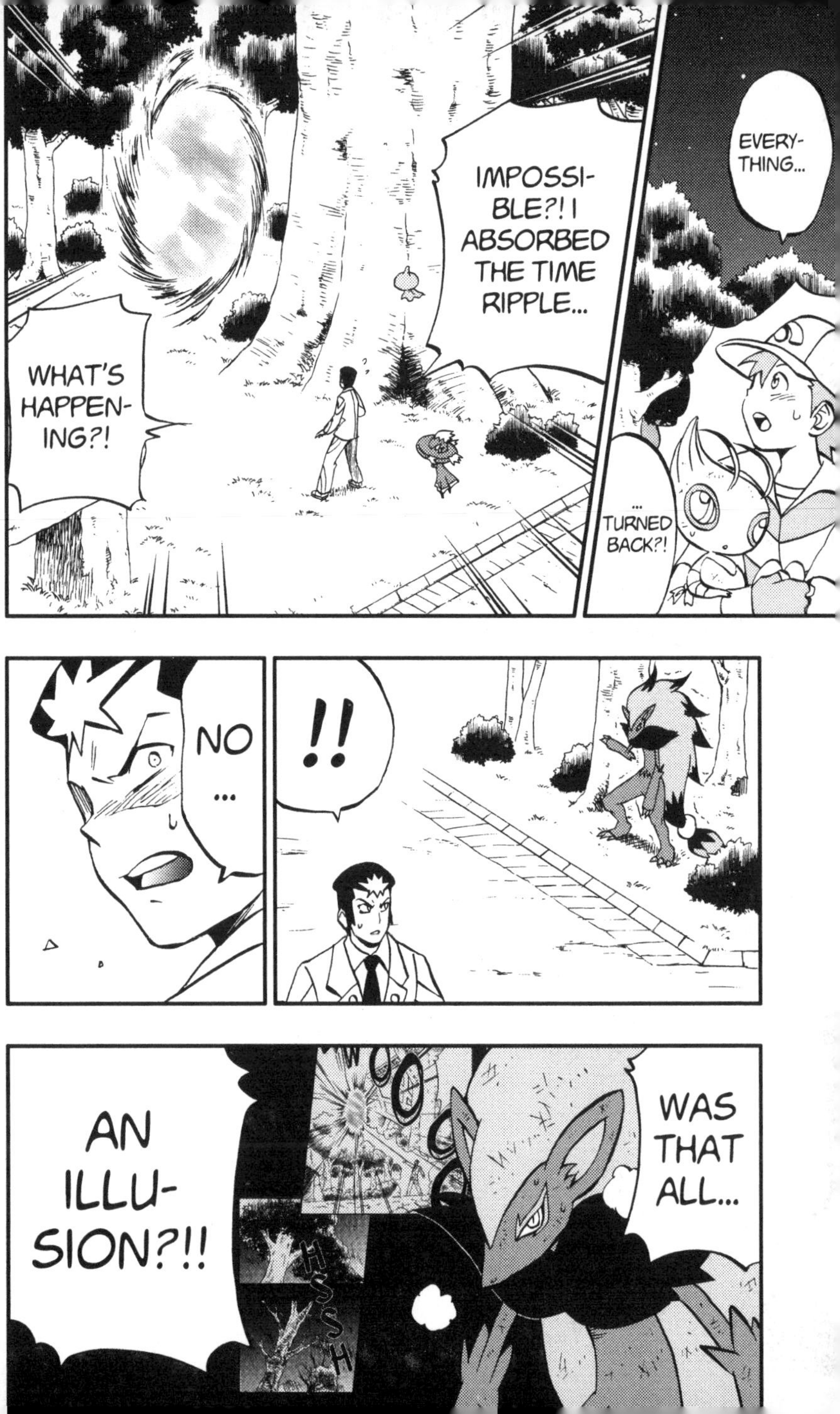
EVERY-THING...
...TURNED BACK?!
IMPOSSI-BLE?! I ABSORBED THE TIME RIPPLE...
WHAT'S HAPPEN-ING?!
!!
NO ...
WAS THAT ALL...
AN ILLU-SION?!!
HSSH

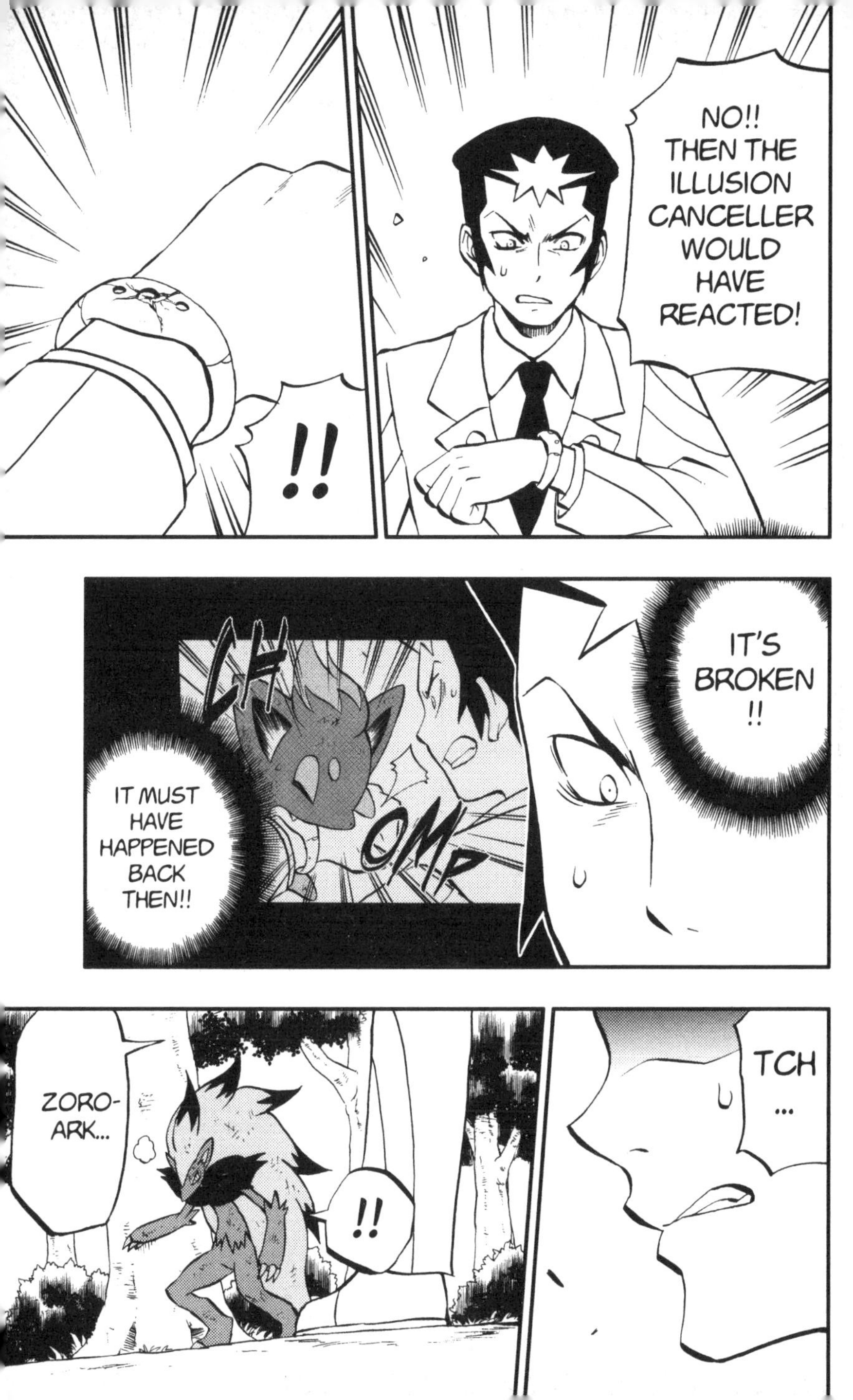
NO!! THEN THE ILLUSION CANCELLER WOULD HAVE REACTED!
!!
IT'S BROKEN !!
CHOMP
IT MUST HAVE HAPPENED BACK THEN!!
TCH ...
ZORO-ARK...
!!

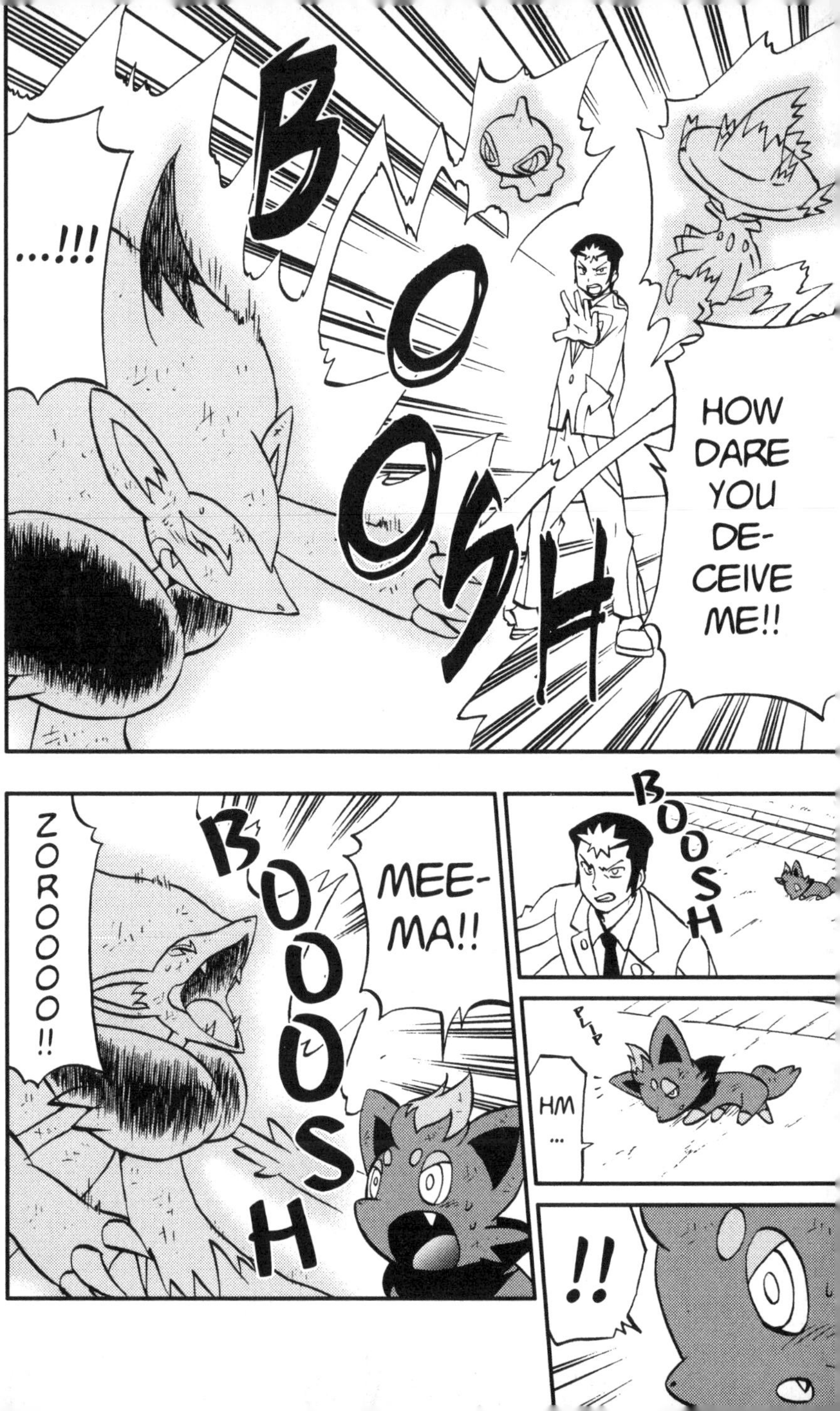
HOW DARE YOU DE- CEIVE ME!!
BOOOSH
...!!!
BOOSH
PLIP
HM ...
!!
MEE- MA!!
BOOOSH
ZOROOOOO!!

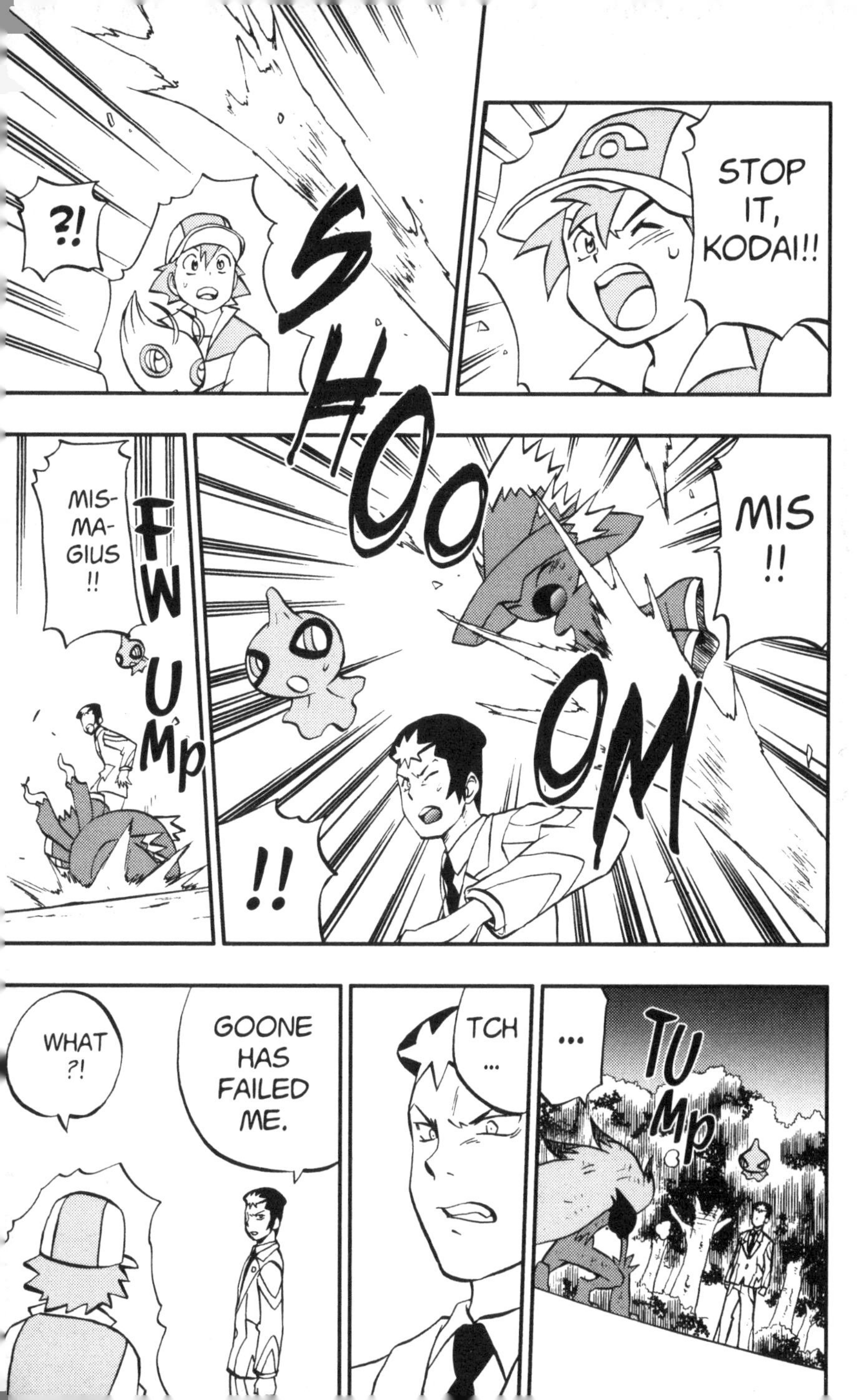
STOP IT, KODAI!!
?!
SHOOOM
MIS !!
!!
MIS-MA-GIUS !!
FWUMP
...
TUMP
TCH ...
GOONE HAS FAILED ME.
WHAT ?!

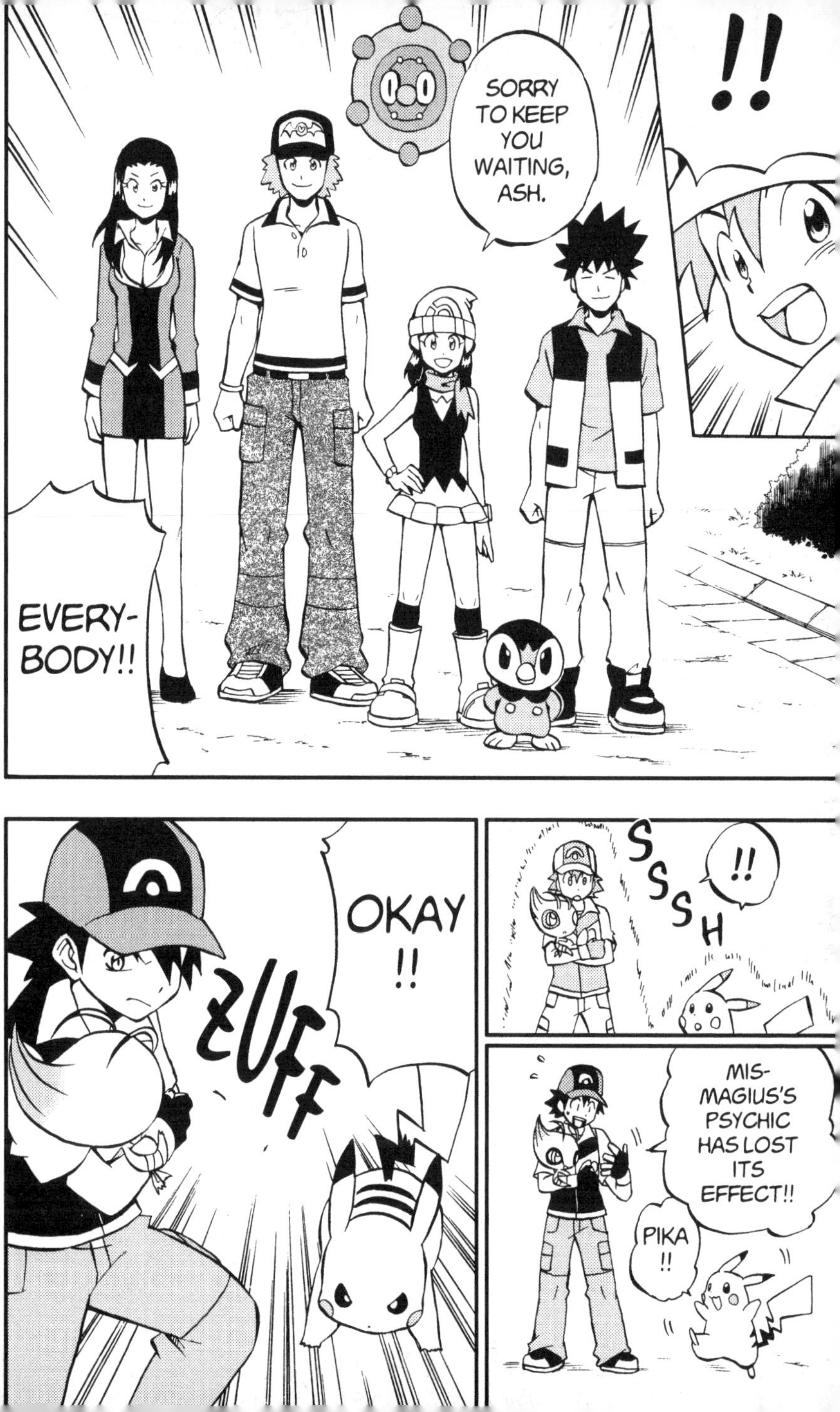
!!
SORRY TO KEEP YOU WAITING, ASH.
EVERY-BODY!!
!!
SSSH
MIS-MAGIUS'S PSYCHIC HAS LOST ITS EFFECT!!
PIKA !!
OKAY !!
ZUFF

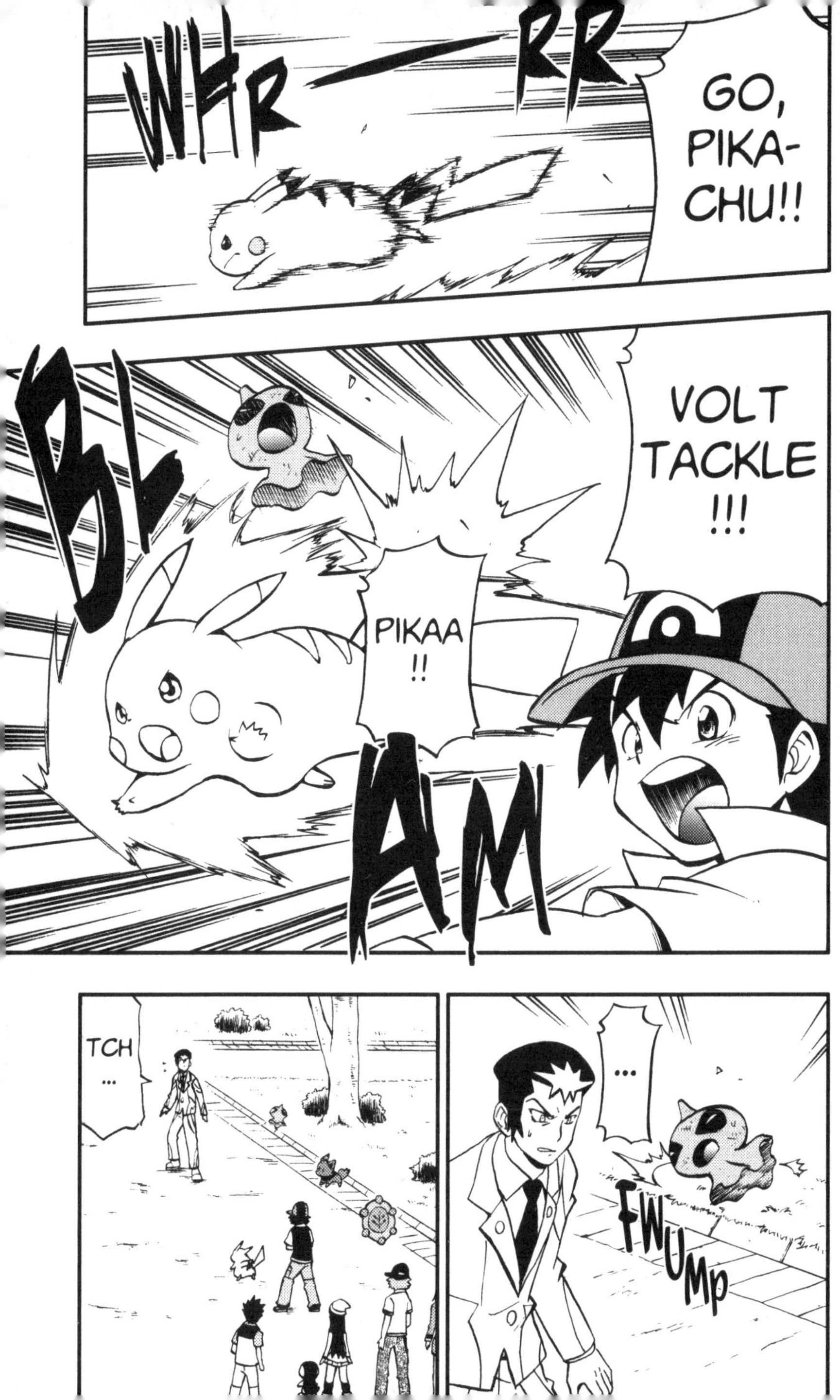
GO, PIKA-CHU!!
WHR—RR
VOLT TACKLE !!!
PIKAA !!
BLAM
...
FWUMP
TCH ...

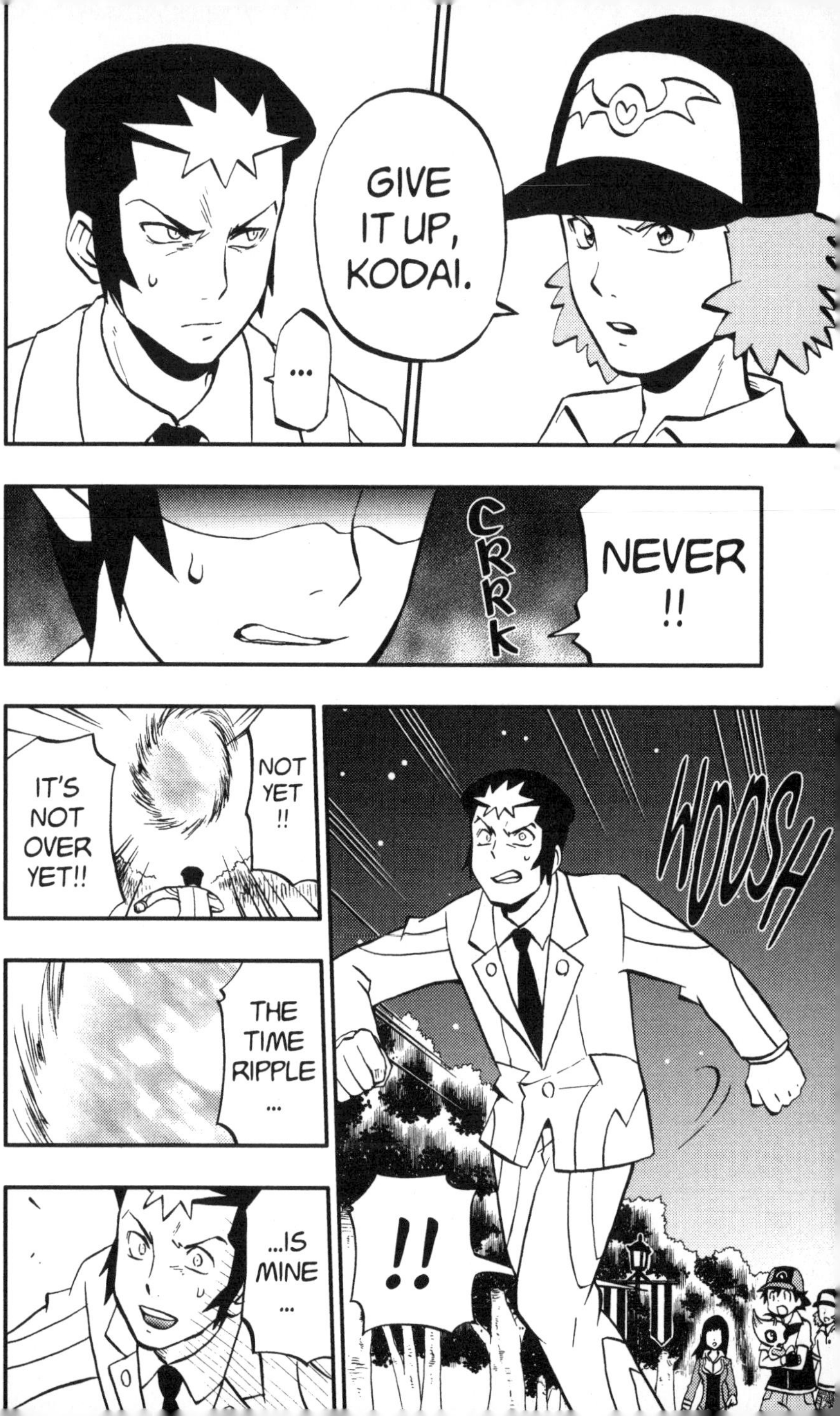
GIVE IT UP, KODAI.
...
NEVER !!
CRRK
WHOOSH
!!
NOT YET !!
IT'S NOT OVER YET!!
THE TIME RIPPLE ...
...IS MINE ...

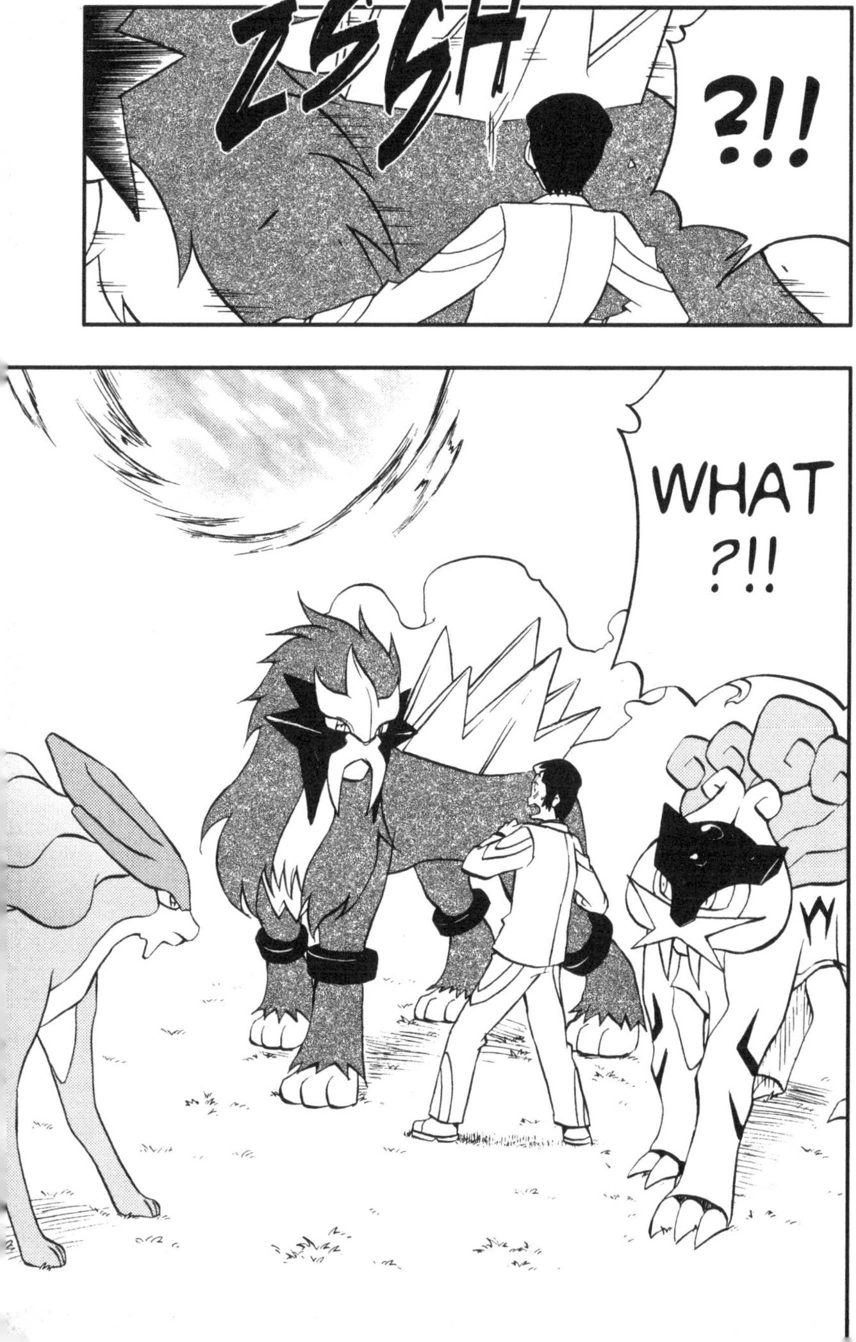
?!!
ZSSH
WHAT ?!!

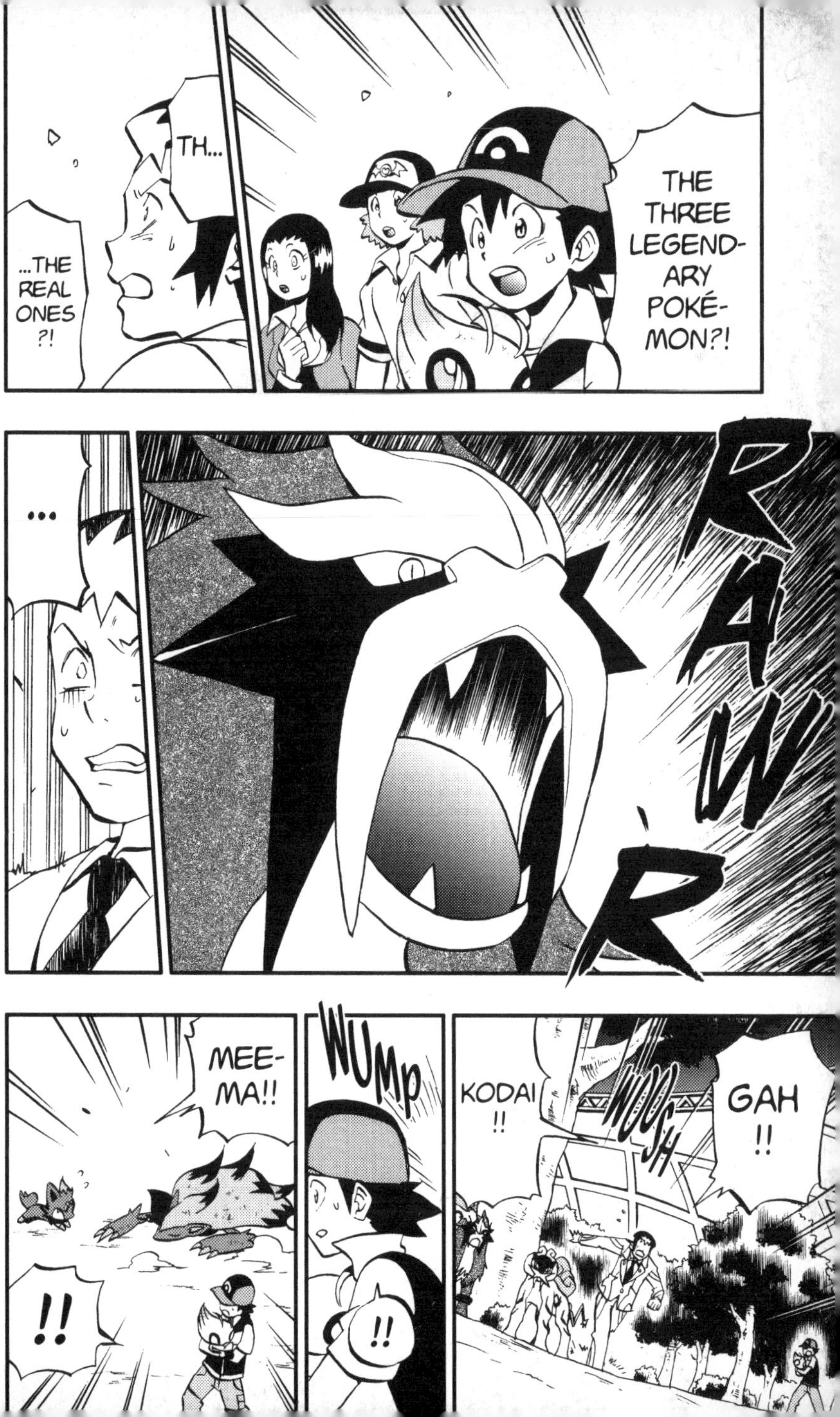
THE THREE LEGEND-ARY POKÉ-MON?!
TH...
...THE REAL ONES ?!
RAWR
...
GAH !!
WOOSH
KODAI !!
WUMP
!!
MEE-MA!!
!!

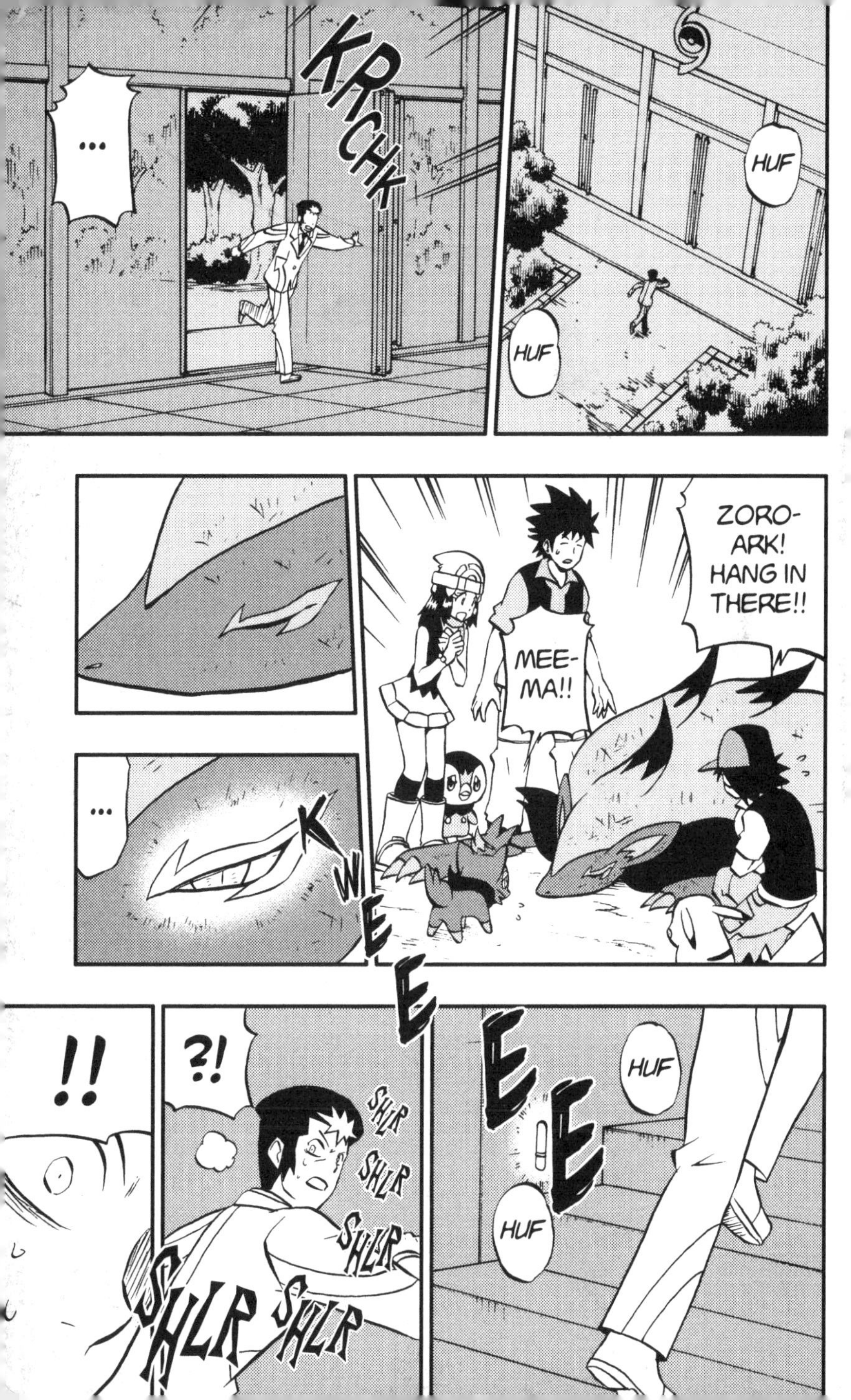
HUF
HUF
KRCHK
...
ZORO-ARK! HANG IN THERE!!
MEE-MA!!
...
KWEEEEEE
HUF
HUF
?!
SHLR SHLR SHLR
SHLR SHLR
!!

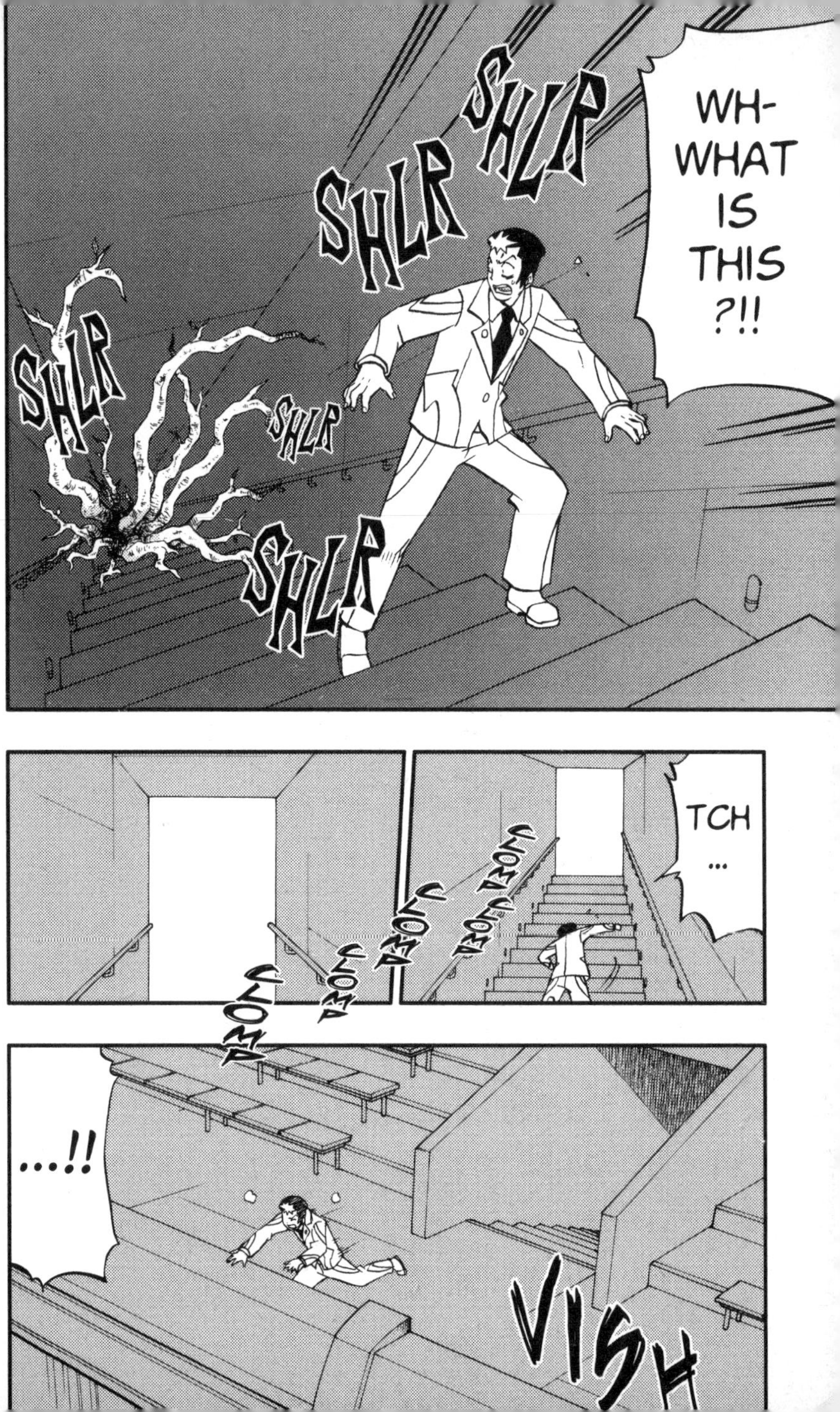
WH-
WHAT
IS
THIS
?!!
SHLR
SHLR
SHLR
SHLR
SHLR
TCH
...
CLOMP CLOMP
CLOMP
CLOMP
CLOMP
CLOMP
...!!
VISH

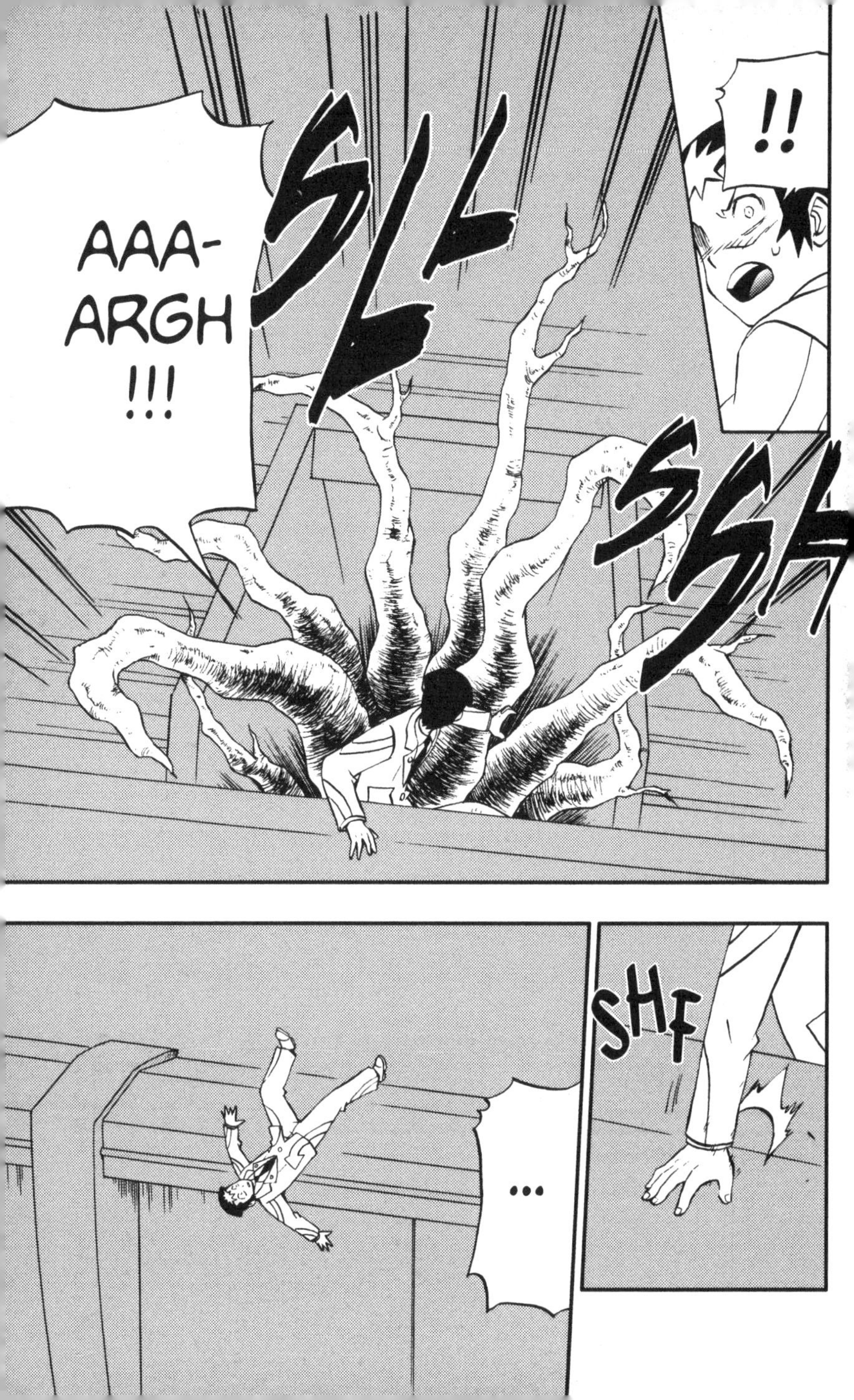
!!
AAA-ARGH!!!
SHF
...

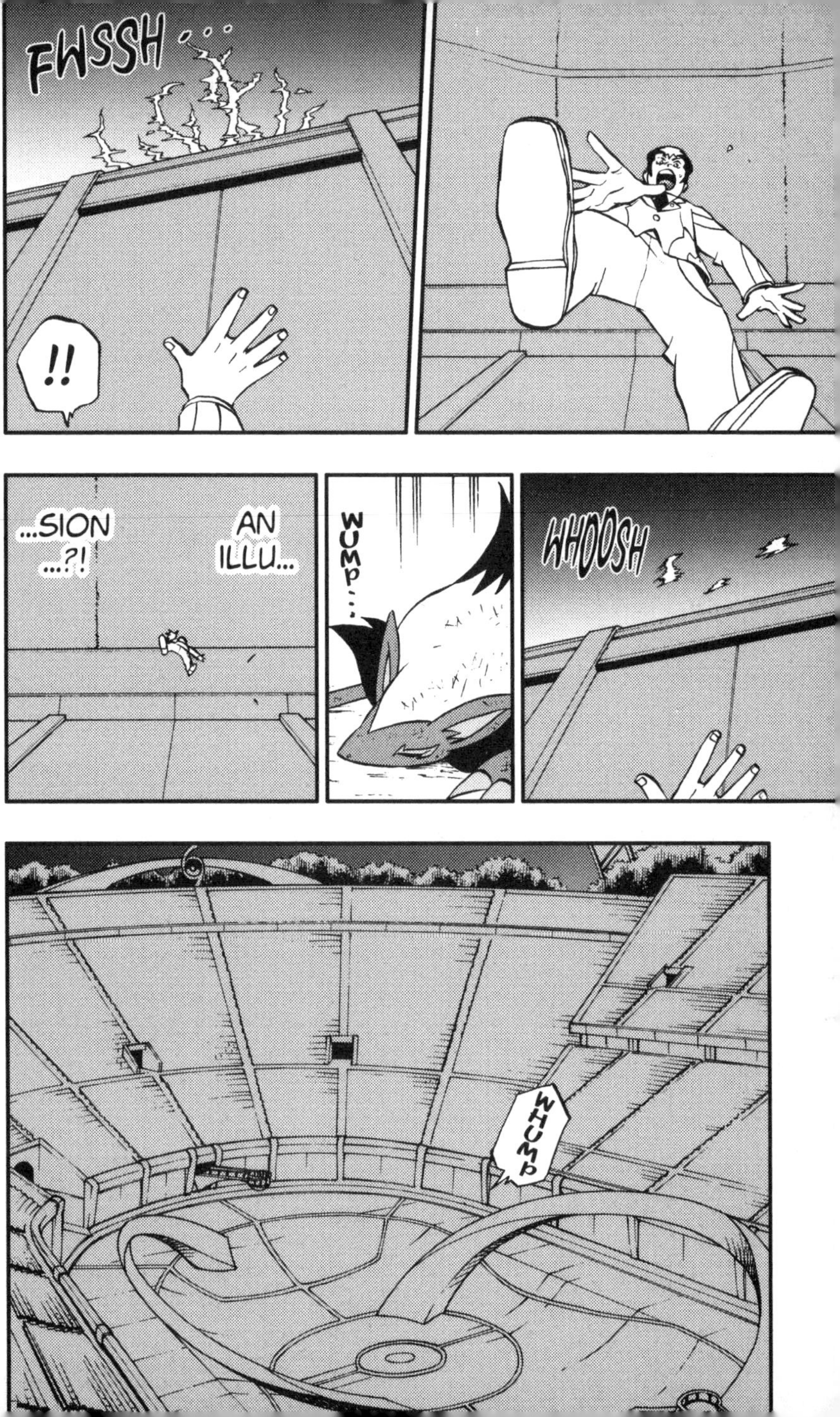
FWSSH
!!
WHOOSH
WUMP...
AN ILLU...
...SION ...?!
WHUMP

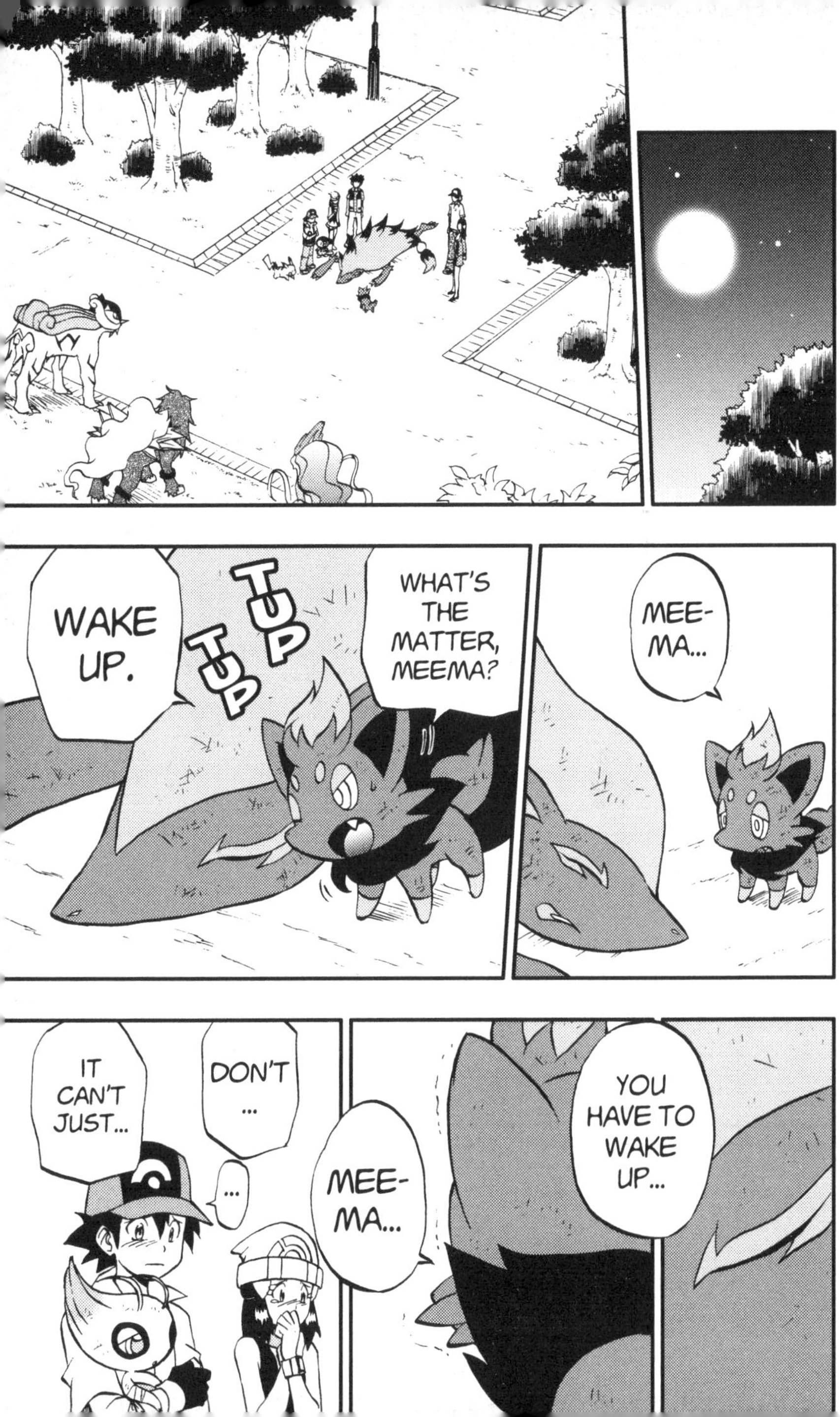
MEE-MA...
WHAT'S THE MATTER, MEEMA?
TUP
TUP
WAKE UP.
YOU HAVE TO WAKE UP...
MEE-MA...
DON'T ...
IT CAN'T JUST...
...

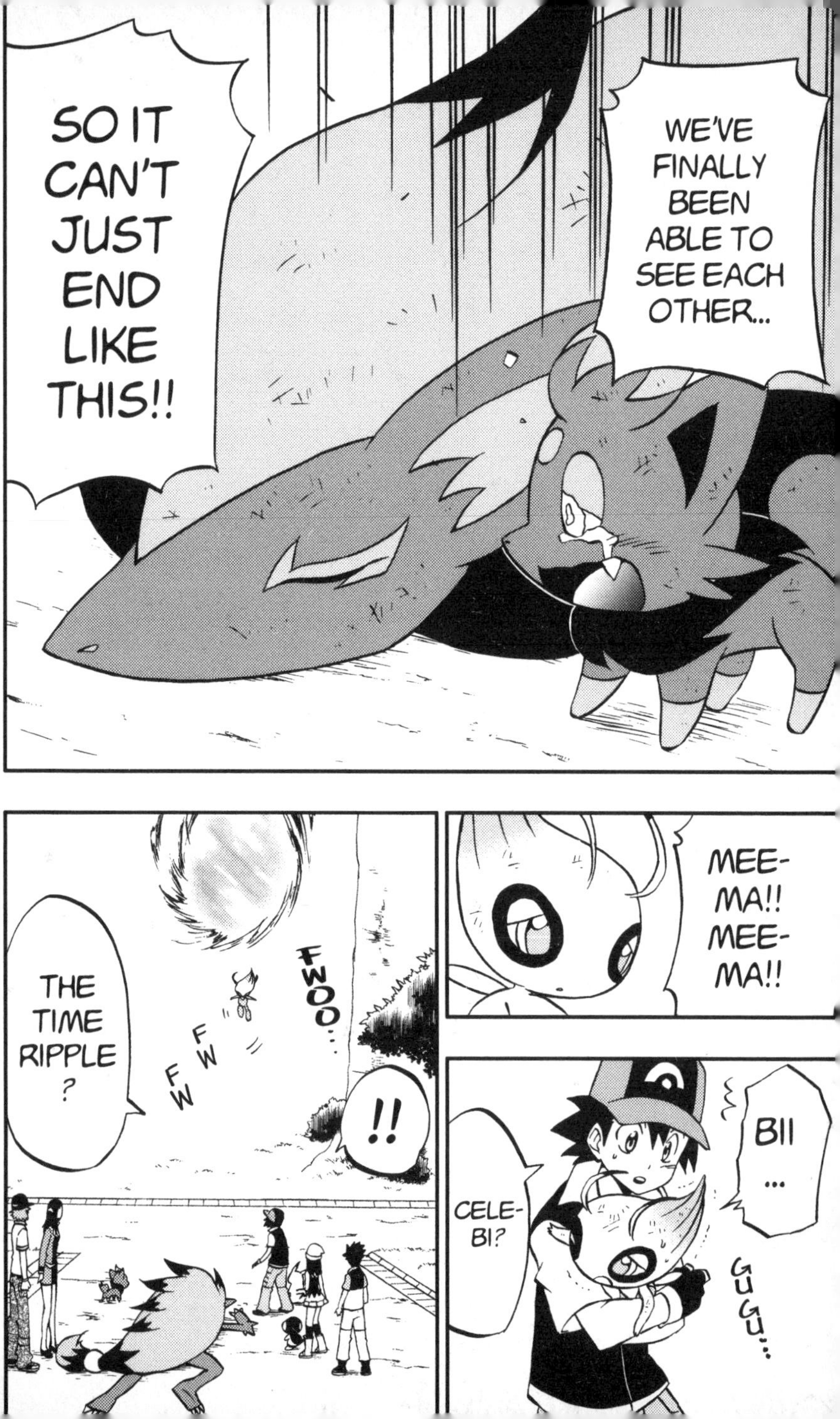
WE'VE FINALLY BEEN ABLE TO SEE EACH OTHER...
SO IT CAN'T JUST END LIKE THIS!!
MEE-MA!! MEE-MA!!
BII ...
GUGU...
CELE-BI?
FWOO...
!!
FW FW
THE TIME RIPPLE?

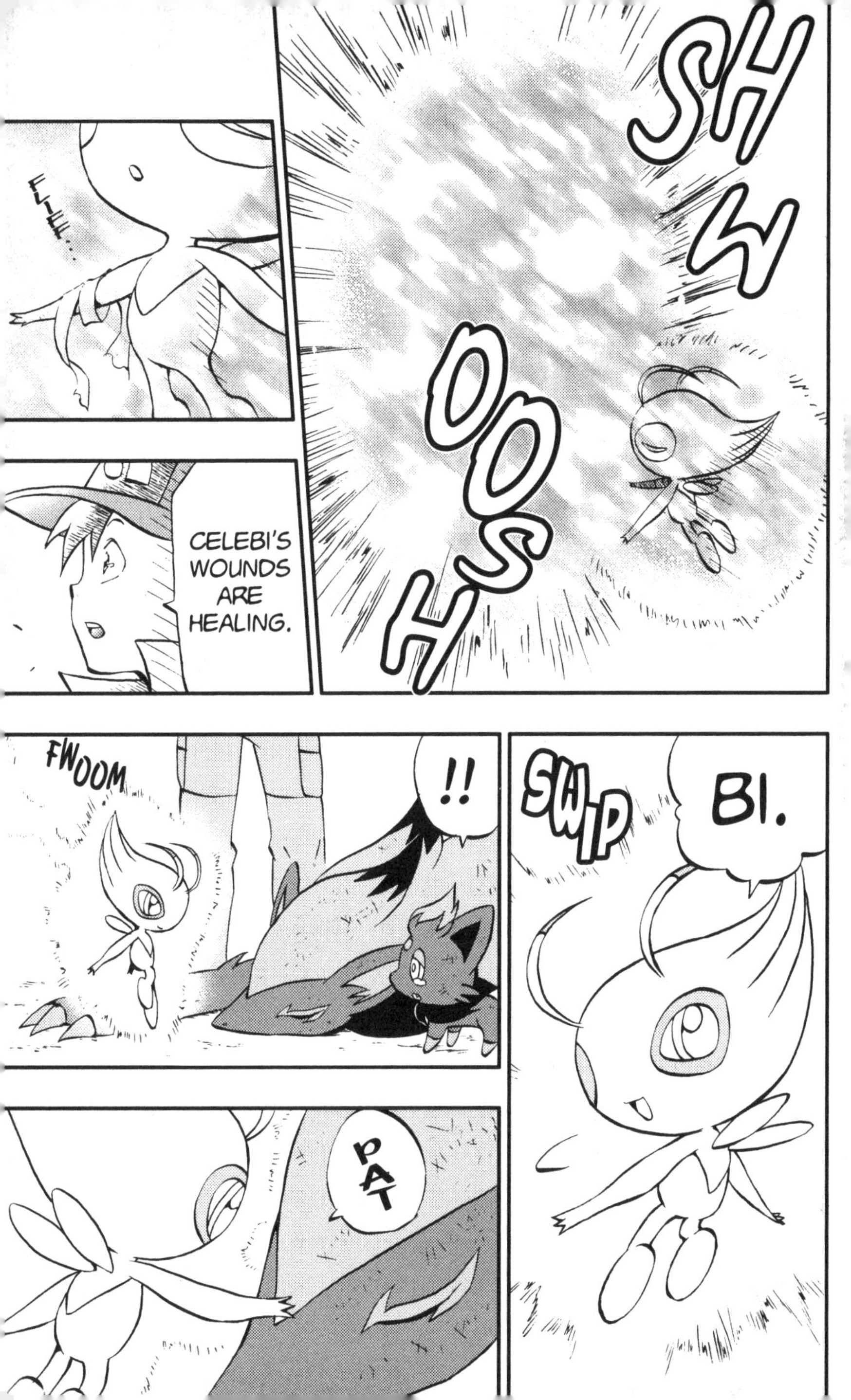
SHWOOSH
FLIFF...
CELEBI'S WOUNDS ARE HEALING.
SWIP
BI.
FWOOM
!!
PAT

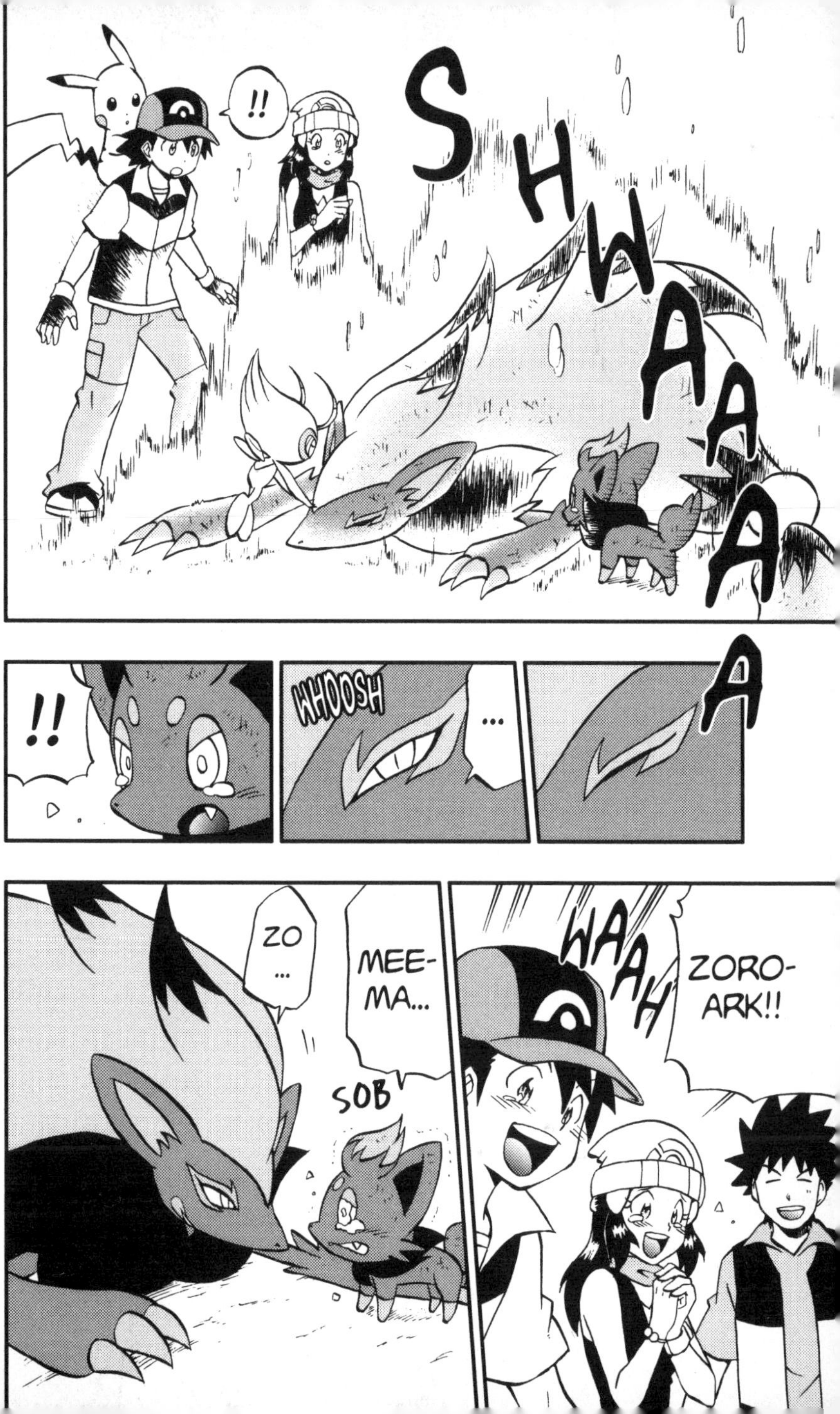
!!
SHWAAAA
WHOOSH
...
!!
WAAAH
ZORO-ARK!!
MEE-MA...
ZO...
SOB

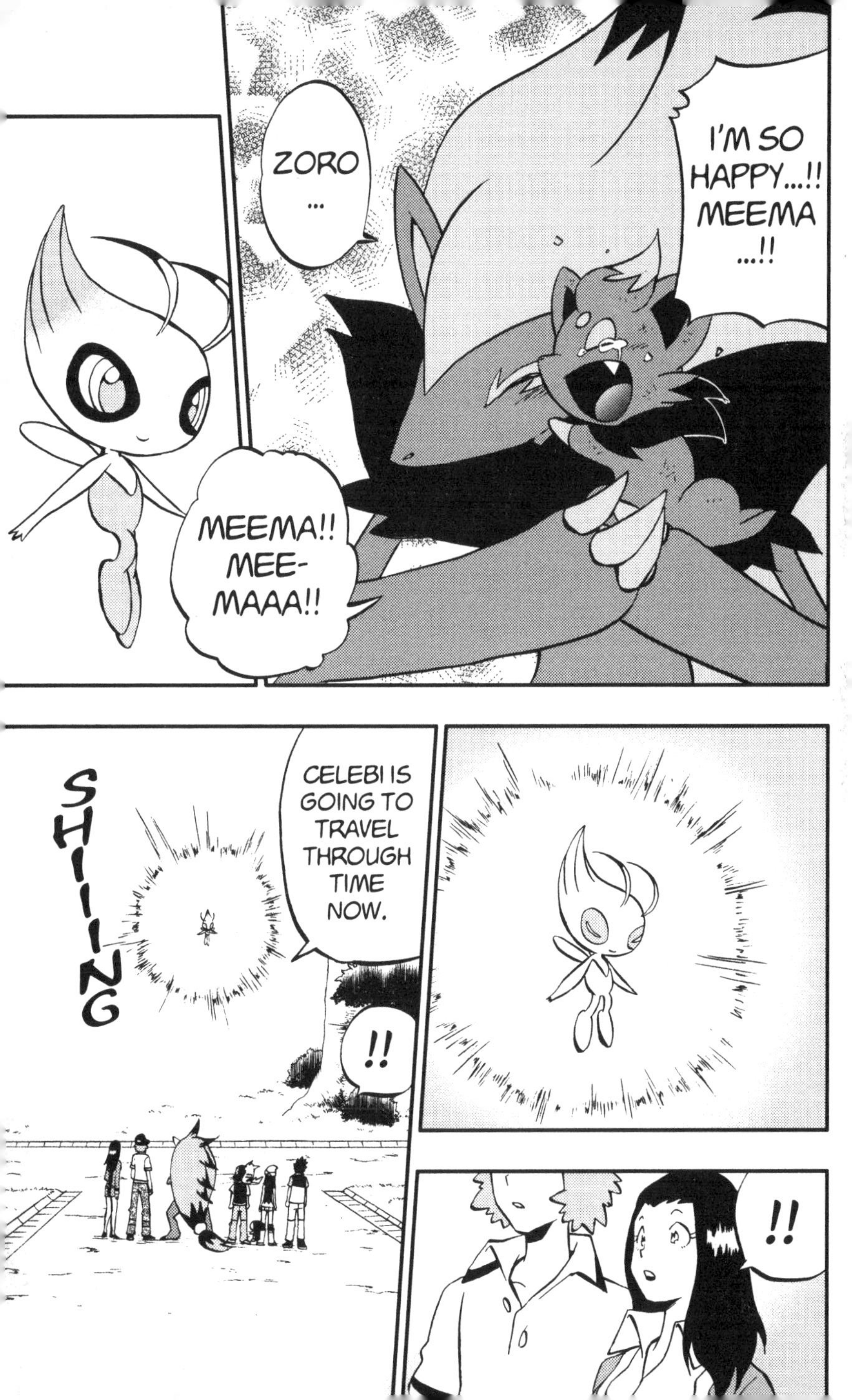
I'M SO HAPPY...!! MEEMA ...!!
ZORO ...
MEEMA!! MEE-MAAA!!
!!
CELEBI IS GOING TO TRAVEL THROUGH TIME NOW.
SHIIING
!!

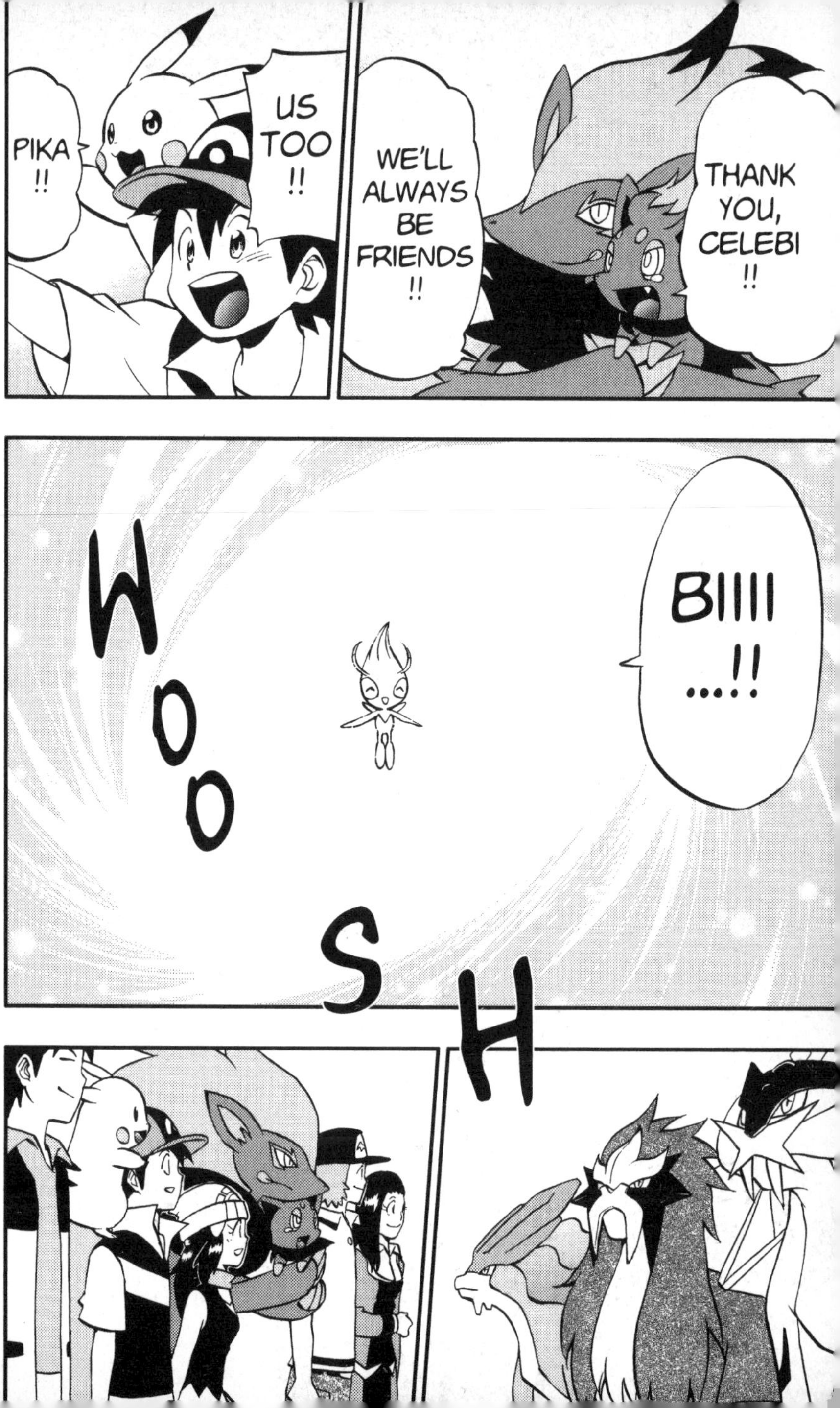
THANK YOU, CELEBI!!
WE'LL ALWAYS BE FRIENDS!!
US TOO!!
PIKA!!
BIIII ...!!
WOOSH

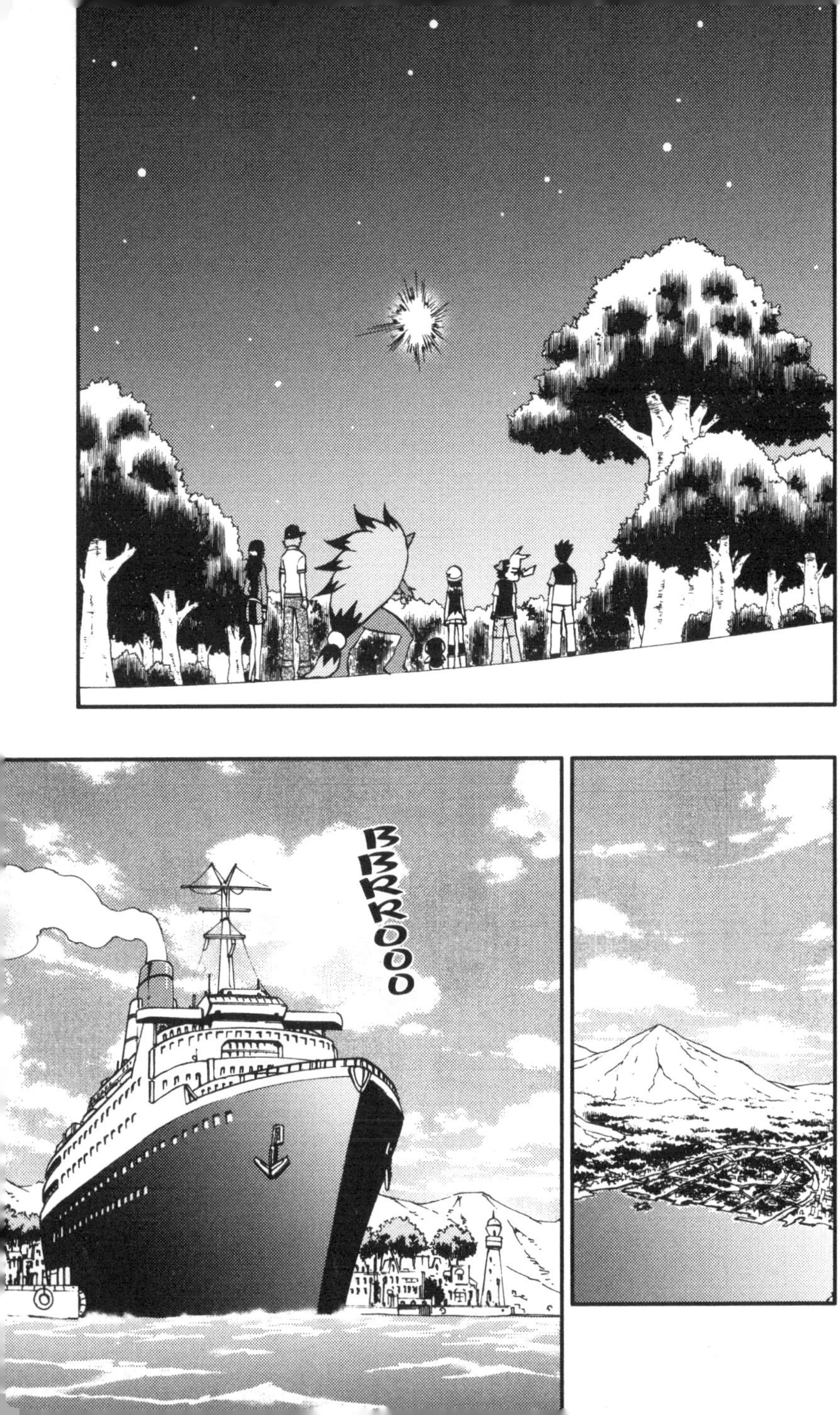
BBRROOO

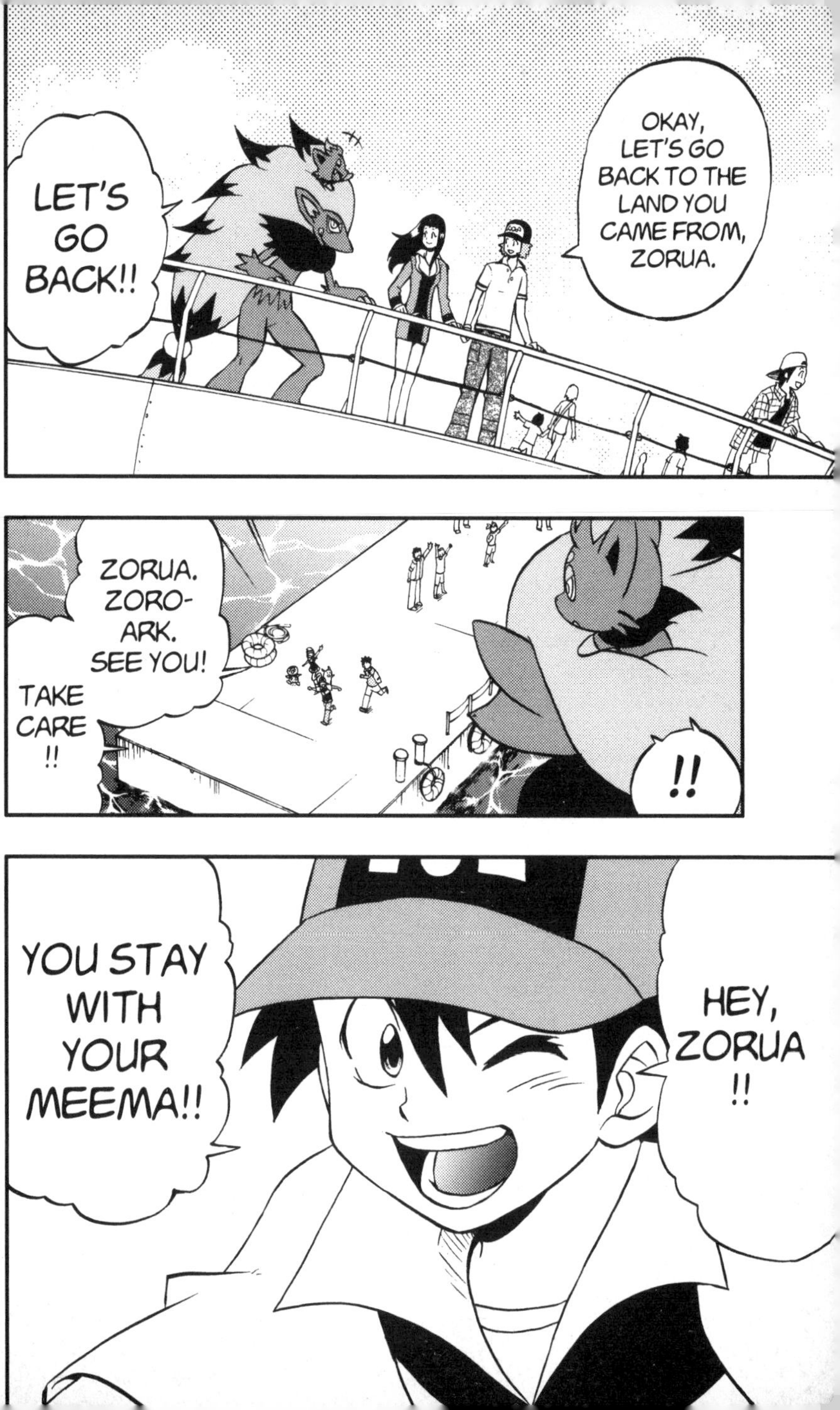
OKAY, LET'S GO BACK TO THE LAND YOU CAME FROM, ZORUA.
LET'S GO BACK!!
!!
ZORUA. ZORO-ARK. SEE YOU!
TAKE CARE !!
HEY, ZORUA !!
YOU STAY WITH YOUR MEEMA!!

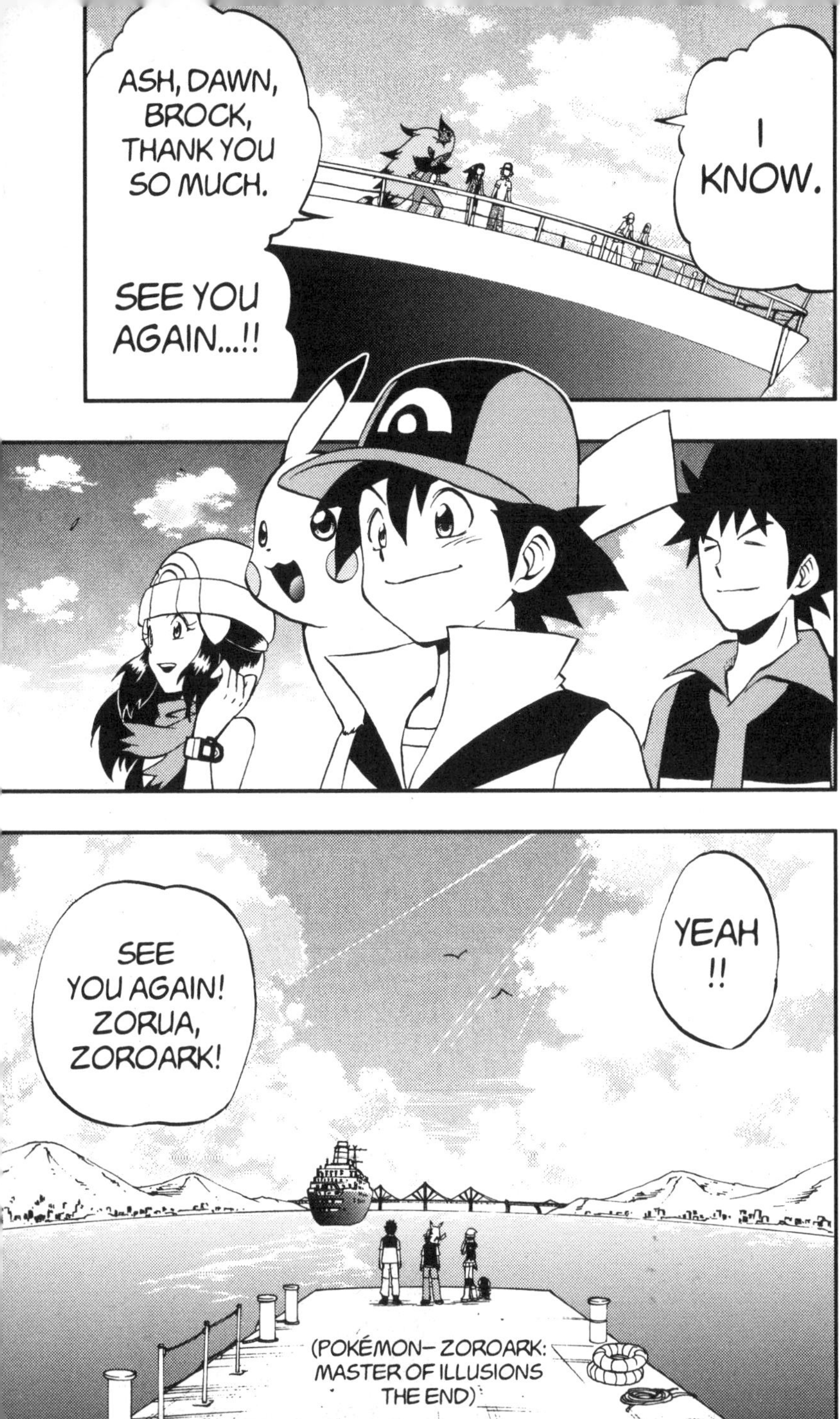
I KNOW.
ASH, DAWN, BROCK, THANK YOU SO MUCH.
SEE YOU AGAIN...!!
YEAH !!
SEE YOU AGAIN! ZORUA, ZOROARK!
(POKÉMON— ZOROARK: MASTER OF ILLUSIONS THE END)

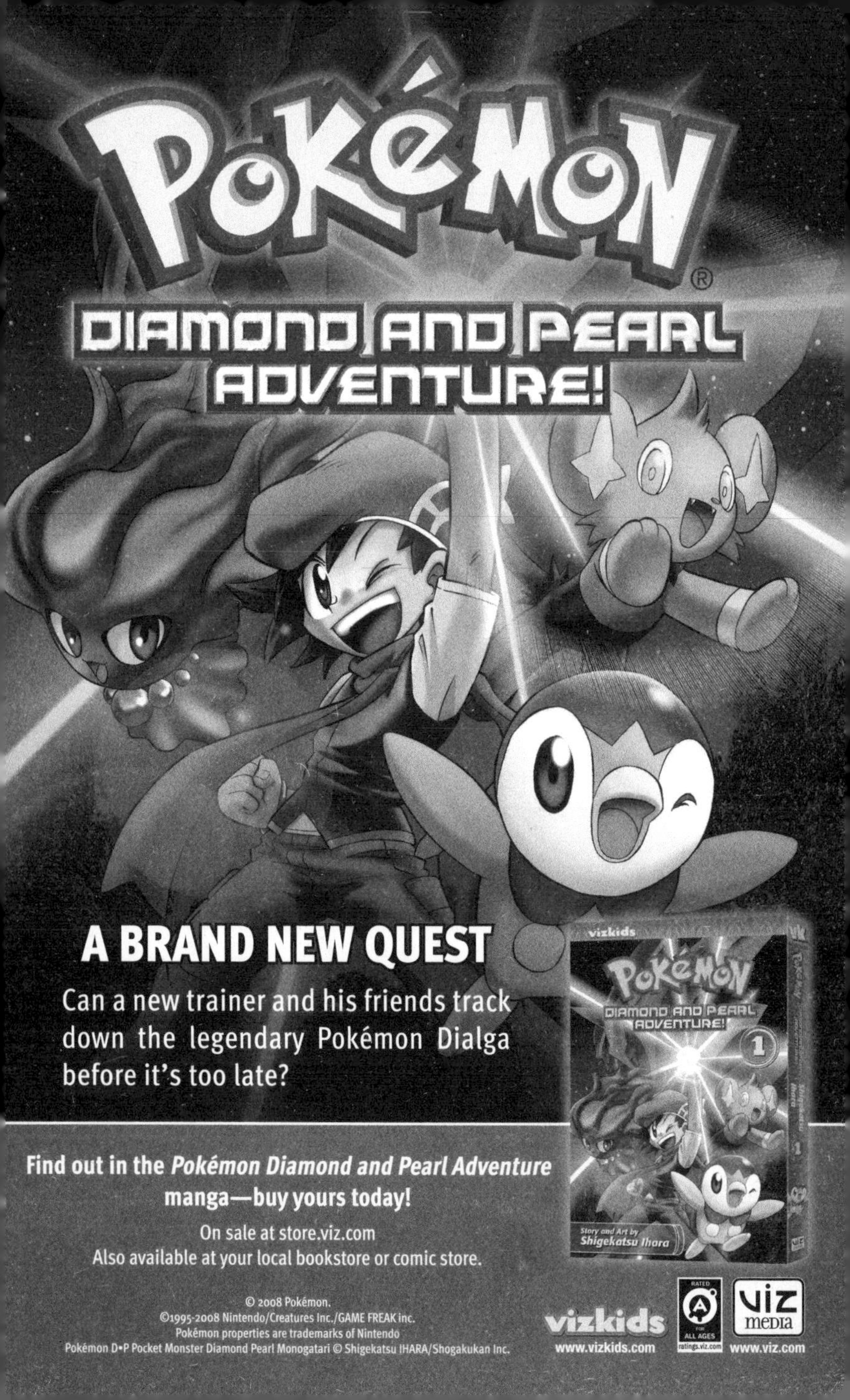
POKéMON®
DIAMOND AND PEARL ADVENTURE!
A BRAND NEW QUEST
Can a new trainer and his friends track down the legendary Pokémon Dialga before it's too late?
vizkids
POKéMON
DIAMOND AND PEARL ADVENTURE!
1
Story and Art by Shigekatsu Ihara
Find out in the *Pokémon Diamond and Pearl Adventure* manga—buy yours today!
On sale at store.viz.com
Also available at your local bookstore or comic store.
© 2008 Pokémon.
©1995-2008 Nintendo/Creatures Inc./GAME FREAK inc.
Pokémon properties are trademarks of Nintendo
Pokémon D•P Pocket Monster Diamond Pearl Monogatari © Shigekatsu IHARA/Shogakukan Inc.
vizkids
www.vizkids.com
RATED A FOR ALL AGES
ratings.viz.com
VIZ MEDIA
www.viz.com